In Love and War

In Love and War

Lesley Lokko

First published in Great Britain in 2014 by Orion Books,
an imprint of The Orion Publishing Group Ltd
Orion House, 5 Upper Saint Martin's Lane
London WC2H 9EA

An Hachette UK Company

3 5 7 9 10 8 6 4

A CIP catalogue record for this book is
available from the British Library.

ISBN (Hardback) 978 1 4091 4250 8
ISBN (Trade Paperback) 978 1 4091 4251 5
ISBN (Ebook) 978 1 4091 4252 2

Typeset at The Spartan Press Ltd,
Lymington, Hants

Printed in Great Britain by Clays Ltd,
St Ives plc

The Orion Publishing Group's policy is to use papers that are natural,
renewable and recyclable products and made from wood grown in sustainable
forests. The logging and manufacturing processes are expected to
conform to the environmental regulations of the country of origin.

www.orionbooks.co.uk

Be of love a little more careful than of anything.
e. e. cummings

All war is deception.
Sun Tzu

Prologue

November 2016, Sidi Aïch, Algeria

A fat bluebottle with iridescent turquoise wings hopped impatiently from louvre to louvre, flinging itself desperately against the net curtain. Heaps of dead flies lay along the length of the sill, drifting en masse every time the door opened and a gust of cold winter air blew in. In the furthest corner from the door, a young woman with cropped blonde hair sat with her hands wrapped around a steaming mug. It was very early in the morning and the cafe was empty. A sad-eyed old man in a long embroidered white *thawb* manned the counter, looking up every now and then, clearly hoping for trade that no longer passed by. The minutes slowly ticked down; ten, fifteen, thirty … an hour. Her tea grew cold but she made no move to drink it. Finally, just before eight a.m., two stocky men in suits and dark mirrored sunglasses walked in. 'Mademoiselle Sturkees?' The shorter of the two pronounced her name with some difficulty.

Lexi Sturgis, thirty-six years old, seasoned war correspondent for the highly respected network NNI, nodded. They were obviously professionals. She hadn't even heard a car pull up. '*Aiwa*. Yes, that's me.'

'You're the reporter?' He looked her up and down suspiciously, muttering something about her age and size, obviously not caring if she understood or not. His companion merely shrugged. 'OK,' he said decisively. 'Come. We go now.'

Lexi's heart began to beat faster. She grabbed the bag that contained her camera, recorder, passport, money, mosquito repellent and a box of tampons – in these regions more useful than a gun and just as hard to find – and followed the men out of the cafe. 'How long?' she asked the one who was busy making preparations to bind her hands together. 'How many hours until we get there?'

He didn't answer. He was no fool. He wasn't about to reveal the location of the interview *that* easily. 'Move.' He gave the cord one last tug and pushed her towards the car. She caught a brief glimpse of an old white Peugeot 504 – no dents or marks that she could see – and then she was bundled into the back seat, where a third man was waiting. He quickly shoved a hood over her head and the world abruptly disappeared. The driver took off at speed. Left, right, left, tyres squealing in protest. For a brief, gut-wrenching second she thought of home. She saw again the look on Magnus's face whenever he saw a suitcase on the bed. 'Mummy's going away.' It wasn't even a question. She pushed the thought to the back of her mind. She couldn't afford to think about him. Not now. Not until she'd got the interview and was on her way back home.

No one spoke to her. There was the occasional brief, terse exchange between the men in a dialect she couldn't follow, and once a mobile rang but no one moved to answer it. From the sound of the engine, she could tell they were climbing, either into the hills that ran south of the city, towards Guelma and Sedrata; or into those that lay to the east, in the direction of Souk Ahras. She'd done her homework all right. There wasn't a town within a couple of hours of Sidi Aïch that she couldn't locate. But after climbing steadily for half an hour or so, they suddenly began to descend. It grew colder inside the car. There was another short climb, then an abrupt turn, and then another descent. She was confused. They were now somewhere in the Atlas Mountains. But where were they headed? As far as she remembered, there were no big towns nearby, only small villages and tiny hamlets, none of which seemed likely destinations for the man she'd flown all the way here to meet.

Another half an hour passed, during which she lost all sense of direction and distance. It was no use panicking, she told herself, over and over again. The security arrangements they'd asked her to make had been so thorough and complex; it didn't make sense to go to all that trouble if they intended to harm her. She tried to concentrate on the interview ahead. Was she being unduly reckless? When her contact had called her to confirm the details, she'd agreed to everything he'd asked without checking with Donal first. If she hadn't, she quickly pointed out afterwards, he would simply have gone to someone else – Al Jazeera or Sky. Unthinkable.

'I couldn't take the chance.'

'Yes, fine. You had to make the call. But you don't know these people, Lexi.'

Acknowledgements

The list of books I consulted during the writing of my own novel would be a novel in itself, but I'm particularly indebted to the great Robert Fisk, the late Tim Hetherington and all of Janine di Giovanni's work, as well as countless other articles, insights, memoirs and travelogues of reporters, correspondents, journalists, news presenters, past and present, whose work in and on the Middle East proved both insightful and absolutely riveting.

As always, I asked several people to help with the translations into Arabic, Swahili and Polish: to Mahmoud Soliman, Caroline Kihato Wanjiku and Jan Misiewicz, I'm deeply grateful (as I am to Mary Long and Chris Howard who led me there!).

Thanks go to my agent, Kate Shaw, and the team at Orion, and to the indefatigable Simon Appleby of Bookswarm, who has single-handedly kept my Facebook profile alive this year.

'I know Marwan. And he said they'd asked for me. Why would they do that if there was something fishy about it? They know who I am.'

Donal said nothing. He just looked at her in that maddening way of his that said everything anyway. *What about Magnus?*

She bit her lip so hard she tasted blood. It had been years since she'd followed a lead without being absolutely sure of its source. It was the sort of risk she'd have taken in her twenties, when she was first starting out and had no one to think of but herself. Now she had a husband and a child. She had responsibilities.

'You've already made up your mind, so there's no point me telling you not to go. But be careful, Lexi. I know what they asked for, but I'm going to send Jim out with you, just in case. I don't want you out there completely on your own.'

'Fine. He can wait for me in Algiers. I'll be gone for a day, no more,' Lexi lied. She had no idea how long she'd be gone, but the opportunity to interview the group who were behind a string of recent attacks on Western interests right across the region, from Morocco to Sudan, was too good to pass up. Although there'd been little loss of life at any of the oil refineries or pipelines the organisation had targeted, damages ran into the billions. They had no known affiliations, no political ties, made no statements. They were as capable of blowing up a refinery or destroying a pipeline as they were of shutting down an entire network. Speed, precision and the ability to disappear without a trace were their calling cards. They were high on Washington's 'most wanted' list, sought by half a dozen foreign intelligence agencies, including Interpol ... but all to no avail. No one had ever seen them or heard them speak. And then one day, out of the blue, one of Lexi's contacts from Algiers had called. The group's spokesperson wanted to talk. To *her*.

'OK.' Donal sighed. It was as close to a compromise as he was likely to get. Donal understood: of course he did. Lexi Sturgis went where the story was. End *of* story. It was a standing joke at Network News International that eight out of Lexi's nine stone were composed of her guts.

'I'll be fine,' she'd said, as lightly as she could. 'I always am. You know that.'

Now, heading into the unknown on her own with three strangers, she wasn't quite so sure. A tremor of fear rose in her throat. She swallowed it as quietly as she could. She mustn't show fear. Above all, she knew, she mustn't show fear.

Suddenly the car made an abrupt U-turn and skidded to a halt. For a split second, her weight was thrown against the man next to her. Something of his own nervousness communicated itself to her in the abrupt touch of their forearms. He jerked away immediately and got out. Someone opened her door, reached in and pulled her out. Still blindfolded, she was handed down a line of waiting hands and pushed through a doorway. Finally she was shoved awkwardly into a chair. A door opened and closed somewhere behind her. All around her were the sounds of footsteps, hushed conversations, whispered instructions. After a few minutes, someone approached and abruptly lifted the hood off her head. She blinked slowly, dazed. After what seemed like hours of near total darkness, the light was blinding. She looked around. Across from her sat a young boy; next to him, a man – his father perhaps – who drank slowly from a glass of tea, his little finger crooked fastidiously, elegant as a matriarch in a Kensington tea room. The boy's eyes, wide with surprise, were fixed on Lexi, but the man's glance landed for a moment then quickly slid away.

She was in a room with high clerestory windows, grubby pale blue walls and an intricately patterned tiled floor. There was a single door to the outside, guarded by two armed men, and in the far corner, behind a desk, a second door, also guarded. A refrigerator hummed loudly in the background. The man opposite continued sipping his tea, smoking quietly. The boy continued to stare at her.

After a few minutes, the door behind the desk opened. The guards stiffened to attention. Two men came into the room and scanned it quickly. They barked out a sharp command to the pair sitting on the bench. The man jumped up, grabbed hold of the boy's arm and hurriedly left the room. Seconds later, a tall, lean figure appeared in the doorway, a black-and-white checked scarf bound all the way around his head and neck, obscuring most of his face. He took a seat behind the desk and motioned to the guards to bring Lexi forward. She was hauled upright and led to one of the two white plastic chairs in front of the desk. The man jerked his head at the guards in dismissal. They withdrew, closing the door behind them with a sharp, disapproving click, and suddenly they were alone.

The silence in the room was so profound it was another element, like water, or air. The man began to slowly unwind his scarf. Lexi's eyes widened as his bearded face emerged. Her heart began to thump wildly.

4

A small muscle moved at his temple, a faint but discernible tremor beneath the surface of his skin. He looked at her, his gaze steady.

'Lexi.' He smiled. 'Ah, Lexi. I knew you'd come.'

PART ONE

November 1991

1

Amongst the stragglers walking up the hill in the full glare of the midday heat was a white schoolgirl in a red-and-white gingham dress, her blonde hair pulled into two untidy pigtails. She dragged her satchel along the dusty ground. Her socks lay in untidy heaps around her ankles and her face was flushed and sweaty. It was a long walk from her school on Busuma Road to her home on Sable Road, on the other side of the golf course where her father played at weekends and her mother sat with all the other wives on the shady veranda, sipping their sweating G&Ts. She'd refused the offer of a lift from Mrs Bates, who sailed into the schoolyard in her big air-conditioned car and looked at her pityingly from behind the steering wheel. 'Hop in, darling. It's not far. We're practically going that way anyway.'

Lexi shook her head obstinately. 'No thanks. My mum'll be here any minute.' She looked at Mrs Bates without blinking. It was a lie and they both knew it. Mrs Bates shook her head and drove off.

Vincent, the school watchman, had looked at her warily from the shaded interior of the sentry box. He was quite used to seeing Lexi Sturgis sitting under the shady acacia trees for hours and hours on end until someone finally remembered to fetch her. But today it looked like she'd decided to walk.

'I'm going home now,' she told Vincent sternly. He looked at her uncertainly. The vertical crease of worry between his eyes was lost on her. He was powerless to stop her and they both knew it. She picked up her satchel, walked out of the schoolyard and disappeared up the road.

At last she reached the white picket fence with the plaque that announced, grandly, *Hightops: Residence of the British High Commissioner*. Home. She pushed open the gate and let it bang shut loudly behind her. The shiny black ambassadorial Rover was parked underneath the portico at the front of the house. She peered into it curiously as she walked past. There was no one inside, not even the driver.

She wandered into the house, sniffing the air for signs of danger, alert as any animal out there in the bush beyond the city. The house was eerily silent. She dumped her satchel on the console in the hallway and wandered down the corridor to the kitchen. Anna, the maid, was at the sink, dreamily washing up. She turned as Lexi walked in.

'Where's Mummy?' Lexi asked, eyeing the fruit bowl that stood on the table. She was hungry. She'd opened her satchel at break time to find it empty. Her mother had forgotten to pack her mid-morning snack. Again.

Anna's hands flashed magenta-painted nails through the suds as she shook them free. She picked up a cloth and began drying the dishes with the absent-minded attention of a lifetime spent repeating the same tasks. She didn't answer at first. Lexi picked out a green tangerine from the bowl. They were her favourites, sharp, not sweet, with papery skin that shucked off with ease.

'Your mummy is sleeping,' Anna said finally. 'You mustn't disturb her.' *You maasen distab ha.* When the family had first arrived in Lusaka, Anna's almost impenetrable accent had been the source of much amusement between Lexi and her younger brother.

'Where's Toby?' she asked.

'Toby, he's at his friend's house. Your daddy says I must go at four o'clock to fetch him.'

'From David's?'

Anna giggled. 'Me, I don't know any David. I only know Master Cunningham. Yes, he's at that house. Will you come with me, lovey?'

Lexi sighed. Nora Cunningham was the wife of the Deputy High Commissioner, a nervous, weak-willed woman whose energies were largely taken up ensuring the proper degree of deference was paid to her by servants, colleagues, friends and visitors alike. In the tiny diplomatic community in Lusaka, she was universally disliked, even by the children. 'All right,' she said reluctantly. 'What's Daddy's car doing here?' she asked through a mouthful of soft citrus flesh.

'Your daddy's home,' Anna said slowly.

Lexi's eyes widened. 'Daddy's home?'

'Yes, but lovey … don't go to him. Not just yet.'

'Why?'

Anna carried the stack of dried dishes to the cupboard. Her mouth was working as though she didn't know what to say. 'They was fighting,' she said after a moment. 'I think he's angry. Yes, he's coming very, very angry.'

Lexi picked another tangerine from the bowl and walked out of the kitchen. She tiptoed past her father's office and crept upstairs. Her parents' bedroom was at one end of the long upstairs corridor and hers was at the other. In between was Toby's room and the two spare rooms, neither of which was ever used. When they'd first arrived, her mother had set one of the rooms up as a sewing room, where she'd tried unsuccessfully to teach Lexi the difference between a running stitch and a cross stitch. Now her big woven basket of beautiful scraps of material that she'd collected in all their foreign postings lay untouched, like everything else of hers in the house – her books, her paintbrushes, her scrapbooks. Nothing interested her any more, least of all her children. It was all on account of the *affair*. The word was a whispered, shameful secret, even though everyone knew. 'What's an affair?' Ellen McIvor asked in class one day, and Olga Marjanovic, the Yugoslav ambassador's daughter, couldn't help herself and blurted out, 'It's when your mum loves someone else's dad!' and everyone laughed except Lexi. Because it was true.

She shut her bedroom door and dropped her bag on the floor. She pulled her school uniform over her head, freed her feet from her sandals and took off her socks with relief, then found a pair of shorts and the T-shirt she'd been wearing the previous day and hurriedly put them on. She pulled her hair out of its pigtails and shook it free. At last she was divested of everything girlish and constraining.

It was nearly three p.m. She had an hour until she and Anna would walk down the road, across the golf course and up the short hill that led to the Cunninghams', where she would endure Mrs Cunningham's inquisitive gaze and her probing questions over an orange juice, and then she, Toby and Anna would walk home together, Anna and Lexi swinging seven-year-old Toby in between them, squealing with delight. It was anyone's guess whether their parents would make it down for supper. Deep down, secretly, she hoped neither of them would. She couldn't bear the sight of her father's angry, broken face, his fingers picking desultorily at whatever Anna put in front of him, or the sound of her mother's peculiarly cheery voice, asking them about school and homework and all the things she thought she ought to be interested in but clearly wasn't.

She walked over to her bedroom window, hoisted it open and looked out. The gardens sloped away from the house down towards the jacaranda trees, huddled together in a storm cloud of mauve and violet flowers. In the other corner, wide blood-red flamboyants spread their branches over Anna's quarters. In the middle, a gigantic mnondo tree sat over the flower beds like a serene Victorian glass bell. Jethro, the gardener, was weeding. She watched him for a moment, his thin dark arms rising and falling, rising and falling, the steel of his blade catching the sunlight, scoring a flash across her eyes. Next year she would leave all of this behind. She was going to boarding school in England. Whenever she thought about it, a bodily pain gripped her in her solar plexus, making her short of breath. It wasn't that she didn't want to go. In many ways, whatever strangeness awaited her there was preferable to the strangeness that held their entire household in its hot, tight grasp.

'Lexi?' A little while later, Anna stood below her window, squinting up, shielding her face from the sun. She'd tied her scarf properly and carried a basket slung over one arm.

Lexi pushed open the window and leaned out. 'It's not four o'clock yet,' she called down.

'Eggs is finished. I'm going to buy some. Are you coming?'

Lexi nodded vigorously. She slammed the window shut, grabbed her flip-flops and ran downstairs. There was a Portuguese greengrocer down the road where Anna went two or three times a week. Tiago, the owner, was a short, rotund man whose smile matched his girth. He liked Lexi, called her *moranga* – on account of her strawberry-blonde hair, he told her – and often made her the gift of a peach or a smooth yellow apple, whose price he would impatiently wave away.

It was another world at the greengrocer's, far from the regimented order of the International School and the hierarchy of the British Club, which were the only other spheres Lexi knew. Barefoot neighbourhood children curled protectively around the legs of their mothers, hankering after chewing gum or a packet of sweets; middle-aged white women, some with their hair in rollers, having dashed out to buy a bottle of wine before a dinner party, waltzed frantically up and down the short aisles, looking for this or that. Nannies and housegirls, like Anna, some with their little *mzungu* charges in tow, bought vegetables, clucking authoritatively over the price or the firmness of a piece of fruit. Outside, black men like Jethro and Chilonga, the nightwatchman who came at dusk and left at dawn, lounged on car bonnets or sat around in groups, cigarettes rolled between thumb and forefinger, African-style, gossiping like old women. Lexi's eyes and nostrils widened pleasurably as she took it all in.

Anna bought the eggs and a loaf of the sweet, doughy sugar bread that she ate every morning whilst Lexi and Toby struggled over half-finished bowls of cereal, and, clutching Lexi firmly by the hand, negotiated their way through the small knot of men at the entrance, who called out greetings and jests in the language that Lexi did not understand. Anna's body jiggled with laughter as she threaded through them. Lexi tripped along after her, humming to herself, the warm, sandy earth beneath the thin soles of her flip-flops as soft as cream.

2

Something woke her, deep in the middle of the night. She sat bolt upright in bed, her heart racing. There was a sudden thud, then a muffled noise, halfway between a shriek and a scream. She held herself very still, straining to hear what was going on. They were arguing, of course, but something was different this time. There was an unfamiliar quality to the air. It had been there all week, sharp and brittle, like the atmosphere before a storm. The previous day, a Saturday, she'd wandered into her mother's bedroom and watched her put her face on in front of the mirror, utterly absorbed in the task: powder, mascara, lipstick, pressing her lips together, and then the bit Lexi loved most, the way she dabbed a wafer-thin tissue against her lips and the glossy imprint came away, perfectly shaped.

'Mum,' she'd begun, wanting not so much to *tell* her anything as to have, even for a minute or two, her mother's undivided attention.

'Hush, darling,' her mother said, carefully brushing her eyelashes, one after the other. 'I've got to concentrate.'

'But—'

'Alexandra! Will you please just shut up? I can't hear myself *think* these days!'

Lexi's mouth fell open in stunned protest. It was the oddest thing to say. *I can't hear myself think?* There'd been nothing but silence in the house for weeks … months, even. She couldn't remember the last time they'd had anything like a proper conversation. She could barely remember when her mother had last been in the house for more than half an hour. She was always either on her way out, or just come back in and already preparing to leave again, all because of the *affair*. Lexi felt the by-now-familiar hot sting of tears behind her eyes. She'd stored up weeks and weeks of things to tell her mother, waiting desperately for that moment when she'd look up and see her eyes on her again, *properly*, the way they used to be. Now there was a vacant, distracted look in them that meant only one thing: her children were already – always – *out of mind*. She'd stared resentfully at her for a moment, then slipped out of the room. Her mother didn't even notice her going.

There was another muffled yell. Lexi's skin shrank. Her bedroom door creaked. It was Toby. 'Come on,' she whispered, lifting up the sheet. 'Hop in. Quickly.'

He ran across the floor and clambered into bed with her. His thin little body was shaking. 'They're fighting again,' he whispered. She could hear his teeth chattering, despite the warm night.

'No, they're not fighting. They're just talking.'

'I heard Daddy say a bad word.'

'No, you didn't. They're just talking. It'll be all right in the morning,' Lexi lied. 'Shall I tell you a story?'

He nodded. His chin was sharp against her arm. 'Yes please. But make it a good one, Lexi. Make it one with a happy ending.'

She swallowed hard on the lump in her throat. She was eleven, and already she knew there was no such thing.

The next morning, the house was quiet. At some point during the night, Toby must have woken up and gone back to his room, though his warmth and scent were still there. She pushed back the thin cotton sheet impatiently and got up. It was a Sunday. One more luxurious, do-as-you-like day, then school again. She slipped her cotton nightdress over her head, pulled on her shorts and T-shirt and tiptoed down the corridor to the bathroom. Toby had already been in, she noticed, wrinkling her nose. His sodden pyjamas lay in a heap by the toilet. At seven, he still regularly wet the bed, though thankfully generally only his *own* bed. She cleaned her teeth and brushed the sleep out of her hair, then went downstairs to make breakfast. Sunday was Anna's day off, and although

Lexi hadn't quite mastered the art of making an omelette to Anna's exceptionally high standards, scrambled eggs was easy.

Toby was in the living room, watching a video. His face turned towards her as she came through. She felt her heart tighten painfully. These days, his expression was one of permanent confusion, as though he was unsure not just of himself, but of the whole of the world around him. Over the past few months she'd watched helplessly as the two sides of his nature – one free and sunny and inquisitive, the other dark and sad – struggled with each other, the end result a caged wariness, as though he couldn't quite trust the world as he saw it. She knew why. It was simply his response to their parents' mercurial changes of temperament. Her mother's impatience to be somewhere else, even when she was present, was overwhelming, settling over the house like dust. Her father's anguish was palpable, tangible, as were his attempts to pretend that everything was normal, as though having a wife who came home at midnight smelling of alcohol and another man's aftershave was an everyday occurrence. They all knew *who* the other man was – in the small, tightly bound diplomatic community in which they lived, there were no secrets – but Lexi couldn't remember ever seeing him. In her mind's eye he was tall and blonde, with pale blue eyes and fair, sun-pinked skin, but she had no way of knowing. To ask a question or utter his name would have been to make it real and therefore true – and she didn't want *that*.

'Hul-*lo*,' she said, reaching down to ruffle Toby's hair. 'Have you had breakfast?'

Toby shook his head, his eyes returning impatiently to the screen. The make-believe world of Captain Daredevil was infinitely preferable to theirs. 'Not hungry,' he murmured.

'If I make pancakes, I bet you'll be hungry,' Lexi teased. She chewed the inside of her lip. She'd watched Anna make pancakes the previous Saturday ... it couldn't be all that difficult.

She straightened up and wandered into the kitchen, pulling open the heavy fridge door and surveying the contents. Everything was kept in the fridge, protection against the humidity as well as the tiny red and black ants that devoured anything and everything left in their path. Flour, eggs, milk ... oh, and sugar, of course. She took out the heavy glass jars, one by one. Mixing bowl, whisk, frying pan, oil ... she lined everything up neatly and was just about to begin cracking the smooth, pale brown eggs into the bowl when she heard someone coming down the stairs.

'Mum?' she called out hesitantly. 'D'you want some pancakes? I'm just making some—' She stopped, looking at her mother in fright. 'What's happened to your face, Mum?'

'What?' Her mother stood in the doorway, feigning surprise. 'Oh, that ... it's nothing. I ... I banged it last night.'

'How?'

'I don't know, darling. It ... it just happened. I must've hit something.'

Lexi looked at her mother's cheek. A bruise the size of an orange was forming underneath the pale, freckled skin.

'Where's Toby? Is he up yet?' Her mother changed the subject.

Lexi pointed wordlessly to the living room. She swallowed hard and turned back to the pancakes, hoping the bruise would disappear.

But it didn't. It deepened and spread. All morning when she looked at her mother, it was like looking into the face of someone she didn't know. A damaged face that wasn't just to do with the stain that dominated it. There was an evasive, distracted look in her mother's eyes that frightened her. Her father didn't come downstairs, and later, after she'd given Toby his pancakes and made her mother a cup of tea that she didn't drink, her mother went back upstairs to bed.

The next morning, neither her mother nor her father was anywhere to be seen. Anna accompanied her and Toby to school. Lexi spent the day in a state of distracted nervousness, absently chewing one of her plaits, worrying about something she could sense, but not see. When she came home at lunchtime, her father's car was in the driveway. She knew at once that something dreadful had happened. She looked into her father's face, made stiff with dread and anger and defeat, and something inside her cracked.

His words made no sense. 'She's gone to make another life.'

Lexi stared at him uncomprehendingly. What did that *mean*? She already *had* a life, didn't she? Here in Lusaka, their fifth posting, with her husband and her two children? Or had she decided that that life wasn't worth keeping? She looked past him to where Toby sat on the living room floor, trying not to hear. *She* would be all right, she knew, with a fierce certainty that almost frightened her. But what about Toby? What would happen to Toby without their mother?

3

In the next-door room, the one with the bay window looking out on to the garden and the neat row of terraced houses that began where the flowers and the grass ended, her mother lay dying. The terrible fact of it gave shape to their days, which had previously centred around other things – meals, school, work, evenings in front of the television, the soft murmur of her parents' conversation the backdrop to her homework, night after night, during the week. Now the routine of the house was given over to others – nurses, health workers, neighbours. Her mother no longer cooked and there were days when her father did not go to work, but hung around the house trailing whichever nurse or neighbour had been appointed to administer the never-ending supply of pills, ointments, creams, medicines, liquids and needles that marked out the passing of the day.

The routine was unchanged and unvarying. One of the nurses – either the loud, cheerful Australian one, or the quiet, serene-looking Irish one – came in at six to dispense the early-morning drugs that made it possible for her mother to face the day. After a wash and a change of sheets and clothing, Jane was allowed in. For the past month, her mother's meals had been reduced to a bland, smooth mush that had to be spooned into her like a baby. Jane perched on the edge of the bed, trying not to notice how little space her mother's legs now took up, barely more than twigs under the brightly patterned coverlet. It was impossible to fathom how those once-sturdy limbs, encased in shiny nylon stockings in winter or lightly tanned in summer, had, like the rest of her, simply wasted away. At eight, just before leaving for work, her father would come in, signalling that it was time for Jane to go to school. He often brought out a packet of mints from his pocket, surreptitiously slipping her one to disguise the scent of decay.

Her mother was dying. The fact of it was still a slap in the face, a stiff shock of surprise when she opened her eyes each morning and heard, through the thin wall of what had once been her parents' room and was now occupied by her mother's mechanical medical bed, that living, breathing battery of machines that ran on continuously, day and night, mysteriously keeping her alive. Sometimes, when she leaned in to hear a whispered wish, she would feel her mother's skin against hers, papery and thin, like an insect's wing, changing and preparing itself for death.

But today was a Saturday, and there was no school. She could hear her father shuffling from the room where he now slept to her mother's room, bringing magazines and the Saturday papers that her mother was too weak to hold. 'Shall I make you a cup of tea?' She heard his voice through the partially open door.

Perched awkwardly on the edge of the bath, she brought the hand-held magnifying mirror to her face. She lifted the scissors with her left hand and gingerly began to cut her fringe. It was something her mother had always done. Every fortnight or so, for as long as she'd had a fringe, she'd sat on the edge of the bath as her mother ran a steady, practised hand across her eyes … snip, snip, snip … it was done. Not any more. As her mother slipped further and further away, Jane sat alone on the porcelain edge and tried, unsuccessfully, to cut it herself.

'Who the hell cut your fringe?' It was the first thing Becky Alperton said to her when she walked into school the next morning. 'Was she *blind*?'

'Shut *up!*' hissed Amanda Hodges, avoiding Jane's anguished, nervous glance. 'Don't you know her mother's *dying*?'

Her mother's dying. Her mum's got cancer. Her mum's really, really sick. The words were like an echo, a shadow that followed her everywhere she went. In a terrible way that she would never, ever be able to express to anyone, her mother's illness had earned her some respite from the dreadful comments that were otherwise the backdrop to her life at school, though even daring to think about herself at a time like this was enough to slice a clean, clear pain through her ribs. How could she be so selfish? But she couldn't help it. No one knew what it was like, no one. She'd been there for nearly two years and nothing had changed. She hated it. After nearly ten years of scrimping and saving, denying themselves holidays, a new washing machine, a new car, her parents could finally afford to send their only daughter to St Augustine's, the private girls' school in Caversham, across the river and a whole world away from the two-up, two-down semi-detached house in Southcote where Jane Elizabeth Marshall, aged sixteen, had lived her entire life. It was the culmination of their dreams, the moment her father, a postal worker who'd risen to mid-level management through dint of sheer graft and tenacity, had been waiting for his whole life.

She sat the entrance exam, passed easily and was awarded a small bursary to boot. The day the letter came, her father excused himself from the breakfast table and, according to her mother, went upstairs to cry in private, the expression of an emotion he would never, ever allow himself to show in front of his wife and daughter.

Peter Marshall wasn't like the other fathers in Southcote. To begin with, his real name wasn't even Peter Marshall. Jane was six or seven years old when she came across a letter on the doormat addressed to a Mr Piotr Marszalek. She stared at it for ages, then took it into the living room. Her mother looked at it for a few minutes before taking down the Polish–English dictionary that stood in the cabinet next to the fireplace. It was a thick, heavy book with a cracked leather spine and faded gold lettering.

marszalek: marshal, denoting anything from a high court official, a field marshal, or the chairman of the Polish parliament, to a servant in a great household.

Jane looked at the explanation, struggling to read the unfamiliar words. She knew her father wasn't English in the way her friends' fathers were. He had odd little habits, a slight hesitation before pronouncing certain words, and – the dead giveaway – there were no relatives on his side – no grandparents, uncles, cousins. Her maternal grandparents had long since died, and although there was an uncle and cousins somewhere in Leeds, her mother's family had never seemed particularly close-knit. It was just the three of them, and it seemed to suit them fine.

Peter Marshall never spoke of his life 'back there'. It fell to Jane's mother to explain why he always ate his food so fast, and why he pre-ferred spending hours outside in the garden, coaxing vegetables – never flowers – from the stony ground. It was to do with hunger, she said, and the fact that the first eight years of his life had been spent more or less on the run, along with fourteen other boys who later made the crossing to England. He ate as though there would never be enough, though he was as thin and lean as Penny, Jane's mother, was round and soft. 'It's because of the war,' her mother whispered to her. 'It affected him.'

The war. A distant, far-off event in a distant, far-off place – her father's childhood – that cast its long, ugly shadow over 7 Ashampstead Road, where the curtains seemed permanently drawn and sunlight never ventured in. Their one ray of hope was Jane, and it would have killed them both to know that she'd never been unhappier in her life than the day she earned a place at the school where she would never, *ever* belong.

Her mother's dying. It was this fact that momentarily put a halt to the sideways glances, the snobbish looks, the snide whispered comments that put her firmly in her place. *Not one of us.* You couldn't say that to a girl whose mother was wasting away. Mandy Hodges knew, because she was one of three girls who'd been instructed by their form mistress to visit Jane one weekend, and the only one who'd actually turned up. The brief visit was torment for everyone concerned, not least Jane, who'd had no idea that she was coming, or that anyone at St Augustine's even knew where Southcote was.

'Oh,' was all she'd said, opening the door to find Mandy Hodges standing outside.

'Oh. Er, hi. Miss Griffiths ... she thought ... well, she thought it would be nice if ... if ...' Mandy trailed off, embarrassed. Behind Jane, the sitting room door was open. Her father was dozing in his armchair.

'Who is it, love?' her mother called from upstairs.

'It's ... just ... just someone from school,' Jane said weakly. Shame washed over her in waves.

Her father woke up, startled by the noise, and then she had to invite Mandy in, and it was all exposed – the mean and shabby little sitting room with the TV in one corner, the bookcase in another and the Formica-topped dining table where Jane still did her homework every night. Two sets of mismatched curtains and a loud shag-pile rug in front of the gas burner. Mandy Hodges stood in the hallway, a wilting bunch of flowers in her hand, her eyes wide with surprise as she took it all in. Jane wished the ground would open up and swallow her whole. She took Mandy upstairs to see her mother, and hung around in the doorway as they made small talk, then led her back downstairs in complete silence.

'Um, thanks ... thanks for coming,' she mumbled, practically pushing Mandy out the door.

'Oh. You're ... well, it was Miss Griffiths really ... I didn't ... my mum said ... Well, I ... I hope your mum feels better soon. I'd ... I'd better go.' And she ran across the road before either of them was forced to say another word.

That was a month ago. If there was something other than withering condescension in Mandy Hodges' eyes after the visit, Jane chose not to see it. She withdrew even further into her shell and refused to meet their eyes. *Only two more terms to go*, she whispered to herself on the bus to school every morning. Her mother was dying. Nothing could be worse than that. Not even two more terms at St Augustine's. No, not even *that*.

4

'We give thanks for the life of Penelope Mary Wilson, beloved wife of Peter Marshall, devoted mother of Jane. We give thanks for Our Lord's grace and His favour in ...' The priest's soft voice droned on. Jane gripped the wooden pew in front of her and tried to stop herself slipping forwards. Next to her, his lips moving awkwardly, silently, her father stood stiffly to attention. Across the aisle were a smattering of neighbours and old Mrs Denning from the Marshalls' Kennington days, before Jane was born, with whom Penny had kept in touch once a month, religiously, either by letter or by phone. Mrs Denning was in her eighties, her face buried behind her hat, which was probably just as well, since she hadn't managed to stop crying since she'd arrived that morning by taxi.

St Michael's Church in Tilehurst, a few miles from Southcote, was her mother's choice, though neither Jane nor her father really knew why. It turned out she'd been in touch all along with the rector, a tall, kindly-looking man named the Right Reverend Richard Rodgers – an alliteration that would in other circumstances have made Jane giggle – who seemed to know more about Penny Marshall's last wishes than either her husband or daughter did. The cremation, a simple, dignified ceremony that lasted half an hour, had taken place earlier that morning. Now there was the matter of the service to get through, and then the day would be over.

At the altar, the silver urn containing her mother's ashes stood surrounded by flowers and wavering, flickering tea lights. The priest raised his arms, gathering the small circle of family and well-wishers into his benevolent embrace, his voice rising above Mrs Denning's choked sobs. He brought his hands together in one final prayer and then, abruptly, it was over.

It took a few minutes for people to exit the pews, stopping before Jane and her father to express their sympathy with a word or two or a hand laid softly on an arm; then she felt her father's hand on her back and together they followed the last guests out of the church. She got into the car between Mr Spaulding, her father's boss, and his wife, who kept up a steady, inconsequential patter of words all the way home, to which Jane muttered alternately 'yes' or 'no', which seemed to satisfy her.

One of the neighbours had been round to the house before the service and helped Jane lay out coffee, tea and cake for the handful of mourners making their way back to Southcote. She moved amongst her mother's best china cups and saucers as though in a dream, refilling the two teapots and the tall nickel-plated coffee pot and making sure there were cakes and biscuits for all.

After what seemed like an eternity, it was suddenly five o'clock, and the sun sank behind the trees. The house grew cold, the teacups were abandoned, and finally the last neighbour closed the door and Jane and her father were alone. They washed up together in silence, Jane taking care to dry the plates as thoroughly as if her mother were still standing over her, watching. By seven, everything was back in place and the kitchen and tiny dining room were returned to their usual quiet emptiness.

The long evening stretched before them. How, she wondered, watching her father settle himself in his armchair, would they fill it, and the one after that ... and all the long days and evenings ahead? Her father was nearly sixty-five; he had another few months until retirement. Aside from work and his vegetable garden, he had no hobbies that Jane knew of, no friends other than the neighbours and work colleagues who'd come to stand awkwardly beside him as he buried his wife. What would he do now? Jane had never been close to him, not out of any difference of opinion or adolescent tension, but because he'd never really encouraged it. There was a distance in her father that only her mother seemed able to cross. It had always been that way. But now ... how would it be now?

PART TWO

August 2010

5

It was raining. Not the tearful spittle-lick of an English summer, but the hammering, fist-sized blows of a tropical downpour. Coming back up the beach with the awkward slow-motion gait of someone walking in sand, Lexi was caught out. She was wearing a bikini top and a pair of denim shorts, and soon she was soaked through. She hadn't seen the storm coming. For three days now the skies had been clear and smooth, a taut sheet of cobalt stretched overhead, moving from iridescent blue to smoky lilac at dusk in the time it took her to polish off a G&T at the bar. But not now. Now the sky was the brooding, bruised colour of plums.

She staggered the last few yards to her cottage and pushed open the unlocked front door. She stood for a few moments in the doorway, looking around, water pooling at her feet. The room was immaculate. It had been swept and cleaned as soon as she left that morning. She found it unsettling. It reminded her of her aunt's Holland Park flat, buffed and polished hourly by her invisible staff. She blew out her cheeks. *Relax, Lexi. Just relax. You're on holiday*. An enforced holiday, granted. Jane had practically frogmarched her on to the plane. 'Donal's instructions. Go. Take a holiday. *Go!*' She woke each day to the yawning in-and-out sound of the ocean, the shoreline a few hundred yards from where she slept. A cool early-morning breeze blew in through the shuttered windows, filtered light turning the bedroom into a dancing play of shadow and light.

Mustafa, the young butler-cum-cook, for whom she was the only guest, came every morning just before eight with a tray of perfectly sliced fresh fruit and a still-steaming Italian-style coffee pot. '*Habari, missus. Habari ya asubuhi.*' His greeting was delivered with a smile so wide and impossibly sincere it seemed to belong to another age. On her first day, still dazed after her overnight flight from London and an uncomfortable three-hour bus journey to the coast, she'd watched him walk back up the beach to the hotel, his skin very black against the pale sand, legs and arms in stark contrast to the starched-stiff whiteness of his uniform. Every now and then he stopped, gazing out at the sea as it stretched away to hazy infinity. A group of children shyly showed him something in the curved palms of their hands. When they wandered off again, bored by his response, he continued dreamily on his way as if no interruption had taken place.

She looked down. The water at her feet had gone cold. She kicked off her flip-flops and walked through the small living room to the bedroom, untying her bikini top as she went. She wriggled her way out of her shorts and looked around for a towel. Suddenly, the rain stopped. She lifted her head in surprise. For the past half-hour she'd been deafened by the roar. Now, as quickly as it had started, the fierce drumming of raindrops was gone. She smiled to herself, a slow, private smile. Africa. She was back in Africa again. She turned on the shower and stepped inside.

He spotted her as soon as she walked in. In her faded denim shorts and loose white T-shirt she stood out like an angry, beautiful thumb amongst the oiled, tanned flesh and yards of trailing diaphanous garments. She hesitated in the doorway, scanning the room for an empty seat, then walked over to the bar, sliding on to an empty stool close by. It was the third or fourth time he'd seen her in the past couple of days. She was small, compact and lithe, with the sort of self-possession that hinted at days, weeks, perhaps even months spent on her own. He'd watched her walk down the beach earlier that morning, his attention caught by the strong, slim tendons of her ankles, hollowed away delicately on either side. Her blonde hair was cut short, and now, as he stole a sideways look at her, he saw that her profile was just as striking – the deep cave of her eye marked by a strip of glossy eyebrow and long dark eyelashes, a combination at odds with the smooth fairness of her skin and hair.

'Drink, miss?' Goodwill, the barman, was upon her in a flash.

'A gin and tonic, please.' It was the first time he'd actually heard her speak. She was English. Her voice was unexpectedly low and husky. He felt his pulse quicken with interest.

'Ice and lemon?' Goodwill was solicitous, as he always was with lone women, beautiful or not.

'Mmm, thanks.'

Goodwill looked up and caught Mark staring at her. The two men

26

grinned briefly at each other. Mark watched as the alcohol swirled oilily at the bottom of the glass. There was the satisfying hiss of tonic over the crushed ice, and then Goodwill laid a thin, translucent slice of lemon triumphantly across the top and slid the drink across the counter with a flourish. She took a sip, then reached into her pocket and pulled out a crumpled packet of cigarettes, tapping one out against the counter. Someone sidled up to her immediately. Mark recognised Philippe, the hotel's resident Lothario.

'D'you need a light?' he asked hopefully.

She turned round. 'No,' she said shortly, in a tone of voice that would have sent most people running.

But Philippe wasn't so easily put off. He flicked open his lighter, holding the flame steady in front of her. 'You're here on holiday?'

There was a second's pause. She bent her head to accept the flame. 'Thanks,' she said calmly, straightening up. 'Do me a favour, though, will you? Piss off.'

Philippe's mouth dropped open, but before he could reply, she'd picked up her drink and her cigarettes and moved off further down the bar. Mark's mouth twitched. Ballsy, too. He winked at Goodwill and followed her.

'A tad brutal,' he murmured, turning his head to where Philippe stood staring glumly into his drink. 'Phil's a bit of a pest, granted, but he's harmless enough.'

She turned towards him. 'Do I know you?' she asked coldly.

'No. I'm Mark.' He held out a hand.

She eyed him cautiously. 'Alexandra,' she muttered finally, blowing smoke out of the corner of her mouth. She had a nice handshake: firm, brief, to-the-point.

'Really? You don't look like an Alexandra.'

She looked faintly amused. 'Whatever.'

'Bad day?' he asked mildly.

She frowned and shook her head. 'Sorry,' she muttered finally. 'Long one.'

'Come off it. You've hardly stirred from your cottage.'

'How would you know?'

'I've been watching you,' he said simply, as if it was something she should know.

She turned her head to look at him properly, her eyes narrowing.

Hazel eyes, he noticed, distracted by the freckles across her nose and cheeks, burnished where the sun had caught her. Lioness eyes. 'Why?' she asked finally. 'Why've you been watching me?'

He shrugged. 'Why not?'

'Is that how you spend your holidays? Watching lone women?'

He laughed, amused. 'Three things, lady. First of all, I'm not on holiday. I live here. Secondly, you're hard to miss.' He picked up his beer and on impulse, in a move that was surprisingly bold even for him, laid the still-cold neck on her arm, tracing a line from elbow to wrist. There was a pause.

'What's the third?' Her voice was suddenly unsteady.

He drew in his breath sharply. 'Wait and see.'

And suddenly, there it was. Desire. Overwhelming desire.

He was very tall, a rangy, strong, restless body. Walking alongside him in the dark, back to her cottage, she was conscious of barely reaching his shoulder. Was she mad? *A rest,* Jane had said to her sternly. *Get some rest.* Not meet-a-stranger-in-a-bar-and-take-him-home kind of rest. She nudged the front door open with her foot.

'Nice,' he murmured, dipping his head as he followed her in. She walked over to the couch and switched on a lamp, watching him warily as he looked around. He was certainly good-looking. Tanned, with lovely strong arms and long, muscular legs in baggy khaki shorts; wavy dark brown hair that fell to his shoulders, deep blue eyes and a permanent humorous slant to his mouth. 'Don't have much, do you?' he said finally, his eyes coming back to rest on her.

'I'm only here for a couple of days.' She pulled her T-shirt over her head and wriggled out of her shorts. 'Bedroom's in here,' she tossed over her shoulder as she walked towards the door.

'Steady on,' he laughed, suddenly sounding oddly taken aback. She turned in surprise. Suddenly, for all his boldness, he was the one ill at ease, his demeanour at odds with the easy, confident swagger he'd displayed earlier. 'Don't you want a drink first?' he asked.

Lexi looked up at him impatiently. 'Why? We've already had a drink. Three, as a matter of fact.' She stood in the doorway to the bedroom.

He walked towards her, still nervous, but when his hands went around her back, pulling her towards him, he found his ground again. 'You smell nice,' he murmured against her hair. She pushed her face into his white shirt, breathing deeply. There was nothing like it; that heavy, heady mixture of sweat, aftershave and cigarettes that was so specifically male. She tilted her head back slightly to look at him. Yes, blue eyes, the colour of a summer sky. He was tanned all over, she noticed approvingly as she peeled back his shirt. She ran her hands down his stomach, following the line of silky hair until it disappeared beneath the waistband of his shorts. He was rock hard already.

It took him less than a second to divest himself of his own clothes. She moved first, pushing him gently back on to the low double bed, feeling the mattress give way underneath the unaccustomed weight. There was no time to waste. A knee on either side of his torso, her lips on his, her tongue stiff and seeking ... She swallowed him, literally, drawing his soft lips into her mouth, biting him, just as her body pulled and sucked his penis inside her. If he was surprised, he made no protest, meeting her hunger with his own. It was exactly what she needed: wild, urgent sex. They fought a little. She didn't want him on top of her, the way it usually was for first-time lovers and one-night stands. She preferred it the other way round. She won, of course.

'Jesus,' he groaned, half an hour later, one hand padding about on the small night table for his cigarettes. 'Are you always this ... this ...?' He seemed lost for words.

'This what?'

'This *direct?*'

She grinned. 'Always. Here, gimme one.' She reached out a hand for a cigarette, pushing her face into that splendid, solid chest once more, taking the scent of him all the way down into her lungs. 'Thanks.' She took the lit cigarette and inhaled gratefully, and they smoked together in easy, shared silence. When she made to switch on the bedside lamp, he put out a hand and stopped her.

'I like the darkness,' he murmured, his free hand going around the nape of her neck, his thumb coming to rest gently on her skin. He stroked the cropped hair absently, almost fondly. She closed her eyes. An unexpectedly tender blast of warmth stole over her, and she had to hold back from pulling him inside her again. 'So, where're you from, Alex? I mean, where are you *really* from?'

She stiffened. 'What d'you mean?'

He chuckled softly. The sound reverberated deep in his chest. 'You *sound* English enough but there's something else there ... I can't put a finger on it. I don't know, just a hunch. An army brat, maybe?'

She blinked. He was surprisingly perceptive. She shook her head. 'No, not an army brat.' She took another drag. She was used to being recognised, and she was certain he hadn't recognised her. She hesitated for a second, then shrugged. What the hell ... she wouldn't be seeing him again. 'My dad was a diplomat.'

'Ah. A diplomat brat. Well that explains it.'

She was silent for a moment, then she suddenly rolled off him and walked to the bathroom, closing the door firmly behind her. She leaned against it for a second, then turned on the tap, scooped a little water into her palm and washed herself between her legs. She wiped herself dry and picked her kikoi off the floor. Wrapping it tightly around herself, she opened the door. He'd switched on the light and was sitting up, thumbing through the book she'd been reading. 'Good book?' he asked mildly, holding it up.

'*If* you don't mind.' She reached across him and plucked it from his hands.

'So, now that we've established that we're both colonial brats, what *do* you do for a living, Alex?' he asked, making himself more comfortable. He patted the space beside him.

She ignored the gesture and walked over to her discarded shorts, fished a cigarette out from the pocket and lit it. 'Look, Mark,' she began slowly. 'I had a really good time tonight and I'm sure you're a great guy, but I prefer to sleep on my own and I'm actually really tired. Could we just—'

'Could I just shove off, you mean?' he interrupted gently.

'Yeah, something like that.' She smiled faintly, hoping he wouldn't take offence.

'Sure.' He took the news without pique, swinging his legs easily out of bed. He really was beautiful, she thought as she watched him pull on his clothes, putting his gorgeous olive-skinned body out of reach. He buttoned his shirt and ran a hand through his hair, tucking it behind his ears unselfconsciously. Then he walked over to her and lightly kissed the top of her head. 'See you around. How long're you here for?'

She shrugged. 'Couple more days.'

'Cool.' He pulled open the flimsy wooden door and stepped out, closing it behind him. The cottage suddenly seemed very empty.

She tucked her kikoi under her armpits and turned to the window. She pushed open the shutters, which Mustafa had clearly closed on account of the rain, and perched rather awkwardly on the sill. She smoked quietly, watching the moon dance across the surface of the water, carving a solid bobbing line of light all the way to the horizon. She leaned her head against the window frame and closed her eyes. In the morning, she'd be gone. It was too complicated to explain, too difficult to change. What was the line from that film she'd seen and liked so much? *Have no attachments. Allow nothing in your life that you cannot walk out on in thirty seconds flat if you feel the heat coming round the corner.* Robert de Niro. She smiled wryly to herself. *Have no attachments.* Yeah, well ... no fear of that.

'Gone? What d'you mean, gone?' He stood in front of the hotel receptionist, struggling to take it in.

The young woman inspected her nails with a bored air. 'She left this morning. Checked out.'

Mark scratched his head. 'But ... she ... wasn't she supposed to stay a few more days?'

The receptionist shrugged. The woman had paid for a week's board and lodging, in full, up front. The fact that she'd left after only three nights was of absolutely no consequence to her. She'd already rented the cottage for the following night. Everyone won. Everyone, it seemed, except the man in front of her. She stifled a yawn. 'I think she caught the early bus. To Nairobi.'

He stared at her as though she'd gone mad. '*Sawa, asante,*' he said finally, and walked off. She went back to filing her nails.

Gone? He sat down at a table, confused, struggling to understand what he'd just been told. Was it something he'd said ... or done? Or *not* done? They'd had a good time; he was sure of it. She wasn't the type to fake it, he'd sensed that about her the minute he saw her. She wasn't really his type: small, short hair, boyish-looking ... no, not his type at all. But there was something about her ... the way she held herself, held her own. She was alone, but unlike most women he knew, she wasn't lonely, setting herself very clearly apart from the other tourists. He knew next to nothing about her, other than the fact that she was a diplomat's kid. He didn't know where she lived, or what she did for a living. There was an intensity about her that burned its way through her skin; something in her eyes that bothered him. What could someone like her have seen to provoke such a troubled look?

He shook his head in amazement. It had been a long time since he'd met someone he wanted to know more of, rather than less. 'Fuck it, you're getting soft, Githerton,' he murmured aloud.

Looking up, he caught the waiter's eye and ordered coffee. As if to reprimand himself, he added sternly, 'No sugar.'

The coffee, when it came, was good, thick and strong. He stirred the little demitasse slowly, breathing in its scent. In his mind's eye, he pictured Alex as he'd seen her last night, her slim, pale body on top of his, small pink-tipped breasts swaying slightly as she bent forward, the smooth skin of her stomach and the taut, round swell of her hips, her closed, dreamy face with the light smattering of freckles across the bridge of her nose ...

He swallowed the coffee in a single mouthful. What the hell had he done wrong? He *liked* her. With a petulant, exasperated sigh, he pushed the empty cup away from him and stood up. He was aware of a faint shadow of gloom hanging over his day, like a bruise beneath the skin of a particularly lovely and delicious piece of fruit. He left a handful of notes on the table and walked out.

She pushed her way through the usual throng of tourists, travellers, and friends and relatives of passengers returning to Britain, America, Canada, Germany. A handful of big-bellied uniformed men patrolled the entrance, pushing back non-ticket-holders with nervously twitching sjamboks. A bored-looking policeman glanced at her ticket and passport and stood aside to let her pass. It was crowded inside the terminal building. Long queues formed around solitary islands of officialdom: passport check; baggage check; ticket check; weight check. She took her place in each, shuffling patiently forward, seemingly no closer to completion.

At last she was through. She handed over her small bag and watched it disappear along the worn black tongue of the luggage belt. On her way up to the departure lounge, she stopped at the restrooms. As she opened the door, she almost fell over an elderly blind woman holding out a pannier full of coins. 'Any shillings, madam?' She fished in her pocket and deposited the last of her local currency. She had no need of it: she wouldn't be coming back.

An hour later, she was again in a line. This time she put out a hand to grasp the metal rail of the steps that had been wheeled to the aircraft. 'Welcome aboard.' The smiling flight attendant's head bobbed this way and that, left and right. 'Welcome aboard.' Lexi took her place at the rear of the hot, airless plane, threw her rucksack into the overhead locker and pulled out her earphones. It was a nine-hour flight to London. She would spend the rest of the weekend with her aunt, which was about all she'd be able to stand, and then her enforced leave, which she'd cut abruptly by three days, would be up. She would go into work on Monday morning bright and early. By evening, with any luck, she'd be back on a plane again.

The engines growled into life and the plane was pushed slowly away from the stand. She leaned back in her seat and closed her eyes. Overhead, the speakers crackled and pinged. There was a momentary pause as the plane steadied itself, then it began to gather speed, throbbing and shuddering as it lifted into the sky. She looked out of the window. Below her, spreading out like a dense blanket of stars, Nairobi began to slip away. They circled the city gracefully, and turned northwards. Far below she could see the inky darkness of Lake Victoria, the inland lake that was as vast as a sea. Away to her right was the coast, and the island she'd left early that morning. Somewhere on that island, she knew, was a rather bemused man, probably at that very moment knocking on her cottage door. Not her problem.

She plugged her headphones into her iPhone, switched it to flight mode and settled herself as comfortably as the seat would allow. The mellow sounds of Zero 7 flowed over her. Within seconds, a habit born out of a lifetime of overnight flights, she was fast asleep.

PART THREE

The following day

6

There was a faint click as the front door closed. Jane's eyelids flew open. At last she could stop pretending to be asleep. She pushed her hair out of her eyes, sat upright and looked across her vast Clerkenwell loft to the front door, now firmly shut behind the man who'd just vacated her bed. He hadn't even said goodbye. For a brief, scary moment, she thought she might actually cry. He'd seemed so ... well, *nice*. Normal. Interesting and interes*ted*. An entertainment lawyer. She'd met him at a cocktail party after work on Thursday; it was now Saturday. A wait of two days. Rubbish by anyone's standards except hers, of course. She drew in a deep breath and reached for the phone.

Lexi answered it on the third ring. Bless her. A lone tear trickled down Jane's nose. She couldn't help herself. 'Where are you?' she asked, hoping Lexi wouldn't be able to make out that she was crying. 'You sound as though you're underwater.'

'I'm in a cab. I'm on my way back.'

'Back from where? Oh, shit ... yes, sorry. Your holiday. How ... how was it?'

There was a derisive snort. 'Fine. What's the matter? Why are you crying?'

No such luck. Typical Lexi. Straight to the point. Jane sighed. 'Nothing. Well, no, not nothing ... Oh, it's ... look, d'you want to meet for coffee? I ... I need to talk to you.'

'You're talking to me now,' Lexi pointed out mildly.

'Yes, but it'd be easier in person.'

'Why? What's happened? What have you done now?'

Jane sighed. It was impossible to hide anything from Lexi. 'N-nothing. Well, it's not exactly nothing ... Look, I'd much rather talk about this over coffee.'

'Fine, but I've only just got in. Give me a couple of hours. I'll meet you in Soho. And before you ask, no, I'm not coming out to the East End. Soho or nothing. Your choice.'

'All right. Bar Italia. See you there at ten.'

'Cool.'

Jane hung up the phone and sat with her chin propped in her hands, a glum expression on her face as she looked out across the mezzanine to her lovely loft below. Usually the sight of it never failed to put a smile on her face, but not now, not today. Thank God Lexi was back. No one understood her like Lexi.

It was two years since Alexandra Sturgis had walked into Network News International's offices, just off Old Street, surprising the hell out of everyone by quitting her job at the BBC to join Donal Pearson's risky new venture. Although there were few people in the news industry who *hadn't* heard of Donal, his bold move to take a group of news correspondents out of the big, established networks and consolidate them into a small, tightly knit crew whom he sent into the riskiest places on earth was considered mad by some, irresponsible by others and professional suicide by the rest.

NNI opened for business on 9 March 2004. Two days later, at 7.37 a.m., the peak of rush hour, ten explosions rocked the city of Madrid, killing nearly two hundred people. Six months after Madrid and two days after suicide bombers detonated another string of bombs in an Egyptian holiday resort, Donal scored another coup. He persuaded Jane Marshall to leave her comfortable, well-paid job as a producer at ITN and join NNI, with the promise of company shares and a slice of future profits to compensate for a substantial drop in salary. Jane and Donal had worked together at ITN 'back in the day', starting out within weeks of each other when both were fresh out of college. Jane had begun as a studio assistant and Donal, several steps ahead of her, as a trainee producer. After nearly a decade of climbing (and occasionally clawing) their way up the proverbial ladder, both had had enough. The persuasion process entailed several phone calls, two dinners and an evening of drinks at a Soho bar which might have ended up elsewhere – Jane's flat in Clapham, for example – had Donal not had the presence of mind to drink water rather than whisky.

'That's the funny thing about old Jane,' he told someone a few weeks later, when the deal was signed and Jane Marshall, Associate Producer,

ITN, became Jane Marshall, Creative Director, NNI. 'She's fucking hopeless when it comes to blokes, but when she's at work she's a different beast, I tell you. She can come up with a brilliant idea in less time than it takes you to blink. She's shit hot. Always has been. We're lucky to have her.'

The move paid off. It took NNI three years to move out of the red, but when they did, Jane's first bonus was her deposit on a cavernous empty loft in Saffron Hill and a year's fees at the expensive residential home in Oxfordshire where her father now lived. She loved her loft and she loved her job. When Lexi Sturgis joined them a year later, the two women slowly began to realise that they would not only be good colleagues, but also good friends.

In many ways, it was an unusual friendship. Lexi was six years younger than Jane, and on the surface, they couldn't have been more different. Jane, for all her anxieties about fitting in, finding a group to which she could properly belong, was an extrovert, a smiling, eager-to-please and friendly face who was forever being let down or disappointed in friendship as well as love. She had one friend from university – Amanda – whom she met once or twice a month for coffee and the occasional dinner, but the truth was, at thirty-seven, she was single and childless while most of the girls she'd known over the years had settled more or less happily into marriage and motherhood and their lives had diverged. She and Amanda still liked one another enough to keep in touch, but Jane found it increasingly difficult to summon up the enthusiasm required to pore over each of Amanda's three children's school reports or keep up with who was who at the couples-only dinner parties to which she was no longer invited. 'There's nothing more dangerous than an attractive single woman,' Donal always said breezily whenever she complained. 'And you're more single than most, darling.'

'What the hell's that supposed to mean?' Jane asked indignantly.

'Nothing. Now, where are we on ratings?

At first, Jane was put off by Lexi Sturgis's air of self-possession. Her steely independence was impressive to witness. She came out of her interview with Donal, long blonde hair pulled back into a ponytail, her mouth a slash of glorious bright red lipstick and her bright, lively green eyes completely free of make-up (unlike Jane, who didn't dare leave the house without her armour of eyeshadow, eyeliner, mascara, powder, eyebrow filler and YSL Touche Éclat). Bare-faced, impossibly fresh and sharp as nails, Lexi looked exactly as she did on camera: tough, uncompromising and totally in control. Jane's first reaction was to be afraid. No one could possibly be that self-sufficient, could they?

It wasn't long before Jane saw another side to her. Lexi had been in Iraq for a couple of weeks, one of the first Western reporters on the scene in the town of Kataniyah, near Mosul, where a string of bombs had gone off, killing nearly six hundred people, one of the war's single most deadly attacks. She covered its aftermath, hour by hour, day by day. After almost a week without sleep, she was pulled off the story and brought back to London for an enforced rest. Sitting in a bar on the far side of Old Street a few days later, Jane watched as Lexi raised a glass of neat whisky to her lips. Her hands were shaking slightly. Donal was outside, smoking and talking on his phone.

'You OK?' she asked quietly.

'Yeah,' Lexi muttered after a second. For some reason – quite out of character, it had to be said – Jane didn't press her any further. She took a sip of her own drink and waited. Lexi said nothing more.

As they got up to leave, Jane suddenly blurted out, 'Tell you what, if you're free tomorrow, why don't you come round to mine? I'll make supper. Nothing fancy. I'm a rubbish cook.'

Lexi looked up in alarm. 'Supper?' she echoed. 'At yours?'

'Yeah. I'm literally round the corner. I know you've got a meeting with Donal at five … you could come back with me afterwards.'

There was a moment's silence. 'Yeah, all right,' Lexi said finally. 'Er, thanks.' And that was it.

As they drove back together to Jane's flat the following night, both women were quiet. The streets were slick with rain. It was Tuesday. On Friday, Lexi would be heading back to Baghdad. Jane had just OK'd the idea of a story following the lives of an ordinary Iraqi family whose father and two sons had been killed in the assault on Fallujah. 'I'm itching to do something different,' Lexi had said to Donal as soon as she arrived back. 'Something with a bit more depth. I'm sick of blood and guts and gore.'

'Fine. Come up with an idea and pitch it to Jane. If she likes it, I'll go with it.'

So she did. A half-hour story, covering an ordinary family caught up in extraordinary circumstances. It ticked all the right boxes – compassion, drama, redemption, hope – and the fact that Lexi had picked up a little Arabic didn't hurt either. Jane liked it. 'Yeah. Run with it. Let's see where it goes.'

No one was more surprised at their friendship than Jane. In the six years she'd been at NNI, the only one of her work colleagues to make it past her front door had been Donal, and even then, only a handful of times. The truth of the matter was that Jane had few friends. Almost none, in fact. She'd never quite been able to put her finger on why. It had always been that way. She was easy to get on with: easy-going and easy to please. At work, she was well liked in a light-hearted, superficial kind of way. At school, she'd never had the close, girlie sorts of friendships that she'd seen others enjoy – there was always the matter of being in the wrong school, or with the wrong crowd, or the fact of her mother's early death and her father's painful withdrawal from the world.

At St Augustine's, after Penny died, she'd thrown herself into her studies, winning almost every term prize going and surprising everyone by turning down a place at Cambridge to study economics at LSE instead. Three years later, with a string of short-lived, unhappy liaisons under her belt, she'd left without making any more proper friends than the two she'd had almost from the start, Amanda and Paul. They'd all met at Freshers' Fair in their first week and were in the same halls of residence together. When college ended and Jane walked across the road to Bush House and into an internship at the BBC, Amanda moved into a flat in Shepherd's Bush with her boyfriend, Rory, and Paul went overseas. Apart from the sporadic postcard, Paul more or less dropped out of her life. A year later, Amanda and Rory got married and their first child was on its way. And that was pretty much it. Two more children quickly followed, Amanda gave up her job as a primary school teacher and the family moved to Victoria Park. When Jane followed her eastwards a few years later, buying the unfinished building on Saffron Hill, she hoped briefly that it might mean a renewed closeness. It didn't. Amanda took one look at the dusty, empty space that Jane had set her heart on and grimaced. 'You're mad. How on earth are you going to turn this into a home?'

Lexi Sturgis displayed no such qualms. 'This is it?' she asked incredulously as the taxi pulled away from the kerb and Jane fished out her keys. She looked up at the facade of what had once been a timber merchant's yard. The lettering – J. G. Biglow & Sons – was still a ghostly yellow shadow imprinted into the brickwork.

Jane nodded. 'Yeah. I bought it last year. It's not quite finished ... well, you'll see.' She opened the door and switched on the light.

Lexi clapped a hand to her mouth. She stood in the doorway and gazed up and around her. The dramatic double-height space unfolded in front of them, painted in Farrow & Ball's gentle Cornforth White, with the reclaimed wooden balustrade that ran alongside one wall leading up to the mezzanine-level bedroom. The floor was a sea of shimmering polished concrete, sealed with a high-gloss resin that had been far more expensive than Jane had anticipated – nearly three times what it would have cost her to carpet the place – but it was money well spent. Light poured in from the enormous south-facing windows and bounced off the floor, sending gleaming rivers dancing all the way across its surface, instantly lifting the mood and feel of the whole apartment. She'd deliberately kept it as empty as she dared; a low charcoal-grey Molteni & C L-shaped couch that was big enough for six – not that she'd ever had six people over – a classic Noguchi sculptural glass coffee table and a long wall of bookcases were practically the only pieces of furniture in the living room portion of the loft. There was an old, slightly bowed French wooden kitchen table that served as a dining table, with six – that odd number again! – Hans Wegner Wishbone chairs, a staple of almost every interiors magazine she'd ever opened, and a sleek white kitchen partially hidden behind the three enormous wooden posts that held up the mezzanine.

'Fuck,' Lexi said dazedly, looking around. 'What a flat! It's ... incredible!'

'Really?' Jane said, delighted. 'D'you really think so?'

'No, I say this to everyone,' Lexi said drily. 'No, I mean it. It looks like something out of a magazine.'

'Oh, no ... it's just ... well, yes, I quite like interiors and ... and things like that.' Jane was suddenly self-conscious. 'Nothing special.'

'It's gorgeous. Shit, I thought my aunt had good taste ... plus it's *huge!*'

'Yeah, it is big.' Jane gave an embarrassed laugh. 'Sometimes I think it's a bit mad ... There's only me knocking around in it, but ... what the hell. I like it.'

'Me too.' Lexi grinned. Jane stared at her. She'd hardly ever seen Lexi smile, she realised suddenly. Her face was completely transformed.

'You should do that more often,' she said impulsively, still staring at her.

'What?'

'Smile. Laugh. It suits you.'

'Yeah, well, Iraq was hardly a bundle of laughs. I'm out of practice.'

'How about a glass of wine whilst I cook? I've got a bottle of Rioja somewhere.'

'Sounds good. Can I look through your books?'

'Be my guest.' Jane waved a hand. 'Toilet's through there, if you need it.'

It was well after midnight when Lexi finally called a taxi to take her back to her aunt's place in Holland Park. 'Come again when you're next in town,' Jane said, handing over her coat and bag.

'I will. And thanks … I … I enjoyed it.' The two women stood in the doorway, awkwardly avoiding each other's eye. Despite having polished off nearly two bottles of wine between them, Lexi hadn't yet dropped her guard. Jane had learned only the barest minimum about her, but what she had learned intrigued her. Lexi was a loner, but with a depth and compassion to her that was surprising and touching at the same time. Jane had never met anyone quite like her.

Somehow, against the odds, something in the way they approached each other seemed to work. Slowly, with much hesitation on both sides, they inched their way over the next few months towards friendship. To everyone's surprise – and Donal's great amusement – the friendship stuck and held.

7

The taxi turned off Holland Park Road and drove up Campden Hill Square, stopping just before number 14, the only red-brick building in the square. Home. Lexi paid the driver, hoisted her rucksack on to her shoulder and walked up the path. She opened the front door quietly. Her aunt would still be asleep. She had a couple of hours to take a bath and change her clothes before meeting Jane in Soho. She stood for a second in the hallway, breathing in the familiar, unmistakable scent of her aunt's home: beeswax furniture polish, Chanel No. 5 and heady, pungent lilies.

Then she opened the inner door, let go of her rucksack and kicked off her plimsolls.

She wandered down the corridor to the kitchen, stopping to poke her head round the living room door on the way. The spacious, elegant room was immaculate; not a cushion, plant or coffee table book out of place. An enormous snowy orchid stood in front of the window, offering a seductive glimpse of the plush interior to passers-by. She walked into the kitchen and had to suppress a grin. It had only been a couple of months since her last stopover in London, but already Aunt Julia had altered things again. She remodelled her interiors the way some people changed their clothes. The kitchen had been completely redone. The entire rear wall of the house had been knocked out, replaced by an enormous glass window opening on to a starkly beautiful Japanese garden. Giant bamboo stems cast spiky shadows on the ground, an intricate, swirling pattern of black and grey pebbles, smoothed into shape each day by some poor gardener. There were enormous pots of lush, stark plants with names only the interior designers would be able to pronounce, and in the corner, climbing all the way up the back wall, a magnificent hydrangea bush, bursting with thick white and pale pink globes of flowers.

She dragged her eyes back to the acres of gleaming white-and-grey marble, the enormous black Aga (which Aunt Julia wouldn't even know how to switch on and off, she thought drily) and the glossy grey cabinets, and smiled wryly. For the past two years, she'd lived out of her rucksack, returning every now and then to the Cairo hotel where everyone stayed, with the occasional week in London when Donal insisted on seeing her. The frenetic pace and unpredictability of her job suited her perfectly. She couldn't imagine living in one place for more than a week at a time; it was why she'd joined NNI in the first place. Donal had offered her what she'd always been looking for – an escape from the humdrum of everyday life, from the countless little commitments and obligations that a settled existence seemed to bring. She didn't want to join the endless circle of dinner parties and trips to the theatre and boutiques that made up Aunt Julia's routine, and she certainly didn't want to spend the rest of her life checking and rechecking facts for a stroppy news anchor, which was pretty much all she'd done at the BBC. Donal had offered her a way out of all that and she'd grabbed it with both hands.

'Lexi!' Her aunt's voice broke into the silence. Lexi almost jumped out of her skin. 'You're back!' Aunt Julia said, smiling widely. 'When did you arrive? And why didn't you tell me you were coming? I'd have sent a car to pick you up.'

'No, there's no need,' Lexi said quickly. 'I took the train to Paddington, then grabbed a cab. It's what I always do. You know that.'

Aunt Julia smiled tolerantly. Then she frowned. 'What on earth have you done to your hair, darling?'

Lexi put up a hand self-consciously. 'Nothing.'

'I can see *that*. Let me make an appointment with—'

'No, it's fine. I'm fine, Aunt Julia. I'm only here for a couple of days. I'll be heading out soon.'

'Where've you been?' Aunt Julia asked, peering at her. 'You look *dreadful*, darling. As though you've been dragged through a bush backwards.'

Lexi sighed. 'I've been on holiday, actually. Lamu.'

'Oh, *Lamu*. Yes, yes, you did tell me you were going. How *divine*. Did you meet anyone interesting? Did you go to Princess Caroline's place? The last time I was—'

'No, I didn't go to Princess Caroline's house, and no, I didn't meet anyone interesting,' Lexi broke in quickly. 'I was only there for a few days. Look, I'm going to have a bath. I've got to meet Jane in Soho in an hour.'

'But you've only just arrived! And I've hardly seen you,' Aunt Julia protested.

'I know. But … I'm busy,' Lexi said, moving quickly towards the door. The last thing she felt like was an in-depth conversation with her aunt. They always ended in the same way – frustration on Lexi's part and incomprehension on her aunt's. 'I just don't understand why you choose to live like this,' was Aunt Julia's favourite complaint. 'I'll … I'll be back later,' Lexi said vaguely, and slipped out of the kitchen before Aunt Julia could say anything more.

She hurried up the stairs to the two-bedroom flat on the top floor that had been hers and Toby's since boarding school days. She paused in the doorway to Toby's room, just for a second, her hand going automatically to her throat. She touched her skin lightly, pressing her fingers against the pain that lay just beneath the surface, and took a few deep breaths to steady herself. Aunt Julia had brought in the decorators shortly afterwards, thinking that wiping the room clean would bring some relief, but it hadn't. It was four years since he'd died, but everything about the room was his, still. Always. To her credit, Aunt Julia had offered to sell the house immediately afterwards. '*Anything*, darling … whatever you want. We can move somewhere else … Chelsea? Kensington? Wherever you choose.' But Lexi couldn't bring herself to move. The room at the top of the stairs was all she had left of Toby. That and the scent of him that was as strong as his ghost.

She turned away, shutting the door tightly behind her, and walked into the bathroom. It had once been a large, high-ceilinged bedroom until the interior designers had ripped it up and turned it inside out. Only the blonde oak parquet floor remained, together with the corniced walls, now painted a soft shade of chalk. The antique bath stood in the window, overlooking the front garden and the street; the windows had been sandblasted to provide privacy whilst allowing the light in. A long, pale cream marble plinth held the sink and the few products the design- ers had grudgingly allowed on display. Lexi walked over, divesting herself of her clothing, and picked up the midnight-blue Neal's Yard bottles, one by one. The names appeared to belong to another age, a medieval era of apothecaries and alchemists. *Purifying Palmerosa Toner. Soothing Starflower Daily Moisturiser. Frankincense Facial Wash.* They looked good enough to eat.

She turned on the taps, catching sight of her reflection in the mirror as she straightened up. She stopped and put a hand to her cheek. Aunt Julia was right. There was no denying the fact that she looked tired. No, not just tired … exhausted. Even the faint tan she'd acquired on Lamu couldn't quite cover the strain of the past six months. She dragged her eyes away from the mirror and picked up one of the pots. *Rosemary and Elderflower Bath Salts.* She tipped it slowly into the water, watching the salts fizz gently in a cloud of soothingly scented steam. She stepped into the tub. The scalding water swelled over her. She pinched her nose, held her breath and submerged herself, the way she used to as a child.

8

Lexi was late. Jane looked at her watch and sighed. She'd been rehearsing her story, building up to the moment of indignation when the front door closed behind him and another one-night stand slipped out into the early-morning light without so much as a goodbye, and every minute's delay was threatening to deflate the impact. No pun intended. *Wham, bam, thank you, ma'am.* Truth was, there hadn't even been much of a 'bam'. They were both drunk. He more than she. If there was one thing she'd learned over the past decade of (mostly) one-night stands, it was that the more they drank, the less able they became in *all* departments, not just in the little matter of maintaining an erection. So why get drunk in the first place? She didn't even like the taste. No, *she* drank because it was the quickest way to get over the crippling shyness that rendered her deaf, dumb and stupid in the presence of fanciable men, thereby ruining whatever chances she might have had if she'd only *known what to say*. It was a secret she kept to herself. Jane Marshall? *Shy?* Most people would've laughed out loud at the mere thought of it.

'Sorry, sorry I'm late!' Lexi pushed her way through the throng at the counter, preventing Jane's despondent train of thought from descending even further into bleakness and despair. 'I took a cab at the last minute … I'd have been quicker walking. Sorry.'

Jane waved a hand magnanimously. 'No worries. I was just … thinking.'

'Don't,' Lexi advised. 'Don't think. Just tell me what happened. What're you having, by the way?'

'Triple-shot macchiato, full-fat, and with extra cream. I need the rush.'

'Sure you do. An espresso for me,' Lexi instructed the grinning barista. 'No sugar.'

'And that's why *you* never worry about your weight and I do,' Jane said glumly.

'Never mind your weight. What's wrong?'

Jane drew a deep breath. 'You remember that drinks thing I told you about last week? The one at Berners Street Studios? Well, I met someone.'

Lexi said nothing; just waited for her to continue. Jane could see by the expression in her friend's eyes that she'd already guessed how the story would end.

'What *I* just don't understand,' Lexi said carefully, when Jane had finally finished, 'is why the hell you care so much.'

Jane frowned at her. 'Of course I care! He … he seemed like a nice guy.'

'Well, clearly he wasn't. Nice guys say goodbye. Or "see you later".

Even if they don't mean it. But what do you care? You're not going to see him again, are you?'

'But … but … that's the whole point!' Jane looked upset and bewildered. Lexi resisted the temptation to shake her.

'What?'

'I never see any of them again! And it's not by choice! My choice, I mean.'

'Well, it should be. Look, you're in a win-win situation.'

'*How?*'

'You wanted a fling, you got a fling. What's the problem?'

'But I wasn't *looking* for just a fling,' Jane wailed.

It was Lexi's turn to look surprised. 'You met him on Thursday, right?' Jane nodded miserably. 'You went out for a drink with him on Friday? And he wound up coming back to yours on Friday night. Tell me, how does that *not* make it a fling?'

'Well … I just thought … I don't know … I thought—'

'Look,' Lexi said briskly, cutting her short. 'I'll tell you what *he* thought. It'll save us both a bit of time. *He* thought, "Great. She's up for it. Met her last night, we've been out for a couple of drinks … she's a grown-up, knows what she wants … no hassle. I got lucky." That's what *he* thought, I promise you. But I bet you thought you'd go out for breakfast, spend the morning together, that kind of shit.'

Jane felt tears beginning to smart behind her eyes. 'But why's that so unreasonable? We had a good time, didn't we? Why shouldn't we go out for breakfast? I'm not asking him to move in, for Christ's sake!'

Lexi sighed. 'It's out of character. No, not *your* character, silly. The character he *thinks* he got. The character he'll be looking for next weekend, and the one after that, and in a year's time he'll *still* be looking for her and it just won't dawn on him that she doesn't really exist. You know what your problem is?'

Jane sighed. 'You're going to tell me. I can feel it.'

'It's simple. Either you learn to tell them what you *really* want, up front, right from the start. Or you stop pretending that what *they* want is what *you* want. You don't want a one-night stand. You keep on *saying* you do, and you keep on behaving as though you do, but you don't. You want a proper boyfriend – don't ask me why – but you keep on choosing the least likely candidates out there.'

'And you don't?'

'What? Choose the wrong candidates? No, I choose the right candidates. I don't want a boyfriend. I choose the same guys you do ... the only difference is, I'm happy with my choices. I don't want any more.'

'I don't believe you.'

'It doesn't matter. The point is, *you* want one and you haven't got one. I don't want one, and I don't have one. It's as simple as that.'

'Oh, Lexi ... it's never that simple,' Jane sighed.

'It is. You're the one making it complicated. Now, d'you want another coffee, or d'you fancy something stronger?'

Jane shook her head. 'No, if I have a drink, I'll wind up in tears. Probably worse.'

'I doubt it. You're over him. Come on. Let's go to Blacks. It's just across the road.'

'Blacks? Isn't that a members' club?'

Lexi grinned. 'Yeah. Aunt Julia. She belongs to most of 'em.'

Jane smiled faintly. 'I keep forgetting. Christ, if you think there's a contradiction between me and the men I choose, try the one between you and your aunt!'

'I know. But I can't help who I'm related to. She comes in handy every once in a while.'

'It's a bit more than that,' Jane sighed, picking her bag off the floor. 'You're bloody lucky to have her, Lexi Sturgis, and you know it.'

9

Kensington, London

The day was hot and sticky, making Inès Kenan think longingly of the swimming pool at the bottom of the garden at the house in Zamalek, in the centre of Cairo. Her hair was curled damply around the nape of her neck and it wasn't even yet midday. She pulled it impatiently into a ponytail and fanned herself with a piece of paper yanked out of the printer. The windows were wide open, but here, unlike Cairo, there was no air-conditioning, no cooling breeze from the trees outside her window, no shutters to protect the rooms inside the apartment from the sun.

In her bedroom on the first floor of the flat she shared with her sister, Deena, there was nothing but the heat and the humid, smog-scented air from Kensington High Street that somehow found its way down Wright's Lane, turning the corner at Iverna Court and floating directly up to the windows of the bedroom that overlooked Iverna Gardens ... *her* room, in other words. Deena's room was on the other side of the corridor and stayed cool all summer long.

She scraped the last few tendrils into place and tried to focus on something other than the rivulet of sweat that was making its leisurely way down her back. She stared at the title of the essay she'd been writing for what seemed like months: 'Modernism, Sex and Redemption through the works of Wagner and Freud'. She had four weeks to finish it, and there were days when she felt no closer to completion than she had been when she started. She could have kicked herself for choosing it. Modernism *and* sex? She knew precious little about either.

She looked away from her computer screen. Her eye fell on *Hello!*. Anne Hathaway's bold new look gazed sleekly back at her from the cover. She picked it up. People always commented that she looked like the Hollywood star, although Inès couldn't see the resemblance, especially not now. Anne's tumbling locks were gone, replaced by a short, snappy cut that wouldn't have looked amiss on a boy. Inès flicked quickly through the photographs. She'd have given anything to cut her hair off, especially in this heat. She had the same thick, lustrous dark brown hair that all the Kenan women had – had *always* had. Grandmother, mother, sister, aunts, cousins ... a glossy, cascading signature of curls. She put down the magazine suddenly, abruptly. It was time to do it before she lost her nerve.

An hour later, she sat in front of the mirror at the Vidal Sassoon salon around the corner, holding her hair away from her face and neck. 'All of it,' she said firmly, pointing to Anne Hathaway.

The head stylist's eyes widened. He stared at her in the mirror. '*All* of it? You've got such beautiful hair.'

'Yes.' Inès swallowed. 'Just like hers.'

'Brave girl. But it'll suit you, you know. You've got very similar features. Right, let's get you shampooed before you change your mind!' He grinned reassuringly at her.

*

'Inès?' Deena looked up at her in alarm as she walked into the living room. 'Oh my God! What have you done to your hair?'

'What's the matter?' Her mother, ever alert and ready for all kinds of disasters, hurried through from the kitchen. She caught sight of Inès and almost dropped the teapot. 'Your hair! What has he done to your hair!' she shrieked. She was preparing their afternoon tea, a transplanted ritual from Cairo that she insisted upon whenever she and her husband came to England from Paris to spend time with their daughters.

'I ... I asked him to,' Inès began nervously.

'You. Asked. Him. To.' Her mother appeared to be struggling with the words. '*Leh?*' There was genuine confusion on her face.

'Because I'm tired of it.'

'Tired? How can you be *tired* of your hair?'

'Ma, it was too long. Plus, it's hot.'

'Hot? You call this *hot*?' Her mother swept an arm around her, pulling the whole of Kensington into her disbelief. 'This is London, not Zamalek! It's *never* hot.'

Deena's face registered both shock and admiration simultaneously. 'Ma, it's been a hot summer,' she interjected soothingly. 'And it'll grow back. Soon,' she added hopefully.

Her mother drew herself up to her full height of five foot three inches, her bosom quivering tremulously underneath her black silk abaya. Her kohl-rimmed eyes filled with easy tears. 'I don't understand. Your hair ... your beautiful hair.' She dabbed her cheeks carefully with the linen napkin and her lips took on a tight, disappointed line before she delivered her killer blow. 'What will your father say?'

For the rest of the day Inès waited for her father's return with queasy nervousness. Her father could go from gentle to roaring in a heartbeat, and if there was one thing she feared, it was his disapproval. In the event, he said very little. 'You've cut your hair,' he murmured as he sat down to dinner. There was a pause of a few seconds in which everything in the room stopped, even the clocks.

'Y-yes, Abu, this ... this morning.'

He sighed. 'It seems to be the fashion nowadays, hmm?' He glanced at his wife. 'They're all wearing it short.' And that was the end of it, the explosion that never came.

10

You had to hand it to her sister, Deena thought, looking at Inès that evening at dinner, half in irritation, half in admiration. Somehow – Deena had no idea how – she managed to get away with it. If Deena herself had calmly walked up the road as if she were going to the park and lopped all her hair off, all hell would have broken loose. It was partly an eldest child thing. She was three years older than Inès and therefore had to 'show an example'. What their parents failed to realise was that Inès never took any notice of examples, good, bad or indifferent. She'd always steered her own path, made her own decisions and chosen what she wanted to do, rather than what she was expected to do. The fact that she managed to do it without incurring any wrath whatsoever was testimony to her modus operandi, a skilful combination of outright disobedience and maximum charm. But there was something else, something Deena couldn't quite put her finger on. It was almost as if they were afraid of Inès, of provoking or pushing her too far. Deena had never been able to fathom it. Perhaps that was just what happened when, instead of hiding and masking your true feelings, you let them show.

Deena had always been the reasonable one, the calm, reliable one who never lost her temper or relinquished control. In contrast, Inès was prone to outbursts and tantrums, quicksilver changes of mood and fits of tears. When they were much younger, Deena could remember quite clearly wanting to throttle her sister. But Inès's moods and outbursts had always been tempered by a nature that was sweeter and kinder than that of almost anyone Deena knew, herself included. There wasn't a manipulative bone in Inès's body – she was simply as she was. It made it impossible to be angry with her for any length of time ... except now. Now Deena wanted to throttle her all over again. She looked good with her hair all short and feathered. No, she looked *great*. Deena would have given anything to cut her own hair. Especially now.

She glanced up and caught Inès's enquiring glance. Something of what she was thinking must have shown on her face. She bent her head quickly to her soup.

'What time is your exam?' her father asked suddenly.

'First thing. Nine o'clock,' Deena answered. Her stomach gave a small lurch.

'There's nothing to be anxious about. You'll sail through. Just like I did.'

'Yes, Abu,' Deena croaked. She swallowed a mouthful of soup, avoiding Inès's eye.

Deena was a fourth-year medical student at St Thomas's Hospital in Westminster, a brisk thirty-minute walk from the flat. She'd just completed her last three-month stint, in emergency medicine, and, assuming she passed the following morning's final examination, of course, was about to begin her final rotation in general surgery. In just over a year's time, at the end of the gruelling four-year programme, again assuming she made it through, she would finally qualify as a surgeon, fulfilling her parents' every last wish and ambition ... and her own, of course.

'When will you know?' Inès asked innocently.

'Probably right away,' Deena replied. Her stomach gave another little lurch. The thought of coming home to tell them she'd failed the exam was making her feel quite faint.

'Nothing to worry about,' Abu repeated firmly. 'Nothing to worry about at all. The Kenans *never* fail at anything. Remember that.'

Deena nodded, too nervous to speak.

The rest of the meal passed in uneasy silence. As soon as she'd finished helping Inès and her mother wash and dry the dishes, Deena escaped down the corridor to her room. She shut the door behind her and leaned against it, closing her eyes. If she were entirely honest, the fluttering in her stomach was only partly to do with the thought of the exam. When she closed her eyes, it wasn't the face of Mr Medda, her surgical consultant, that she saw ... it was someone else's. His. She saw him as she'd seen him the other night, the smooth, taut muscles of his arm stretching towards her as he reached across to light her cigarette. They were standing next to one another, there in the flat where she'd first seen him, wrapped in that special stillness that he had, soft and content. There was a quietness about him that drew the eye; just like the others, she was mesmerised by his calm authority. A shiver of almost unbearable anticipation moved through her and she opened her eyes, blinking slowly, as though coming out of the dark tunnel of night.

She walked over and sat on the bed. Her mattress creaked a little under her weight. She kicked off her shoes and lay down, smoothing the eiderdown on either side of her. He loomed in her mind in a series of images, outlines, expressions, glances ... until the air thickened with his presence, almost as if he were there in the room with her. His face began to move through her mind in light and colour, filling her consciousness ... she moved towards him, then away again ... closer, further, near and far.

11

'*There* she is! Inès!' Someone called to her from across the street. Inès stopped and turned round. On the opposite side of the road was her father, and beside him, her uncle Khaled, her father's older brother. Uncle Khaled held up his walking stick, waving frantically at her as though she were blind. 'Inès! Over here!'

'Uncle Khaled!' she yelled back, her face breaking into a smile. When had he arrived? She waited for a cyclist to pass, then hurried over. 'I didn't know you were coming!' she cried.

'I only just got here. Just now. But your hair! You've cut your hair!' he exclaimed, looking to his brother, as if for confirmation or explanation.

'Yes, yes, the other day,' her father muttered impatiently. 'It's old news now.'

'Is Tante Soraya with you?' Inès asked quickly. The last thing she wanted was a discussion about her haircut.

'No. Not this time, I'm afraid,' Khaled chuckled. 'You'll have to make do with me.'

'Where have you been?' her father asked, frowning.

'At the library. I've only got another three weeks, Abu. Remember?'

'Ah, such a diligent student. Just like her mother,' Uncle Khaled said affectionately. 'D'you remember, Ibrahim, how we used to—'

'Come now,' her father interrupted him. 'Inès doesn't want to hear all that again. Let's go.'

'I don't mind,' Inès said quickly, squeezing her uncle's arm. 'But where are we going?'

'Your uncle wants an ice cream,' her father said, sighing. 'He's been asking for one since he arrived.'

Inès smiled. 'Where would you like to go, Uncle?'

'Dino's,' Uncle Khaled said happily, raising his stick to press the pedestrian crossing button. 'Haven't you ever been to Dino's?' He loved showing Deena and Inès that he knew more about London than they did.

Inès shook her head. 'No, never. Where is it?'

'Just over there.' He raised his stick again, pointing in the direction of Kensington Church Street.

Inès laughed. 'How do you know all these places, Uncle?'

'There are many things I know,' he said cryptically. 'Come.' The lights turned red. Arms linked, the three of them walked slowly across the road.

Inès watched as Uncle Khaled took his last dainty scoop of vanilla ice cream. He patted his lips and moustache carefully with the linen napkin and signalled to the waitress. *'Un doppio espresso, per favore,'* he said smoothly. Both he and her father watched with automatic male interest as the pretty waitress cleared away the dishes. 'There's someone I want you to meet,' he said suddenly, turning back to Inès.

'Who?' Inès looked at him in surprise. She saw the two men exchange a quick glance. Her pulse started to race. 'Why?' she added sharply. A little *too* sharply.

'Inès,' her father murmured gently, lapsing into Arabic. 'Don't be rude.'

'Abu, I'm not being rude,' she replied, as calmly as she could. 'Who is this "someone", anyway?'

'His name is Talal,' her uncle interjected. 'He's an outstanding young man, from a *very* prominent family, the Ghalibs. I'm sure you've heard of them.'

Inès shook her head. 'Are you starting up a marriage bureau, Uncle Khaled?' She tried to turn it into a joke, to disguise the panic fluttering inside her.

The waitress returned, bearing her uncle's *doppio espresso*. He was silent for a few moments as he stirred a lump of sugar around the thimble-sized cup. 'Of course,' he said simply, with his slow, quiet smile, 'ordinarily, it'd be Deena's turn. She's older, after all. But she has her studies to finish, and what man wants a medical student for his wife?'

'Uncle! How can you say that?'

'There's no need to exaggerate, Khalu,' his brother remonstrated. 'Deena will make a very good wife, medical student or not.'

'I can't *believe* you two!' Inès exclaimed. Her father could be surprisingly conservative, often when she least expected it. 'Mummy was finishing her studies when you married.' She looked at him accusingly.

'It was different back then,' Abu said darkly. His eyes went to her hair.

'Well, *you* insisted on sending them here,' murmured Uncle Khaled, finishing the last drop of his espresso. 'All this "Inès" and "Deena" business. Inas and Dafiyah, that's who they are. Who is this "Inès"? Is she French?' He lapsed into Arabic with his brother. 'Didn't I tell you? You should have left the girls at home, Ibrahim. You'd have a lot less to worry about. Look at our two. Both happily married, two children each, Fatimah with another on the way. God has been good to us, blessed be His name. Still, it's not too late.'

Inès looked away. She could feel the old, familiar resentment beginning to build in her chest. She heard Deena's voice in her ear; her sister knew how to handle them. *Stay calm, don't provoke; don't answer back. Let it all wash over you and then get on with your life. Just as before.* In her unflappable way, she'd somehow managed to avoid the fate that was now threatening to descend upon Inès. *Meet whoever they put in front of you. Be polite, smile nicely and then tell them that you don't like him. Make it seem as though you've actually considered it. Don't say no outright. No one can force you, Inès. It's your choice.* It was easy enough for *her* to say. Deena's medical studies seemed to take precedence over everything, including marriage.

'Don't you at least want to meet this young man?' her father asked.

Inès sighed. She twisted the strands of the pearl bracelet she was wearing. 'No, Abu, I don't. But you're going to make me anyway, so what's the point of telling you how I feel about it?'

She saw her uncle glance accusingly at her father. No doubt he would report her churlish behaviour back to the family members in Cairo, who'd turn to each other in the same disapproving way. *Well, that's what happens when...* and the rest was left unsaid. It was a familiar refrain. 'When *what?*' she'd once yelled at her mother, as a teenager. She knew now that it referred to a multitude of sins, all stemming from the single decision Ibrahim Kenan had taken to send his daughters overseas to an English boarding school, where they'd surely mixed with all sorts of modern, unsuitable types. What else did he expect?

'Fine, I'll meet him,' she said, capitulating suddenly. There was no point in fighting them, at least not openly. She would join in the farce and meet whoever it was they were talking about. She would do exactly as Deena said: find half a dozen reasons not to like him and then gracefully let the idea die. The problem, of course, was that this was just the beginning. Before the year was out, she'd have had a dozen such men paraded in front of her, and how long could she reasonably be expected to keep on saying no?

She saw her father and uncle exchange glances. Her father looked relieved, but Uncle Khaled looked uneasy. He knew that it wasn't in her nature to capitulate so quickly. That was Deena's way; Inès must have something up her sleeve. She could read his discomfort like an open book.

'Come, Abu, Uncle,' she said decisively. 'Let's finish up. Mummy will be waiting for us.'

She stood, and waited for them to get to their feet. Her uncle got up stiffly, levering himself on to his silver-tipped cane, impatiently waving off any offers of help. His bad leg – the result of an old accident – had begun to worsen, though he refused to acknowledge it. Inès watched him recover just before he was thrown off balance. The twinge of pity that rose in her throat caught her out. She coughed hurriedly and turned her face away. It was the one thing her uncle couldn't stand: pity. She understood him well. In that, too, they were unexpectedly alike.

12

'Come in, come in!' The man holding open the door couldn't have been more pleased to see them. He practically reached out and dragged them in. 'Asya! Asya!' he shouted over his shoulder. 'They're here! The Kenans are here! Come in! It's good to see you, Ibrahim, good to see you! It's been a long time ... too long, in fact. Come in and meet my wife, and

Ammar, of course. Ammar!' He barely drew breath before yelling for his son.

'Meet? Marry, you mean,' Inès hissed indignantly under her breath to her mother as they were shepherded down the narrow corridor.

'Oh, Inès,' her mother murmured. 'You *do* exaggerate.'

No exaggeration necessary, Inès thought crossly, taking a seat opposite a stout, rather sour-looking woman in a patterned hijab and a long black abaya, whom she took to be Mrs Ghalib. The very air reeked of matchmaking. Her mother sat next to her, leaving the two men, Dr Kenan and Mr Ghalib, standing, looking down on their womenfolk with tentative, persuasive smiles of encouragement.

'You're comfortable? Not too warm? Something to drink, perhaps?' Mr Ghalib was beside himself.

'Fadi, Fadi ... let our guests settle down,' his wife protested. She turned to Mrs Kenan and in a voice that was every bit as insistent as her husband's asked, 'You'll take some tea?'

Inès saw her mother's hand go to her throat in an unconscious gesture of self-protection. Oh dear. They hadn't even met the young man and already it was going wrong. She had to bite the inside of her cheek to stop herself smiling. Oh, how she and Deena would giggle over this one! She cast a surreptitious glance around the living room. It was typically overstuffed. Too much furniture; too many pictures; too many silver-framed photographs of relatives past and present. Garish Oriental rugs covered almost every square inch of a dun-coloured carpet, and a sombre-looking wooden cabinet took up nearly all of one wall, casting an uncomfortable pall over the gathering. It was the polar opposite of their own light-filled, airy apartment in Kensington. A sure sign, if she needed one, that any potential match was doomed.

'How do you take your tea, my dear?' Mrs Ghalib turned to Inès holding a cup aloft. 'With milk and sugar, like the English?' Her tone implied that nothing could be worse.

Inès quickly shook her head. 'No thank you. Just as it is.'

Mrs Ghalib nodded approvingly as she passed it over. Inès tried not to catch her mother's eye. The whole thing was ridiculous, *so* last century!

She looked at her father, who had accepted a cup *and* a slice of cake. 'Wonderful, wonderful,' he was murmuring appreciatively. Inès looked on, half amazed, half amused. 'Such wonderful cakes, Mrs Ghalib! Wonderful! And wonderful to see you, Fadi, wonderful!' One more 'wonderful', she thought mutinously, and she'd stand up and leave. Her mother changed the subject with alacrity.

'So, I understand your son is studying engineering?' She turned to Mrs Ghalib.

Mrs Ghalib nodded heavily. 'He wants to do his doctorate,' she said, unable to fully disguise her pride. 'He already has a master's degree, you know. Both of them, yes, both my sons. But the expense! Both boys, still living at home! What can I do? I prayed for boys so that they could bear their father's name and partner him in his business, but they have no interest in—'

'What sort of engineering?' Inès spoke suddenly, cutting her off mid sentence. The words were out of her mouth before she could stop them. Her mother frowned at her.

Mrs Ghalib looked confused. 'He's an engineer, that's all—'

'Mechanical engineering.' His father spoke up from across the room. He lifted his head and bellowed for the second time. 'Ammar!'

'I'm here.' A voice spoke from the doorway. 'What's all the fuss about?' They all looked up. Inès's eyes widened. He was short *and* fat. There was a sudden pause, and then the room sprang into action once more.

'Ammar! There you are, *habibi*!'

'I've been shouting for you for half an hour! Come in, come in … come and meet some new friends.' His father stepped forward, welcoming him in. 'Come … this is Dr Kenan … you remember I told you about him? Uncle Khaled's older brother … and this is his wife, Lateefa … no, no, please … please don't get up … and *this* … this is their youngest daughter, Inas.'

Everyone in the room turned to Inès. She felt the heat rising in her cheeks. An image suddenly popped into her head of a prize cow she'd seen on television being led out to auction. She was now that unfortunate cow. She hurriedly swallowed the rest of her tea, scalding her tongue.

PART FOUR

December 2010–January 2011

13

He knew the runway at Lamu airport like the back of his hand; every tree, every pothole, every bump. The small island airport was actually on Manda island, which technically wasn't an island at all, but a fist-shaped bump of land that jutted out from the mainland, curving protectively around Lamu. He adjusted his headphones, picking up the static-filled voice from the small air tower. 'Papa Alpha Zero Two Seven. Are you clear for take-off?' He looked quickly left and right. The murmuring metallic water ebbed and flowed around him. Above, in all directions, the warm winter skies were clear. To his left, across the narrow strip of water, lay the Corniche Path, the long line of homes-turned-hotels and swaying palm trees that bordered the harbour. Dozens of squat wooden boats and elegant yachts with tall, billowing sails were tethered to the jetties like animals drinking at a trough, bumping gently against one another. The ornate stuccoed facade of Lamu General Hospital swung briefly into view as he nosed the small plane around, steadying himself and his three passengers for take-off, and then disappeared again as he faced the ocean.

'Papa Alpha Zero Two Seven. Requesting runway clearance.'

'You're clear to go. Blue skies, Githerton. *Tutaonana.*'

'*Asante.*' He grinned. He'd known Jefferson, the guy in the control tower, since primary school. They sometimes drank a beer together at the Peponi, the same hotel bar where he'd met Alexandra that night. His mind skittered over the events of that evening yet again, producing a bittersweet longing in him that he quickly fought to clear. *Concentrate. You're about to take off.* The dark strip of runway stretched out in front of him. There was very little crosswind. The plane, a small four-seater Bellanca Cruisemaster, generally had good rudder control, but he'd struggled with a strong headwind on landing the previous week. Today he was ferrying an American couple back to their safari base at the foot of Kilimanjaro. 'It's my wife,' the man had said to him, a touch sheepishly, puffing on one of those giant cigars that only Americans ever seemed to smoke. 'She got fed up with all them damned animals. She'd rather be lying on a beach somewhere. You know how it is.' Mark had looked at him uncomprehendingly.

Across the narrow aisle from where the Americans were sitting were two giant cooler boxes of medical supplies, including several pints of blood, scheduled for delivery to the British Army, temporarily head-quartered at the Fairmount Hotel just outside Nanyuki. Each year they sent a battalion out to Kenya, ostensibly to acclimatise the troops to places like Helmand and Basra, and Mark had seen the aftermath of a bar brawl after the lads had been in town. The blood he carried was simply a precaution. He was looking forward to Nanyuki. He'd had a rather cryptic message from Mike Smith, one of the officers with whom he'd become friendly over the past couple of years. *Heard you're coming up on Friday. Meet us at the Zebar after you unload. Might have something for you.* He wondered what the 'something' might be.

He pushed the throttle forward and felt the sweet, satisfying tremor of the engines underneath his thighs. The plane shuddered for a split second, then surged ahead. Its climbout rate was good; just over two thousand feet per minute. The land beneath him fell away as they lifted with very little sway, ocean and sky merging for a minute and then separating again as he swung the nose away from the horizon. He continued climbing steadily upwards, bursting through the light haze, puncturing it like a needle through skin, and then they were above the mist, looking back down at the earth through its veil.

Behind him, in an intimacy that was a little too tight for his liking, the American couple excitedly ooh-ed and ah-ed, pointing out landmarks come upon slowly through the distorting perspective of distance. He slipped on the headphones, and at once the chatter behind him receded to a soft murmur. He was in his favourite spot in the whole wide world: at the controls of his own plane. The vast continent below rippled out-wards, the patchwork of geography that he'd known all his life. He could trace it as they flew: first the knotty, stubby green of the lowlands sloping towards the sea, shrouded in thin cloud at the coast. At Matondoni, he nosed the aircraft gently westwards, heading towards Lake Kiboko. A burst of radio static from another aircraft, floating above or below him, broke into his dreamy concentration. *Echo Zulu One Nine… Go ahead, Echo Zulu One Nine… Permission to—* The transmission was abruptly cut, the thread of conversation lost for ever. He flew steadily on, following the roads: Mombasa–Malindi; Garissa, and then the A2 northwards – Thika, Makuyu, Nyeri, skirting the Mount Kenya National Park until the familiar shapes and forms of Nanyuki swam into view.

He brought the plane down to earth, the controlled shudder travelling up his arms as he steadied her over the bursts of crosswinds at three thousand feet, then two, then a thousand … then the last few hundred rushing towards them as they approached Nanyuki's small runway. A thud, a bounce, then the brace as the flaps went up and the air solidified into a wall, forcing them to a standstill. His passengers were pleased; earth once more, and a chance to smoke. Puffing like a chimney stack, the man led his disgruntled wife away as a handful of young boys hurried over to offload their many cases. He parked the plane in its usual spot behind one of the empty sheds and pulled out his flight paperwork. He glanced at his watch: it was nearly five. It would take him ten minutes to fill out the log and have a quick cigarette. His battered jeep was waiting in the airport car park; with any luck, he'd be at the bar at the Fairmont within the hour.

His phone buzzed into life. He pulled it out. Major Mike Smith was already at the bar. *Get over here, Githerton. Pronto. Crowther's just arrived.* Mark grinned. In spite of their many differences, he genuinely liked the officers who came out to Archer's Post on their yearly exercises. It was Smith and Crowther's third visit together, and already Mark knew how the evening would end. They reminded him of the boys with whom he'd spent six years at an English boarding school on the edge of the South Downs, sick with longing for Kenya.

His phone beeped again. *Hadley's just walked in. MOM. Fuck.* He grinned again. Lieutenant Colonel Hadley was the CO. MOM. Mind our manners. Hell, it was nearly six on a Friday evening. Smith and Crowther might have to mind their manners, but not him. *He* wasn't in the army, thank God. He was a free agent. Just as he'd always been, and just the way he liked it. But as he tucked his phone back in the pocket of his jeans and started to close up the plane, he was aware of something niggling at him, a sense that something wasn't quite right, or that he'd missed something. Or, rather, some*one*. He sighed, exasperated with his inability to shake off the ghost of a woman he'd spent one night with four months ago. *One* night? What the hell was the matter with him?

He shouldered his bag, pulled down the shutter doors and fastened the padlock. He had three days and two nights in Nanyuki, and he was determined to make the most of them – and to forget about Alexandra whatever-her-name-was. He gave a short laugh. He didn't even know her last name.

'Githerton! At long fucking last! What time d'you call this?'

He slid on to the empty bar stool beside Crowther and Smith, already well into their second – or possibly third – beers. He signalled to the barman. 'I'll have the same, thanks.'

'Good to see you, mate,' Mike said, raising his half-empty glass in welcome.

'You too.' Mark closed his fingers around the neck of the cool, already sweating bottle. He raised it to his lips and took his first sip. It was ice cold, and sharp against his tongue. He felt himself begin to slip into place, into play. The flight up from the coast wasn't merely a matter of geographical distance; there was a bridge to be crossed in himself, too. In Lamu, hundreds of miles from the farm at the foot of the Aberdares where he'd grown up, he'd found himself unexpectedly freed. There he was just another *mzungu* who came and went. He'd rented a cottage that had once been the servants' quarters of a house belonging to a wealthy Dane who summered in Nice and wintered in Lamu. Mark had met his landlord twice. On the first occasion, they both got blindingly drunk in the Peponi. Niels knew nothing about the tall, rangy Englishman. At the bar, he overheard him speaking Swahili to one of the waiters. 'Picked the language up, have you?' was his only comment. It was unclear whether he knew the difference between an Englishman and a white Kenyan. In any event, Mark's name meant nothing to him. The terms of the lease had been concluded over a beer. Niels looked over his shoulder as he signed, and murmured, 'Mark Githerton. How very English.' And that was that. He didn't read the sorts of papers in which Mark's work appeared, and it was unlikely he'd ever have connected Mark Githerton, photojournalist, with Mark Githerton his tenant.

In Nairobi, it was different. There, amongst certain people, his past clung to him like smoke. 'Mark Githerton? You're not Sally's son, by any chance, are you?' they would ask curiously, seeing in him the resemblance that only they would spot. Sally Houldsworth–Githerton. Mark's mother, the second wife of Basil Houldsworth, the 4th Baron Fermeroy, an Anglo-Irish aristocrat, landowner, twice-married adulterer, alcoholic and convicted felon whose death had been mourned by no one, least of all his wife and son. When Basil died, Mark immediately dropped Houldsworth from his name, partly out of respect for his mother but mostly to rid himself of any trace of his father. And for the most part, it worked. It was only amongst the crowd who'd known him as a child that the connection was made. To everyone else, he was simply Mark Githerton, just another white man who'd long ago uprooted himself from the Kenyan valley where he'd been born, and made himself anew. Most people thought he was English. As his mother's friends died off, one by one, so too, thankfully, did Mark Houldsworth.

But all that was a long time ago. He put his father firmly out of his mind and looked around him. The Zebar at the Fairmount was full of wealthy, satisfied-looking tourists and harried, nervous-looking staff – much like luxury hotels anywhere, he supposed. Nanyuki attracted a very different type of visitor from Lamu: corporate, older, though not necessarily wealthier. Lamu's wealth was European and bohemian; Nanyuki's was anything but. Half the people in the bar were American businessmen who'd slotted in a safari on the return leg of their business trip, preferably without their wife. The other half – at least for the next eight weeks – were men like Dave and Mike, British army officers taking a temporary break from their regiments. The setting was stunningly idyllic. As the flaming sun settled beyond the ridge of pale, smoky blue mountains, a flock of birds rose lazily into the air. The sky threw up its dusk colours – vermilion, sunflower yellow, hazy mauve, iridescent pink – before settling into the bruised topaz of dusk. Nightfall on the equator was a brief, sudden event. Within thirty minutes, light and dark had swapped places.

Mark turned back to Mike. 'So, what was it you wanted to see me about?'

'Got a small job for you,' Mike said, lowering his voice suddenly.

'What sort of job?'

Both Mike and Dave glanced over at the far end of the room, where Hadley, the CO, was sitting with a group of men. 'Strictly off the record, mate. It's a pick-up, that's all. Some friends of ours are looking for a pilot, someone who can get people in and out of a situation in a hurry.'

Mark took another sip of beer. 'What sort of situation?' he asked warily. 'Where?'

'Algeria. Close to the border with Libya. Oil rig. Bunch of expats.

Something's brewing out there and BP don't like it. There's protection for the Brits, of course. Foreign Office'll send us in to get everyone out who needs getting out, but let's just say not everyone's on the list. There's an opening for someone like you. *If* you want it.'

Mark nodded. He was fast running out of money, and his reluctance to pick up a camera again meant he was also running out of options. Other than his skill behind a lens, his pilot's licence and his ability to get along with just about anyone, he possessed absolutely nothing of any value. Not even a bicycle. It was the great irony of his upbringing. The 4th Baron Fermeroy had squandered every last penny of whatever aristocratic fortune there had once been. When he died, there was nothing left but the title and the shame, and you couldn't eat either.

He pondered the offer. It had been three months since his last assignment, in Misrata, which he'd sworn would be his last. 'In and out, you say? Low risk?'

'Minimal risk. You'll be on standby somewhere relatively safe ... Cairo or Tripoli, somewhere like that. They'll organise all your permits and flight path clearances. It's an easy job. Just a bunch of oil execs and a few businessmen. You know how it is. There's always some dickhead who won't leave when he's told. Your job'll be to ferry them to the nearest city, and their own people will take over from there.'

'They usually do, don't they?' Mark said with a wry smile.

'Yeah. No reason why you shouldn't grab a slice of that pie, though, mate,' Dave broke in. He signalled for another round of beers. 'If you're interested, we'll hook you up.'

'Yeah, I'm interested,' Mark said slowly. It was exactly what he needed, and not just financially. He needed to get away from Lamu for a little while. Kyrgyzstan had finished him, physically and emotionally. When he'd boarded the flight from Osh to Moscow in June, nearly six months earlier, he'd sworn never to pick up a camera again. He'd spent nearly a fortnight covering the riots that had unexpectedly broken out between the Uzbeks and the Kyrgyz, and although it was by no means the most violent or bloody conflict he'd covered – not by a long shot – somehow it had tipped him over an edge that many said he'd been teetering on for years. He'd copped a lift from Bishkek to Osh with a Russian army platoon and sat the entire journey with his head in his hands, strangely defeated by what he'd seen. The Russian soldiers had helped secure him a flight to Moscow, and from there he'd headed home. Aside from a couple of weekends in Nairobi, he hadn't left Lamu since. He'd wrapped his cameras and the rest of his equipment in a bed sheet and stuffed the bundle into the back of a cupboard under the sink. The only person who opened the cupboard was the girl who came in once a week to clean. That part of him was finished.

But he had no idea what to do next. He'd been a photographer almost his entire adult life. The third-class degree in philosophy he'd scraped from Oxford was about as useful to him as a suit and tie. No bloody use, in other words. He'd gone to university mostly to please his mother. As soon as he was able, he was out there, drinking in the world and all its messy contradictions the only way he knew how: through a lens. He bought a second-hand Leica with the first money he earned as a bartender, and took to photography like a duck to water. It was *his* medium, *his* way, *his* story to tell. Something about his upbringing, his sense of apartness that wasn't aloofness, and his easy, affable manner communicated itself to the people he met, and a bond was forged that allowed him access no other photographers could. He went to Sarajevo a year before the siege ended. The *Sunday Times* bought his first pictures, and there was no looking back. For the next fifteen years there wasn't a hotspot – war, disaster, famine, you name it – that Mark Githerton hadn't covered. Yet for all that, he managed to stay out of the spotlight. The world knew his photographs; it didn't know *him*. He wasn't one to stick his picture under a byline or attend awards ceremonies. For all his fame, few would be able to pick him out in a crowd. It was better that way. Better for him, better for his work. He didn't want anyone to know him. Somewhere underneath it all, he wasn't sure they would like what they found.

He looked down at his beer. Yeah, a month or two spent ferrying people out of harm's way might give him a better sense of perspective, something different to do. Something that would help take his mind off a woman he'd barely met four months ago. A woman he would really rather forget.

14

Jane tapped her pencil against her teeth. 'She's not going to like it,' she murmured, looking down at the sheet of paper Donal had just given her. 'The Middle East's *her* territory, not Dominic's.'

'What are you talking about?' Donal looked at her, exasperated. 'It's nobody's *territory*. It's whoever I think is going to do the best job, that's whose territory it is.'

'She's not going to like it,' she murmured again, a warning note in her voice.

'And don't you go saying anything to her.' Donal glowered at her. 'Not before I've had a chance to tell her myself. I know you two are as thick as thieves.'

'That's not fair. This is between the two of you. I'm just saying—'

'All right, all right,' Donal broke in irritably. 'I know what you're saying. But I just don't think it's a good time to send her back out. She's exhausted. She's running on empty and I don't want a repeat of Gaza. It's too risky for a woman right now, especially a woman who looks like *her*. I'd rather just send Dominic.'

'You sound like one of those corporate suits you're always banging on about, Donal,' Jane said mildly. 'Has she ever let you down? And you know Gaza wasn't her fault. It could've happened to anyone.'

'Yes, but it happened to *her*. And I'm not taking another chance like that.'

'Fine. Send her in with backup. Send Dominic in *with* her, not instead of her.'

Donal shot her a withering look. 'Are you kidding? She'll eat him alive. You know that.'

There was an urgent tap on the door. They both looked up. It was Susie, the receptionist. She looked worried. 'What is it?' Jane called through the glass.

'It's Lexi. She's at Old Street. She's on her way in. This morning I … I accidentally … I sent the email to her instead of Dominic … I'm so sorry ... it just sort of *went* ... it just disappeared before I could stop it ...' Her voice trailed off.

'Oh, for fuck's sake!' Donal's whole body jerked as though he'd been hit. 'Lexi's on her way in? Now?'

'Nice work, Susie,' Jane snapped, rolling her eyes. She turned back to Donal. 'Well there you go. Now you don't have to worry about *me* telling her. You can tell her yourself. Uh-oh, watch out ... here she comes now.'

Lexi came barrelling through the door, brushing Susie aside as though she were an irritating insect, even though Susie was easily the largest person at NNI, and by quite a considerable margin. Lexi's face was as dark as thunder.

'I'll leave you to it. I'll be in my office if anyone needs me.' Jane slid past Lexi and hurriedly left Donal's office.

Lexi's voice was a howl of barely suppressed rage. 'How *could* you ...'

'Nice one,' Jane repeated to Susie, who was trying unsuccessfully to hide behind her computer screen. '*Very* nicely handled.'

'It wasn't *entirely* my fault,' Susie bleated.

Jane ignored her and looked over to where Dominic was sitting. She felt a sharp stab of irritation. She understood well enough why Donal had hired him, even if she disliked him almost as much as Lexi did. In spite of his youth, he was a throwback to the good old-fashioned public-school correspondents of the seventies and eighties. Prep school, Eton, Cambridge. Not quite aristocracy, but almost. Donal thought he complemented the team. Jane thought him a pompous, overbearing prick. Lexi detested him. There was an extra edge to her antagonism towards him which Jane hadn't quite worked out, but she couldn't help feeling sorry for her. To be upstaged by Dominic was one thing. To find out about it in a stray email from Susie was another altogether. Utterly galling. She could see Lexi gesticulating wildly at Donal in the meeting room. She could also see Dominic smirking. Her fingers itched to smack him. What was Donal *thinking*?

15

Lexi's lips tightened as she looked through the window at Dominic's desk. It was almost completely buried in books and magazines. *Her* books. Several of the titles were clearly visible. *The Great War for Civilisation: the Conquest of the Middle East. Pity the Nation. The Origins of Arab Nationalism. A Savage War of Peace.* 'I gave him those,' she said tersely.

'What?'

'Those books on the Middle East. You asked me to give him a bit of *general* background, or have you forgotten? You didn't say you were planning to give him my job. And don't you *dare* pretend you don't know what I'm talking about.'

'I do know what you're talking about. But let's not discuss it here. Not like this.' Donal stood up. 'Come on, let's get you a cup of tea.'

'I don't *need* a cup of tea!' To her alarm, Lexi heard her voice beginning to wobble. 'I just need you to tell me what's going on.'

Donal didn't answer. He gripped her forearm and half dragged, half pushed her out of the door. Susie was hovering anxiously in the background.

'Donal, I'm really sorry, it's all my fault—'

'Not now, Susie. Tell Dominic to come and see me later. And bring us two cups of tea. Right, Lexi, in here.' Donal pushed open the door to the boardroom and shut it firmly behind them. He finally let go of Lexi's arm and pulled out a chair. 'Sit. Sit down, shut up and listen.'

'Donal, I—'

'Lexi, will you just *listen?*' He sat down heavily and spread his arms in a gesture that seemed to indicate his own helplessness.

'Why *him?*' Lexi asked. Her lower lip began to tremble, and she fought hard to control it.

Donal looked at her closely for a second before answering. 'Because he's the right person for the job. For now, at least. And before you ask, no, Jane *didn't* know. I didn't discuss it with her. This is my decision and my decision alone. I'm not sending you back there, not right now. You need somewhere quiet. Somewhere you can get a decent cup of coffee and a paper to read. I'm not sending you anywhere where you'll be dodging bullets. Just look at you, Lexi. You look fucking *shattered*. And what the hell have you done to your hair?'

Lexi looked away. She couldn't handle his concern – anyone's concern. And why was everyone still so fucking concerned about her hair? She *liked* it short. End of story. She tried to bring the subject back to the matter at hand. 'The Middle East's *my* area, Donal, you know that. I'm the one who's been out there the longest. I've spent *months* with my ear to the ground. Something's going to happen, I just *know* it. How can you let him cover it?'

'You've been out there too long, it's that simple. I should've pulled you back in the summer, after you came back from Lamu. You're a *wreck*, for fuck's sake.'

'Wh-where're you sending me?'

There was a moment's pause. 'Brussels. The EU are just about to announce a rescue package for Ireland.'

'*Brussels?* You're sending me to *Brussels?*'

Donal nodded. 'The deal will be announced on Friday. You can catch the Eurostar tomorrow night.' He reached out and laid an arm on her forearm. 'Trust me, Lexi, will you? *You* might not have noticed it, but the rest of us have.'

'What?'

Donal sighed. His hand remained where it was. 'It's been tougher on you than I think you realise. I know, I know ... Gaza could've happened to anyone. But it didn't. It happened to you.'

'I'm no good at sitting around, Donal. I need to be busy. It's my job to be busy.'

'And it's *my* job to make sure all my correspondents function in the way they should.'

'Are you saying I'm not functioning?'

'No, I'm not. But carry on the way you're going, and you'll wind up in trouble again. You're not at your best and we both know it. You need a break. Take one in Brussels.' He let go of her arm. 'It's a great city. Lots of bars, lots of good restaurants, galleries, museums ... whatever you like. Stay there for a couple of weeks. Get your mojo back, then let's talk. You're absolutely right. Something's brewing in the Middle East and we've got to be there, covering it, whatever "it" turns out to be. But let

Dominic do it for now. *You* go to Brussels, report on the bailout and then we'll see. If things look like they're heating up ...' He paused, and held up a restraining hand. '*And* if I think you're properly rested, I promise I'll send you back. But not a moment before. I mean it.'

There was a moment's tense silence. From the expression on Donal's face, Lexi knew that argument was futile. 'Fine,' she muttered eventually.

Donal looked at her. 'And try not to be so fucking ungrateful, darling. Any other editor would've grounded you. Without pay, too. Now get out of here before I change my mind.'

16

'Deena? Is that you? Hang on a moment ... I've got some news for you.' Deena turned at the sound of her name. It was Dr Stubbens, Deena's immediate boss. She was hurrying down the corridor towards her, smiling widely. 'I just heard the news from Mr Larcombe. You passed! I thought you'd like to know.'

'I did? Really?'

Dr Stubbens nodded enthusiastically. 'You did very well. Mr Larcombe was pleased with your performance. So it's official. You'll be with myself and John Falconer next.' She frowned. 'Is something wrong?'

Deena swallowed. 'No ... I ... I'm just surprised, that's all. I thought ... I didn't think I'd done *that* well.'

Dr Stubbens smiled. 'You did brilliantly. I'm probably not supposed to say this, but you came out top. Well done. It's a difficult rotation.'

Deena nodded. She had the sudden urge to sit down. 'Th-thanks,' she said dazedly. 'I ... I'd better run,' she added quickly. 'I'm supposed to be doing ward rounds.'

'Of course. But I'm glad you'll be joining us. John's thrilled, too. I know we'll make an excellent team.'

'Y-yes, th-thanks,' she stammered again. She watched as Dr Stubbens sailed back down the corridor, a sinking feeling starting to take hold. She ought to be thrilled. Abu would be thrilled ... Inès, her mother ... everyone would be pleased. And she was pleased, too, of course. Emergency medicine was one of the hardest rotations, and it was just her luck that she'd had it first. But she'd passed.

She looked at her watch. She did have ward rounds to make, but no one would miss her if she nipped out to the balcony for a few minutes. She hurried to the lifts and went up to the fifth floor. It was nearly two o'clock. Everyone would be either hurrying back from lunch or already following the consultants round the wards. She stepped out on to the balcony, wrapping her white coat tightly against the stinging rain. A winter's storm had broken over the city earlier that morning, sending sulphurous flickering tongues of electricity flashing across the skyline, anticipating the onslaught of freezing rain. She looked up into the enormous darkening sky and felt again the strange shifting and turning of the elements that mirrored the changes going on inside and around her, changes she couldn't admit to anyone, not even Inès.

Her mobile buzzed furiously in her pocket. She fished it out and peered at the flashing screen. It was from Huda. *Mtg tonite, Riverfleet, 7 p.m.* Her heart started to beat faster. She hurriedly typed her reply – *Tx. C u there* – then drew in a deep breath to steady her nerves and hurried back inside. She would have to think up some excuse as to why she wouldn't be home for supper. It would be the third time this month. She was pushing her luck. Very little escaped her mother. Luckily for her, Inès's attention had been taken up lately by her own exams, but deep down, Deena knew it was only a matter of time before someone noticed something, and then the game would be up. She punched the lift button impatiently and descended swiftly to the second floor.

'Deena? Where've you *been*?' Clarissa, one of her fellow foundation doctors, hissed at her as she joined the crowd following the two senior consultants into the wards.

'I had to make a phone call,' Deena whispered. 'Did I miss anything?'

Clarissa was prevented from answering by their arrival at the bedside of a young woman whose face was turned to the wall.

'Name?' barked Mr Humphreys, the surgical consultant. A young doctor sprang forward to consult the chart.

'Um, Nadine ... I can't read the surname. Twenty-two years old, pre-sented this morning in ER, dizzy, very high fever and nausea. She was admitted to ward just before noon. She's a first-year student at UCL,' he added, somewhat unnecessarily.

'Notes.' A few moments' respectful silence followed as the consultant scanned the brief notes. Then he walked around the side of the bed and lifted the young woman's hand. Even from where she was standing, Deena noticed how listless the girl was. The consultant reached into his breast pocket, extracting a small pen-light. 'Dr Kenan,' he barked out suddenly.

Deena pushed her way forward, heart thudding. 'Er, yes, sir?'

'Check her pupils. I'd be looking for light sensitivity and cranial pressure. I'd perform a lumbar puncture if I were you. *Neisseria meningitidis.* Right, let's move on. Next.' He thrust the penlight at her and strode away, sweeping up the remaining ten students in his wake.

The room was suddenly quiet. Deena bent forward and lifted the young woman's arm. It was burning, hot and clammy to the touch. She bit her lip. Her father's words came back to her. *A good doctor is a good diagnostician. There's no substitute for instinct. Find out what's wrong first, and then treat it.* She looked at the girl's face. Her eyes were closed, but there was a faint flickering under the lids. She wasn't asleep. Deena lifted the chart. Nadine Mossaieb. It was a Lebanese name, possibly Jordanian. She looked back at the girl's face, shiny with fever. Nadine's eyelids flickered open. For a second, they stared at each other. Then Deena leaned forward.

'*Nadine, eh il hassel-lik dilwa-ati?*' she asked her softly, in Arabic. *What just happened to you?*

The girl shook her head slowly from side to side. A lone tear trickled down the side of her nose, settling into the corner of her mouth. Her eyes were glassy with tears. She opened her lips, but no sound came out. Deena stared at her, then slowly put the penlight away. It wasn't a lumbar puncture that was needed. She touched the girl's arm, squeezing it lightly.

'You'll be fine,' she murmured. 'It's an infection. Complications from your procedure. I'll start you on antibiotics right away.'

The girl swallowed. Even in her fevered state, she knew that Deena understood. '*Shukran,*' she whispered, closing her eyes.

'You're welcome. Don't worry about a thing. In a couple of days you'll start to feel better. Do you have family here?'

'*Aiwa.*'

'I'll speak to them. Don't worry. They'll never know.' Deena squeezed her arm again and picked up the chart. *Clostridium sordelli. Bacterial infection. Ceftazidime, intr., tazobactam, oral, 100mg.* She quickly wrote out the prescription and left the room. She'd recognised the look on the girl's face immediately. A mask that was a mixture of fear and longing, shame and regret. As soon as she saw it, she knew. The mask was a mirror of her own.

17

Lexi hurried across the bewildering intersection that was Old Street, her coat belted tightly against the cold, and stepped into the small coffee shop on the opposite corner. She spotted an empty seat by the window and plonked her bag down, then ordered a cup of hot chai, still fighting back the angry tears that had very nearly spilled out in Donal's office. She'd resisted the temptation to storm into Jane's office – that wouldn't have gone down well with either Jane or Donal. She took a sip of tea, nearly scalding her tongue. *Slow down*, she cautioned herself. It was exactly this combination of rage and frustration that had tipped her over the edge that night in Gaza City, the closest she'd ever been to fear. She'd been lucky. One of the Israeli soldiers who'd seen her leave the barracks had followed her. If he hadn't, there was no telling where she'd have ended up. Or how. When she'd calmed down sufficiently to see the world without the veil of anger that obscured everything, including reason, she'd thanked him for it, much as it galled her. And afterwards, facing the incandescent IDF commander who'd ordered her out of Gaza hadn't been half as bad as facing Donal.

But there it was. She couldn't help it. The mere sight of someone being bullied was enough to make her lose control. Earlier on that day, on patrol with the soldiers, with whom she'd built up a sort of grudging trust, she'd seen a group of them teasing a handful of ragged-looking Palestinian children with sweets that they alternately held out and snatched away. She'd yelled at them to stop it, her whole body immediately suffused with rage, but the soldiers only laughed at her and continued on their merry, tormenting way.

'Cool it, Lexi,' murmured her photographer, who was sitting next to her in the armoured patrol car. 'Just forget about it. That's not what we're here to cover.'

'Forget about it? How? They're just kids.'

'You call them kids?' the platoon commander snapped at her. 'Don't be so naïve,' he added contemptuously.

Lexi stared at him. The air was suddenly full of tension. Jim looked up. 'Lexi,' he said warningly. 'Don't.'

But she couldn't help herself, of course. An argument broke out that ended up with Lexi and Jim being summoned to the IDF control room back at base – and then things just got worse. She'd actually only slipped out of the barracks to get some fresh air, she tried to explain to Donal when they were safely back in London.

'Fresh fucking *air*? Are you insane? You were in the middle of a ground offensive and you thought it prudent to go out and *get some fresh air*?' He was nearly purple with rage.

'I … I'd been stuck in that jeep with those assholes all day,' Lexi said defensively.

Words seemed to fail Donal. He stared at her for a full minute before shaking his head. 'Get out now,' he said quietly. 'Before I say something we'll both regret.'

'Come on, you know it's only because he cares,' Jane told her later, over the first of many glasses of wine. 'You can't imagine how scared he was. How scared we *all* were.'

'I know what I'm doing,' Lexi said stubbornly. 'I don't understand what all the fuss was about.'

'Oh, come off it. If that soldier hadn't followed you, Christ knows what would have happened. Can you imagine how I'd have felt, getting a phone call in the middle of the night? Don't ever put me through that, Lexi. Don't put anyone through that.'

Lexi was silent. Jane would never know how close she'd come to hitting the mark. Lexi *did* know how it felt. She had once been the one who'd had a phone call announcing a death. 'Another drink?' she said after a moment, forcing a note of lightness back into her voice. 'My round.'

'Fine. I won't argue with *that*. See if they've got any crisps, will you?'

Lexi looked down at her hands now. They were still shaking slightly. She glanced around the cafe. It was full of the usual mix of creative types, smart office workers and dishevelled students – a far cry from the Old Street she'd known in her university days. She'd gone out once with an art student who lived somewhere nearby, sharing an enormous, draughty warehouse with a group of other students and a few thousand old car tyres. Like most of her relationships, it hadn't lasted long – a week, a fortnight? She couldn't even remember.

An image popped into her mind suddenly of Mark, the bloke she'd met in Lamu in the summer. She frowned, annoyed with herself. But she couldn't help it. She closed her eyes, picturing him, surprised at the ease with which she recalled details she wasn't even aware she'd noticed at the time. A small dark mole, just below his left eye; the way the thick, wavy dark brown hair brushed the nape of his neck; the telltale tan line that ran around his biceps, the mark of a man who lived his life in the sun. She shook her head. It was odd the way he'd remained so fresh in her mind, even now, four months later. She was suddenly aware of a warm flush rising up through her body, almost as though he were touching her still.

She snapped back to the present, stood up abruptly and grabbed her bag. There were more important things to think about. In just over twenty-four hours she'd be on a train to Brussels to report on a crisis she knew next to nothing about. No, make that *absolutely* nothing, she thought grimly as she pushed open the door. She had twenty-four hours to find out everything she could about EU reaction to the recently-announced Irish bailout. A whole day? Piece of cake. As Jane would say.

18

'But what's *wrong* with him?' her mother asked, frowning. She was at the sink, carefully washing large dark-green bunches of parsley, preparing to chop them into tiny fragments for the tabbouleh salad. Inès sat at the table, squeezing lemons as she'd been directed. Deena had just come home from work and Abu was still out somewhere.

'Nothing,' Inès said slowly.

'Then why?'

Inès sighed. 'Because I don't *like* him.'

'But who says you have to like him? Immediately, I mean? *Ya'ani* …
it takes time.'

'Not for me, it doesn't.' She pushed the lemons aside and stood up.

'Where are you going?' her mother asked sharply, turning round.

'To watch TV,' Inès said, and walked out before her mother could
launch a fresh assault.

The living room was empty. She flung herself down on the settee,
her lower lip trembling mutinously. She hated these conversations with
her mother. When would they understand? She wasn't going to marry
some young man *just because they'd chosen him!* Listlessly she picked up
the remote control and turned on the television. As usual, it was tuned
to the news. Something had just happened in Tunisia. She stared at
the screen. Crowds were chanting in the streets, holding banners aloft,
running from tear gas. The poor newscaster was doing his best, struggling
with a string of unfamiliar names.

'Turn it up, will you?' Deena came into the room, towelling her hair
dry. She'd just taken a shower and her skin was dewy and pink. Both
girls stared at the screen.

'*The Tunisian street vendor Tarek al-Tayeb Mohamed Bouazizi, who set
himself on fire in protest against trading restrictions in his home town of Sidi
Bouzid, has died as a result of his injuries. According to friends and family,
local police officers had allegedly targeted and mistreated Bouazizi for years,
regularly confiscating his small wheelbarrow of produce—*'

'Why's the television so loud?' Their mother suddenly joined Deena
in the doorway. She was still holding her chopping knife.

'He died,' Deena murmured quietly.

'Who?'

'Bouazizi.'

'Who's Bouazizi?' Her mother looked at Deena, puzzled.

'The street vendor. The one who set himself alight.'

'Oh, *Deena!*' Her mother's voice rose in protest. 'Why do you watch
such horrible things?'

'It's the *news*, it's not some silly horror film!' Deena's voice was unusually loud. 'This is happening back home, right now!'

'Home? It's Tunisia, not Egypt! Such a thing would never happen in
Egypt!'

'It *does* happen,' Deena said urgently. 'You just choose to pretend it
doesn't.'

Inès looked nervously from one to the other. It was so out of character for Deena to say such a thing. She waited for her mother's response, but to her surprise, she didn't reply, just turned and marched back down the corridor to the kitchen. There was a wary silence.

'Don't,' Deena warned.

'Don't what?'

'Don't say anything.' Deena turned and walked off. Inès was left sitting on the couch, listening to the newscaster with her mouth open in surprise.

An hour or so later, she was lying on her bed, reading – or trying to read – when there was a gentle tap at the door. 'Who is it?' she called, hoping it wasn't her mother.

'It's only me. Can I come in?' The door opened a crack. Deena was dressed as though ready to go out. Her hair was loose and she was wearing lipstick.

'Where're you going?' Inès asked curiously. 'It's nearly dinner time.'

'To meet some friends.' She hesitated for a moment. 'D'you want to come?'

Inès looked at her in amazement. Deena *never* invited her along to meet her friends. It was an unspoken rule between them that, aside from family matters, they didn't socialise together. 'Which friends?'

'You don't know them.'

Inès hesitated. Her curiosity got the better of her. 'OK, I'll come.' She swung her legs out of bed. 'Where're we going?'

'A friend's house.'

'Where?' Now Inès's curiosity was well and truly piqued.

'You'll see.' Deena turned to leave.

Inès jumped up and quickly ran a brush through her hair. She grabbed her handbag and coat from behind her door and ran down the stairs. Their mother was on the phone to a relative, her voice rising and falling in indignation over some far-off drama unfolding at home.

'We'll be back in a couple of hours,' Deena shouted through the living room doorway. 'Come on,' she mouthed to Inès. 'Let's go.'

'Won't you at least tell me where your friend lives?' Inès asked as they hurriedly closed the front door.

'King's Cross.'

'King's Cross? Who do you know in King's Cross? Who *are* these people, Deena? How come you've never mentioned them before?'

'Wait and see. Come on, there's a bus that goes all the way. I hate taking the Tube.'

Deena hated taking the Tube? It was beginning to dawn on Inès that there was actually quite a lot she didn't know about her older sister.

Ten minutes later they were on the top deck of the number 10 bus, moving slowly along Kensington High Street towards Harvey Nichols, surrounded by loud teenagers in shiny fur-trimmed parkas and Arab women in long black robes who chattered incessantly to one another like excited starlings from underneath the safety of their veils. It was nearly five o'clock and almost already dark. Deena was quiet. She pulled out her phone and concentrated on sending text messages. No surnames, Inès noticed, surreptitiously glancing downwards. *Bassam. Walid. Talal. Huda.* She'd never heard Deena refer to any of them.

Deena lifted her head, and for a second, their eyes met. There was an expression on Deena's face that Inès didn't recognise. She looked away in embarrassment and confusion. Something was happening – had already happened – that she didn't fully understand. All through their childhood, she'd been the one with secrets, the one who'd broken all the rules. She'd read books they weren't supposed to; she was the first to see films that had been banned. She smoked her first cigarette long before any of the other girls in her class did, and once, when she was thirteen or fourteen, when they'd still lived in Paris, she'd begged Chrissie Gemayel's mother to bring her back a boob tube from London, which she'd worn down to breakfast, giving her mother palpitations. She suppressed a smile, thinking of it now. Deena had given them no such trouble. She was an open book. She was simply *all there*; nothing withheld, no secrets. Yet now it was Deena's face that presented itself as half closed, a beguiling, almost guilty look in her eyes.

Inès looked out of the window. She felt an unfamiliar trembling in the pit of her stomach. Something was about to happen. But what?

They got off at King's Cross, Deena leading the way. It was dark by now, and in the yellow sodium glare of the street lights, everyone they passed had a furtive air. They walked up one of the side streets. Inès looked up:

Birkenhead Street. There was a small post office on the corner and an off-licence around whose door a huddle of drunks argued in muted tones.

'Got any change? Got any change, love?' A man appeared suddenly out of the shadows and stood in front of them, blocking the way. Deena calmly stepped around him. Inès flung a worried look over her shoulder as she hurried after her. At the top of Birkenhead Street, they passed through a set of enormous steel gates that led to the first of four high-rise council blocks, one stacked neatly behind the other, with a concrete patch in front of each, and a lonely, solitary swing.

'What sort of place is this?' Inès whispered.

Deena smiled faintly. 'It's a housing estate. A council estate. Don't tell me you've never been to one?'

Inès shook her head. 'No, never.'

'Come on, don't be scared. It's perfectly all right.'

Inès's eyes only widened further. There was an elevator at the foot of the stairwell. Not the sort of elevator with which she was immediately familiar, she thought, wrinkling her nose as the doors closed nosily behind them. This one stank of sour urine and the walls were covered in graffiti, which she chose not to read.

'Couldn't we have taken the stairs?' she asked, wrinkling her nose.

'Safer.'

'Oh.'

On the fifth floor, the doors ground slowly open again. In front of them was a long, dim walkway, patchily illuminated along its length. An overhead fluorescent strip flickered as they walked. At the second-to-last door Deena stopped. 'I just want to warn you,' she said quickly, pressing the buzzer.

'Warn me? About what?' Inès asked, alarmed.

But before Deena could answer, the door was flung open. A man stood in the passage, silhouetted against the light. The rain suddenly intensified, drumming against the metal railing behind them. A gasp of chill wind gusted down the walkway. Against the increasing roar of falling water, Inès looked up, her eyes travelling the length of the man's frame to his face. A face of extraordinary beauty, she thought distractedly, saved from a Hollywood plasticity by one or two oddities: a slightly crooked front tooth, a scar that ran across his left eyebrow, ploughing a thin furrow in what would otherwise have been a thick, glossily smooth dark line. She swallowed nervously. Through the open door behind him, she saw a room full of people, the rising plume of bluish cigarette smoke and a hazy curtain of lightly falling rain against the far window pane. He turned without saying anything and led them inside.

'*Ahlan*, Deena.' *Welcome*. Several people looked up, obviously recognising Deena.

'Hi, everyone. This is my sister. My younger sister, Inas.' Deena spoke in Arabic.

Inès looked around. She didn't know or recognise any of the young men and women crowded together in the living room, though their names were strangely familiar. *Bassam. Walid. Mireille.* They were the names on Deena's phone, she realised, as the introductions were made. She perched on a chair at the edge of the gathering, her handbag tucked awkwardly under her legs, sandwiched between a girl with curly dark hair who introduced herself as Wissal, and a young man with terrible acne and a limp, hesitant handshake.

There were perhaps twenty people crammed into the little room, sitting wherever there was a spot to be had. She'd never been in a gathering quite like it. Although the Kenans certainly mixed with other Egyptian families in London, they were generally families much like their own – middle class, Westernised, liberal, if culturally conservative. Inès had never been in the company of young Arabs like these. They talked in loud, urgent voices in a mixture of English, French and Arabic, all focused on the burning of Bouazizi, whom they'd seen on television only hours before, and the effect it was having on the region. They were anywhere between twenty-five and thirty-five years old, serious-looking young men and women, cigarettes held aloft, and for some, a glass of wine or whisky at their elbow. There were half a dozen laptops lying scattered about the room, and in the far corner, sitting at the small dining table facing them, two young men were busy setting up Facebook pages. Every now and then one of them would raise his head and ask something of the group. 'Saturday or Sunday, what d'you guys think?' or 'What about "in memory of" or "in recognition of"? Which sounds better?'

Deena took her place amongst them, her eyes darting from one to the other, the conversation and arguments rising around her, working in her blood like alcohol. There was a commanding confidence about her that made Inès's heart suddenly swell with pride. She argued a point here, conceded another there. Laughing one minute, deadly serious the next. When one young man heckled her over something she was saying, his neighbour lifted his head and said, quite loudly, 'For fuck's sake, Nassim, listen to her! She's a doctor. She knows exactly what she's talking about.' There was a brief pause, then everyone nodded. Inès listened, open-mouthed in admiration.

'So who *are* they?' she asked Deena, a couple of hours later, as they made their way back down in the creaking lift to the ground floor.

'I told you. They're friends.'

'Come on, Deena. There's more to it than that. I'm not blind. What exactly is this organisation?'

The doors opened and they began to walk across the now deserted and completely dark forecourt to the main gate. Something moved in the shadow of one of the smaller buildings in front of them; Inès only just managed not to grab on to Deena's arm in fright.

'We're activists,' Deena said simply, as though that answered everything. 'We're helping various groups across the region organise themselves.'

'Various groups? What groups? Deena, what's going on?'

'Inès, don't you watch the news? Come on, how can you pretend to be so blind?'

'I'm not pretending!' Inès replied, stung. 'Of course I know what's going on. But ... why are *you* involved with them? What does it have to do with you? With us?'

Deena stopped and looked at her. In the half-light of the street lamp, her eyes flashed urgently. 'We're *doing* something, Inès, that's the point! Things are happening back home! Everything's changing.'

'But ... I've never known you to be even *remotely* political,' Inès protested, genuinely puzzled.

Deena was silent. They reached the Euston Road. Cars whooshed past in both directions, trailing streaks of glowing red lights. Inès looked at Deena closely, as if trying to make sense of her, but saw nothing more than she already knew. In her neat camel-coloured coat, dark blue jeans and sensible low-heeled boots, she looked exactly as she'd always looked – practical, demure, contained. The image was completely out of tune with the fiery, radical young men and women with whom they'd spent the past couple of hours.

The crossing signal suddenly beeped. 'Come on,' Deena said quickly, changing the subject. 'Let's go home. Mummy'll be worried.'

'Deena, you still haven't answered me,' Inès insisted as they reached the other side. The cavernous entrance to the Underground loomed in front of them. For a moment, the two sisters faced each other, not speaking; there was a sudden uprush of feeling between them.

Then Deena laid her hand on Inès's forearm. 'Join us, Inès. Join us.'

'Me? What can *I* do? What use could I ever be?' Inès asked, bewildered.

Deena looked at her and smiled. 'Whatever you like. The future's *ours*, Inès. Do whatever you like.'

PART FIVE

February 2011

19

The ground below leaned this way and that, rising again as the aircraft straightened itself out on approach. They touched down just before dawn, golden rays of sunlight swinging an arc across the convex glass of her window. She was one of the first passengers off the plane, walking briskly, her rucksack and camera slung over her shoulder. At immigration, she passed carefully under the watchful gaze of the soldiers who flanked the walls. There was a nervousness in the air that she hadn't experienced since Abidjan, almost two years earlier. There she had witnessed the same strange tension, a whole country holding its breath, pretending collectively that everything was normal, an absurd distortion of reality brought about by the war: that it was quite usual for a jeep full of soldiers to pull into a street, cast their eye around and haul off a pineapple vendor or some unlucky fellow selling lottery tickets. No one shouted out in protest for fear they would be next. The whole city was a hall of mirrors where everyone's gaze was directed both inwards and outwards. She had that same sense of trepidation now.

The customs official looked intently at her passport and press credentials, gazing at his screen as though his life depended on displaying the correct level of attention to detail.

'*Enti sahafeya?* Journalist?' He shot the question at her suspiciously.

'Yes.'

'You speak Arabic?'

'A little.'

He thumbed through the pages. A fly buzzed uncomfortably close to her ear. The air was warm and stale. Behind her, people shifted uncomfortably. Suddenly a commotion broke out further down the line, a scuffle taking place in almost total silence. A man was hustled into an adjoining room by two soldiers as his womenfolk looked dumbly on, their fear hidden behind their veils. The door slammed shut. The queue, which had broken up momentarily to watch the outburst, re-formed once more. All was quiet, as if the interruption had never happened. The hairs on the back of her neck stood up. Something was about to happen. She could almost smell it.

She took back her passport and hurried through the queues of passengers waiting for their baggage to be delivered. The exit doors flew open at her approach and she stepped into the brilliant, blinding sunlight, relieved to be out of the atmosphere of oppressive gloom. There was a man standing beside a taxi, parked a few yards away. She gestured to him – free? He nodded quickly and opened the door. She slid in, threw her rucksack across the seat and shut the door.

'Hotel Flamenco, just off Gezira Street. You know it?'

He nodded. '*Aiwa.*'

'Let's go.' It was a relief to be back in Egypt, despite the tension and foreboding in the air. She'd practically gone down on her knees in front of Donal, begging to be given her old turf back again. The whole region was going up in flames. After the immolation of the Tunisian street vendor, there was no stopping the unrest. Like one of those uncontrollable bush fires in the Australian outback, the protests had spread: Tunisia, Jordan, Yemen, Bahrain, Libya ... and Egypt. It was time for her to return to Cairo.

Cairo. *Her* city. She knew it better than anyone at NNI and certainly better than Dominic. In some ways, it felt more like home to her than London. She was certainly more comfortable in its crowded, chaotic streets, full of the noise and bustle of her childhood, than she was in the manicured opulence of Aunt Julia's house. There she felt like a visitor, amongst the thick white towels and the cushions that were plumped always just so. The heat and dust of Cairo suited her; she drew energy and empathy from the din and the bodies that jostled and hustled for space.

She turned her head to look out of the window. The freeway was thick with early-morning traffic heading into the city. It was exactly as she'd left it nearly seven months ago: chaotic, bustling, dynamic, moving to its own inward beat and rhythm. The driver changed from lane to lane, weaving what seemed like an impossible path through the congestion. A string of glass beads hung from the rear-view mirror, jangling as he jerked forward and sideways, seeking a minute's advantage here or there. Lexi rolled down the window and leaned her head on her arm. Bursts of conversation in other tongues, blasts of carbon monoxide and glimpses of lives on balconies or the rooftops of apartment blocks whose interiors remained closed to her came at her as they paused at a red light or stalled in traffic.

They crossed the river on the 15th of May Bridge, coming down to street level in a smooth rush. All of a sudden she was at eye level with men in snowy-white *thawbs* who sat smoking at roadside cafes before going to work. No one took much notice of her. They passed the All Saints' Cathedral on the corner and turned into Ibn Maiser. The Hotel Flamenco was halfway down the narrow street. The driver pulled up in front of the door with a screech.

Lexi looked up and smiled faintly. As a concession to its name, there were a few random Spanish touches – wrought-iron balconies, a low red-tiled roof and a few azure-and-yellow tiles placed haphazardly along the whitewashed walls. In a narrow street dominated by greying utilitarian office buildings, the effect was curious. A relic from another age, another past, another version of events. She'd stayed at the Flamenco many times. She liked its out-of-the-way character and its faded charms. Unlike many of the foreign correspondents who jetted in and out of town, she avoided the big hotels. Most of them stayed at the Ramses Hilton, just across the river, but Lexi hated the faux-camaraderie and the heightened sense of importance that journalists seemed to acquire whenever they moved together en masse. Much better to stay under the radar, out of sight. *She* wasn't in it for the glory.

She glanced at the driver. His limpid dark-brown eyes were fixed on her with an expression she couldn't read. She opened the door and hurriedly got out. 'No, no ... I'm fine. I can manage.' He tried to prise her rucksack away from her but soon gave up. She walked into the hotel lobby, all gilt mirrors, heavy chandeliers, wood-panelled walls, the driver trailing disconsolately behind her. In the silvery watermarked mirror behind the reception desk she could see the reflection of scores of well-padded businessmen in the bar, a mixture of Westerners and the locals they had come to seduce – or was it the other way round? Sometimes it was hard to tell.

'Ah, Miss Sturgis. Welcome back.' The manager behind the reception counter was chummily familiar. 'May I take a copy of your passport? Thank you.' She handed it over. He passed it to the receptionist next to him, and as he turned back to her, he nodded imperceptibly to someone behind her. She glanced over her shoulder, but there was only the driver who had brought her in. Something had passed between the two men, but it was so fleeting she wondered if she'd imagined it. She turned back to the manager, who quickly brought his gaze up to meet hers. 'You're here for a fortnight?'

'Yes. And there should be a room booked for Ian Conroy? He'll be here later today.' Ian, her cameraman, was coming in that afternoon from Amman.

'Yes, yes, there's no problem. Everything is booked. You would like smoking or non-smoking room?'

'Smoking. Definitely smoking.'

'No problem.' It seemed to be his favourite phrase. 'Room 315. Overlooking the river.'

'Thanks.' She took the old-fashioned key and picked up her bag. She fished in her pocket for a tip for the waiting driver, but to her surprise, he raised his hands in horror. 'No, no … please.' He seemed genuinely alarmed. She put away the offending notes, puzzled, and made her way to the elevator. She overheard him say something to the receptionist, but her Arabic wasn't good enough to catch it. She pressed the lift button and waited. Just before the doors opened, some instinct made her turn to face the reception desk again. She saw the manager miming to the driver, *I'll call you later*. So she *hadn't* imagined it. Odd, she thought, frowning. There'd been no open sign of recognition when they'd first walked in.

The lift doors closed abruptly, blocking off her view, and the lift rushed up to the third floor. She walked down the corridor to room 315, still puzzled, and opened the door. The air was slightly stale, but the room was large and clean. She tossed her rucksack on to the bed and walked to the window. The heavy sliding doors that led to the small patio were stiff, but she managed to drag them apart and stepped out. After the stuffiness of the lobby, the air felt fresh and sweet.

She walked to the edge and looked across the city. A cluster of new flats opposite wasn't yet high enough to block out the view. Beyond the thin fringe of trees she could just see the wrinkled brown skin of the river. It was nearly noon, and the sun hung low and hard in the winter sky. The leafy streets below rang with laughter and chatter. The sounds of children returning from school or servants walking back with laden bags from the shops and neighbourhood markets slithered up the walls to meet her. Their cries and half-jeering shouts, the full-bellied, waxy sound of car horns and the waspy stutter of motorcycles washed over her. The building next door, an elegant *fin de siècle* mansion with a lush, semi-tropical garden of mango and palm trees, turned its sleepy, blank gaze towards her. As she stood there smoking quietly, the air pressure shifted and deepened, signalling an afternoon storm. She looked up into the sky. The clouds had an architecture all of their own; now breaking up, now colliding, now dissolving. She watched them chase each other, their ephemeral shapes holding on to the last rays of the sun before a graphite blanket appeared on the horizon and a prowling roll of thunder reverberated through the air. Soon it would rain.

She turned back into the room and tugged the sliding door shut behind her. Inside, all was quiet. She switched on the television and flicked through the channels until she found CNN, then began to unpack. Rain started to fall against the window panes, a steady pitter-patter that drowned out the voice of the newscaster.

It took less than ten minutes to empty her rucksack. She closed the wardrobe doors and took a quick look around the room. Everything was as it should be. Her clothes and possessions were packed away; her laptop and notebooks were lined up neatly on the small desk next to the bed, waiting for her to file her first report. She sat down on the edge of the bed and unzipped her boots, then took off her socks and wriggled her bare toes against the thick, fluffy pile of the carpet. She lay back slowly into the spongy mattress with its cover that smelled of chemicals and detergent, allowing the bed to absorb her weight. Her mind had suddenly gone quite still. Her eyes moved across the ceiling, following every crack; the damp patches above the air-conditioner; the electrical conduit that ran along the surface and down the length of the wall. For the first time in ages, the back-and-forth shuttle of her mind was still. A sensation came over her that was like the one she'd had as a child, going to lie down in the long, uncut grass in the garden – which garden? She remembered at once how everything around her was silenced, the world outside receding until all she was left with was the drumming of her own blood in her ears, making her think she could feel the earth turning underneath her. She huddled in close against it, drawing her knees up to her chin, not falling, yet falling, falling.

20

All morning, far out to sea, where the purple line of the mountains began and the dazzling line of the horizon ended, a dark mass had been taking shape, lifting itself off the flat edge of the world, rolling slowly towards them. Sitting on the roof terrace of the Ali Baba Hotel, beside the Red Sea, Mark finished his demitasse of thick, dark espresso and stood up. In a few minutes, a taxi would come for him and take him out to the makeshift airstrip that lay some five kilometres outside the town. He had two stops to make before nightfall – one a little further down the coast at Quseer, where three American oil executives were waiting nervously; the other about an hour and a half due west at an oil rig near Al Kharga, closer to Libya, from where a group of French engineers were being evacuated. He was to bring both groups of men to Cairo, stay overnight in the city and then head back in the morning.

In the two months since he'd met up with Crowther and Smith in Nanyuki, he'd flown almost two thousand miles, picking up people who needed to be rescued in a hurry and brought to safety, usually to one or other of the nearby capitals – Tripoli, Algiers, Cairo. But those capitals were becoming increasingly dangerous. The unrest that had started in Tunis three months earlier had spread. He'd warned his handlers that Cairo might not be safe, but his advice had gone unheard.

He shrugged on his jacket, slipped on his sunglasses and headed downstairs. Even though it was winter and a storm was approaching, the sunlight was still blinding. He hurried out to the waiting taxi. He wanted to be off and in the air before the first rolls of thunder split the skies.

The taxi pulled up in front of the small hangar. Mark tipped the driver, grabbed his rucksack from the back seat and strode across the stony ground. The two young mechanics who manned the airstrip were readying the plane. With a length of nearly twenty metres, it was almost twice the size of his own machine, which he'd left behind in Lamu. The Cessna 680 Sovereign was capable of flying from coast to coast across the United

States and could seat eight passengers in comfort, twelve at a push. He would miss it when the job was over, he thought, as he climbed into the cockpit to begin the pre-flight safety checks. One of the mechanics clambered up after him and they quickly went through the drill.

'Weight?'

'Six hundred and forty-two kilos, sir.'

'Fuel?'

'Everything ready, sir. Here's the flight plan. You can go.'

'Thanks.' Mark took the handwritten sheet and glanced at it. He'd been assigned a cruising altitude of 37,000 feet in a westerly direction, away from the encroaching storm. He settled himself comfortably into the seat and started the engines. The roar was immediate and satisfying and he felt his body relax. Start-up and take-off were the moments of flight he liked best. Nothing in the world compared with the feeling that he and his plane were one.

He nosed the aircraft slowly over the bumpy tarmac, avoiding the worst of the potholes and grassy knolls. The wheels strained against the terrain; underneath his fingers, the throttle hummed with life. He gave the mechanics a thumbs-up and signalled his 'OK' to the controller, then taxied out to the northern end of the strip, readying the plane for flight. As the engines revved, the ground swelled beneath him. He pulled the throttle lever towards him and the plane gathered speed, flying over the rough grassy tussocks and stones, straining like a racehorse at the bit. The earth tilted and then was abruptly left behind.

The air was elastic and cushioned, first impenetrable, then milky and fluid, finally becoming solid. He shot upwards, carving a graceful arc into the light blue sky, conscious of the darkening mass of cloud behind him. He was flying away from it, over the wrinkled grey-and-brown hills of the Sinai, the shimmering blue Gulf of Aqaba left far behind. It would take him less than an hour to reach Quseer, where the first batch of passengers awaited. With luck, they'd take off again almost immediately and land in Al Kharga by three. If everything went according to plan, he'd deliver his passengers safely to Cairo by nightfall, spend the night at one of the hotels close to the airport and take off again just after dawn.

A thousand feet; two thousand feet; four thousand feet – the earth slipped away. Below him, glinting angrily, a silver flash of water appeared through the thinning cloud as though a hand had reached down to polish it. He saw his own shadow upon the ground, a wavering presence marking out his journey. The finger of the Gulf of Suez swam into view, bordered on both sides by a thin ribbon of black road. He flew steadily over it, his eyes and mind flickering between the dials in front of him and the vast panorama through the windscreen. He was an instinctive, intuitive pilot, preferring what he could see in front of him to what he'd been taught abstractly. In his mind's eye he held the map of the world as he'd always known it, lying face down on the lawn in the front garden, observing the comings and goings of beetles, slugs and ants with the intense concentration of a child. Up there in the skies, where there was nothing solid to hand, he found it comforting to think of that view of the earth, intimate and real, as he alone knew it.

21

She woke with a start. There was an urgent rapping at the door. She sat up. *Tap, tap, tap.* A few seconds later, it started again. *Tap, tap, tap.* Louder this time.

'Who is it?' she croaked out. There was no answer. 'Who is it?' Still no answer. She stood up, instantly alert, and crept barefoot towards the door. A fat, clumsy moth suddenly flew across her line of vision, falling limply against the wall sconce. A thin tremor of fear rose up through her belly and chest. She peered through the convex glass eye, looking right and left as far as she could see, but there was no one there. She opened the door a fraction, making sure it was on the chain, and peered out. The corridor was still and empty. She slid the chain off and opened the door wide. The air was tinged very faintly with cigarette smoke. A careless giveaway, she thought. Whoever had been outside her door was male. Women rarely smoked in public. Her heart began to thud. She kept one foot against the door, propping it open, and leaned out as far as she could. There was nothing, no one, no sound, just the empty, acrid drift of smoke.

She shut the door again, making sure it was locked, then padded back to the bed and pulled her laptop out of her bag. She looked at her watch. It was almost four. She'd slept for four hours straight. She wondered where Ian was. She picked up her mobile and was scrolling through the contacts to send him a text when she heard another tap at the door. This time someone spoke. A man's voice. 'Miss Sturgis?'

She got up and moved cautiously forward. 'Who is it?'

'It's the manager. From the reception desk.'

She half recognised his voice. She opened the door a crack, still keeping the chain on, and peered out. It *was* him. 'What is it?' she asked. 'What's the matter?'

'There isn't time to explain things properly, but you need to leave the hotel. Come with me.' His English was suddenly accent-free, almost American.

She gripped the door frame. 'Where? Why? What's happening?'

He flashed a quick look up the corridor, then turned back to her. 'You're not safe here.'

A cool wave of understanding washed over her. 'It's started, hasn't it?' On the way into the city from the airport, she'd seen the protestors converging on Tahrir Square, streams of young men and women walking across the bridges that separated Zamalek island from the city. She'd turned her head to stare at them, but something about the way the driver had darted her a quick backwards glance had made her unusually circumspect.

There was no need to elaborate. He nodded. 'We have to leave. Now. I'm going to take you to the Hilton. That's where most of the foreigners are. You'll be safe there.'

Lexi had lost count of the number of times in her working life she'd had nothing to go by in a situation other than her own intuition. Standing face to face with complete strangers – soldiers, rebels, militiamen, thugs – she'd had to make split-second decisions with nothing to back them up apart from what she felt deep in her gut. *Can I trust this man? Should I?* She looked at the face in front of her and made one such snap decision. 'Let me get my stuff.'

She turned and grabbed her small nylon holdall, thrusting her laptop, wash bag and a change of clothing into it. She picked up her phone, remembering to yank the charger out of the wall, and ran back to the door. 'What's your name?' she asked. *Establish the beginnings of a bond.* It was textbook stuff, straight out of the section headed 'Hostage Crisis'.

'Faisal. Come on. Let's take the stairs.' He propelled her towards the emergency stairwell.

97

'Why did you come for me?' Lexi asked as they clattered down the stairs together.

'We know you.'

'We? Who's "we"?'

But there was no time to answer. Faisal burst through the exit doors and on to the street, still holding her arm. A car was waiting in front of them, its door swinging crazily ajar. Lexi glanced to her left and saw a mob of men running towards them. Faisal pushed her into the back seat and clambered in after her. She looked up and with a start, she recognised the driver who'd brought her to the Flamenco from the airport. Her heart was thumping. Her mind began to race. She'd been singled out from the start. She'd felt something was amiss in the lobby. She should have seen it coming.

'*Yala!*' Faisal instructed the driver, shoving Lexi's head down into the seat. The smell of old leather rose to meet her nostrils. Her face was pressed almost flat against the crinkled skin of the seat. She could scarcely breathe. The driver peeled away from the kerb, swerving left and right, cursing under his breath as they raced away. After a while, Faisal eased the pressure away from her head and she sat up.

'Where are we going?' she demanded. They were accelerating away from the city. 'This isn't the way to the Hilton.'

'No, it's not. We need you to do something for us first,' Faisal said, sounding almost apologetic.

'What? Where are you taking me?' She couldn't tell in which direction they were headed; the lights of the city were strung out in front and behind them, disappearing in each direction into a thick, tense blackness that seemed pregnant with menace.

'Alexandria,' Faisal said at last. 'There's someone we want you to meet.'

22

Mark laid the aircraft gently down on the makeshift runway at Quseer, straining to see through the cloud of dust. He taxied up to the hangar where the three portly Americans were waiting, tension etched on their faces, panic showing in damp patches of sweat on their shirts. It took them less than ten minutes to board and then they were away again, ploughing a furrow through the same dust cloud before breaking free and soaring into the cloudless cerulean sea. He kept his headphones on, partly to stay abreast of what was happening on the ground but partly too to block out the incessant chatter behind him, relief at their sudden rescue sending their voices high with fright and indignation.

He flew on to Al Kharga, landing there just after noon. This time, things were a little more complicated. As he began his descent he could already see, from his height of ten thousand feet and dropping, the telltale plume of dust that signalled a vehicle travelling at speed. He looked left and right and saw similar plumes that meant the same thing. He made a swift calculation, giving himself no more than fifteen minutes to load the executives and get the hell out of there before there was a confrontation of some sort. He wasn't armed and was sure the Americans sitting nervously in the rear were similarly defenceless.

The Egyptian, Libyan and Algerian workers at the rig were nervous. They loaded the foreigners into the back of the aircraft like cargo, clearly desperate to get rid of them. The last thing Mark saw was the arrival of the first of the trucks packed with men brandishing guns, heading to the hangar they'd just left. He didn't hang around to find out who they were or what they wanted. He took off at speed, thundering down the runway and leaving behind whatever trouble was brewing. The silvery glint of a lake in the distance scored across his line of vision as the plane tilted to the east, then righted itself northwards, heading for Cairo. He flew steadily north, measuring his progress along the thin finger of the Nile. The men in the back were silent as they gazed down upon the danger from which they'd just escaped. But their abrupt departure from trouble turned out to be just the lull before the storm.

About an hour later, on their approach to Cairo, air traffic control informed Mark tersely that the airport was closed to all domestic and international flights. Alexandria was similarly shut. He circled Cairo for a further forty minutes, fast running out of fuel, desperately seeking permission to land. He was finally granted a slot at Giza, some twenty kilometres south of Cairo. He touched down with the fuel gauge flashing angrily and the sweat running down his back. His passengers clambered down hurriedly, their legs unable to carry them any faster away from the plane. The Americans were met by representatives from their embassy – a country clearly well versed in taking care of its own – but getting hold of someone to relieve him of the Frenchmen took another hour. Finally, just before five, two French soldiers arrived to take them off his hands.

'What the hell's going on?' Mark asked as the men scurried into the waiting vehicle.

One of the soldiers shrugged and spat into the ground. 'Who knows? It's better for you to go to the Hilton. We'll take care of these two, but you're on your own, *mon ami*.'

Mark looked around. His plane was safely parked away in one of the side hangars. The wad of cash with which he'd started the day was almost gone. There was clearly no hope of getting any fuel – aside from the skeleton staff needed to run the airport, everyone else had vanished. 'Where's the Hilton?' he asked resignedly.

'Centre of town. Look, we'll drop you off as close as we can. Come on. Let's get these fuckers out of here.'

Mark needed no second invitation. He flung his rucksack into the back of the vehicle and climbed in. He pulled his mobile out of his pocket, but he was already out of juice. He would call his handlers in the morning and try to figure a way to get out of this mess. It was just his fucking luck. He'd spent the past year trying to avoid warzones, and here he was, flying right into one.

23

Dusk was beginning to fall by the time the driver pulled off the main highway into Alexandria. The streets thronged with protesters and police, and the air was filled with the acrid smell of burning tyres. Faisal instructed her tersely to keep her head down until they were clear of the crowds. Finally, after what seemed like an eternity, he told her she could sit up again. *Saleh Basha*. She caught a glimpse of the street name as they turned the corner. A few minutes later, the driver pulled into an empty parking lot and killed the engine. They coasted silently into a space and came to an abrupt halt. She looked up at the tall grey apartment building.

'Are we here?' she asked, not fully expecting a reply.

'*Aiwa*.' Faisal looked cautiously up and down the street. 'Let's go.' He opened the door.

'Who're we meeting?' Lexi asked.

'You'll see. We want you to interview someone. It won't take long. Half an hour, maybe a bit more. But it needs to go on air on Friday morning. Can you do that?'

'It's not up to me,' she said slowly. 'It's not my decision what gets selected for airing. It depends if it's interesting enough.'

The two men exchanged a quick glance. 'Oh, it'll be interesting all right,' Faisal said. 'Just make sure it goes out on time.'

Lexi was silent as she followed him into the building. Friday prayers had become the rallying point for demonstrations up and down the Middle East. In spite of her uncertainty about what lay ahead, she could already taste the familiar thrill of excitement on her tongue.

The stairwell was dark and damp and smelled of urine. She put a hand to her nose as she ran up the stairs sandwiched between the two men. Narrow corridors branched off left and right, leading into darkness. Up and up they went, until they reached the eighth floor. A metal security door protected the corridor. In front of it, barely discernible in the shadows, were two armed men. There was a quick, urgent exchange in Arabic that was too fast for Lexi to catch, then the metal door swung open. Both men wore the distinctive red-and-white Palestinian-style scarves wrapped closely around their heads. Only their eyes were visible. Lexi felt their scrutiny like a physical patting-down as she walked through.

'Come.' Faisal led the way, stopping halfway down the corridor in front of an incongruously cheerful yellow door. He knocked briskly, twice, and the door opened slowly to reveal a large sitting room. All the furniture had been pushed back against the walls – two worn brown sofas, cushions flattened out of shape, and a cluster of small tables and stools – and the centre of the room was taken up by desks and chairs and an impressive array of computers, fax machines and modems. Two young men, heads almost touching, were crouched behind a screen. They looked up briefly as Lexi entered, faces illuminated by the ghostly light. There were perhaps a dozen people in the room, all working furiously. Her presence seemed to illicit no response.

'Where's the boss?' Faisal asked no one in particular.

'He's asleep. He's been up for days.' Someone looked up from a task. 'Wake him. Tell him the reporter's here.'

The man nodded and hurriedly left the room. In the lull that followed, Lexi looked around her carefully, noting the details that might come in handy. Oddly enough, she felt no fear. The instinctive certainty that had made her follow Faisal down the hotel corridor was with her still.

There was a sudden movement at the door. She looked up. Everyone's eyes were drawn to the man standing in the doorway. He hadn't uttered a single word, but he unsettled the room, somehow refocusing its energies towards him as he moved forward into the light. He was tall and rangy, dressed like all the others in jeans and a thick hooded sweatshirt. He shoved his hands into his pockets, feeling for something. A cigarette. There was a quick, sharp flare as he lit up, then he turned his head and looked directly at her. Dark-brown eyes fringed with impossibly thick lashes, the shadow of a beard coming through his golden skin. He'd been asleep, someone had said. As Lexi looked at him, her impression wasn't of someone who'd just got up, but of a man who hadn't slept at all.

24

'What can I get you, sir?' The barman addressed him as if pouring his drink was the most important thing in the world. Thirty storeys below, a revolution was taking shape, but to the half-dozen staff struggling to man the long bar, now full to bursting with semi-hysterical journalists, the long-suppressed revolt was a secondary consideration. Mark shook his head. He was shattered.

'Whisky. No ice.'

The drink appeared within seconds. Mark took it and pushed his way through the throng pressed up against the bar. He spotted a lone empty table by the window and hurried towards it.

There was tension in the air, shifting dangerously from relief to fear. Around him, on every table, every surface, lay piles of recording equipment, bulky cameras, furry-ended microphones, laptops and mobile phones plugged into every available socket, boxes of duty-free cigarettes and bottles of booze. People yelled without pause into their phones, trying to send reports out of the country, trying to get through to their desk editors, line managers and bookers. He'd been plunged straight back into the world he'd done his best to escape. He tried not to look at the cameras and tripods that were once as familiar to him as parts of his own body. There was a sinking feeling in the pit of his stomach, as if he had recognised the signs of the descent into madness before anyone else around him.

He turned away from the room and looked out of the window. A spectacular sunset was slowly taking hold. Buildings, trees and telephone poles were punched black against the dusk sky, into which fresh loads of colour appeared to be tipping, staining and spreading with more and more intensity until the whole city was bathed in a light so strong that people around him slid back the doors, not so much to look at the sunset as to be in it. From far down below and behind them came the muffled roar of the demonstrations building in Tahrir Square and across the city. Gunshots rang out, puncturing the night air, and somewhere, at disturbingly close range, an ambulance siren began to wail. Yes, the descent had begun. He was right back in it, in the thick of it. That place he'd promised himself he would leave behind.

25

He spoke quietly, with an intensity that was so at odds with his polished cut-glass English accent that she had to keep checking herself. She listened, mesmerised. He could have been Toby, or any of the young men she'd been at school or university with. Nice, exceedingly well-brought up young men whose only experience of war might have been a grandfather who'd served with the Coldstream Guards, or a tray of polished medals from the Great War that lay, buried and forgotten, in a drawer in the Queen Anne chest that stood in the hallway. She didn't dare interrupt him. He had a fluency that spoke of hours of silent mental preparation and a kind of readiness and ease in front of her recording equipment. Whether or not she agreed with his assessment of the situation and where he thought things were headed was irrelevant. *Fourteen minutes.* 'Whatever happens in the Arab uprisings, nothing can take away what's happening in Tahrir Square. We have nothing. No weapons, no tanks, no firepower … just us.' *Twenty-two minutes.* 'People ask me all the time if what's happening with the youth here is in any way connected to what happened in America, with Obama's campaign. You know, the whole "yes we can" thing. Here, it's different. We're not doing this because we can. You think Bouazizi set himself on fire just because he *could*?' His eyes caught and held hers for a moment. Lexi suppressed the urge to shake her head. It wasn't a question, she knew. 'They were brought up on Al-Jazeera. On Facebook. Twitter. They're confident in a way their parents weren't, and it's not just freedom they're demanding. It's a new sense of dignity.'

'You say "they",' Lexi began hesitantly. It was the only time she'd dared interrupt. 'Don't you mean "we"?'

It was as if she hadn't spoken. *Thirty-seven minutes.* 'The more desperate a regime becomes, the more willing it is to send men to torture cells and then arrange for their disappearance. But the strategy backfired. Police abuse unites this nation, not divides it. It happens to everyone. Young, old, educated, peasant, women, men, Muslim, Christian. It's the one thing that everyone understands.' *Fifty-two minutes.* 'Whatever comes next, Egyptians know that freedom and democracy aren't given. They must be taken. That's what you shouldn't forget.' He stood up abruptly, signalling the end of the interview, and looked down at her, his tall body blocking out the light. 'Did you get it all?' he asked, a faint, almost sardonic smile lifting the corners of his mouth.

Lexi glanced down at her recording device. The red button was still switched to 'on'. She replayed a second or two of the interview. 'Yes.' She nodded. 'It's all here.'

'Good. One thing: it's got to go out before noon on Friday. Can you do that for me?'

She nodded again. 'I'll do my best.'

'No. Make sure it goes out. I'm counting on you, Lexi.'

She looked up in surprise at the sound of her name. The door closed behind him and he was gone.

26

Jane came off the A40 on to Oxford Hill, drove past the King George's Field playing fields, now covered in white, and turned right on to Woodgreen Hill. It was six o'clock and the countryside was shrouded in darkness. She was late. She hadn't been able to get out of the office before three, despite it being a Saturday, and the traffic heading out of London had been thick. She passed the cemetery, which always made her shudder, and carried on along New Yatt Road, with its pretty low stone walls and centuries-old cottages on either side. The nursing home, once a stately home nestled in the Oxfordshire countryside, was down a slip road to the left. The journey was deeply familiar to her. Every month, sometimes twice, for the past nine years, she'd driven up here, despite the fact that for the last year there'd been little point. Her father's memory was now so bad that it made no difference whether she came for five minutes or stayed for five days. His face was a mask of almost complete indifference out of which he looked dazedly on the present, often failing to recognise his own daughter.

She parked in the car park, flipped down the mirror to check her face and carefully applied a fresh smear of lipstick. She wanted to look her best. 'Oh, it's *you*, Jane,' the matron always said as soon as she saw her. 'You look lovely, my dear. You *always* look lovely.' Silly as it seemed, it mattered to her that the nursing staff whom she paid an absolute fortune to look after her elderly father should approve of her. It was the great irony of her father's life, she sometimes thought, that the middle-class decency he'd struggled to provide his whole working life had finally been achieved in his dotage. Except now his brain was too addled to appreciate it. *Oh, Dad. If you could only see yourself now. In a stately home at last.*

'Oh, hello, Jane. You're late today.' The staff nurse greeted her as she came through the entrance doors into the lobby, where there was no sense of time, no sense of the day of the week or even the seasons outside. Inside, the warm, faintly methylated air was kept at a regular temperature; the soft carpets deadened footsteps and light classical music played through discreet speakers in the communal areas. Lilies and vases of freesias brought the scent of decay to mind.

'I know, I know. Traffic was bad. How is he?' Jane asked, looking past the nurse to one of the living rooms that overlooked the beautiful gardens. Several of the home's occupants sat around in chairs: a few white-haired old ladies, who always seemed to outlive the men. Except her father, of course. At eighty-five, he was one of the oldest residents.

'Not too bad, not too bad.' The nurse smiled up at her. 'Elizabeth's in with him now. She's just given him his bath.'

'At this time? Isn't he about to have supper?' Jane raised her eyebrows.

'Oh, he had a little accident earlier.' The nurse smiled sympathetically. 'But he's fine now. Go ahead. I'm sure he's already dried and dressed.'

Jane nodded and walked down the corridor to his room. She paused outside the door for a moment, then grasped the handle and stepped inside. Her father was sitting in his chair by the window, staring unseeingly out. He was in his habitual shirt, tie and soft woollen cardigan that he seemed to wear whatever the weather. His eyes flew open as he caught sight of her and Jane saw the terror expand his face.

'Who's that?' he cried out in horror.

'It's only Jane,' called Elizabeth, the impossibly cheerful Zimbabwean nurse, coming through from the bathroom with a collection of towels and bed sheets in her plump, capable arms. 'It's Jane, your daughter, *baba*. She's come to visit you. Isn't that nice?'

Jane crossed the room quickly and bent to kiss him. 'It's only me, Dad. It's Jane.'

'Where are my teeth?' Her father's hand went up to his mouth as he accepted her kiss. 'Why aren't my teeth in?'

'They're in, *baba*,' Elizabeth said, laughing and shaking her head at him. 'Don't you remember? We put them in after your bath this morning, remember?'

'Oh.' Her father's face suddenly emptied. Jane looked away.

'I brought you some flowers, Dad, for your birthday.'

'My birthday? How old am I this time?'

'Eighty-five, Dad.'

He pulled a face. 'Horrible. Horrible. It's too long. I've been around too long.'

'Don't talk like that, *baba*,' Elizabeth broke in cheerfully. 'Eighty-five is nothing, nothing! My *gogo* was more than a hundred when she passed. Can you imagine that? More than a hundred!'

Jane could see her father's mouth working in distress. 'Why don't I put these in a vase for you, Dad?' she broke in quickly. 'They can go here, by the window.'

'He doesn't like the scent,' Elizabeth explained. She knew more about the old man's likes and dislikes than Jane could ever hope to.

'We'll put them in the bathroom, then,' Jane said soothingly, swallowing hard on the lump in her throat. He'd always loved flowers, always. Not any more. 'You'll be able to see them, but you won't smell them.'

Her father looked at the nurse. 'Who is that?' he asked, pointing a finger, his face growing hard with suspicion.

'Oh, it's only me,' Elizabeth sang cajolingly. She began to bustle around. 'It's only me, *baba*. Your favourite nurse.'

Her father dismissed her explanation with an impatient wave. 'Why is she here? Who is she? What's she doing here?'

'I'm the one giving you a bath, *baba*, don't you remember? I feed you, I bring you tea … I make everything nice for you.' Elizabeth began to catalogue her tasks in a soothing lullaby, but Jane saw that for her father, the nurse had ceased to exist. His hands, knotted and gnarled from years of hard labour and gardening, twisted one against the other in agitation. Then, just as suddenly, his attention steadied and his face broke into a smile.

'*Co jemy na obiad?*'

'What's that, Dad?' Jane asked, frowning.

'He's doing that a lot these days,' Elizabeth remarked as she folded away the last of the towels. 'He's speaking in another language. I don't know what it is.'

'Dinner. What are we having for dinner? You speak Polish, don't you? Didn't I teach you?'

Jane looked at her father. His eyes were red-rimmed and watery. She swallowed and patted his hand. 'Yes, of course you did, Dad. I've just forgotten, that's all.'

Her father nodded, satisfied with her answer. His chin slipped, and within minutes, just like a newborn baby, he was asleep.

Jane sat with him for a while, then got up, avoiding Elizabeth's concerned glance, and went into the small en suite bathroom. She shut the door slowly behind her, leaning against it whilst she steadied herself.

Her usual hour was almost up. If he woke, she'd take her leave with a bright smile and a promise to visit next week. If she didn't show up for a month, he wouldn't know the difference. On her last visit, he'd turned to her as she was picking up her handbag and keys and asked plaintively, like a child, 'What happened?' The question had brought tears to her eyes. 'It's old age, Dad. That's all. Nothing's happened. It's just age. Time passing.' She'd stroked his hand awkwardly. Old age. There wasn't much more to say.

She opened the bathroom door and looked over at him. He was fast asleep. She picked up her bag and coat and smiled her thanks at Elizabeth, not wanting to disturb him, then let herself out. Outside, she walked quickly across the car park to her car. It was nearly the end of February, but winter showed no sign of letting go. The air was razor sharp and cold. She switched on the engine and waited impatiently for the heater to warm things up. The news came on; it was just past seven p.m. *Fierce fighting has broken out in Tahrir Square, in the centre of Cairo. Sources say—*

She fumbled for her phone. Lexi was in Cairo. She'd landed this morning. How many hours ahead was Cairo? She tried to remember. Two? Three? She dialled Lexi's number but it went straight to voicemail. She scrolled through the list until she found Donal's. He picked up on the first ring.

'Have you heard from her?' she asked anxiously.

'No, not yet. Ian's still stuck in Amman. The airport's been closed all afternoon, apparently. It looks as though the army were anticipating this.'

'So she's there on her own?'

There was a second's pause. 'Yeah. But she'll be fine.' Donal was trying to sound reassuring. 'She'll be fine.'

'Call me as soon as you hear from her. I don't care what time it is.'

'Don't worry. She'll be fine.'

His words carried no reassurance whatsoever. They both knew Lexi well. Only *too* well.

27

The driver muttered something to Faisal as they turned off the bridge and descended the off-ramp towards the river. There was a quick exchange between them that again she couldn't follow. Faisal turned to her.

'He says he can't get you any closer than this.'

Lexi looked around. They were on a narrow side street just off Tahrir Square. It was empty, but she could see roadblocks and the ominous clumsy shapes of armed personnel carriers and barricades ahead. The mood of the protesters had turned ever more belligerent, and the regime's response had been brutal. There was real fear in the air, along with the dawning recognition that the protests couldn't be stopped. 'The hotel's just there, on the corner. Come on, I'll walk with you.'

'You don't need to. I'll be fine.'

'No, it's not safe.' He opened the door and got out. Lexi picked up her bag and followed. The air was chilly. She drew her jacket around her tightly and retied the headscarf Faisal had given her before leaving Alexandria. It was dangerous to draw attention to her blonde hair, especially now. Together they hurried along the street, heads firmly down. They took a left just before the square, pushing against the crowds coming in the opposite direction. The air was thick with smoke and the faint, sharp residue of tear gas. The sky was lit up with an eerie orange glow that fought the sunset for dominance. Lexi pressed the sleeve of her jacket against her nose and forced her way forward.

It took them nearly fifteen minutes to reach the forecourt of the hotel. It was jammed full of BMWs with blacked-out windows, and big, sleek American cars. There were scores of emblazoned news agency vans – everyone from CNN and the BBC to Al Jazeera. The sight was immediately reassuring.

'How can I contact you?' Lexi asked.

'You can't. But we'll be in touch. This isn't going to be over any time soon.'

They stood looking at one another for a few seconds, not saying anything. Lexi felt a sudden surge of sympathy for this man who in another life and place would have been a university student or a young professional just embarking on a career. Faisal must have caught something of her mood. He smiled briefly, almost sadly, and then strode away, merging into the growing darkness. Lexi touched her bag, just to be sure everything was in it, and hurried across to the hotel. She tried Ian's number for the umpteenth time, but the networks were still down. He would have arrived at the Flamenco to find her gone and would probably be frantic by now. She would try calling him from the Hilton.

The lobby was packed and the mood inside was hysterical. Everyone was talking at once, shouting to each other across the heads of the anxious-looking hotel staff. Lexi stuffed her scarf in her bag and headed for reception.

'Sorry, no room, madam, no room! Hotel is full!' the harried-looking receptionist shouted at her when she finally managed to approach the desk. Lexi shrugged. There'd be someone she knew in the bar or the restaurant from whom she could bum a mattress or couch. The receptionist looked at her closely. Perhaps he recognised her, or perhaps it was something in her expression that made him relent. 'I'm sorry. I try to find you a room. Maybe somebody's cancelling tonight.' He lifted his shoulders. 'What can I do? Everything crazy right now.'

Lexi smiled. 'Don't worry. I'm sure I'll find something. Is it possible to use the hotel phone?'

'Yes, yes.' He handed it over.

She dialled Ian's mobile number but it went straight to voicemail. She tried the Flamenco, and on the third attempt managed to get through. No, Ian Conroy wasn't there. He hadn't arrived. God only knew where he was. The airport was closed, hadn't she heard? Lexi hung up. 'Is there anywhere I can use my laptop?' she asked the concerned-looking receptionist.

'You want internet? You need internet?' She nodded vigorously. 'Go to restaurant. Top floor. There is a satellite transmitter.'

'Thanks. Thanks for your help.' She smiled at him and turned to push her way through the crowded lobby to the lifts, where she squeezed in amongst the Dutch, German, American and British journalists heading for the thirty-sixth floor, all talking at the tops of their voices. Squashed against someone's flak jacket with a camera jammed uncomfortably at her back, Lexi was silent. She'd spotted a few famous faces from the major networks, tense with anticipation and excitement. This wasn't their fight, but they were witness to it all the same.

Suddenly, incongruously, something her father had once said popped into her head, a quote from Winston Churchill: *The further backward you look, the further forward you see.* What would her father make of all this? she wondered. For the first time in years, she wanted to know what he thought might happen. It was one of life's supreme ironies that in a roundabout way, they'd both wound up trafficking in current affairs, though on opposite sides of an invisible divide. Years earlier, in one of their more spectacular arguments, he'd thrown the accusation at her: *you're only doing this to spite me.* She'd laughed it off, of course, and walked out, slamming the door behind her so hard the panes rattled. She quickly forced herself back to the present, annoyed with herself. For all her steely determination *not* to think about him, he had an uncomfortable way of popping into her head, just when she least expected it.

The lift doors opened suddenly on to the babble of noise and movement that was the rooftop restaurant and bar. She followed two German news reporters out. She was impatient to get down to Tahrir Square amongst the protesters, talking to people, recording events as they unfolded, but first she had to speak to Donal and send him the interview she'd just done . Once it was safely gone, if there was still no word from Ian, she would go out into the streets alone. It wouldn't be the first time. Donal would have a fit, but the coverage would be worth it. She had a small hand-held camera and her microphone, enough to convey the atmosphere and the urgency of events.

She scanned the room, looking for an empty table. All around her people were talking at full volume, *at* one another, *to* one another, *behind* one another, yelling into their telephones, struggling to establish ISDN links to their various desk editors and colleagues overseas. Conversations in English, French, Arabic, German and countless other languages she couldn't identify rose and fell around her like rainfall. In the corner of the room she spotted a table with a single chair that someone had just vacated and made a beeline for it.

As she pushed her way through, she briefly noticed a man sitting a few tables away, staring at her. She slipped off her jacket and hung it over the back of the chair before pulling it out. Suddenly, she was aware of some extraordinary source of tension behind her. Her shoulder hunched, as though someone had touched her there. She turned slowly. At that exact moment, a series of earth-shattering explosions ripped through the air, followed by the terrifying whistle that preceded a bomb blast. Four, five, six … the roars were louder than any thunder crack, and then the *whump* that seemed to shatter glass.

In the confusion that followed, everyone surged towards the windows. The shout went up like a chorus: 'The army's been deployed!' Somewhere at the back of the room, a woman, stupidly, dramatically, began to scream. Lexi stared at the man, who was staring right back at her. The clamour and chatter receded abruptly. He got up, and the noise of his chair scraping against the tiles seemed to her to be the only sound in the room.

28

They gazed at each other, neither, it seemed, able to speak. Mark's mouth had gone dry. *Alex. Alexandra.* How many times in the past six months had he said her name out loud, only to shake his head, embarrassed at himself? His heart was thumping recklessly inside his chest. What the fuck was she doing here, standing in front of him exactly as he'd seen her in his mind's eye countless times since that night? But before he could gather himself sufficiently to ask her, another explosion rocked the building, splitting the air. Sirens began to wail, followed by the frightened staccato of gunfire. He had no idea who she was or how she came to be in a hotel bar in Cairo, but there was no time to ponder it.

'Come with me.' The instinct that had seen him through nearly two decades of war reporting kicked in. He put out a hand to grab hers, but she was already gone. He stared after her.

'Stairs, not the lift.' She tossed the instruction over her shoulder as she pushed her way through the crowd towards the emergency exit. There was no time to question it. Incredulous, he followed her, dodging the surging bodies as people rushed to and fro, most heading for the lifts en masse. As one, they burst through the first set of safety doors leading to the fire escape. Whoever she was, he thought dazedly, she knew exactly what she was doing. She ran, sure-footed, straight down the stairs, clutching her small rucksack tightly with her free hand. She was fit. As fit as he was. Above them he could hear others shoving open the doors and clattering down the staircase. The lifts were clearly jammed or suspended. Down, down, down they ran, each concentrating on keeping balance, sticking together. At last they reached the bottom. She halted him and stood for a moment with her back flattened against the exit door, listening intently.

'Who are you?' he whispered urgently.

She shook her head violently. 'Later. Just follow me.' She pushed open the doors, ignoring the wail of the alarm, which was quickly swallowed up by the noise coming from all around them. They were in a small courtyard, sandwiched between the main and service entrances to the hotel. She ran lightly across to the single gate leading to the street. It was padlocked. There was a wall at chest height running all the way around the compound. They looked at each other questioningly, but before either could say a word, there was the sudden whistle of a stray bullet and a *ping* as it hit the brickwork. With the same impulse, they scrambled over the wall, landing hard on the other side. She was up first. She brushed herself down, ignoring his look of amazement. 'Come on,' she said firmly, urgently. 'Let's go.'

Luckily, the street was empty. Abandoned cars were scattered haphazardly all the way down its short length and the street lights were out. The city had the eerie sense of a place on the edge of an apocalypse. Some way off, a blaze burned, sending a warm orange glow into the sky. She pulled a scarf out of her pocket and quickly covered her hair. 'Follow me,' she said brusquely. 'Keep up. Don't lose me.'

She moved quickly, slipping easily between cars, crossing the road, one hand curled protectively around her rucksack. He followed her blindly. She seemed to know the city like the back of her hand. She led him down El Sheikh-Rihan Street, walking against the molasses-slow flow of traffic heading in the opposite direction, a slim, petite figure with her hair and face covered, indistinguishable from any of the women around them.

'Where are we going?' he asked as they stopped for a second. They were on a quieter side street. All the lifeblood of the city had been drained away to Tahrir Square, now almost a mile up the road.

'See that alleyway between those two shops?' She pointed to a passageway, so narrow he'd have missed it. 'Some friends of mine live just down it. We'll be safe there.'

They crossed the road and slipped into the alleyway. She stopped for a moment to check they hadn't been followed, then rapped softly on a door about halfway down. Two short raps, followed by a long one; a pause, then two more. It was obviously a code. He stared at her.

'*Me'en da?*' A man's voice came through the grille.

'It's me, Ahmad. Lexi. Open up.'

'Lexi?' The grille slid back immediately. 'Lexi? What the …?

The door opened slowly to reveal an Egyptian man in his mid thirties, staring at them both in disbelief. He looked Mark quickly up and down, assessing him as best he could in the dark, then stepped back to let them in. Mark's head was reeling. Lexi? He looked down at her, recognition slowly dawning. Lexi Sturgis! The news reporter. How the hell had he missed it? But before he could say anything, Ahmad urged them to step inside. 'When did you get here?' he asked, closing and bolting the door behind them. 'I didn't even know you were in town. And how the hell did you get *here*? The whole place is going up in flames!'

'I know. We walked,' Lexi said, kissing him gravely on both cheeks. She avoided Mark's eyes.

'Walked? From where?'

'The Hilton. The RTT's just been hit.'

Ahmad stared at her and shook his head. 'It's crazy out there. I got back about an hour ago. Giovanna's been going out of her mind. Come on, let's go up. You *walked*? Lexi, you're mad, you know that?' He led them upstairs, still shaking his head. 'Gio,' he called out as he opened the door. 'Gio? It's Lexi.'

In a daze, Mark followed Lexi down a long corridor. At the end was an enormous, high-ceilinged room overlooking the street. His jaw dropped as they entered. It was like an eighteenth-century Parisian apartment, complete with ornate plasterwork and a crazily beautiful geometric-tiled floor that seemed to stretch on for ever. The walls were covered in a rich array of hand-painted wallpaper, some reaching all the way to the gilt-edged ceiling. The furniture was an eclectic mixture of antiques and modern designer pieces. Giant artworks and sculptures adorned the textured walls. It was theatrical in the extreme, adding to his sense of unreality.

A woman turned as soon as they entered and he saw she was carrying a baby. 'Lexi! Oh my God! Are you all right? How did you get here?' She hurried over. She was tall and slim, with long, silvery hair that was at odds with her beautiful, youthful face.

Lexi hugged her tightly. 'We came over from the Hilton. Have you got internet, by the way? Is it working? Can I upload a video?'

Ahmad nodded quickly. 'It's patchy, but we can try, yes.'

'I've got to send something out tonight.'

'No problem.' He turned to Mark. 'So, who're you? Her cameraman?'

Mark looked quickly at Lexi. She gave him a quick, almost imperceptible nod. 'Er, yeah. I'm Mark.'

'Well, nice to meet you, Mark,' Ahmad said. 'You picked the right day to arrive.'

'Can we try sending my file out?' Lexi asked impatiently.

'Sure. Come on. Gio, get Mark a drink, will you? He looks as though he could use one.'

Gio nodded, smiling, as Ahmad and Lexi disappeared down the corridor. She moved past Mark to the kitchen counter, gently patting the baby. 'What'll you have?'

'Anything. Whatever's going.'

'I don't know about you, but I could use a glass of wine. And it'll help put him to sleep.' She looked down at the baby and smiled. Mark watched her, the sense of surreal estrangement growing even more strongly in him, as she opened the refrigerator, took out a bottle, already uncorked, and poured wine into the elegant crystal glasses standing on the marble kitchen counter as if waiting for guests to casually drop by.

29

Ahmad was right about one thing: the internet connection *was* slow. She sat next to him, her eyes switching between the modem and her laptop screen, watching the flickering lights trip happily up and down, silently willing the connection on. Without turning her head, she felt his attention on her.

'He's not your cameraman, is he?' he asked quietly after a moment.

She hesitated, then shook her head. 'No.'

'So who is he?'

She hesitated again. 'He's ... he's just some guy I met,' she said finally.

There was a moment's silence. She turned her head. Ahmad's dark, questioning eyes came to rest on hers. 'That's not like you,' he murmured. 'You always keep things … separate. Who is he? What does he do?'

'I do. I mean, I … it's just … we just bumped into each other at the Hilton, completely by accident. I met him last year. On … on holiday. I don't know what he does, to be honest.' She was aware of the flimsiness of her answer. A deeper question was being asked.

'And you brought him here?'

She nodded slowly. 'Yeah. Look, don't worry, he's safe. I … I can't explain why, but I trust him.'

Ahmad looked doubtful. For a moment they stared at each other, neither saying anything. Then he nodded thoughtfully. 'Go easy on him, eh, Lexi? He seems like a nice guy.'

She flushed, but said nothing. Ahmad knew her only too well. She'd met him and Giovanna in Gaza a few years earlier. They'd both worked for UNHCR in Gaza City and had left to get married, returning to Cairo, where Ahmad had grown up. Now Ahmad was one of Egypt's most popular political bloggers and Giovanna had a part-time job with the European Commission. Ahmad was right. Bringing Mark to them was a risk. But somehow, despite the fact that she knew next to nothing about him, deep down she knew that he posed no threat whatsoever. At least not to their cause. No, Mark whatever-his-name-was embodied a different kind of danger. She wasn't even sure she could put it into words.

He closed the bedroom door quietly behind him, making sure it was shut before turning to her. The room was bathed in the dim light from the bedside table. For a few moments they simply looked at one another, not saying anything. She was aware again of the way his skin retained the sun, glowed from within. She looked at the rosy brown patch of skin vibrating between his collarbones as he spoke, the bronzed breastplate where a few tufts of thick dark brown hair disappeared beneath the V-neck of his jumper. Skin that in another time and place she'd seen and touched.

He was the first to speak. 'You're Lexi Sturgis. I should have recognised you, even though we've never met. You work for Donal, don't you?'

It was her turn to look surprised. ' How do you know Donal?'

'I worked for him, ages ago. When he was at ITN. I'm a photojournalist. Or at least I used to be.'

'What's your last name?' she asked, her brows knitting together in a frown.

'Githerton.'

She put up a hand to her mouth. They stared at each other. Slowly, she began to laugh. 'Mark Githerton? You're Mark Githerton? *I* should've recognised *you!* Why didn't you tell me who you were?'

'When? The next morning? If I remember rightly, you just vanished without a trace.' There was an unexpected tightness to his voice that made Lexi flush.

'I ... I had to go.'

'Yeah, sure you did.'

'It's ... complicated.'

'Sure it is.'

'Look, I don't need to explain myself to *you*,' she said quickly. 'I didn't think I'd ever see you again. I just didn't want ... complications, you know?'

'And saying goodbye automatically leads to complications?'

She looked at him warily. 'I didn't know who you were,' she began hesitantly.

'Would it have made a difference?'

She sighed. She wasn't handling the conversation well. She shook her head. 'I'm ... I'm sorry. I just ... I just thought it was better that way.'

'It's never better that way.' Seeing the expression on his face brought a flush of shame to the surface of her own. He was hurt. She hadn't meant to hurt him. She hadn't thought she could.

'I'm ... sorry,' she said again, meaning it. 'I ... didn't think.'

'I *liked* you,' he began, then stopped. He ploughed a hand through the thick curtain of his hair, and turned away, embarrassed. Then he turned back to her, smiling almost sheepishly. 'I ... I didn't expect to. It's usually the other way round. I'm usually the one who runs.'

Relief began to flood through her. He was making it easy for her, for both of them. 'So we're a pair, then, it seems.'

He nodded, still smiling. The wide double bed behind her was an unspoken invitation. She saw his eyes move away from her to the expanse of sheets and pillows. 'So what now, Miss Sturgis?'

She shrugged. They looked at each other warily. Neither spoke. He began to unbutton his shirt. She watched him undress in the half-light, the sense of unreality deepening as he shed his clothing, revealing again that strong body with its thick, glossy pelt of dark brown hair spreading across the chest, tapering down the lean, muscled torso, disappearing beneath the waistband of his shorts. She was surprised at how much of it she remembered, how much of their brief encounter she'd subconsciously taken away. He was watching her too, those deep, indigo-coloured eyes fixed steadily on hers with a knowingness that somehow saw beneath the surface of her diffidence.

She knew his work; who didn't? It was bold, gutsy, brave beyond measure, yet warm and humane, too. She'd seen his images – again, who hadn't – read his descriptions of some of the most cruel and violent spots on earth and been amazed time and again by the humanity he managed to extract from people caught up in the most out-of-the-ordinary events. The name Githerton was as familiar as some of the best-known photographers: Cartier-Bresson, McCullin, Natchwey, Hetherington. She knew vaguely that it had been over a year since his last assignment, and that he'd dropped out of circulation, temporarily or otherwise. She'd heard the rumours – a breakdown, burnout; stock-in-trade risks of the profession they'd chosen or that somehow had chosen them. In some ways it was curious that they'd never met, but he was one of those who, like her, avoided the limelight when he wasn't working. Glitzy awards ceremonies and the crowded, popular hangouts weren't his scene, just as they weren't hers.

Yet knowing who he was and where he'd been, understanding in a way that few others could what he'd witnessed and done, what she saw in him now was a complete surprise. She wasn't prepared for his easiness. It was the last thing she'd have expected. He threw out his charm like a net, sweeping her up in it, so that she was unable to resist it or him. There was a lightness in him that was all the more powerful for being unforeseen, yet part of it was that he expected her to see through it, to sense that his ease and playfulness hid another, deeper seam that might lead elsewhere. The compelling mixture of intensity and insouciance left her unprepared, and she could feel her guard begin to disintegrate, come tumbling down.

He sat beside her. She was perched on the edge of the bed, fully dressed, her mind a confusing, conflicting jumble of emotions. 'Come here,' he murmured, putting out a hand and pulling her against him. She pushed her face into his neck, breathing deeply. She was astonished again by how familiar he seemed. His scent flooded her nostrils and her mind. Behind them, through the shut and curtained window, the sky was lit up periodically by dull glowing explosions and the fluorescent green streaks of tracer fire.

It was different this time. He was different; *she* was different. That last time had been about the simple need to be as physically close to someone as possible, nothing more. She'd been the one in control; of him, of her own body, her own pleasure. Remembering it, she felt a hot flush of shame at the way she'd pushed aside all other thoughts: what he might feel or think; what he might – God forbid – *expect*. It had all been about *her*, no one else, least of all the man whose body she'd used so selfishly. It was the way she was used to doing things. It sometimes came to her that she knew no other.

Sitting next to her, he sensed her hesitation and was careful with her. The thick tartan blanket that Giovanna had placed at the end of the bed had wound up covering her knees, like the pelt of a warm animal settled over her. His hand slipped beneath it, finding hers, lacing their fingers together. There was no need to make any response. Time slowed and stopped. The only sensation she could distinguish was the clasp of his hand against hers. The thick, fleshy pads of muscle at the base of their thumbs were pressed tightly together, as one. She closed her eyes and gave herself up to his direction. He released her hand gently, but his own didn't emerge from beneath the rug. Instead he began to trace a slow, hesitant path along her jeans-clad thigh, stopping at the thick ridge of the zip – a question? His fingers remained there, pressing oh-so-lightly against the seam of her jeans, the lightest of touches a jolt that ran through her as if he'd entered her already. She unzipped herself quickly, pushing them down to her knees, and was about to wriggle out of them altogether when he stopped her, shaking his head, his mouth busy against the skin of her neck.

'Leave them on,' he murmured indistinctly.

'But ...'

'Just leave them on.' His hand continued its leisurely exploration of her flesh, sliding into the crevice between leg and body, stopping at the thin elastic edge of her underwear and moving slowly into the soft hair there, probing, stroking, touching the slick wetness that was a fluency and language all of its own. She'd been found; he'd found her. She had no clear idea of where he was, or where his hand was. They weren't kissing, but all she could think about was his mouth on hers, his tongue against hers, feeding on him ... He brought her skilfully to the edge of the sweetest, sharpest pleasure and then stopped to watch her crash.

When she was present again, and she dared to open her eyes, she saw in his face such naked honesty and longing that she squeezed her eyes tightly shut again and held her breath.

30

Inès looked at Deena fearfully. She felt as though she'd been hit in the solar plexus, stabbed by Deena's announcement. 'Right now? Right this very minute?' she asked, her voice shaking, betraying her fear.

Deena nodded. She picked up a jumper, folding it neatly, and placed it in the suitcase lying on the bed. 'They'll be here soon.'

'But what will I tell them?'

Deena paused. 'They'll understand,' she said after a moment.

'No they won't,' Inès said quickly, miserably. 'They'll just blame me.'

'Don't be silly. Why should they blame you? It's got nothing to do with you.'

'But they'll ask me why I didn't stop you. Or tell them, at least.'

'Then say you didn't know.'

'Oh, Deena, I *can't*. What if ... what if something happens to you? Don't go, Deena. *Please* don't go.'

'Inès, stop it.' Deena snapped her case shut. 'I'll be with MSF, I won't be on my own. I'll be with hundreds of other doctors. You *know* that.'

'I know. But ... I'm scared, Deena.'

'Well I'm not. I'm a doctor, Inès, and doctors are needed. It's that simple. I can't just sit here and watch what's happening back home on the news. I'm sorry.'

'But it's not our home. Not really. And I want to come with you.' Inès felt the sharp prick of tears behind her eyes.

Deena shook her head. 'No, we've been through this a hundred times. You stay here. Look after Mummy and Abu, that's your job. It'll be over soon, everyone knows that. They can't keep us down for ever.'

Inès said nothing. Part of her wanted to scream at Deena: *us?* Who's *us?* There was a lump the size of an orange in her throat and she thought for a moment she might actually be sick. Deena was leaving for Cairo. She and two other colleagues from St Thomas's had signed up with Médecins Sans Frontières to join the team of doctors and paramedics already stationed out there. It was impossible for her *not* to go. Even if she hadn't been so politically involved, she couldn't sit at home night after night watching her friends and colleagues risk their lives. Inès could only stare at her in awe. She was seeing a side of her sister that she'd never even suspected existed. She talked of the organisation, activists, bloggers, demonstrations, petitions, podcasts ... it was another world to Inès and another side to Deena. It was bitterly unfair. Just at the point where her admiration for Deena had grown tenfold, she was about to lose her. And in an all-too-real sense.

Deena's phone rang suddenly. She picked it up and answered in Arabic. 'I'll be right down,' she said finally. She picked her suitcase up off the bed and turned to face her sister. For a moment, neither said anything. Deena's expression was impossible to read. Inès studied her, searching for some sign, some assurance that everything would be all right. She found none.

'Look after yourself, *habibi*,' Deena whispered, hugging her fiercely. 'And look after *them*. Promise me, whatever happens, you'll look after them. I wish I could tell them myself, but I can't. Just be gentle with them.' She broke off abruptly.

Inès's head was swimming with questions, just as her eyes were swimming with tears. Their parents were out visiting friends. When they returned, Deena would be gone. It was as simple as that. Inès would have to break the news of where, and why. She nodded, but she couldn't speak. She watched mutely as her sister lugged her suitcase to the door. Deena turned briefly, gave Inès a quick thumbs-up and closed the door firmly behind her.

Inès's legs finally gave way and she sat down on the edge of the bed. Her hands were shaking. She hated goodbyes, always had. When Deena had gone to boarding school in England, Inès had hidden under the bed when the time came to take her to the airport. She couldn't bring herself to say goodbye then, just as she couldn't bring herself to say it now. She heard the car door slam outside and the engine start up. She ought to get up and go to the window for one last glimpse. She couldn't. She waited until the engine had died away before she moved across the room and tentatively held aside the curtain. The street below was quiet; nothing moved, not even the leaves on the trees in the small private gardens opposite. She hung back, one hand clutching the pale blue silk curtain, listening to her sister's voice again, as if there was a message contained within it that was only for her. There was none. The clock on the mantelpiece ticked down the seconds slowly. From the street came the *phut-phut* of a motorcycle turning the corner, growing fainter with each passing tick.

31

'First of all, she's fine.' Donal lifted his hands as if to ward off an invisible blow. 'I heard from her this morning. She's fine. She's with someone.' He had a half-smile on his face that drew a frown of puzzlement from Jane.

'Who?'

'You'll never guess.'

'Who?'

'Mark Githerton.'

'Mark *Githerton*? What's *he* doing there? I thought he'd quit,' Jane said in surprise.

'So did I. So did we all.' Donal chuckled quietly. 'Trust Lexi.'

'What d'you mean? She's got him to work again?'

Donal shrugged. 'Dunno. She just said they'd bumped into each other and that he was hanging around for a bit. Ian's coming in overland. He couldn't get to Cairo so he flew into Tripoli instead. He bummed a lift with an Italian film crew on their way to Alexandria. He should be there by tomorrow evening. In the meantime, believe it or not, Mark Githerton's using her camera.'

'Fuck. That's … that's amazing. Can we afford him?'

Donal grinned. 'That's my job. I'll make sure we can. Now, where are we on programming for next year?'

Jane felt a flush of embarrassment flood her face. 'I … well, the thing is, I've been sort of distracted … by … by Lexi and everything that's been happening out there and—'

'Spare me.' Donal's hands went up again. 'We're running out of time, Jane. I need something to go to our next board meeting with and I'm counting on you. New ideas, new directions, new avenues. The meeting's in April. That's barely a month away, and you've given me squat. You've got a week to come up with something. And something good. The competition's knocking at our heels and you know it as well as I do. If Draycott doesn't like what he hears, he'll pull the plug. That's how these guys work.' Donal shook his head in annoyance. 'I don't know why I'm even bothering to tell you this. You *know* the kind of pressure I'm under. Pull your finger out, Jane. Come on.'

Scott Draycott was their American investor, the money behind NNI. If Donal was worried about what Draycott might think, they all ought to be. 'I … I'm sorry,' she stammered.

'Don't be sorry. Just come up with something. Something good.'

Donal bent his head back to his laptop. Jane opened her mouth to say something but quickly thought better of it. She hurried back to her own office, uncomfortably aware of Susie's eyes on her as she scuttled away. She closed the door, sat down at her desk and switched on her computer. Nothing happened. She pressed the button impatiently. Still nothing. The screen stared blankly, blackly back at her.

'Oh, for fuck's *sake*,' she hissed under her breath, looking around to see if the cleaner had perhaps unplugged it by mistake. No, the snaking cables that ran underneath her desk were all firmly connected. She tried it again. *Still* nothing. She picked up her phone. 'Susie? My computer's not working. What? Yes, of course it's plugged in. No, I can't. Just get someone to look at it, will you? And hurry up. I've got a ton of work to do today. I can't afford to be without it.' She put down the phone and took a deep breath. Stay calm. Get a cup of coffee. Maybe even a Kit Kat. She stood up and grabbed her coat.

'Oh, hi.' The young man sitting in her chair looked up as she came back in. He stood up and immediately knocked over the pot in which she kept her pens, scattering them across her keyboard and desk. 'Shit, sorry.' He quickly tried to scoop everything back, making matters worse.

'Just leave it,' Jane snapped irritably. 'Who're you?'

'I'm one of the IT guys. Your receptionist called. I was just taking a look.' He gestured towards her still-blank screen.

'So what's wrong with it?' Jane asked abruptly. Her day hadn't started well, and it was just getting worse.

He shrugged. 'Hard to tell straight off, but I'd say the motherboard's gone.'

Jane looked at him, her mind as blank as her computer screen. 'Motherboard?'

'Yeah. I'll need to take it in. It shouldn't take too long to fix.'

'So what'm I supposed to do in the meantime?'

He gestured towards the enormous rucksack leaning against her desk. 'I, er, brought you a laptop, just in case.'

'How long's it going to take?'

'Hard to say.'

'Yeah, thought you might say that.' She was being churlish, she knew, but she couldn't help herself. He looked even more uncomfortable.

'Look, I'll ... I'll just get this out of your way,' he began hurriedly, sensing that she was in no mood to be placated. 'I'll look at it as soon as I get back to the office. If it's going to take more than a day to repair, I'll make sure you get a replacement first thing tomorrow morning. I promise. I know how irritating it must be to be without a computer. I'll sort you out, don't worry.'

Jane shot him a quick glance. Was he being facetious? He was young: late twenties? Trendy boy-band haircut; hipster jeans; rumpled blue shirt opening on to a T-shirt with the name of some band or other scrawled across it; sneakers ... the sort of bloke who hung around certain bars in Soho, a PR bird attached to his arm. 'All right, fine. Leave me the laptop. And for God's sake, show me how to get my emails and all that shit. I don't have time to start reinventing the wheel.'

'You won't have to, I promise. Here ... gimme two minutes, I'll set you up. Go out and get a coffee. Have a break. I'll be done by the time you're back.'

'I've already had a coffee.'

'Then have another one. Have a Kit Kat.' He grinned at her suddenly.

Jane shot him another glance. Did she look like the type to scarf down Kit Kats? Now he really *was* being facetious. But no, he'd bent his head to the laptop and was busy doing just as he'd said – sorting her out. 'I'll ... I'll just make a couple of calls,' she said, finally, and got up quickly to leave.

Susie glanced up as she passed. 'Everything all right? I told them it was *super* urgent. They sent someone out straight away. He's pretty tasty, too.'

Jane looked at her blankly. 'Who?'

'The IT bloke. He's gorgeous.'

Jane stared at her. 'I hadn't noticed,' she said frostily. 'I'll be in the boardroom if anyone calls' She stomped off. She had more important things to worry about than the merits of some idiot IT hack who'd broken all the points of her carefully sharpened pencils.

32

The coin-clear profile of a man in pale blue scrubs turned towards them as they entered. His surgical mask was pulled halfway down his face, as though he'd forgotten to push it back up. His dark, nearly black eyes were full of expression. Deena was struck by how arresting eyes could be when they were the only feature showing. She followed the two medical officers into the makeshift operating theatre and stopped, letting her suitcase hit the floor. The scene in front of her was bedlam.

The two paramedics who'd met her at the main hospital had brought her to a house somewhere in the suburbs of Cairo; she'd didn't know exactly where. There were dozens of these makeshift clinics scattered around the city, one of them explained. MSF sent their doctors wherever help was needed; this abandoned house, whose occupants had fled when fighting first began, had been turned into the neighbourhood clinic, where demonstrators, protesters and unlucky passers-by were being brought in by the dozen.

'New doctor?' His voice rose momentarily above the screams of the child whose arm he was swabbing.

Deena swallowed and nodded. 'Yes. Yes, that's me. I ... I just arrived.'

He pointed to a bed behind him, where a man lay swathed in bandages. Blood was seeping through a wound in his thigh. 'Sit on him. I'll get to him in a second.'

Deena blinked. 'Sit on him?'

'Sit on his thigh. Just below the wound.'

'Won't ... won't it hurt?'

The surgeon paused and looked up briefly. 'What's your name?'

'Deena. Er, Dr Kenan.'

There was the briefest pause. 'Dr Kenan. There are five litres of blood in the human body. *Five* litres. And it can be gone in three to four minutes. That man has been lying there for ten. Sit on him. It'll help slow the rate of loss. I assume that's what you're here to do ... help?'

Deena swallowed. 'Yes, yes of course.'

The man was unconscious. There was an ugly gash across his face, and one blackened and bruised eye was closed completely. She looked down at his leg. Even through his trousers and the swathes of blood-soaked bandages, she could see where he'd been shot; there was an ominous indentation where his flesh should have been. She swallowed again and pressed down hard, just above his knee. His body responded from the depths of consciousness, twitching under her hands, though whether in pain or simply from the recognition of another's touch, she couldn't say. She looked into his face; beneath the days-old stubble and the dried blood, there was a hint of blue around his mouth that seemed to be deepening. It was a bad sign. She bit her lip and pressed down harder. She couldn't bring herself to sit on him, no matter what the surgeon said.

A minute or two passed. All around her people came and went; children were brought in crying, some screaming, more in distress at what they'd seen than from any injuries they'd sustained. A pregnant woman was helped to a bed in the far corner. From her groans, it was clear that she was in the early stages of labour. The living room had been turned into the most basic and rudimentary of clinics – no humming equipment, no beeping monitors, none of the all-too-familiar sounds of A&E at St Thomas's. The doctors worked quickly and with intense concentration in the midst of the chaos to patch people up and send them on, either to one of the major hospitals in the city centre ... or to the morgue.

'He's gone.' The surgeon who'd spoken to her was suddenly at her side.

Deena glanced up, uncomprehending. She looked back down at the man whose leg she was still pressing. 'Gone?'

He nodded. He pulled his surgical mask free. 'Yeah. Come with me.'

Deena let go of the man and scrambled upright. One of the paramedics moved forward with a thin green cloth. She turned and followed the tall figure of the surgeon out of the room. Her heart was pounding wildly. She'd seen more than her fair share of death as a medical student. This was different. This was something else.

'Dr Kenan, did you say?' There was the short scrape of a match being lit, followed by the acrid scent of cigarette smoke.

Deena nodded and looked at the man standing opposite her. He was extraordinarily handsome; dark eyes under thick, glossy brows; full, delicately scrolled mouth with the classic line of symmetry extending from the upper lip to the cleft in his square, determined-looking chin. She had to look away. There was something else, a faint echo of a face she already knew or had seen before, perhaps? Who was he?

'I'm Dr Stuart,' he said, answering her unspoken question. He didn't offer a first name. He was English. He held out his cigarettes; she declined. 'You don't smoke?' She shook her head. 'You'll start soon enough. St Thomas's, you said?'

She nodded. 'Yes. Final year.'

'But you're Egyptian?'

She nodded again. 'Yes, although I was actually brought up in England. We left Egypt when I was a kid.'

'You speak Arabic?'

'Yes, of course.'

'Good.' He drew hungrily on his cigarette. 'Well, you've seen the way we work . . . the conditions and so on. I don't know how long you'll be with us. Dr Kerkorian's not very forthcoming with the rotation paperwork.' Dr Kerkorian was the MSF director in Cairo. He'd looked at Deena when she'd walked into their downtown offices and instructed the paramedics to 'take her out to the field'. She had no idea why. 'It's pretty basic,' continued Dr Stuart. 'The most important thing is not to rely on anything that requires electricity. The supply's patchy at the best of times. You can see for yourself. We don't do anything here that needs more than the most basic set of skills. But you'd be surprised. We've saved a lot more lives than we've lost. I asked for someone who's not afraid to work in these conditions. I hope that's what I've got.' He looked at her as he took the last draw on his cigarette. Deena swallowed nervously.

'I . . . I think so.'

'You *think* so, Dr Kenan? That's no good to me, I'm afraid. I need someone who *knows*, otherwise you're better off going back to St Thomas's. This is Egypt. We're at war. It isn't a place for dilettantes.'

Deena's back stiffened. 'I'm no dilettante,' she said quietly. 'I've already done an A&E rotation. I *asked* to be sent out here. I know what I'm doing.'

He said nothing for a moment as he ground out his cigarette underfoot. Then he lifted his head and smiled. Again Deena had the distinctly odd sensation of having seen him somewhere before. There was something about the way his face was transformed by his smile, the flash of even white teeth and the folding of those obsidian eyes into the creases of his skin that reminded her of someone ... but who? She couldn't place him or his likeness. 'Good. You've got spirit. You'll need it.' He gestured back towards the door. 'Shall we?'

She followed him back in without a word. What had she let herself in for? For a fraction of a second she thought of Inès and her face as she'd closed the door on her. It was barely a day since she'd left London, and yet already it felt as though she'd stepped into another lifetime, another world. London seemed impossibly far away. And Adnan. He seemed farthest of all. She tried to summon up his face, but couldn't. It was hard to think of him in the midst of the screaming and crying and the cacophony of pain. But it was because of him that she was here. It was he who'd started it all. He was the one who'd opened her eyes, and now it was impossible for her to close them again.

33

Deena. Dr Deena Kenan. As soon as he heard her name, he stood stock still, as if he'd suddenly discovered where he was. Then he quickly busied himself with the child he'd been treating and the moment passed unnoticed, or so he hoped. He'd tried to make it seem as if he didn't know who she was. 'But you're Egyptian?' he'd asked, wincing inwardly as though he'd been hit. Of course she was bloody Egyptian! She was as Egyptian as he was, though no one would ever know it. In those days she'd been Dafiyah. Dafiyah and Inas Kenan. Dr Ibrahim Kenan's daughters. Their neighbours, two houses down. He was eleven when the Kenans abruptly left Cairo. Dafiyah was five; Inas, her little sister, whom he remembered only as a chubby thing who cried incessantly, must have been two or three. Aiden, his older brother, was glad to see them go. Dafiyah was *a fucking nuisance* (yes, even then he'd learned to swear) and her sister was worse. But that was just Aiden all over. Cruel, charismatic, even at eleven, coldly passionate. Dafiyah was besotted. She'd followed Aiden around like a shadow, clinging possessively to his arm whenever he allowed it, waiting patiently, desperately, for his attention to fall on her and bathe her in its warmth. It enraged Níall. Couldn't she see that her too-obvious happiness in his attentions was the very thing that would bring her down?

It baffled him at first. For Dafiyah, no one else existed, certainly not Níall. She would come up the short path escorted by the nanny, and as soon as his mother opened the front door, she was lost. He was too young then to fathom it properly, at least not in the way he understood it now, but even then he saw that she had fallen under Aiden's spell, and that it would destroy her in the end. As young as she was, there was still a feminine edge to her guile, and her manner was naturally, girlishly flirtatious, even though she was far too young to comprehend her own behaviour.

Once or twice, on finding Aiden absent, or, worse, present-but-absent, ignoring her, she would turn to Níall. *Doesn't Aiden like me any more?* In those moments, Aiden's rejection produced such an open, naked longing in her face that it was enough to make his own eyes smart with tears. He liked her, more than he would ever dare to admit to anyone, and he wondered sometimes if those moments when she turned to him were actually a strange and cruel form of mockery. But when he overheard his mother talking to Madame Abou-Chedid, their neighbour on the other side, the phrase she used – *she's keen on him* – shocked him out of his assumption, casting him into a more adult world of emotions than the one he occupied. He realised then how foolish he had been. It wasn't mockery. If anything, she had put herself in his power, making her even more vulnerable, though in trusting him so openly, she was also making sure he would never abuse the trust.

She was keen on his brother. At first he didn't understand what his mother meant. The old-fashioned phrase in Arabic had caught him out. When it was explained to him, the dread that took hold of him came from his own experience of his brother and the fear that he would inflict the same torment on someone else. But if the opposite happened, if

Aiden graced her appearance at his door with a smile, then she would be happily full of herself, sure of her power over him. She just couldn't see it, thought Níall miserably. She just didn't understand that her certainty would in the long run be the thing that would undo her.

And now here she was, twenty years later, the certainty that he'd been so afraid of back then clearly transformed over space and time and learning into a calm assuredness in her own capabilities as a doctor that astounded him. Just like her father, or so he'd always been told.

After the first few days, they began to work together as a team, separate from the other doctors. There was no discussion, no decision taken – they simply drifted together out of an unspoken understanding of their respective skills and got on with the job. They were always within touch. Sometimes he looked at her across the table where they worked and saw the faint lift of flesh at the corners of her eyes that was the beginning of the smile he'd come to know well. She moved quietly among the patients, her hands moving over them as over pieces of sculpture, assessing whilst soothing, receiving them carefully through all her senses, judging, testing, deciding. Her hair was long and occasionally slipped the confines of whatever ponytail or braid she'd fashioned on waking. He had to physic-ally stop himself from reaching out and tucking a loose lock or strand back behind her ear, or simply running his fingers through it, thick and lustrous like velvet or silk. Once, when they'd been working late into the night, stitching up a demonstrator who'd been viciously beaten by the security services, he closed his eyes just for the pleasure of hearing her moving near him. He almost put out a hand where he thought she was passing, but stopped himself just in time.

34

Deena was sitting on one of the balconies overlooking the street, having the rare luxury of a coffee break with Valérie Pinchot, a French anaes-thesiologist who'd given up her holiday time to volunteer with MSF. They were discussing the aloof Dr Stuart. 'I think his first name's Neil,' said Valérie. 'I described him, and my friend thought he was the guy he'd worked with in Afghanistan.'

Deena stared at her. 'That's funny, we used to know someone called Níall Stewart. I was always tagging along after his brother, or so everyone tells me. I can't really remember them. They were our neighbours when we lived in Zamalek. I haven't seen them for years. We never heard from them again after we left. But that's not him. That Níall had reddish hair, not dark brown. I think their father was Scottish or Welsh, something like that. Gosh, I haven't thought about them in *years*. Dr Stuart does remind me of someone, but I can't think who.'

'Good-looking, though, underneath it all,' Valérie said, smiling faintly.

Deena shrugged. 'There's a lot to get through before you get to that,' she murmured, finishing her coffee. 'He's so ... *formal*. So bloody remote. You'd think in these circumstances he'd let his guard down a little. Have coffee with us every once in a while, join in a conversation, you know?'

'That's exactly what my friend said. I bet it's him. Those army doctors. That's just what they're like. They see this sort of shit all the time. Me, I couldn't. I need to know there's a world out there where this doesn't happen. At least not every day.'

'Well, army or not, he's too cold for my liking,' Deena said firmly. 'Don't get me wrong, he's great to work with. I've learned more from him in a week than I've done all year, but I wouldn't want to spend an evening in a bar with him. I'd run out of things to say, wouldn't you?'

Valérie giggled softly. 'I doubt you'll ever get the chance. No bars around here.'

There was a sudden movement behind them. 'Dr Kenan?' They looked up. Dr Stuart was standing in the open doorway. Deena froze. The heat rushed into her face. How long had he been there? 'If you're quite finished,' he went on coolly, 'we've got a couple of casualties coming in.'

'I'll be right there,' she mumbled, avoiding Valérie's startled, embarrassed glance. She collected her cup and saucer from the balcony ledge and went back inside. Damn him. That was the last thing she needed, to feel any more awkward in his presence than she already did.

PART SIX

March 2011

35

Abidjan, Côte d'Ivoire, West Africa

The air was thick and soft, a drowsy, tropical night that was both torrid and languid in the same breath. That breath came to her over the tree-tops, lightly fanning her face and bare arms, momentary relief from the crushing humidity. The chorus of insects – creaking cicadas and the incessant thrum of crickets – and the low, mournful bass of frogs rose and fell all around her. Lexi drew hungrily on her cigarette. The smell of beeswax and insecticide tickled the inside of her nostrils along with the pungent whiff of smoke.

She'd touched down in Abidjan a few hours earlier after a six-hour flight from London and a three-hour stopover in Lagos. Things in Egypt had calmed down for the time being. As soon as it was safe, Mark had retrieved his borrowed Cessna, flown back to Amman and handed it over. His contact wasn't pleased. There were still jobs to be done, people to rescue, supplies to drop off. Mark shrugged. Not his problem. He completed the paperwork and caught the next commercial flight back to Cairo, to Lexi. For the next three weeks, they'd scoured Cairo for the stories that everyone else would have forgotten or overlooked. Donal reluctantly agreed, trusting there was a bloody good reason for her to prolong the assignment. They moved through the city together, aware of the fragile state of suspended reality into which they'd fallen, knowing full well that it would soon come to an end. At night, crawling into the low, wide bed that Ahmad and Gio had so generously provided, the conversations they'd had during the day spilled naturally into another kind of conversation, corporeal, his body achieving a kind of fluency that put into words what he couldn't bring himself to say.

As she came to know and understand him better, she began to see that there was something lying just beneath the surface of his skin – some resentment, some private torment – that welled like oil under the earth, flammable to the touch. For the most part he kept it hidden, masked by his air of easy, sunny affability. But it was there. At times he withdrew

135

from her and everyone around him, moving off into a space and mood all of his own, remote from everything. She began to recognise the signs that led to it and knew instinctively to steer clear. Another lover might have pressed him, mistaking the distance he sought from himself for a longing to be free of her. Not Lexi. She moved out of his orbit, and when he was ready, he returned.

There was another side to it too. Out of those moods of withdrawal he would make love to her with the single-minded clarity he'd momentarily lost in the world outside their small room. She'd never experienced anything like it. A strange balance emerged between the shared experience of their work and the intense intimacy it seemed to provoke. All the time she moved through the city, talking to people, making notes, writing, she was aware of her own body orchestrated by him, singing to a different, deeper tune. For those three weeks, they operated as one. Her happiness might have been to do with something she wasn't conscious of: that long-sought-after balance between her working life and living with a man.

But it couldn't last. Three weeks later, just as they'd expected, Donal pulled the plug. 'I'm moving you out,' he said, his voice coming to her in fits and starts down the crackling international line.

It was just after midnight, and she'd answered her phone on the first ring. She gathered up the bed sheet, bunching it under her arms, and moved into the bathroom, leaving Mark lying naked on the bed, his head buried beneath the pillow as if blocking out the world, which was how he liked to sleep.

'When? Now?' she asked, hoping the lurch she felt in the pit of her stomach hadn't made it into her voice.

'Don't panic.' It was pointless trying to hide anything from Donal. 'He can go with you. *If* he wants. We'll pay.'

'Where?'

'Back to Abidjan. Something's happening down there and I need someone who's been before. Tundé's covering Congo and his French is rubbish. I'd send Caro but she'd be hopeless out there. So it's you, darling. Get yourself back to London for a couple of days and Susie'll organise tickets and cash. Let me know if Githerton'll take the gig. Otherwise I'll send Ian out to join you.'

Lexi swallowed. The previous day, they'd been in Giza, filming and interviewing the sister of a young engineer who'd been badly beaten by the security services. The young woman had told Lexi how her brother had been arrested, beaten to within an inch of his life, then released and promptly arrested again. For six long days and nights the family had waited for news outside the local police station in the suburb of Abdeen, not far from Tahrir Square, but there was nothing. Finally, on the seventh day, they were told he had already been tried and sentenced by the military courts to twenty years' imprisonment, the first two in solitary confinement.

For two hours Lexi listened intently to her story, then she followed the young woman back to her house, where she interviewed her parents. She finished the piece by speaking directly to camera. 'For most Egyptians, the challenge isn't just about getting rid of a corrupt leader. Now the fight is about exposing the injustices of the system that are endemic to everyday life.'

She'd looked at the grieving family, the heightened emotion of the day still evident in their faces. 'That's enough,' she said quietly to Mark. 'Let's give them some space. Poor fucking bastard. Nineteen years old.'

They'd taken a break and gone to sit in a cafe opposite the entrance to the Pyramids. It was cold and dusty outside; the streets were still barricaded, and the situation was tense.

'You're bloody good at this,' he said suddenly as they ate, watching her file copy on her laptop, cursing quietly to herself as the patchy internet connection came and went.

She looked up, puzzled. 'What d'you mean?' Did he expect her to be rubbish at her job?

'The way you talk to people,' he said, sipping the scalding cardamom-scented coffee that the little cafes still somehow managed to produce. 'You're prickly as all hell in person, but when you talk to someone like Ghassem's father, that defensiveness just disappears. You've got such empathy with them. Christ, you make *me* want to confess my deepest secrets.' He stopped suddenly, as if aware of having given something away. 'If I had any, of course,' he added carefully.

She'd looked at him, surprised, but said nothing. It was another reminder that for all the closeness they'd found and shared, there was another side to him that remained firmly out of bounds. It was new territory for her, a whole uncharted landscape of emotion and depth. Some nights they were too shattered by what they'd seen to do anything other than hold each other through the long hours of darkness, locked within their own thoughts. It was hardly Lexi's first experience of war. Liberia, Lebanon, Gaza – she'd covered so much. But it was the first time she'd been in danger with someone she cared about, and whose safety meant something outside the narrow emotional confines of her profession.

Twice before she'd lost a cameraman, and in Beirut, a local colleague was gunned down in front of her, but those were the risks. They created an intense bond between people who worked together but who might not ordinarily know, or even like, one another. She knew everything about Ian, her cameraman, whom Donal had posted elsewhere, and yet she knew nothing. He had seen her at her best and her worst. He'd watched her vomit her guts out after seeing the corpse of a small child. He'd cradled her head in his hands when they'd come upon the mutilated remains of a platoon of teenage soldiers in a ditch just outside Pristina. He'd yanked her bodily out of danger, argued for her release with a loaded pistol at his head, yet he'd never met any of her friends or family, knew nothing of her life when they returned to London and went their separate ways. She knew he had a girlfriend, but that was about it. But it was normal. Knowing too much about each other – or worse, caring too much – would just make it harder.

The past few weeks with Mark had been different. For the first time ever, she moved around with a heightened awareness of the risks, not just because she was taking them, but because the consequences had suddenly intensified. When he surged ahead of her, her camera slung loosely around his neck, she watched with her heart in her mouth. She began to look out for him as well as herself, and at times the strain was more than she could bear. They hardly knew each other, and yet she felt a connection to him that she'd never experienced before, with anyone. Not even with Toby. Her throat suddenly thickened.

'You still there, Lexi?' Donal's voice was impatient.

'Yes, yes ... I'm still here.'

'Let me know what Githerton wants to do. I'll get you on tomorrow night's flight back to London. Oh, by the way, the interview with that family you tracked down came through. It's good. We'll air it on Saturday night.'

'Uh, thanks. I'll ... I'll let you know about ... Mark.'

There was a second's hesitation. 'You sure you're OK, Lexi?' Donal asked, his voice suddenly softening. 'With him, I mean. I don't need the details ... but you're OK, aren't you?'

The unexpected concern in his voice made her wince. 'I ... I'm fine,' she stammered. 'Thanks.'

'OK. Well let's talk in the morning. I'll have Susie wire you the flight details.'

'Who was that?' Mark mumbled.

'Donal.'

'Time to move on?' He was suddenly awake.

She slid into bed beside him, her heart thudding. Would this mean the end? 'Yes,' she said after a moment. 'He's sending me to Côte d'Ivoire. I was there last year ... something's up.'

'How long?'

She swallowed. 'I don't know. A week ... maybe two. Maybe even more. It depends.'

He was silent. She could feel his withdrawal. The terror that swept over her blocked her throat as she waited for the words that would confirm everything she knew about anyone she'd ever loved. *I'm off.*

36

The silence that spooled between them was like oil, thick and swirling and dark. Lexi had finally fallen asleep, weighed down by words she couldn't bring herself to say. No matter. He could hear them as clearly as if she'd spoken them aloud. He was being evasive and he hated himself for it. He knew what she wanted: him. *All* of him, not just the parts of him she'd seen in the past three weeks. And why shouldn't she? Even he, practised as he was at the art of walking away, understood that this was different. Deep down, in that place where he kept those few remnants of tenderness and love that had once, a very long time ago, been his means of making his way in the world, he'd recognised the capacity in her to make him whole again, to bring him back to himself. It was like being turned round and shown who he really was, not who he'd been forced to become. With her, as with no one else, he had the strong sensation

that he could at long last be himself. She saw *through* him, through the
sunniness and the sullenness to what he was scared and ashamed of,
without ever having had it explained to her. There was a darkness in her,
too, but instead of adding to his own shadows, it freed him somehow.
Sometimes when he was with her he felt very strongly the beating of his
own blood, dark and loud, and it scared him. And then she would look
up, sensing the fear in him, and the gentle question in her expression
would loosen it, making him light-headed and happy again, and younger
than he'd felt since his childhood.

He stretched out, lacing his hands behind his head, careful not to
wake her, and looked up at the intricate plasterwork of the ceiling. The
dim light that hung in the centre shone at a point just between his eyes,
but he was too tired to get up. The silence deepened and he closed his
eyes. It was after midnight. He knew this hour. He dreaded it. He got
up suddenly and switched the light off, and the room was plunged into
darkness. He lay down again, and the silence fell upon him once more.
The night stretched out in front of him. He closed his eyes, longing for
sleep.

*It's almost evening, and the sun is rapidly sinking behind the low line of
acacia trees that marks the edge of the farm. In a few minutes, darkness will
fall and the light will drop off the edge of the world. He's walking back to
the house through the dusty undergrowth, his two dogs, Pancho and Briscoe,
running alongside with their alert, strangely feminine faces turned up towards
him, tongues hanging out, lolling pinkly against their foamy jaws. It's dusk,
but the air still holds the day's heat. Every so often he reaches down with his
stick, swiping at the calf-height bushes that cover the ground as thickly as
any carpet. Everything in this landscape has thorns – long, surgical-looking
spikes, clean and sharp as bone; thick, fat, hairy thorns, bristling with needles;
curved, jagged, dull, shiny. The landscape around Lake Naivasha can go from
parched to lush in a fortnight, depending on the rains. Now, in early April,
it's dry as tinder. The rains are late. Everyone's worried. The cattle are thin
and the crops are failing. It'll take more than a good soaking of the earth for
things to come right again.*

*The grasses make a crunching, hissing sound as his foot falls to the earth,
flattening the crisp, dry stalks. Over to his right, the smoky blue outline of the
Aberdares melts into the hyacinth sky. The flat-top acacias turn to silhouettes
against the milky, inky infinity now stretching overhead. It comes so quickly.*

'Good girl.' He reaches down to fondle Briscoe, fingers catching on the little burrs that have attached themselves to her pelt. He crumbles one between his thumb and forefinger; he'll bathe the dogs in the morning. They'll enjoy that. Suddenly a shot rings out – out of the bush, out of the dark silence, somewhere across the mealie fields on his left. Pancho lets out a loud, puzzled bark. Mark stops. The panting of the dogs is in his ears, as is the dying echo of the shot. Someone is out hunting. He wonders who.

'Come on,' he murmurs, and breaks into a jog. The dogs bark their approval. The ground is hard underfoot; small twigs and branches break loudly as they all scramble towards the house.

Issa, their tall, lugubrious cook, is in the kitchen, moving efficiently between the stove and the cupboards, putting the finishing touches to dinner. He looks up as Mark bursts in, and frowns at the sight of the dogs.

'Jambo, Issa. Are they down yet?' He jerks his head to indicate upstairs and quickly shoos the dogs out. Issa doesn't like animals in the kitchen, or anywhere else in the house for that matter.

'Yes. But memsahib, she say she's not eating.'

Mark's heart sinks. That means it'll be just him and his father at the table. His mother will sit on the veranda as she does most nights, staring out into the liquid, slow-moving darkness, murmuring quietly to herself those words that no one else can hear, or fathom, or make sense of. 'I'll go and see her,' he says swiftly. It's the last thing he feels like – yet another silent evening alone at the table watching his father drink his body weight in pale liquid gold whilst the food goes cold.

He walks through the house, past the dark wooden chests and dusty oil paintings in the passageways that have been there since before he was born; past the living room with its faded chintz sofas and threadbare rugs and the animal skins that his mother put up when they first 'came out'. He hates that phrase: came out from where? He goes past the staircase that winds its way inelegantly up to the bedrooms and walks through the arched doorway. His mother is sitting in one of the wicker chairs at the far end of the veranda that runs almost all the way around the house. He hears the soft cooing of wood pigeons, a long way off, and faintly, drifting through the night air, the lively sound of chatter and laughter from the servants' quarters behind the empty pool and the stables, which are empty now too.

'Mum?' He can hear her singing quietly to herself. 'Mum?' He lays a hand on her shoulder, but gently, so as not to alarm her.

141

She turns her face up towards him and her expression is blank. There's nothing in her eyes that indicates she even sees him, let alone recognises him.

'Mum? It's me. Mark.'

'Mike?'

'Mark. It's Mark, Mum.'

'Oh. Oh, it's you. Why didn't you say so? Are you back from school? Did you have lunch?'

'Mum, it's dinner time. Won't you have something to eat?'

She looks at him, and for one heart-wrenching moment, understanding dawns in her expression. He watches the components of her face rearrange themselves once more into the face he once knew, long ago. The feeling is so strong it's as though he can reach out and grab it, grab hold of her and force her back to him ... but it has already slipped away again. Her face becomes crafty, knowing, evasive. 'Oh no, thank you, darling, I'm fine here. I've got my beer.'

So that's it. He turns away and walks back into the house. Issa is putting plates on the table. He looks up, and a flash of recognition passes between them, strong as an electrical current and just as fraught. Then the cook pads away silently. The smell of overcooked mutton comes to him, suddenly, and his nose wrinkles in distaste. The cuckoo clock on the mantelpiece chimes out twice. It's seven o'clock. Dinner time. Better call his father down, get it over with.

He's about twenty yards from the bedroom door when he hears a noise that makes him stop. It's the sound of someone's breathing, but stifled, coming up through layers of weight. The door is partially open and his skin seems to know what he's about to witness before his eyes do. It starts to crawl.

He stops just before the doorway. He knows he shouldn't go on. He shouldn't enter. He shouldn't see what he's about to see because once he's seen it, there's no going back. Cautiously, slowly, he pushes the door open a little. And he sees them. Rising and falling, thrusting and panting, heaving and shoving, a desperate, determined race against some demonic inner clock. His father's shockingly thin white shanks, moving in a frenzied blur against the smooth, dark brown legs of the girl who sweeps the yard in the morning. Tumaini. Issa's youngest. She's ten years old.

He woke up suddenly, drenched in sweat, and sat upright, breathing heavily. He looked down at his hands. His fists were clenched, his forefinger twitching nervously. For the thousandth time since that night, he felt again the cold, smooth curve of the trigger against his finger.

37

She stubbed out her cigarette and turned round. A group of foreign journalists were sitting around a table on the roof terrace, talking quietly. The
situation here was still tense. Three months earlier, a stand-off between
the defeated president and the new president-elect had resulted in chaos,
and there were fears the country would slide towards civil war. A hasty,
fragile peace had been brokered, but the mood was ugly. Reports had
begun to filter in of election fraud and worse. Massacres, intimidation,
even genocide. Everyone was anxious to avoid a repeat of Rwanda. When
word came of the discovery of mass graves, foreign and neighbouring
African countries were quick to act.

She leaned over the rusty balustrade, looking down on to the pool at
ground level and the deserted street beyond the palm trees that shel-
tered the hotel from the road. Someone was swimming. In the milky,
fluorescent-tinged water, all she could see were the trails of light at his
shoulders and the rush of bubbles as he flipped into each turn. The moon
cast a thin beam across the heaving surface. The city was tense, and there
was a sharpness to everything – every little sound, every unexpected
noise – that set her teeth on edge. The Ivoirians she'd met since she'd
arrived – taxi driver, hotel staff, waiters – all refused to meet her eyes.
These were not the same people she'd left a year or so before. Something
had changed.

Her mobile throbbed suddenly against her hip. She pulled it out. It
was Mark. Her stomach gave a violent lurch. 'Hello?' *Keep it light. Keep
it light.* Her new mantra, covering all communication between them.

'Safe and sound?' He too had adopted a new tone, flippant, half teasing, unconsciously easing things between them.

'Safe and sound. I'm in the hotel. Got in about an hour ago.'

'So what's the situation?'

She stubbed out her cigarette. 'Not sure yet. I'm heading out with a
couple of guys from *Corriere della Sera* tomorrow. It's tense ... you know

how it is. That feeling that a storm's on the way? But don't worry about me. I'll be fine.'

'I know you will.'

'How's Lamu?' She changed the subject quickly.

'Hot. I'm not in Lamu, actually. I'm in Nanyuki. Hooked up with a couple of friends … looking around for another job.'

His words sent a bolt of pain ripping through her. She drew in a deep breath. Friends. A new job. A new life. Without her. 'Well, have fun.' She forced the words out. 'I'll see you around.'

'I'll see you, Lexi.' His voice was quiet, knowing. 'Stay safe.'

'You too.' She put her phone back in her pocket and looked through eyes blurred with tears over the edge of the balustrade. Her swimmer was gone. The water had settled itself back to a flat sheet, lit by the moon once more.

Mark switched off his phone and slid it into his back pocket. The annoying voice of a woman sitting just behind him cut sharply into his miserable silence.

'I said to him, honestly, I said it … just like that. I told him. I told you I would!'

'You never!'

'I did! Oh yes, I did!'

He took another long swig of ice-cold beer, dangling the bottle by the neck in front of him. He was sitting in the Zebar at the Fairmount, waiting for Smith and Crowther. He'd been back a week, and the desolation of being without her burned him like a fever.

'Mark?' Mike Smith's voice brought him abruptly back to himself. He turned round, relieved. 'You all right, mate?' Smith hopped on to the stool next to him and signalled to the waiter. 'Whatever he's having. Give him another one, too. You all right?' he repeated, turning back to him.

Mark nodded, then shook his head. 'No. Actually, no. I'm not.'

There was a moment of uneasiness. They'd been friends for long enough, but in the slightly awkward way of many men, the length of time they'd known one another bore no relation to any depth of intimacy. By admitting he wasn't all right, whatever that meant, Mark had crossed a line. Mike knew more about him than most people, the result of a drinking session in the very same bar that had seen Mark blurt out something he normally kept tightly under wraps, but the drunken confession had remained exactly where he'd left it – between them, never again referred to by either man.

'What d'you mean?' Smith asked, eyeing him warily.

Mark ran a hand through his hair. He looked a mess and he knew it. After three days in the cottage on Lamu, he had flown up to Nanyuki simply to talk. He should have known. He should have seen the trouble he'd be in with her. 'It's ... it's stupid really,' he parried.

'What is it? Money?'

Mark gave a hollow laugh. 'No. Not *that*. It's ... it's a woman.'

'Ah. Same one as before?'

'Before?' Mark was puzzled. Insofar as he knew, he'd never once mentioned a woman to either Mike or Dave.

'Yeah. Last time we met, you seemed a bit distracted.'

Mark gave another hollow laugh. 'Oh yeah. Well there you go. I didn't think it showed.' The two men eyed their beer glasses uneasily.

'So what's the problem? Is she married?'

Mark shook his head. 'No, no. Nothing like that.'

'Well what, then?'

'She's a reporter.'

'Match made in heaven, I'd say. So what's the problem? When did you guys meet?'

Mark shifted uncomfortably on his stool. 'She came out to Lamu about six months ago, on holiday. We met at the Peponi and ... well, nothing *much*. One night, you know how it goes. I don't know why I didn't recognise her straight off. She disappeared the next day back to London. That's when I came up here ... just afterwards. I couldn't stop thinking about her. But I bumped into her in Cairo again, completely by accident, about a month ago. After I'd dropped off those oil guys, I headed for the Hilton ... and she was there. She's been covering the region for months. We spent the next three weeks together. Best fucking weeks of my life.'

Mike shook his head, chuckling to himself. 'No offence, Mark, but you might be punching a bit above your weight there, mate.'

Mark looked into his glass. 'Don't say that. Please.'

'What've you told her?'

'Not much. I mean, she knows who I am. She knows my work. But not much else. No one does. Except you two, and I can't for the life of me work out why the hell I told *you*.'

145

Mike blew out his cheeks. 'Well I'd come clean if I were you. She's a fucking reporter. She'll find out eventually.'

Mark bit his lip. 'Yeah,' he said slowly after a moment. 'Thing is, I don't know how to tell her.'

'Try. Either that or forget her altogether.'

'I'm not sure I can.'

'Then do it. Don't be a dickhead. Just do it.'

38

Three days later, he came through the double doorways into the tense glare of expectant faces on the other side of a makeshift barrier. He saw her immediately: a slight figure sandwiched between two burly soldiers, both wearing the light blue berets of the UN peacekeeping force. He lifted a hand but she'd already spotted him, her face breaking into a wide smile. As soon as she started moving towards him, her small body weaving deftly through the throng, her short blonde hair and white skin in stark contrast to the dark hair and faces of most of those gathered there, he suddenly felt – absurdly – that everything could be made right again. He quickened his pace, overtaking the slow-moving couple in front of him, the woman's elaborate headdress swaying in time with her stately pace. His eyes were fastened on her as she moved towards him, like a secret thread that bound them together. Her face wore a look of amazement, as though she doubted his existence. Their eyes held as he crossed the last few steps towards her, and then there was the long-anticipated, almost anticlimactic sensation of holding her again. He buried his face in her hair, and her small, warm solidity was all the reassurance he required. 'You're here,' he murmured against it. 'You're here.'

'So are you.' She tilted her face up towards his.

'So I am.'

'I thought you'd never get here. Let's go, the guys are waiting.'

'*You* need protection?' he teased.

'This is how I roll,' she grinned. 'Come on.'

The road into Abidjan from the airport was eerily quiet. Everywhere there was the debris of recent fighting – burnt-out cars, abandoned vehicles, buildings pockmarked and riddled with bullet holes – and the exuberant, life-affirming, chaotic throng of West African cities that he remembered was gone. In its place was a tense watchfulness. As they drove across the bridge on to the island, passing the *quartiers* of Biétry, Marcory and sprawling Treichville before crossing the lagoon to Plateau and Cocody, where the hotel was located, a song drifted into his head. *Cocody, Cocody, Cocody Rasta.* He hummed the refrain under his breath. It seemed to belong to a different time and place.

There were few people on the roadside, and those that were there eyed the white UN Land Rover suspiciously as they stopped at traffic lights, or waited for a lone taxi or mammy wagon to pass. He'd been to Côte d'Ivoire once before, many years ago, but this was not the place he remembered. Gone were the bustling plantain and coconut sellers who set up makeshift stalls wherever there was a space. Gone, too, were the kids running alongside the cars pushing their spindly bicycles in front of them, and the young women who sold sachets of ice-cold water from tin basins balanced precariously but gracefully on their heads. Instead the streets held groups of sullen-faced young men, clustered together around a transistor or a portable television, keeping one watchful eye on whatever traffic there was and another on the news. He passed his hand across the back of his neck. He was sweating, and just as it had been in Cairo, it wasn't simply the heat.

Her skin gave off a sheen of dampness that was almost cool to the touch. He traced a line down her flat stomach to the whorl of her navel. 'Like an orange,' he murmured, bending his head and touching it with his tongue. He felt the muscles of her stomach contract, sending a quiver rippling across her torso. He loved that about her. Every touch, every caress, every stroke generated an immediate response that he could see, feel and taste. He'd never made love to a woman like her. The tightly held control that she exercised in her day-to-day dealings with the world disappeared as soon as he held her in his arms; the thought crossed his mind more than once – was this always how it was for her? He was surprised to find his insides clutched with the nervous sort of jealousy he hadn't felt since he was a teenager. She was bold and direct and took her pleasure greedily, without any of the coyness he associated with English girls, but she was capable, too, of giving of herself so tenderly, and with so much passion, that it wasn't unusual for him to have a sudden, unexpected hard-on thinking back on some night or early morning that they'd shared.

He reached up and pinned her wrists against the already damp sheets, and moved down between her legs, his tongue seeking out the soft folds and slippery crevices of her body whilst she squirmed delightedly under his touch. Salty, sweet, sharp – he could never make up his mind. She tasted like Lexi, like no one else. He was almost twice her weight, but he already knew her strength. He was unable to pin her down for long. In a single fluid move she was on top of him, urging him into her. His last semi-coherent thought before he dissolved in an explosion of his own sweet relief was that he would have to find a way to make this – it, them, *her* – last. That was all that mattered.

He woke in the early hours of the morning to find her gone. He'd fallen asleep with the wonderful soft weight of her breasts against his back, her arms wrapped around his waist. Once or twice in the night he'd stirred, then felt her warm reassurance willing him back into slumber. But there was no one next to him now. He sat bolt upright. The air-conditioner in the corner of the room was blasting out a purring chemical-scented coolness. There was a light on in the bathroom and he could hear the soft murmur of a conversation. He gathered the sheet to his chest and reached for his cigarettes. Snatches came to him through the half-closed door.

'No, it's fine … Absolutely … What time are you heading out? … No, I don't think so … If you can, that'd be great … Sure. OK, thanks, Fabio. Go safely. See you guys when we get back.'

She came back into the room, naked and comfortable in her own skin in a way he'd known few women to be. She perched on the end of the bed and took the cigarette from his hand.

'Who was that?' he asked.

'Fabio. He's with France-Presse. They're going into the city tomorrow morning, but I think we should head out of town. We got reports of something happening near Toulépleu, which is out west, close to the Liberian border.'

'How dangerous?'

She shrugged. 'No more, no less.'

'Meaning?'

'Very, probably. But that's not going to stop me.'

He chuckled. 'No, somehow I didn't think it would.' He hesitated. He'd offered to double as her cameraman; he'd often switched from still to moving images and felt just as comfortable doing either but it meant they were essentially alone. 'I'd feel safer if we were armed, you know.'

She looked up, surprised. 'Armed? I've never carried a gun in my life. Have you?'

He hoped his voice was steady. 'Yeah.'

'Where the hell are we going to get a gun from in three hours?'

He bent down and picked up his jeans and shirt from the floor. 'Leave it to me. This is Africa, right? *My* turf.' He grinned, kissed the top of her head and grabbed his toothbrush.

Ten minutes later, he was in the lobby on the ground floor, surveying the staff trickling in for the early-morning shift. Somewhere amongst them would be someone whose face would hold the sign he sought. After all, it wouldn't be the first time he'd looked for protection in this way.

39

She had once had a dream in which she found herself walking along a road, late at night or early in the morning, she could no longer remember which; just the particular fading or dawning light that both dusk and dawn provided. She could still recall the strange shock she'd experienced when she understood that she was walking against the flow of people coming the opposite way. She'd stopped and turned round to see what it was they were heading towards ... and then abruptly woken up. The strangeness of it had stayed with her all day. Now, sitting in the back seat of the Land Cruiser next to Mark, looking at the reddish ribbon of the dirt road stretching out in front of them, the same sensation returned. They appeared to be the only ones heading out of town. Everyone else – cars, trucks, vans, buses, bicycles, pedestrians – seemed to be making for Abidjan.

She turned to look at the landscape passing by. In less than half an hour, the city was gone, thinning away to nothing. The greenery thickened and closed in on them, and then there was nothing but the one smooth road in front of them, its sides eaten away by the torrential rains, exposing the fiery orange earth beneath the tar-like muscle and fat beneath the surface of skin. Here and there they came upon an abandoned wooden table, the basic roadside stalls that in Africa stood where traffic signals and direction posts might be found along a European highway. Now and then they picked up the fizzing crackle of a local radio station, but with the closure of the state broadcasting service shortly after fighting had begun, the signals were weak and voices died away, sporadically replaced by a burst of music, then silence. Mark's thigh was uncomfortably warm against her own; they'd switched off the air-conditioning to conserve fuel, and the thick, close air was hot, but it was surprisingly comforting.

He'd come back into the room just before nine. 'All sorted,' he'd said, and that was it. She didn't ask; he didn't volunteer. She'd noticed as they were loading up the car in the crowded hotel car park that his watch was gone. A watch for a gun. *This is Africa.* A stark reminder of the contradictory nature of value in this part of the world.

Tiassale, Divo, Lakota. The musical, haunting names of unknown towns were come upon and left, spun off into the distance. They headed north to Daloa, through rainforest as thick as any she'd ever seen. The landscape here was different both from the coast, where Abidjan was perched, and from the southern African landscape that she remembered from childhood. There, in Zambia, the sky was enormous, stretching over the land in a gigantic infusion of blue. Here it was close and tight, pressed down upon the earth with a stillness that bordered on oppression. Human habitation seemed to claw its way out of the humid fug of plants and stifling air, fighting for breath. Through the thick canopy of forest, trails of smoke could be seen, signs of a small village or patches of cleared earth under cultivation. The trails disappeared almost immediately, becoming lost in the blanket of haze that was both cloud and vapour, hovering just above the treetops, smothering the ground.

At Daloa, they headed due west, towards Douekoe. The road worsened and their pace slowed. They stopped several times, once to clear a log that had fallen across a particularly bad patch of road. It had rained recently, and the air was thick with dying rainflies, those insects that burst into life for a few hours after the rainfall and then fell to the ground, carpeting it thickly before dying in huge drifts and mounds.

'Ever eaten these?' Mark asked, picking one up between thumb and forefinger.

Lexi wrinkled her nose. 'Er, no, thank God.'

'Why not? They're good when they're fried. Pure protein.'

'Thanks. I'd rather have a Mars bar.'

He grinned and wandered over to talk to the driver, Modeste. She noticed how he squatted easily beside him, pulling out a packet of cigarettes by way of greeting. He beckoned her over and she took her place beside him, leaning against one of the mud-splattered tyres.

'How much further, Modeste?' she asked, accepting a light.

He looked up at her shyly from under feminine, beautifully curled lashes. 'Maybe one, two hours. It depend on the road.'

'Want me to drive for a bit?' Mark asked. 'You're not tired?'

Modeste shook his head firmly. '*Non*. Is OK.' *He* was the driver. He would get them there safely; it was his responsibility. They gathered up the empty water bottles and biscuit wrappers and climbed back into the vehicle.

'Can we have the air-conditioning on, just for a minute?' Sweat was running down Lexi's back and pooling uncomfortably in the waistband of her jeans. In a few minutes, the damp heat was replaced by a dry cool that wafted over them like running water. Relieved, she held her shirt away from her body to dry it and looked out of the window. The landscape was so different from anything she'd ever seen that it passed into an unthinking kind of acceptance, unexplored and unknown.

The tall elephant grasses had been cropped by the recent fire so that the ground had the appearance of a shorn head. Everything within the fire's path was blackened, scorched, reduced to a gently smoking heap, brought down to eye level. It was clear that it had been done deliberately. Several plastic jerrycans had been left scattered on the perimeter of the blackened earth, still reeking of petrol.

'Let's do that one more time, Lexi. The sound quality's not great.' Mark started filming again. 'Just the last bit.'

Lexi cleared her throat. 'We're standing in the middle of what looks like a bush fire, except this is no act of nature.' Mark swung the camera around slowly to take in the yellow jerrycans. 'Someone started this deliberately.'

'Great. That's it. We're done.' Mark straightened up, brushing at the tiny particles of smoke and debris that had landed on his jacket. 'Let's get out of here.'

'I want to go into the village,' Lexi said, looking across the scorched ground to a thin track that led into the forest. 'There must be people there who saw something.'

Modeste shook his head. 'That place is a bad place,' he murmured. 'Very bad place. Many bad things is happen for that place.'

'No, it's too risky. You don't know who might still be hanging around.' Mark agreed with him.

'Well, villagers, for one thing. And even if there are rebel soldiers, we're hardly the French militia. We're reporters.'

Mark shook his head again. 'No, Lexi. I don't want us to take the chance. I've been in these situations before.'

'So've I,' Lexi said stubbornly. 'And I'm telling you, it'll be fine. We're no threat to anyone. Let's check it out, talk to a couple of people and get some footage. Modeste can wait here with the car. Let him park under those trees over there and stay out of sight.' She hoisted her rucksack on to her shoulder and began to walk towards the track.

After a second's hesitation, Modeste started the Land Cruiser and headed for the trees. Mark blew out his cheeks in exasperation, but caught up with her soon enough.

The walk across the scorched field let off a stink like a dirty ashtray. The ground was powdery underfoot, made worse by the knowledge of what lay buried there, mixed in with the burnt grasses and reeds. She tried to tread carefully, with respect, but it was impossible. She held a handkerchief against her nose until they were clear of it and had entered the forest. The sudden drop in temperature and light was a surprise. It was cool in there underneath the thick canopy. The path worn by feet and bicycle tyres was clearly well used – they followed its track like a spoor. Sunlight came down upon them in dappled bursts. A whole continent of sound pressed in and around them: snapping twigs, the chitter-chatter of birds, the gravelly croak of frogs and insects she didn't like to think about, the swift clatter of wings as something above their heads moved, disturbed by their passage through the tightly woven fabric.

They walked for nearly fifteen minutes, until the trees started to thin, and then all of a sudden the curtain abruptly ended and they emerged from the forest. They were on the edge of a small escarpment. The land fell away and then rose again around them in a series of small folded hills that stretched to the horizon. The village – a rather haphazard collection of mud huts with thatched roofs – followed the contours of the hills. Palm and coconut trees punctured the sky like slender, accusatory fingers. Mark switched his camera to 'record', and together they moved cautiously forward. There was no one about.

'It's so quiet,' Lexi whispered, looking around. 'Where is everyone?' A few dogs sniffed around in the overflowing gutters and a herd of goats skittered by, the small ones trailing behind, their woeful bleats the only sound in the heat. Sweat ran down her back. Out of the cooling canopy of trees, the heat was once more intense.

Suddenly a shot rang out, shattering the silence. As one, they dropped to the ground. Lexi's heart began to accelerate fast. They waited, palms flat down in the reddish dust, not daring to move. From the distorted perspective of the ground, she could see a dog running along the road in front of them, clearly nervous. She lifted her head and looked quickly to left and right. The village spread around them, butting up against the forest and knitted together with an intricate network of dusty paths and open gutters. There was one building larger than the rest – a church or a meeting house, perhaps? – which stood a little way down the hill. She squinted, calculating the risk. It was too far. There was no telling where the shot had come from.

'See that hut over there?' she whispered. Mark nodded. 'There's a little alleyway next to it. Better to hide there than in plain sight.' He nodded again. 'I'll go first.' He was about to protest, but she was already gone.

They reached the alleyway and waited for a few minutes. There was nothing but eerie silence. Whoever had fired had stopped. They got cautiously to their feet, flattening themselves against the mud walls, inching their way deeper into the ochre-tinged settlement.

She recognised the granary by its conical shape and the opening that was halfway between a door and a window. 'In there,' she whispered. Before he had time to answer, a volley of shots rang out from the direction from which they'd just come. They looked at each other for a brief second, then jumped. She went through the opening first, landing in a cloud of dust thick with the scent of fermenting corn. There was a single shaft of light coming from a small opening in the roof; dust particles floated in it like diamonds. Mark landed after her with a soft thud. His legs all but disappeared, swallowed up by the soft mattress of yellowing kernels. They lay there in total silence, both somehow managing to resist the urge to sneeze. It was cool inside the hut, but there was an oppressiveness in the air that was worse than heat.

Minutes passed, then they both became aware of the ground shaking slightly. The cloud of dust that surrounded them began to vibrate and thicken. A thudding drone could be heard in the distance, coming closer and closer. The chuddering, clattering noise burst upon them suddenly, a racket of blows that split the sky. It produced a high-pitched ringing in their ears and set the ground alive with vibrations. It was a helicopter, coming in to land. They could hear the whirring scythes cutting through the air, then a long rumble of vehicles that seemed to come out of nowhere. Running feet. Voices yelling out commands in a language that neither could understand. Dogs barking. A volley of shots, then silence. There was a shriek, a strangled cry that could have been a man, woman or child, then a single shot. Mark's hand tightened on her arm.

They waited for what seemed like hours, every sense, every nerve ending attuned to whatever was happening out of sight. Finally there was the whirring, pumping sound of the helicopter taking off again and the start-up of engines. More voices, more shouting. The words were unknown but the meaning was clear. *Get out of here. Let's go.* The helicopter lifted, making a circle of shuddering sound waves overhead. The noise level changed, died down and finally faded away. The village was returned once more to silence. Mark's grip on her arm did not slacken until a full five minutes – or ten, she lost count – had passed.

'You OK?' he whispered finally. She nodded. 'I'll go first.' He got up, covering his face with his arm against the perfumed dust. He slipped through the opening, waited a moment, then beckoned her forward. They emerged out of the darkness and gloom of the hut into the full brightness of day. For a second, neither spoke. At the end of the alleyway, something moved. It was a dog. It raised its head to look nervously at them. Its quivering, cowering tail suggested recent fear. It sniffed the air once, twice, then darted off, quickly disappearing from view.

Mark moved cautiously towards the road. Nothing moved. Even the sky seemed to be holding its breath. Lexi looked upwards to where a hazy cloud had drawn a blind over the afternoon, fuming with suppressed heat and light. He beckoned her forward again. She moved to stand next to him. Across the road and a little way down the hill was the church. Lexi could just make out the crude length of iron hanging from a nearby tree that stood in place of a church bell. Unlike the other buildings, this one had a tin roof, and there was a grassy space in front of it that indicated a structure of some formal importance and dignity. Something emanated from it that neither could dismiss. They glanced at each other, then moved forward together.

A faint buzzing noise was coming from within the building, but Lexi couldn't quite work out what it was. She put up a hand to grab hold of the doorknob, but the door was already partially ajar. It swung open with a creak at her touch. The buzzing intensified. As she moved forward into the gloom and the noise, she realised what it was. Flies. She clapped a hand to her mouth and gagged. Mark put out an arm and pulled her close. She turned her face into his jacket. With his free hand he manoeuvred the camera, swinging it left to right in long, graceful tracking shots. He kept her head pressed firmly against him as he filmed, shielding her from the horror inside the gloom. No one had ever offered her the kind of protection he was giving her now: the strong circle of his arms, the solid expanse of his chest and the unshakeable reassurance that whatever happened next, with him she would be safe.

PART SEVEN

July 2011

40

Aunt Julia was beside herself with glee. She'd drafted in two girls who worked at the agency she'd once owned and into which she occasionally popped to call in favours from designers. The girls rushed up and down the stairs with armfuls of clothes that Aunt Julia made them hang on the two racks that she'd had delivered to her rooms on the first floor specifically for the purpose. She herself lounged on the dark green velvet chesterfield in a pair of silk Hermès pyjamas that made Jane's eyes water with envy, directing operations with a wave of her beautifully manicured hand, stopping every now and then to sip at a flute of pale gold champagne.

'No, no ... put the Mourets over there, yes, next to the Legers. Yes, that's right. I want them ordered by *type*, not *length*. Lovely. Lexi?'

Lexi was in a dressing gown, looking decidedly uncomfortable as her aunt instructed the girls to pull out one outfit after another. Jane, whose own wardrobe was considerable by anyone's standards, was struggling to take it all in. Lexi had begged – *begged* – her to stay with her all day, from breakfast at eight through the agonising dress-fitting, a light lunch, hair and make-up and then the Royal Television Society awards at Claridges. 'You don't need to beg,' Jane had said. 'Three things in your favour ... Aunt Julia, Claridges *and* Mark Githerton. I can't believe I'm actually going to meet him!'

'Oh God ... please don't. Don't make me any more nervous than I already am. And please don't say anything about Mark to Aunt Julia. I ... I couldn't face her probing. Not just yet.'

'Fine, but *you*? Nervous?' Jane raised an eyebrow. 'You survived Gaza, Lexi.'

'Which is nowhere near as scary as this, let me tell you. What the hell am I going to wear?'

'That's where *we* come in, Aunt Julia and me. Leave it to us. Trust us. Wars are *your* turf, designer kit is ours.'

'Darling, try on the black one. The Oscar de la Renta. Bring it out, Polly.'

Lexi stood nervously in her underwear as Polly reverently brought out the bouclé wool and chiffon dress and laid it on the bed for Aunt Julia's inspection. She was shivering, despite the almost tropical temperature of Aunt Julia's house. She was such a funny little thing, thought Jane with a rush of warmth. Standing there in a regulation M&S bra-and-knickers set (and not from the Rosie Huntington-Whiteley range, mind you), arms wrapped protectively around her ribs, she looked like a teenager, uncomfortably out of place. Aunt Julia, in contrast, looked like Boadicea.

'What do you think?' asked Aunt Julia, cocking her head to one side as Lexi was zipped up.

Jane shook her head. 'Na, it's too … old. She needs something lighter, something fun. Flirty.'

'Flirty?' Lexi looked up, alarmed.

'I agree,' Aunt Julia said crisply. 'What about that one?' She pointed to a beautiful silk-and-jacquard below-the-knee dress in a bold, stunning floral pattern. 'Yes, the Erdem. Try it on, darling.'

Lexi obliged, allowing Polly to take the de la Renta dress off her with shaking hands. Olivia pulled the zip up and turned her round to face her critics.

'Lovely, just lovely. With the right hair and make-up, you'll be stunning.'

'Make-up?'

'Oh, for goodness' sake, Lexi! You're going to an awards ceremony! They don't come around every day, you know. You're a woman! What's wrong with dressing up? You never know, you might even meet someone. Now that'd make a change,' Aunt Julia said conspiratorially to Jane. 'D'you know, I don't think I've *ever* met one of her lovers.'

'Aunt Julia!' Lexi wailed. Polly and Olivia couldn't keep the grins off their faces. She could only imagine what they were thinking: Lexi Sturgis, seasoned war correspondent, standing in her aunt's bedroom in her knickers listening to her love life being laid bare. As bare as she was.

Jane had to laugh. 'Oh come on, don't be precious! It's been a crap year so far. It's just for one night, Lexi. Let your hair down and let's have some fun!'

'My hair's short, in case you'd forgotten,' Lexi said drily.

'More's the pity,' Aunt Julia shot back. 'If only you'd stop hacking it off with those gardening shears of yours. Oh well. I've got Daniel coming round at two. He'll sort your hair out. Right, let's see what else we've got. How about a Helmut Lang? There's that midnight-blue one ... yes, bring it *out*, Olivia. No use standing there gaping at it. Put it on, darling.'

Jane nodded approvingly as Lexi stepped into the pool of midnight-blue silk. The dress was absolutely made for her, oozing glamour and sophistication in equal measure. Her golden glow, which had as much to do with the time spent in Mark's arms as it did with the sunlight on Lamu, was a beautiful contrast to the dark, silky sheen of the fabric as it slithered over her slight frame.

'Shoes?'

'Don't make me wear heels, please,' Lexi begged.

'Are you *insane*? Of course you'll have to wear heels. Bring us a pair of Blahniks, Polly. Higher the better.'

At four thirty, her breathing partially restricted by the silk-satin Ender Legard underwired bodice that had somehow restructured her body to give her breasts *and* hips, Lexi turned nervously to face the team. The Helmut Lang had been replaced at the last minute by a light turquoise wool-crêpe sheath dress by Michael Kors, with two side-panel slits that opened to reveal a caramel-coloured silk lining. Her legs were bare and she wore her first pair of Jimmy Choos, palest green suede pumps with a stiletto heel and a razor-sharp pointed toe. A matching grosgrain clutch and a sleek silver Chloé cuff finished it off. Looking at herself in Aunt Julia's full-length mirrors, she saw in her own face the dazed air of one who no longer recognised her own image.

'Absolutely stunning,' Aunt Julia said, satisfied at last. 'I couldn't have put it together better myself.'

'You *did* put it together.'

Aunt Julia shook her head. 'No, darling. A team effort. That's what styling's all about. Wouldn't you say, Jane?'

Jane was busy with her own reflection. She'd chosen a Halston Heritage draped double-faced gown in fuchsia silk, which Polly had had to fetch personally from Selfridges since the sample size the agency had sent over was too small – *way* too small. 'Does this come in a twelve?' she had asked hopefully.

'A twelve?' Aunt Julia arched a perfectly-arched brow. 'I doubt it. But we can always ask.' Luckily for Jane, it did. She could hardly breathe, mind, but fit her it did. Just.

'A team effort?' she echoed now, still dazed by her own image. 'Yes, absolutely.'

'Right, one last glass and we're ready to go.' Aunt Julia glanced at Polly and Olivia. 'Girls, pop downstairs to the kitchen, will you? I've asked the housekeeper to lay out lunch for you. Someone'll come and pick up the dresses. Thanks for your help.' Polly and Olivia hurriedly left the room.

Aunt Julia turned to Lexi and lifted her glass. There was a moment's odd hesitation, then she said something that clearly shocked Lexi as much as it did Jane.

'I know I hardly ever say it, darling ... partly because you won't let me, but I'm proud of you. And I know you'll hate me for saying it, but Kitty would be proud of you too. So very proud.'

Lexi turned away, but not before Jane saw the dark flush of some powerful emotion sweep over her face. She shrugged dismissively, but the tightly hunched bones of her shoulder blades were more eloquent than words.

'No, I mean it,' Aunt Julia went on quietly. Jane held her breath. It was suddenly as though there were only the two of them in the room. Jane had all but vanished. 'Listen to me, Lexi. D'you know what she said to me ... just before she left?'

Lexi's shoulders were still tightly hunched. 'I don't care,' she hissed.

'You do. Yes, I know you do. She asked me to make sure I knew you. "I want *you* to know her, Jules." Those were her exact words. That was the thing she most regretted, darling. That she wouldn't get to know you.'

Jane could hardly breathe. She felt her eyes begin to flood. She gathered the silk folds of her skirt together awkwardly in one hand and hurriedly left the room. Her heart was thick and heavy in her breast. Lexi's mother had thrown away the chance to know her only daughter; Jane's mother had had it taken from her. It was an unexpected bond between them that she'd failed to see, and one she knew Lexi would never recognise.

41

His first thought as he saw her coming through the door flanked by two women was that he must have misunderstood. She'd told him once, in the drowsy sweet confidences of bed, that her mother was dead, but wouldn't be pressed to say anything further. 'When I was quite little,' was all she said. But the woman standing next to her was clearly her mother. The resemblance between them was striking, despite Lexi's best efforts to hide it. The older woman was glamorous in the way of film stars, carefully made up and styled to her best possible advantage. In complete contrast, Lexi paid no attention to her looks. What was beautiful in her seemed to have come about by accident, through no effort of her own, a fact that made her all the more compelling to him. He quickly adjusted the sleeves of his jacket, securing his cufflinks – it had been a while since he'd worn anything as formal as a tuxedo – and moved across the floor.

'Who's this?' the older woman said archly as he approached, making it clear that Lexi hadn't said a thing about him.

'Aunt Julia … this is, er, Mark. Mark, this is my aunt.'

Her aunt. So he hadn't misunderstood after all. He held out his hand. Like Lexi's, her grasp was warm and firm. 'Pleased to meet you.'

'Well, well, well. She tells me nothing,' Aunt Julia said, tucking her arm conspiratorially into his. 'I do hope you'll be sitting with us.' From her tone of voice, it was clear there was no question about it. He cast a bemused backwards glance at Lexi as Julia led him off.

In the two hours he sat with Julia Mahon, he learned more about Lexi than he had in three months. Every so often he would catch sight of Lexi's eyes on him, lioness eyes, burning with discomfort. He couldn't quite grasp it all. Some of it he knew already, more from things she'd unwittingly let slip than from anything she'd told him outright. Diplomat father, absent mother, a peripatetic childhood, much like his own. But there was other stuff: her father's disappearance after her mother walked

out; Aunt Julia stepping in to look after the two abandoned children …
his head was spinning.

'There were two of them?' he asked when Lexi had gone with Jane
to the ladies'.

Aunt Julia turned to look at him. Her grey-blue eyes regarded him
frankly. 'She hasn't told you?'

He shook his head. 'No. I … I don't know that much about her,' he
said finally. 'She's very private.'

Aunt Julia nodded. 'Not surprising, really. I never knew a home with
more secrets. Nothing was ever *said*, you know? It was partly Matthew's
fault. Goes with the territory, I suppose.'

'Diplomats, eh?' he murmured.

Aunt Julia flashed him a keen glance. 'Is that what she told you?'

Something deeper was being said. He could feel it. He nodded slowly.
'I've a feeling you're going to tell me something different.'

She shook her head. 'No. That's for Lexi to tell you, not me. I've
probably said too much already, but there's something about you, Mark …
yes, there's definitely something different about you.' She lifted her
champagne glass. 'And now let's change the subject. Here they come.'

He looked up. Lexi's eyes were on his. He felt an uncomfortable flush
of shame, as though he'd been eavesdropping, listening to something not
meant for him. He was in trouble. He could feel himself being pulled
further in, driven by a need to understand this woman who'd managed
to push her way under his skin, seemingly without trying. His head was
reeling, not just from the anticipation of what he might find out about
her, but equally what she might discover about *him*.

She was conscious throughout the long evening of Mark's eyes on her,
searching for something beyond what she could bring herself to reveal. It
had been a mistake to bring him; she hated the way everyone's eyes were
drawn to him, then to her … an unspoken question. *Mark Githerton?
What's he doing here? What's he doing with Lexi Sturgis? Are they …?* She
felt a surge of impatience with it all, the speeches, the accolades, the
toasts … after Cairo and Abidjan and everything that they'd seen and
experienced together, there was something almost nauseating about the
celebrations – the wine, the food, the *excess*. She longed to pull off the
gown into which she'd been poured, kick off the heels in which she could
barely stand, let alone walk, and simply disappear.

From the way Mark looked at her, his violet-blue eyes catching the light so that she felt as though she could see straight through him to a confusion that was as deep and profound as her own, she knew there was more to come, more questions to answer, more truths to face. She felt her skin begin to tingle in an anticipation that was partly fearful, but partly also relief. *Is this what love is?* she asked herself wonderingly, her mind drifting away from the evening that ebbed and flowed around her. *Is this what I've been missing all along?* But before she could answer her own question, or even ponder it further, she became aware of people staring at her, faces bright with expectant pleasure. There was a sudden outbreak of applause. She turned to look at Jane, confused.

'Go on,' Jane hissed, smiling broadly. 'Get up there.'

Where? She looked around her, dazed. Realisation crashed over her. Her name had been called. She'd been awarded something. Something … but what? She felt the calming pressure of Mark's hand on her arm and got up. She looked down at him, and then did something she'd never thought she would ever bring herself to do. In front of Aunt Julia, Jane, Donal, her colleagues whom she'd worked with over the years and scores of strangers she'd never met, she bent down and kissed him. A brief, appreciative murmur went up from the crowd, and then she turned and concentrated on making her way up the stairs to the podium without tripping over.

42

It's hard to believe I've been here nearly four months already. I know it's such a silly cliché but I honestly don't know where the time's gone. Every day is different and yet every day is the same. There's six of us now, we— Deena lifted her head. Her fingers stopped moving over the keyboard. 'What was that?'

She was sitting at the kitchen table, taking advantage of an unexpected lull in fighting that had seen three of the doctors – herself, Valérie, and Christos, a young Greek anaesthetist who'd been with them for just over a week – pop into the kitchen to make coffee and grab something to eat.

Dr Stuart had gone with two colleagues to try and find medical supplies from one of the nearby government hospitals. The air was redolent with the scent of food. A neighbour had just delivered lunch; packets of still-hot falafel were sitting on the counter top, waiting to be unwrapped.

'What was what?' Christos looked up from rolling a cigarette.

'I thought I heard something at the door.'

Valérie was at the sink, busy washing plates for lunch. There was a transistor radio playing in the next room and the level of background noise was raised by the tumble of water.

'I'll go,' Christos said, pushing back his chair. He lit his cigarette, inhaled briefly and disappeared.

The front door was swollen from the recent rains. Deena heard it scrape against the tiles, and then there was a pause in which she dimly grasped that no greetings were exchanged. She got up from her chair at the exact moment a crack splintered the walls and blasted apart the sound of the radio presenter's voice. Something fell in the passageway. There was a sudden shocked silence. She and Valérie stared at each other. A second later, before either had a chance to react, the door to the kitchen slammed open. In the doorway, framed by daylight coming in through the open front door, stood two masked men, weapons pointing directly at them.

Valérie began to scream. Deena's gaze slid past the men to where Christos lay on the floor. She had just enough time to see the pool of blood widening around his head before one of the men moved forward to grab her. Valérie's screams abruptly stopped as one of the men hit her across the face with such force that she fell sideways, soapy water and plates flying as she dropped. Deena's arm was wrenched almost clear of its socket and she was shoved head first against the stockier of the two men. Fear broke out all over her body like a fever, washing through her in great gulping swathes.

A sack was thrust roughly over her head, immediately blocking out the light. In the tunnelled, foul-smelling darkness, she had only her ears and hands to guide her. Her heart was hammering, threatening to burst out of her ribcage. She was roughly manhandled down the hallway, dragged over the inert body of the doctor she'd only known for a week. One pair of hands … no, two … someone grabbing at her legs. Now she was drowning in her own fear. She was being picked up, hoisted over someone's shoulder. A car door opened. She was thrown inside – boot? Back seat? The engine gunned into life, doors opening and closing, someone pressing something – a knife? A gun? – into the crook of her neck. And everything in complete silence. Not a word was exchanged, not a single command issued. A slap on the dashboard, the crazy zigzag motion of the vehicle – a car? A van? – as it shot forward, skidding across the street. Her blood was thundering in her throat. She was being taken somewhere, but where? By whom? And why?

43

It took Jane a full minute to work out that the numbers showing on her bedside clock were 10.07 and not 7.07 a.m. If it was 10.07, she thought drowsily, then it must be a Saturday, possibly even a Sunday. She closed her eyes. Then it hit her. It wasn't. It was a Thursday. The day after the awards ceremony that had seen Lexi pick up not one, but two awards, causing Donal to bring out the champagne. No wonder she'd overslept. Lexi and Mark had disappeared almost as soon as the ceremony was over, leaving Jane with half a dozen drunk, happy male colleagues. Aunt Julia had taken one look at the company and decided, wisely, to leave.

She leapt out of bed, stubbing her toe as she rushed to the bathroom. It was now 10.12 a.m. At ten o'clock, twelve minutes earlier, Donal and Oliver Miles, their chief financial officer, would have gone into the boardroom, together with Zoë and Judith, their two staff writers. By now, the four of them would be looking at each other, wondering where the hell she was. She was due to present her programming ideas for the coming year – a one-page draft that she'd *intended* to work on as soon as she got home from the ceremony but hadn't. Shit, too late to do anything about it. She had no choice but to get to the office as quickly as she could and pray that Donal would forgive her lack of detail.

She was showered and dressed in fourteen minutes flat. A further four minutes were spent running down the street to Farringdon Road and another three hunting down a cab.

'Jane? Where the hell have you been?' Susie looked up as she came through the glass doors at a gallop. 'They've been waiting for nearly an hour! Donal's absolutely fuming!' Jane ignored her and ran straight to the boardroom, pausing only for a second to draw breath before entering. She tucked her hair behind her ears – something she only ever did when she was nervous – and opened the door.

'Ah, Jane. Finally.' It was Oliver who spoke. Jane's skin crawled. There was no love lost between her and Oliver, and with the possible exception of Donal, only Oliver and Jane themselves knew why. One of those it-seemed-like-a-good-idea-at-the-time evenings that subsequently went spectacularly wrong. Despite the seven years that had passed since then, it made Jane shudder to remember the desperate lengths to which she'd been driven, whether by her own demons or his it mattered little. 'Good of you to join us. Late night? Or rough night, perhaps? I seem to remember that's what you like. A bit of rough.'

Jane's mouth dropped open. Was he *serious*? 'I ...' She found to her horror that she couldn't even speak.

'Ah. Lost your voice too, have you? Well, you do know what they say, Jane, don't you? Don't swallow. Bad for the vocals.'

This time there was an audible gasp from Zoë, who turned shocked cornflower-blue eyes towards Jane, incredulity written all over her face. Jane was aware of the stain of embarrassment seeping up her neck and face. She opened her mouth to say something – a retort, a rebuke, a rebuff, anything to put that bastard in his place – but to her horror, her mind had gone absolutely blank. She gulped in a mouthful of air. Zoë and Judith were looking at her expectantly. Surely she wasn't going to let him get away with it? Donal was staring fixedly at his computer screen, damn him! She tried to think of something witty that would take the sting out of Oliver's words and restore the balance in the room to how it had been before he opened his big ugly mouth, but again she came up with nothing. Donal coughed discreetly. They all waited. Jane fought desperately to control her voice.

'Look, I'm sorry, everyone. Something ... something just came up. I'm sorry I kept you waiting.' She sat down with shaking knees, and without preamble opened up her briefcase and took out four copies of her presentation. 'It's not long,' she began. 'And bear in mind it's just a working draft. That's why I asked Zoë and Judith to come in. I haven't shown it to them – I haven't shown it to anyone yet – but I thought today would be a good opportunity to do a bit of brainstorming, throw some ideas around before I start firming it up.' She passed each of them a single A4 sheet, headed *Working Girl © Jane Marshall, Creative Director, Network News International.* As they bent their heads to read, she skimmed her own copy for typos.

Who can forget Melanie Griffith's luminous performance in the 1988 romcom Working Girl? *The rags-to-riches story of a lowly secretary from Staten Island who not only outwits her scheming boss to land herself the top job at an investment bank but snags Harrison Ford into the bargain. Twenty-five years ago, the clichéd image of a female investment banker was enough to carry a movie ... not any more. Investment bankers come in all shapes and sizes – male, female, black, white, working class, posh boys, Sloane Rangers, single mothers, go-getters ... you name it. But what of other professions? In* Working Girl, *an exciting six-part made-for-TV series that looks at women in unusual roles, we're going to shadow six women at the top of their respective games. From war correspondent to nuclear physicist to racing driver, detective and politician, we want to know what it's really like. What sorts of challenges do they face? Is gender a help or a hindrance? What do their colleagues, friends and family think? How do they handle that age-old balance between work and private life? Can a woman really 'have it all'? Starting with one of TV's most committed journalists, NNI war correspondent Lexi Sturgis, we ask her the questions that you, the viewers, can't. What drives her? What keeps her up at night? What is she most afraid of? Over the course of an hour and a half, we bring you an intimate, never-before-seen glimpse into the life of an ordinary working girl.*

She looked anxiously at each person in turn as they read quickly and silently through her proposal. Zoë had a frown that didn't look like concentration between her brows: more like puzzlement. Jane felt the first stab of alarm. What was wrong? Too cheesy? She glanced at Judith and caught her looking sideways at Zoë. A second stab of alarm clutched at her insides. She looked across the table at Donal. He was gazing straight at her, and it wasn't an expression of admiration etched on his face; it was exasperation. Her mouth suddenly went dry.

Oliver was the first to speak. 'What the fuck?' He looked at Donal. 'Is this what we pay her for?'

Jane's stomach hit the ground. 'Wh-what d'you mean?' she stammered. She looked at Zoë, who gave her a quick, sympathetic grimace.

Sympathetic? What was going on? 'What's wrong with it?' she demanded. Her face and neck were flushed with panic. 'Donal?'

Donal was silent for a moment. 'Look, it's not your best effort, Jane. I was hoping for something a bit more ... well, a bit *grittier*. This reads like something out of one of those awful women's weeklies that my wife reads.'

Jane's flush deepened. 'I just ... I just thought it'd be good to do something ... a bit lighter, that's all. You kept saying we needed to sex things up.'

'We're a serious news organisation, not a fucking tabloid paper,' Oliver cut in. 'Sharpen up, Jane. We need ideas, not fantasies. Though as I recall, that's more your department, isn't it? Fantasies and the like.'

There was a sudden chill in the room. Zoë and Judith stared at her.

'Can I see you outside, Oliver?' Her voice seemed to her to have come from someone else.

Oliver looked at her. 'No need to go outside. You can say whatever you have to say in here. We're amongst friends.'

'Outside,' she repeated quietly. Very quietly.

Oliver rolled his eyes and made a great show of getting up. 'Better do as Mummy says,' he murmured, loud enough for Jane to hear. There was another audible gasp from Zoë.

Jane felt the pressure in her chest rise up, threatening to choke her. Somehow she managed to walk out without tripping over or bursting into tears. She closed the boardroom door behind her, stalked ahead to the exit and opened the front door. They were standing in the small hallway at the bottom of the stairs, so close they were practically touching. She didn't care. She had no intention of letting Susie or anyone else in on the conversation. She whirled round.

'What the *fuck* is your problem?' she spat out, almost too angry to speak. 'What's the matter with you?'

'Me? Nothing's the matter with *me*.' Oliver feigned ignorance. '*You're* the one with the problem, Jane.' His face was inches from hers. Her back was pressed against the wall; she tried to stare him down.

'What fucking problem?' she hissed.

He brought a stiff index finger to her face and for one absurd moment, she thought he might actually hit her. 'What's your job title?' he asked. Without waiting for an answer, he went on. 'I'll tell you. Creative Director. What's mine?' He was practically shouting at her. 'Chief Financial

Officer. That means it's *your* fucking job to come up with new ideas for me to produce. New, *creative* ideas. When was the last time you pitched us anything worth listening to? No idea? I'll tell you, darling. Two years ago, Jane. *Two* fucking years ago. Two years is a long time in television history. And history's where both of us will be if you don't pull your *fucking* finger out of your arse and DO SOMETHING!'

Jane was so taken aback she couldn't even blink. 'Don't you *dare*—'

'What? Take you to task? Since when did you become so fucking precious, Jane?'

'You've got a nerve, Oliver. One more comment like that and you'll be hearing from my lawyer.'

'Oh, for Christ's sake! Don't tell me you're sleeping with him *too*?' Oliver sneered.

'I'll have you up for harassment!' Jane yelled, suddenly feeling terribly exposed.

'Harassment? That's a fine one, coming from *you*!'

'What the fuck's that supposed to mean?' Jane felt a cold hand clutch at her insides.

Oliver smiled. 'Oh, I think you know *exactly* what I mean. Sharpen up, Jane. You're running out of time. I want something on my desk first thing on Monday. We've got a board meeting at three. I'm warning you. I'm running out of patience.'

And with that, he turned sharply on his heel and walked away, leaving Jane leaning against the wall behind her, only this time she was leaning against it for support.

44

'Cheer up. Things can only get better. Or that's what Labour promised us. Didn't work for them, mind you. Or us.'

Jane looked up, dazed. She'd fled downstairs to the basement cafe and collapsed into one of the low chairs at the back. Her eyes travelled up the length of a pair of jeans, a white shirt and a thin yellow-and-red-striped tie and came to rest on the smiling face of a young man who looked vaguely familiar. 'I'm sorry?' she said, taken aback.

'He's an asshole. I wouldn't take what he said seriously. I wouldn't take *anything* he says seriously. Seriously.'

'Look, do I know you?'

'Phin Harman,' he said helpfully. 'Phineas, actually. I'm the computer guy. *Your* computer guy. You probably don't remember. I fixed it about four or five months ago. Sorry, I couldn't help overhearing. I was standing in the stairwell for ages, just waiting for him to go.' He grinned at her.

She stared up at him. '*Phineas?*' she asked weakly.

He grinned. ''Fraid so. Could've been worse.'

'How?' She didn't know whether to laugh or cry.

'Look, can I get you a coffee? Or a tea? Or a Kit Kat. We both know you like Kit Kats.'

'I ... I'm sorry,' Jane said, shaking her head. 'I'm fine. I ... it was just ... just a work thing. Wh ... what are you doing here?'

'I was just bringing back someone else's computer. Same problem, actually. Look, forget about stupid computers. How about a drink? You look like you could use one.'

'It's not even lunchtime,' Jane said weakly.

'I meant tonight.'

'Tonight?' Jane stared at him. How old was he? Twenty-five? Twenty-six? 'I ... I'm ...' she stammered, unsure how to respond.

'Come on. Just one. You won't have to go very far, I promise. I'll take you somewhere round the corner. I know just the place.'

She got to her feet. He was a good head taller than she was, even in her heels. He had a nice face and a lovely, strong-looking body. She didn't dare look into his eyes but she thought they were blue. 'How old are you?' she asked abruptly.

'What's that got to do with it?' he parried.

'OK, fine,' she said suddenly, capitulating. 'Where?'

'It'll be a surprise. I'll meet you out the front at six.' He held out a hand. She shook it. A nice firm handshake. A nice bloke. A nice face. A nice body. And a nice smile. Was she dreaming?

'Six on the dot.' He flashed her a quick, easy grin and disappeared.

She spent the rest of the day staring grimly at her computer screen, her mind torn between the terrifying blankness of her empty imagination and the thought of a drink with Phineas Harman – good-looking, charming, but still practically a teenager! She wasn't sure which was worse. She made three trips to the bathrooms to check on her hair and outfit: Diesel jeans; Zara jacket; high-heeled sandals and a slouchy MaxMara suede fringed bag. It would do. It would have to do. She had no other option.

'OK, I have to admit I'm impressed. This *is* rather nice,' Jane murmured, looking round in approval. 'Some view.' They were in the bar at Paramount, on the top floor of the Centre Point building on Tottenham Court Road. London was spread below them like a vast, complex web.

'Thought you'd like it,' Phin said, clearly pleased. 'It feels like your sort of place.'

She took a gulp of her martini. Was he flirting with her? No, he couldn't be. He just felt sorry for her, that was all. Who wouldn't feel sorry for her, having overheard Oliver? 'Yeah, it's nice. Although I have to say it doesn't seem like *your* kind of place.' She took another hurried gulp. 'Look, I know you didn't answer me earlier, but exactly how old *are* you, Phin?'

'Old enough,' he said evasively. 'Age is just a number.' So he *was* flirting with her.

'No, go on. Tell me.'

'People get far too hung up about it, if you ask me.'

'Phin, I'm thirty-seven. *And* I'm a client.'

'So? It's not as if we bump into each other every day.'

'That still doesn't make me any younger,' she said slowly.

'It's just a number, Jane,' Phin repeated mildly, managing in a single sentence to make her feel both old *and* immature.

She gulped down the last of her martini. In the half-hour they'd been there, the unpleasant taste in her mouth that was Oliver was gone, replaced by something that felt dangerously akin to excitement.

'Don't go anywhere.' Phin slid off his stool, seeming to sense her shift in mood. 'I'll get us another one.'

She watched him thread his way across the room to the bar. Tall, good-looking, charming, easy to talk to. The clutch of girls at the next-door table clearly thought so too. They all smiled as he passed, and Jane was alarmed to find herself watching closely for his reaction. There didn't seem to be one. What was more, as he returned with their drinks, the smile on his face seemed to be directed at *her*. She felt the heat rise in her cheeks as he set the glasses carefully down on the table. 'Thank you,' she murmured. She couldn't remember the last time someone had bought her a drink, much less two. She was usually out there waving her credit card before anyone else had a chance.

'Cheers,' he said, clinking his glass against hers. 'Here's to a better evening than the day you've had.'

'Wouldn't be difficult,' Jane said drily.

'He's an asshole. Did I already say that?'

'How come you know so much about Oliver?' Jane asked curiously. 'I didn't think he had much to do with ... well, with anybody, really.'

'Oh, he's always got some issue with his computer or his email account or his software. That's just the way he is. Always looking for problems where they don't exist just to show he's in control. He's a tosser.'

Jane smiled. Tosser. There was something wonderfully uncomplicated about Phin Harman. His voice held just the right note of promise, a quickening vibrancy that set the pulse racing and made her think: why not? But hot on the heels of that exciting thought was another, more worrying one: *he's a good ten years younger than you!* She blushed. Did she just say that out loud? She wasn't sure. To cover her confusion and her rising blush, she polished off her martini and stood up. 'I ... I just need the bathroom,' she said quickly. 'I'll be right back.'

'I'm not going anywhere,' Phin said, grinning at her. 'And walk slowly.'

She darted him a suspicious look. 'Why?'

He winked at her. 'Because I like watching you.'

She stumbled away from the table, too stunned to speak.

In the ladies', trying to recover some of her poise, she slowly turned off the tap and picked up one of the hand towels. She looked at herself in the mirror. Jane Marshall. Thirty-seven years old. Five foot nine inches in her bare feet, ten and a half stone. On a good day. She was attractive. Not beautiful, no, but even she had to admit she still got more than her fair share of attention. On a good day she could pass for thirty. Tousled dark-brown hair, becoming more auburn with each trip to the hairdresser. A choppy, slightly messy fringe, which suited her rock-chick image and hid the fine lines that ran diagonally across her forehead. She was always careful with her clothes and make-up: nothing too flashy, no garish colours. Sultry, smoky, sexy ... that was her look. Good legs, a nice firm ass and a reasonably flat stomach, though her upper thighs had started to spread ever so slightly lately. If she stood in front of the long mirror in the hallway and craned her neck, she could see the dreaded ripple of orange peel. No amount of Pilates, yoga or pounding the treadmill seemed to be able to get rid of it. Once, catching sight of herself rolling around with someone (to her shame, she couldn't actually remember who), she'd been so horrified at the sight of her thighs that she'd promptly taken the mirror out of the bedroom. She'd rushed out that weekend and spent a small fortune at Agent Provocateur, stocking up on garments whose names she either promptly forgot or couldn't pronounce. The Esme playsuit, the Veronikka body, the Caitlin waspie, the Alina basque. Not that any of the one-night stands she'd had lately would've noticed. Her last four lovers had all been rather too inebriated to notice what she was wearing. Their comments ranged from 'Mmm, sexy. Now take it off' to 'What the hell's *that*?'

No, she wasn't doing too badly for someone approaching forty, but was it really enough to attract – and hold – the attention of a twenty-four year-old? *Fuck it. Who cares?* She mouthed the words defiantly, added a quick touch of lipstick and a squirt of perfume. Two martinis on an empty stomach had sharpened her mood pleasurably. She blotted her lips and tossed the paper towel in the bin.

When she got back to the bar, she saw that the table was empty. Phin had disappeared. She slid on to her stool a touch self-consciously and looked around. Where could he have gone? She drummed her fingers on the table. She caught the bartender's eye and was just about to signal for another drink when she noticed the girls at the next table whispering amongst themselves. They seemed to be talking about her. She caught the words 'ridiculous' and 'at her age, too'. She flushed. Standing in front of the mirror critically assessing herself was one thing, but to be openly ridiculed by a bunch of twenty-year-olds was quite another. She felt the stain of embarrassment surge up through her face. Where the *fuck* was Phin?

Fifteen minutes later, there was still no sign of him. By now the girls were openly laughing at her. She'd been stood up, well and truly played. She couldn't bear to sit there any longer. She picked up her bag and marched over to the bar. 'A single whisky,' she instructed the bartender. 'No ice.'

'Coming up.' He hurriedly poured her a single measure which she downed in a single gulp. He looked at her warily. He'd evidently also noticed that she'd been stood up. 'Anything else?'

'Nope.' She slid a ten pound note across the counter. 'Keep the change.' She turned to go.

'And your, er, friend ... d'you want to leave a message?'

'Tell him I got tired of waiting and I've gone,' Jane tossed over her shoulder and walked out, her cheeks flaming. What a jerk! She took the lift back down to the ground floor, burning with a mixture of humiliation and anger.

'Are you sure he'd actually gone?' Lexi murmured sceptically later that evening. 'He might've just gone to the toilet. You could've waited a bit longer.'

'I waited nearly half an hour!' Jane protested. 'You don't leave someone sitting on their own for half an hour, not in a bar like that. The girls at the table next to me were having a field day. I could just hear them!'

'Oh don't be silly. I'm sure they weren't. But I believe you,' she added hastily. 'What a weird thing to do, though. And he hasn't phoned or anything since?'

'He doesn't have my number and I don't have his. Oh well ... I guess I'll bump into him in the office at some point and then I can tell him what a jerk he is.'

'Don't do that. Just ignore him. Pretend it never happened. That's much more dignified.'

Jane nodded and reached for a cigarette. 'Yeah, you're right. Hang on, I'm just going to light a fag.'

'Thought you'd given up.'

'Only on men. Christ, they're all the bloody same.'

'Don't say that. They're not *all* the same. Just the ones you seem to pick.'

'But I didn't pick him! He picked *me*! What was the point in asking me out for a drink? *And* I paid for them.'

'Well, I still think you could've waited a bit longer. Anyhow, one way or the other, you'll see him in the next couple of weeks. Let him explain – *if* there's anything to explain. If he isn't big enough to apologise at the very least, he's not worth wasting another thought on.'

Jane took a long, deep drag. 'Yeah, you're right. Anyhow, I'd better go. After my run-in with Oliver this morning, I've got to come up with something better for Monday. Fuck, why'd I choose *this* career of all the bloody careers out there? Why couldn't I have done something safe and boring? Why'd I have to go and choose something where I've got to *think?*'

Lexi snorted. 'You? Safe and boring? Don't worry, you'll pull it out of the bag. You always do.' She chuckled and hung up.

Jane threw her phone down and switched on the television. She needed some distraction from the question going round and round in her brain: why had he asked her out if it was only to run off on her? For one brief mad moment as she'd walked to the bathroom, conscious of his eyes on her, she'd actually wondered if this time she might get it right. Perhaps a younger man was the solution. Well, there was only one answer to that question: clearly not. More fool you, Jane Marshall, she thought grimly. *No man at all* seemed to be the correct answer to the question. *Will I ever find someone? Anyone?*

45

Inès was looking idly out of her bedroom window, watching a bird pick its way delicately across the grass at the front of the house, when she saw a car pull up and stop opposite the flat. She watched the couple walk across the road, the woman pressing down on her skirt as the wind playfully whipped around her. They disappeared from view, and seconds later, she heard the buzzer sound.

She slid from her bed and hurried into the hallway. Her father was taking an afternoon nap in his study and her mother was in the kitchen, preparing the evening meal.

'I'll get it,' she yelled. She opened the door.

'Inès Kenan?' The woman spoke first.

Inès's chest began to heave. 'Yes?' She looked from one to the other in alarm. Their faces were impassively solemn.

'Are your parents home?'

'Y-yes … why? Who are you?'

'May we come in?'

'*Me'en da? Me'en henneck?*' her mother called out to her from the kitchen. *Who is it?* And then it all happened at once.

After they'd gone, she realised she didn't really know who they were. Police? Aid workers? Intelligence? She had no idea. They'd sat in the living room on either side of her parents, cups and saucers balanced on their knees as they calmly went through the chain of events. Her father took the news stoically, as he would. It was her mother who went to pieces.

Inès turned away from her bedroom window and let the curtain fall. She tiptoed quietly down the corridor. The door to her parents' bedroom was still closed. Her mother had been sedated by their neighbour, Dr Humphreys. 'Let her rest for now,' he said, patting her father awkwardly on the arm in a gesture that indicated both his solidarity and his professional concern. He was Welsh, and, Inès supposed, understood little of the ripple of terror that had gone through them all, not just her mother. Deena had been detained. *Detained.* What would a kindly Welsh doctor know about such things? When the woman said the word out loud, Inès's breath caught and she had to sit down. Deena, locked up somewhere in a police cell, or worse. All in, six doctors working across the city were being held, the man informed them briskly. 'We've no reason to suspect they're being mistreated in any way,' he added authoritatively. 'We're in constant contact with the various embassies and consulates. It's a good job there are six of them.'

'Why?' Inès's voice wobbled.

'Well, with so many foreigners involved … that's a lot of embassies bringing pressure to bear.'

'But Deena's Egyptian too!' Inès burst out. 'They must know that. Won't … will they treat her differently?' She avoided her parents' anxious glances.

He shook his head firmly. 'No, not necessarily. She's with an international organisation, after all.'

'As soon as we have some more concrete information, you'll be the first to know,' the woman supplied helpfully. 'And please don't distress yourselves . Just because we haven't heard from them doesn't mean the worst has happened.'

'Yet.' Again, the word escaped Inès's tightly pressed-together lips.

'Inès.' Her father threw her a warning glance. He turned back to the two officers. 'Please keep us informed. Please. It's … it's very worrying.'

'Of course. I'm sorry. It's distressing news. MSF is a powerful organisation, don't forget. Their local liaison office is doing all they can.'

'Thank you.' Her father's face had taken on a tight, closed aspect that Inès couldn't recall ever seeing. She looked at her mother, but her mother's glance slid past her. As her father showed the couple to the door, her mother drew her hijab over her face, hiding it, as she began the theatrical wailing that Inès had often seen other women do. The sound of it was awful, like glass breaking.

'Mummy—' she began, but her father came back into the room and intervened.

'Leave her to me, *habibi*,' he said firmly. 'Go next door and see if Dr Humphreys is at home. Ask him to come round if he's there.' Inès ran from the room, her heart hammering.

Now she hovered outside their door, torn between wanting to go in and fling herself on her mother's bed, and running out the door to grab a cab to Heathrow. Detained? By whom? And why?

46

A pearly dawn broke over London, sending pigeons flying overhead, tracing a line across the uncurtained window. It was a Saturday morning. Mark woke before Lexi. He lay in her wide double bed, his body at ease with itself, his equilibrium suddenly restored. Beside him, Lexi slept on, worn out by the demands of the media circus following her win. He'd been in London all of two weeks and was restless, half eager to move on, yet oddly reluctant to go. It was time to make a decision. He pushed aside the covers, careful not to wake her, and stood up. He picked up a pair of sweatpants and a T-shirt from the untidy heap on the floor and quietly left the room. He walked lightly down the stairs, stopping to pick up his running shoes, and opened the front door. He needed a run to clear his head. He crossed over the square and headed for the park. The tarmac was hard and unyielding, so different to the sandy roads around

Lamu where he ran every morning, but as he began to find his pace, he ceased to notice it.

He ran for an hour or so, crossing from one Royal Park to another, coming finally to rest somewhere in the middle of Hyde Park, not far from where he'd started. A metallic, steely light bounced off the Serpentine. He walked towards the water's edge, leaning against the railings, resting his arms and catching his breath. The water lapped gently back and forth, rocked by the passing drag of a canoeist. He closed his eyes briefly, taking the scents and sounds of the city down into his body.

He can't look at him, not directly, anyway. He tries, but his eyes won't hold, they won't focus. They slide off his face as if they can't bear to rest there, not even for the most fleeting of moments. They've been brought in separately, some last-minute discretion ordered by the judge. Whose crime is the greater? One has killed; the other has not. They stand there facing one another, flanked by their respective lawyers but not looking at each other. He hears the murmur from the stands where members of the public are sitting. The few whites are clustered together, as much out of loyalty as class – or anything else. Everyone strains to have a look. It's not every day that something of this sort happens, not out here. For the older onlookers it's Happy Valley all over again. Bit distasteful. All sorts of rumours.

Somewhere in that little group of whites is his mother. She's being propped up, either by one of their neighbours, or by her sister and brother, both of whom have flown out to Kenya to act as support – though it's not clear whom they're supporting, or who is most in need of it. Certainly not Sally Githerton. She's almost unaware of what's happened. Mark says 'almost', because in the days that followed the shooting, after both he and his father had been taken away, she let it slip that she'd known what was going on in that bedroom ... had always known. 'Good on you, boy,' she murmured once when she came to see Mark in the cell where they'd taken him.

He glances at the lawyer who's come up from Nairobi – and before that, Stellenbosch, where, he said blithely, 'this sort of thing happens all the time'. Mark isn't sure which 'thing' he's referring to – the rape of a ten-year-old or the killing of one – but he doesn't suppose it really matters. What matters is that Tumaini is dead, and that both Mark and his father, Basil Houldsworth, the 4th Baron Fermeroy, are charged with her murder. But only one of them is guilty. Which one? That's for the jury to decide.

There's a murmur from the gallery. Someone else has walked in. It's Issa.

Tumaini's father and their erstwhile cook, though Issa is almost the same age as his father. Mark can't meet his eyes either. It's as if he's suddenly been struck blind. He sees things, but he doesn't, not really. He's been unable to see anything since that night, since the terrible chain of events that led to a death – but not of the person whom he wished dead. The other one. The mistake.

Lexi was in the kitchen when he came in. She looked up, and there was an urgency in her face that he recognised.

'What's happened?'

'Donal just rang. There's reports of a young Greek doctor being killed in Cairo ... he's one of a bunch of doctors from Médecins Sans Frontières ... one of the other doctors has been detained, though they're not sure who by. A British doctor. A woman. Donal wants me to go back out and report on it.'

'When?'

'Tomorrow, day after ... depends how quickly Susie can arrange everything.' There was a second or two of hesitation.

'And you want me to come with you?'

She nodded. There was a look of fiercely suppressed trepidation in her face. 'Only ... well, only if you want to,' she offered, uncharacteristically shy. He felt his heart tighten. He knew only too well what she was asking; not just the immediate job, but everything that came with it, everything that would come after.

He was nineteen, in his first, miserable year of university in London when he met the man who would change everything for him. Leon Bullard was a war photographer to whose exhibition Mark had been dragged by a girl he was seeing at the time. Funny how he couldn't remember anything about the girl – not her name, not her face or body – but everything about the evening remained in sharp focus, even now, almost twenty years later. He'd been standing nursing a glass of warm white wine, his eyes roving from image to image, stunned into wakefulness and out of the torpor of his first-year studies in economics that he'd somehow stumbled into and had no interest in. They got chatting. Leon was looking for an assistant. It was 1992. Nelson Mandela had just suspended talks with the South African government following an attack on ANC supporters at Boipatong township just outside Johannesburg.

'You sure about this?' Leon appraised the tall, rangy young man. 'I wouldn't, if I were you.'

'Why the fuck not?' Mark was surprised. It had been Leon's suggestion, after all.

'Not unless you're prepared to change everything. You won't be the same afterwards. You won't be able to go back.' He waved a glass around, drawing in the summer evening, the exhibition venue somewhere off Bond Street, the leggy blonde – yes, she *was* blonde – all of it. Mark shrugged.

'I don't want to be the same. That's the whole point.'

Leon looked at him. He had the physical brightness of someone who lived his life not just in the sun, but in the full, brutal force of everything the world had to offer. He was holding a door open. It was a way out. Mark took a deep breath, and in that moment rejected everything that had been set up for him – partly out of concern, partly out of guilt – and walked through it. He hadn't stopped walking, working ... wading through. Until two years ago in Kyrgyzstan, when something inside him finally snapped and he woke up unable to carry on.

Now Lexi was asking him to go back.

47

Outside, the air was thick with summer heat, the dense fug of traffic fumes, birds, insects and the comings and goings of whatever building she was in. There was a single window in one high corner of the cell; a crude metal grille scored the only glimpse of sky. Deena was lying on the thin mattress that had been pushed up against the wall so that one end of it doubled as a pillow. The floor smelled of damp and dust and another, sharper smell that came to her suddenly as blood. She recognised it from the operating theatre. All her senses were concentrated on the knot of pain that was her stomach. Like most women her age, she'd known hunger before – one or other of the fad diets she'd tried as a teenager. But always out of choice, always a matter of willpower, never beyond her control. Now it was different. She'd been in the cell for almost twenty-four hours – she'd had to calculate it by the light outside and the position of the sun; they'd taken her watch along with her jewellery as soon as she was brought in. In that time, she'd had nothing other than a small bottle of water. Twenty-four hours with nothing to eat. She'd never gone that long without food in her life.

Her fingers went automatically to her wrist, where she wore the bracelet that Inès had given her on her sixteenth birthday ... only it wasn't there. Her wrist felt thin and naked, and horribly vulnerable. She felt the prick of tears behind her eyes. Fear, like hunger, she was only now beginning to realise, was a physical thing, not mental. It came off her like sweat, a cold film that coated her eyes, nose, mouth ... all her senses. After the first night, it was no longer possible to distinguish between hunger and fear. Both gnawed at her insides, focusing her mind and energies so completely inwards that she began to lose all sense of time, of the minutes passing in the pitch darkness before the first rays of light picked out the grubby pinstripe of the mattress, and she was no longer sure whether she was awake or asleep. Time passing was measured only by her capacity to take it all in, and that was slipping, moment by moment.

Suddenly there was a noise outside her door. She stiffened and scrambled upright. The bolt slid back and there was the noisy jangle of keys as first one was tried, then another. Her heart thudding, she stood with her back to the wall, waiting. At last the door opened. A policeman stood in the opening, a thick truncheon in one hand which he tapped softly against the other, saying nothing, just looking at her. Deena forced herself to return his stare. Someone was hovering behind his bulk, holding something. She saw with a sudden treacherous rush of saliva to her mouth that it was a tray of food. Her whole body trembled, but she wasn't about to reveal that to him, or to anyone. To make matters worse, beneath the threshold of hunger she was dimly aware of another pain: the leaden, dragging ache of her period. Her legs were trembling, and she had to bite down hard on the inside of her lip to stop her whole body from welling up.

'Put it down,' the policeman instructed the young man hovering behind him. He darted forward and laid the tray on the ground. 'Ten minutes.'

Deena forced herself to answer. 'And then what?'

'And then someone will come for you.'

'What for? Where am I?' Deena asked, but he had already turned his back. The door banged shut again and the key was turned firmly in the lock.

She looked down at the tray. A plate of beans, a folded-over pitta bread and a bottle of water. There was no crockery. She didn't care. She forced herself to eat slowly; she knew the risks better than most. Burning fat and protein instead of carbohydrates could potentially result in a cellular loss of electrolytes. Even after only a couple of days of starvation, the sudden shift from using her own body's reserves of fat could trigger an insulin rush, leading to cardiac arrest. In her medical studies she'd seen it happen twice. It wasn't about to happen to her. She drank slowly too, her eyes darting around the cell for something – anything – to use in place of a sanitary towel. She had no idea where they would be taking her, or for how long. She quickly tore a strip off the dirty mattress, turning it over to its cleaner side and had just readjusted her skirt when the bolt on the door slid back again and the policeman stood once more in the light.

In silence he nodded to the two men standing respectfully behind him, and they reached forward to grab Deena by the arms. She was marched between them past half a dozen similarly locked doors until they reached the end of the corridor. A change came over the bulky man who was clearly in charge. He hesitated before the last door and, in a gesture that was curiously self-conscious, slicked back his hair with the flattened palm of his hand before knocking, almost reverentially.

'*Et fuddal.* Come in.' The answering gruff shout penetrated the thick wooden door. The policeman opened it and again beckoned to the two men to bring her forward.

Deena found herself in an office, large and airy, with high clerestory windows that looked on to the same blue sky. A portly, moustachioed man sat behind a desk in one corner of the room. He said nothing for a few moments, then he removed his glasses. There was absolute silence in the room. Behind her, though she couldn't see them, she could feel the presence of the two police officers, breathing faintly, fingers resting lightly on the cool metal of their guns. She swallowed as quietly as she could.

'So,' he said finally, his eyes moving dispassionately over her face and body. 'Here she is. The Kenan girl. Looks like him, don't you think?' He tossed the question out, but it was clear he didn't want an answer.

Deena's head was reeling. Who did she look like? Who was he refer-ring to? One of the guards moved forward and grabbed her by the arm.

The fear lying just beneath the surface of her skin erupted like a rash, prickling her with its intensity, turning her inside out. The room swam before her.

48

Jane woke suddenly, her neck stiff from having fallen asleep on the couch. The television was on in the background, a dull, static flicker that hovered on the edge of her consciousness. She pushed herself slowly upright, wincing. Her head ached from the glass of red wine she'd downed before dropping off. An unmarked yellow foolscap pad lay on the glass coffee table, uncomfortable proof of her inability to come up with a single idea. Two horrid humiliations in as many days had left an unpleasant taste in her mouth, despite her best efforts to forget both. She got up slowly and walked over to the fridge. Water, aspirin, coffee, and in that order.

She'd just swallowed the last mouthful of her coffee when an image on the television screen caught her eye. It was of a young, dark-haired woman, very pretty, with dark, almost jet-black eyes. She was wearing a white coat – a medical coat? – and her hair was partially covered with a scarf. She frowned. *Foreign Office accused of not doing enough to secure the release of British national.* The ticker-tape headline ran across the screen. She walked back to the couch and fished for the remote control. *The twenty-five year-old medical doctor hasn't been seen since Thursday, when masked gunmen shot and killed one of her colleagues, Dr Christos Pitsillides, in the temporary clinic south of Cairo where they'd been working for several weeks. Dr Kenan, a second-year medical intern at St Thomas's Hospital in South London …*

Jane stared at the screen. She reached for her mobile phone. An idea had just come to her.

She risked looking at Donal's face as he read. It was impassive – was that a good sign? She couldn't tell. She'd decided against involving Oliver at this early stage. Somewhere in the background a phone rang. She heard Susie shouting instructions to someone; the office was in full swing. Lexi was due to head back to Cairo to cover the story of the missing doctor … which was where Jane's idea had come in. They would send Lexi back to Cairo to cover the story of the missing young doctor. It ticked all the right boxes – human interest, current affairs, a region in turmoil … the fact that the girl in question was beautiful was a bonus. She winced. There were days when she hated the shallowness of her job … but not today. She was desperate for a good idea and one had just come to her.

Donal nodded as he came to the end of the sheet, and Jane felt the tight snake of worry loosen its grip deep inside her belly. 'Yeah, it's good. I can see why it'd work. But we've got to move fast. Brief Lexi straight away. She'll have to set up a few interviews before she heads out. I want her there the day after tomorrow, latest. Who knows what'll happen in the next couple of days.'

Jane nodded vigorously. She looked again at the photograph of Deena Kenan that she'd pulled from the internet. She had a small, delicate-boned face; thick dark-brown hair, parted in the middle and falling over her shoulders. Her eyes were dark and luminous under thick, perfectly shaped and tapered brows. But it was her expression that caught and held the attention. There was a serene directness to the young doctor's gaze that hinted at something infinitely more profound than surface beauty. 'I'll get on to it,' she said, getting up. 'Thanks, Donal.'

He looked up at her. There was a moment's hesitation between them, the memory of their last encounter still fresh. Jane could feel the blush beginning to stain her face. 'Good work, Jane,' he said brusquely, and bent his head back to his laptop. It was the closest he would ever come to an apology. Jane swallowed and beat a hasty retreat.

She'd just finished typing a reply to someone when a tap on her door interrupted her. She looked up. Someone was standing in the doorway. It took her a second to work out who it was. It was him. Phin. A sharp flush of annoyance immediately travelled up her chest and throat. 'What the hell are you doing here?'

'Before you say anything, will you just let me explain?'

'Explain? Explain what?'

'I … I had to do something. I shouldn't have left you sitting there for so long, I'm sorry. I didn't have your number … in fact, I *still* don't have your number and—'

'It's fine,' Jane said quickly, cutting him off mid-sentence. 'It's not a problem.'

'No, it's not.' He shook his head. 'I … it was an emergency, honestly. I came by the day after but you weren't in, and I was off-site all day yesterday. I would've called your secretary but I didn't want to leave some sort of pathetic message. I'm really sorry, Jane. Honestly. Will … will you let me make it up to you? Please?'

Jane glared at him. Whatever else, he had some nerve, marching straight into her office like this. She could see Susie squinting curiously in her direction. She frowned and turned her attention back to him. She couldn't recall ever seeing a man look quite so embarrassed. Whatever the emergency had been, there was no doubting his present discomfort. 'Look, it's really no big deal,' she said again dismissively.

'But it *is*,' he insisted. 'And you went and paid for everything, too. Please let me take you out again. *Please?*'

Jane struggled to remember the last time a man had sounded quite so keen. She sighed. 'OK, fine. One drink.'

It took him a second to work out that he was being thrown a lifeline. 'Oh, thank *God*,' he said fervently. 'Fuck, you're terrifying when you're angry. How about Friday? This Friday?'

She had to bite back a smile. His unguarded enthusiasm really was rather sweet. 'All right. Last chance, Phineas Harman.'

He grinned at her. 'Can I at least have your mobile number? If I'd had it last time … well, I probably wouldn't be in here begging pathetically like this.'

'OK,' she said finally. 'But only for emergencies.'

'On my honour. But there won't be any more emergencies, I promise. So, Friday, then? I'll think of somewhere special to take you. And it's on *me*, OK?'

'Fine. Now scram. Some of us have got work to do.' She bit back another smile.

'Friday.' He flashed her another one of his heart-wrenchingly genuine grins and disappeared.

She leaned back in her chair. Well, well, well. She hadn't expected *that*. Perhaps her luck was about to change.

A couple of hours later, her mobile bleeped, reminding her that she hadn't checked her messages all afternoon. She fished it out of her handbag and peered at it. There was a message from Phin. Her heart gave a lurch. Was he about to cancel? *Been thinking about u all afternoon. Wish it was Friday.* She stared at it for a few moments, savouring the warmth that spread through her. How long had it been since she'd had the pleasure of knowing that someone, somewhere, was thinking about her, wondering where she was, *how* she was? The men she'd met in the past few years were far too cool to send text messages that weren't simply a matter of logistics or protocol. Phin's directness was unsettling in its simplicity. Aside from his slightly odd sense of time and a few off-colour jokes, there appeared to be no edge to him, nothing to fear.

She quickly typed out a reply. *Hi there, on my way home. Look forward to Friday.* She hesitated, then quickly deleted the 'Hi there'. It sounded as though she'd been expecting to hear from him. *On my way home.* No, too abrupt. *Just on my way home. Yes, looking forward to Friday.* Yeah, better. She pressed 'send' before she could change her mind (again). Less than a minute later, his reply lit up her screen. *Gr8! Roll on Friday!* She giggled. *Jesus, Jane Marshall!* It was ridiculous. *She* was ridiculous. But hell, it felt good.

49

Lexi put her pen down and sat for a moment lost in thought. Her notebook lay open next to her, covered in her semi-decipherable handwriting – names, dates, telephone numbers, email addresses. After her meeting with Donal and Jane earlier that morning, she'd disappeared into one of the empty offices with her laptop and a frown of concentration etched on her face. She hadn't said anything to either of them, but the young woman's name – Deena Kenan – had jogged a long-dormant memory. After an hour of searching and four phone calls, she had it. She looked at her phone. There was a fresh message from Jane. *Make it personal, Lexi, as personal as you can. It's not our primary aim, I know, but it'll help with the ratings. Sorry.* Well, with what she'd just found out, it couldn't possibly be any more personal. She wondered what Inès Kenan already knew.

The phone was answered on the first ring, as though someone was standing guard over it. 'Hello?' A young woman's voice, breathless with a heart-wrenching mixture of hope and trepidation.

Lexi felt her own heart contract. 'Inès Kenan?'

'Yes. Who is this?'

'Hi, my name's Lexi Sturgis. I'm a reporter and—' Before she had a chance to complete her introduction, the line went dead. Inès Kenan had hung up. Lexi couldn't say she blamed her. She looked at the address. Kensington. Well, at least she knew the girl was at home. She grabbed her bag from the back of her chair.

She got out at Kensington High Street and hurried through the arcade, cutting through Marks & Spencer, pushing her way past the shoppers clustered indecisively around the sales racks. She turned right and ran down Wright's Lane to Iverna Gardens, stopping at the bottom, just before the corner, and looking up at the handsome red-brick building. A small brass plate announced the building's residents. *Kenan. Dr T. Humphreys. M. & J. Cunningham.* She pressed the Kenans' buzzer. Just like the telephone, it was answered on the first ring. 'Hello?' It was the same voice.

'Hi, this is Lexi Sturgis ... I rang about half an hour ago. Look, I *know* you don't want to talk to me and I promise I won't harass you any further, but I'd just like to speak to you for a few minutes. I'm thinking of doing something that might help your sister.'

There was a click, as though Inès had hung up again, but seconds later, the door buzzed. Lexi quickly pushed it open. She stood for a second in the dim, cool hallway, looking around, and then heard someone come out on to the landing above her.

'First floor.' Inès Kenan's voice floated down the stairwell. 'Second door on the right.' Lexi hitched her bag firmly over her shoulder and ran up the stairs.

The flat was small and quietly tasteful. The walls of the entrance hall and the living room where Inès led her were a pale mint green, offset by one or two pieces of dark, polished antique furniture and a rather lovely aubergine-coloured sofa with ornate scrolled feet and giant oatmeal cushions. There was the usual collection of family photographs on a long, low console by the window and some striking original artwork on the walls. The Kenan sisters were clearly short of neither money nor taste. Lexi took in the details, automatically mentally filing them away for later recall.

Inès turned to face her. 'I know who you are,' she said quickly, before Lexi could say anything further. 'And we've got nothing to say to the press. We were warned not to talk to anyone. The men from the Foreign Office said it would be counterproductive.'

'They always say that,' Lexi said gently. 'And in general, I have to say I agree. But I didn't come here looking for a scoop. I know this must be a really difficult time for you all. I can imagine how worrying it is.'

'No, I don't think you can.' Despite her politeness, there was a suppressed hostility in Inès's voice. It was understandable. Lexi knew she would have to tread carefully in order to get what she'd come for.

'Actually, I can. But that's not why I'm here.'

'So why *are* you here?'

'D'you mind if we sit down?'

Inès blinked. 'Sorry. Yes, of course.' Her manners got the better of her emotions. She indicated the couch and sat down opposite on a leather pouffe with her knees pressed tightly together. 'Why are you here?' she asked again.

Lexi leaned forward. 'Inès, does the name Bassam Kenan mean anything to you?' She watched her carefully, looking for the signs that might give her away. But there was nothing but puzzlement in the young woman's clear dark-brown eyes. She shook her head.

'Bassam Kenan? No. I have an Uncle Khaled, Khaled Kenan ... and my father is Ibrahim. We're not a very big family. There's just us ... my parents, Deena and I. And a few cousins. Why? Who is he?'

Lexi bit her lip. She was quiet for a few seconds. Finally she drew a deep breath and lifted her head. 'I think it's something you should talk to your parents about,' she said quietly. She got to her feet. Inès remained seated, her lovely brows knotted together in a frown of incomprehension. Lexi held out her card. 'I leave for Cairo tomorrow night. Please call me. I can't promise anything, I have to be honest. But you need to talk to them about Bassam Kenan. Don't ask me why, but I have a feeling Deena's disappearance is connected to him.'

Inès was quiet. The silence in the room deepened. A curious feeling came over Lexi. Her shoulders hunched suddenly, pulling together, as though someone had placed a hand on the small of her back, surprising her. She knew that touch. The circumstances were different, but the trepidation of anticipation was the same. Inès's world was about to be turned upside down. She put the card down on the glass table. Inès made no move to take it. She left the room and let herself out of the building.

There was complete silence in the flat after Lexi Sturgis had gone. Inès sat where she was, unable or unwilling to get up. Her mother would have been appalled to learn she hadn't even shown her visitor out. In the Kenan household, good manners prevailed above all else. She listened to the sounds outside – birds, a car door opening and closing, the rattle of wheels on the pavement – and to the familiar noises of the house – the clock in the kitchen with its soft chime, the creaking of the floorboards as Dr Humphreys or his wife moved around upstairs. At last, she got up and walked down the corridor to Deena's room. The door was partially open. She stepped inside and closed it behind her.

The room still held her sister's scent – a combination of the perfume she always wore – Poison – and the smell of her hair. She washed it once a week, on Sunday afternoon, and spent the early part of the evening combing it through with the mixture of coconut and olive oil that their mother swore by. Inès looked at the dressing table in front of the window. Deena's things – the silver hairbrushes, a few bits and pieces of make-up, an unopened box of cotton buds – were spread across the surface as though she'd only just left the room. Her bed was neatly made and there was a stack of books on the floor beside it, the usual mix of medical books, journals and crime novels. Everything looked as it always did, as though waiting for her to come in after work, kick off her shoes or boots and flop backwards on her bed, letting the stress of the day seep slowly out of her before coming into the kitchen to make herself a mug of camomile tea.

She heard a creak behind her. The door opened as she turned round. Her mother and father were standing there.

'Oh … I didn't … I didn't hear you come in,' she stammered, embarrassed. Her mother's face was swollen, as though she'd been weeping.

'We just got back,' her father said. He was still wearing his jacket. 'We went to see the Lahiris.'

She knew she ought to wait until they were settled, had had time to take their coats off and were sitting in the living room before she opened her mouth to ask the question that had been burning on her tongue from the moment Lexi Sturgis left, but she couldn't. She couldn't wait another second. 'Abu, Mummy,' she burst out urgently. 'Who is Bassam Kenan?' Out of the corner of her eye she saw her mother's head jerk upwards.

No one spoke. Her mother pulled a handkerchief from her sleeve and dabbed her eyes. Her father's mouth opened and words, the like of which she'd never heard before, began to tumble out.

PART EIGHT

March 1961

50

No one ever spoke about the means by which the family had come to live in the beautiful old house in Maadi, the quiet neighbourhood just south of the bustle and noise of Cairo proper. It seemed as though it had always been theirs. In the late afternoons, Madame Kenan and her friends played backgammon and patience in the shade of the splendid bougainvillea that exploded across the veranda like a giant celestial parasol, periodically dropping pink and cerise-coloured leaves as papery and delicate as butterfly wings on to the black-and-white tiles, to be swept away by the servants every morning. Her late husband, Kenan Pasha, had extended and improved the gardens so that people who came to visit were often sidetracked by the wondrous explosion of scent, texture and colour that surrounded the house, almost overwhelming it.

For the three Kenan boys, who'd grown up in its shade and splendour, it was their own Garden of Earthly Delights, their tropical paradise. Aside from the bougainvillea, there were storm-cloud amaranthine jacaranda trees imported from South Africa that turned lavender, lilac and magenta as the blossom season went on; blood-red flamboyants; snowy, musk-scented jasmine bushes, grown large as trees; bulbous, garish tulip trees and acres of sweet-smelling roses of every possible colour and size. Even now, with the elder two married, with successful careers and families of their own, when they came home it was to the garden they always went first. There they sat under the little pergola on the terrace that overlooked the Nile – flowing past smooth and stately, swollen with the flood waters as surely as any tide – drinking coffee from silver-embellished *dallahs* and smoking the thin cheroot cigars that Bassam, the eldest, brought back from his trips to conferences in America and beyond.

Inside the house, the two daughters-in-law sat somewhat less comfortably under the watchful eye of Madame Kenan, self-consciously touching a stray lock of hair or smoothing down the thin silk of their skirts. Both Bassam and Khaled had married within the ever-decreasing circle of well-to-do, cosmopolitan Egyptians like themselves. Both girls came from families who were intimately known to Kenan Pasha and his formidable wife. Irène, Bassam's pretty, vivacious twenty-six-year-old wife, was the only daughter of a couple whose ancestry dragged half of the Ottoman Empire in its wake. Soraya, Khaled's wife, was a year older, but still a decade younger than her husband, and was half Italian, half Persian, the daughter of an illustrious biologist whose forebears had settled in Alexandria from Baghdad a whole century ago. Only Ibrahim, the youngest, had still to make the right match, but there was no hurry, Madame Kenan declared tartly, not whilst she was still scrutinising what was left of the pool of young ladies from which she could confidently choose her youngest son's bride.

It was on a mild spring morning in 1961, almost five years after the Suez Crisis had ended, that the first inkling surfaced that something wasn't quite right. Bassam, a hydraulics engineer, was on his way to the airport, due to deliver a paper at the IAHR conference in Rome, when he was apprehended by two men who pulled up in front of him in an unmarked car, forcing him to stop. That night, there was no phone call from the hotel room where he'd been booked for four nights, on the Via di Ripetta, close to the Piazza del Popolo – just a few minutes' walk from the conference centre, he'd told Irène the night before his departure, pleased. Irène was pregnant with twins; three year-old Fouad was looking forward to the presents he'd been promised, among them an astronaut robot and a giant bulldozer that ran on batteries. Irène was more irritated than worried; it was typical of Bassam to forget to call.

When there was no phone call the following night, she confided her annoyance and mild worry to her sister-in-law, Soraya. Soraya's mother, Giulietta, was prevailed upon to contact a relative in Rome, who called in at the hotel. The gentleman at the front desk at the splendid Residenza di Ripetta was more than helpful. No, Signor Kenan hadn't arrived as scheduled. His four-night stay had been paid in advance by the Egyptian Institute of Engineers, so there was every indication that he was supposed to turn up, but so far, unfortunately, he hadn't. Yes, yes, he would telephone Signora Marciano immediately if there was any sign of the gentleman. The conference was due to end the following day. Most odd.

The news of Bassam's failure to arrive at the hotel was duly relayed back to his wife in their smart new two-bedroom apartment in the up-and-coming district of Lazoghli, where Kenan Pasha had bought the newlyweds their first home, and to the gracious house in Maadi, whereupon Madame Kenan went pale. 'What do you mean, he never arrived? Where is he?'

'I don't know, Umm Bassam. I don't know where he is.'

There followed three days of incessant phoning and calling on anyone – friends, colleagues, clients – who might know of Bassam's whereabouts. On the fourth day, just before midday, a car pulled up outside the house in Maadi and a man got out. He stood for a moment unsteadily in the street, blinking in the sunlight as though his eyes were unaccustomed to it, then the car slowly pulled away. He crossed the road, pushed open the gate and the family dog, recognising his scent, if not his uncertain manner, barked joyfully.

'Bassam? Bassam? Oh, *habibi*! It's you! Madame Kenan! Madame Kenan! Bassam's back!' Yenta, the elderly housekeeper, caught sight of him as she walked back to the kitchens from the vegetable plot behind the house. Her shrieks brought everyone outside, running; even Madame Kenan, who'd forgotten her headscarf in her haste. Bassam was brought into the living room, made to lie down on the black leather Corbusier chaise of which Kenan Pasha was so proud, and Yenta was dispatched to bring water, dates, cakes ... flaky hot samosas ... *anything*. He looked so thin! And so tired! And what were those marks on his face and arms?

There was a time and place for Bassam to give an account of himself. Not now. Not just yet. For two days and nights, everyone tiptoed around the house. Irène and Fouad moved into one of the many spare rooms. With only a few weeks to go until her daughter-in-law was due to give birth, Madame Kenan declared it better for everyone to stay close by. On the third day, Bassam woke and emerged from the room where he'd been sleeping, his face almost obscured by a beard. He washed and shaved and presented himself at the breakfast table, where everyone was waiting. Layla and Hasna, the two servants whom Madame Kenan ruled with an iron hand, ran back and forth, bringing out plates of *ful*, pale, creamy fava beans glistening with olive oil and a sprinkling of lemon juice; panniers stacked with pitta bread, fresh from the oven; bowls of creamy snow-white moussaka; plump green and black pitted olives and shiny hard-boiled eggs. Coffee and mint tea were served, alongside tall glasses of freshly squeezed pomegranate juice, sweet as honey. Madame Kenan watched anxiously as her son toyed with his food. Everyone waited for the explanation that never came.

'It was the Mukhabarat,' Kenan Pasha whispered to his wife in bed that night. 'We will not speak of it again.'

'But—'

'*Kifea! Mish hanitkalim tenni aleh.* We will not speak of it again. Let us put it behind us. He's back, unharmed. That's all that matters.'

Gihaz al-Mukhabarat al-Amma. The Egyptian General Intelligence Service. Set up by Nasser in 1954, charged with protecting national security. In the dark, Madame Kenan swallowed hard on her fear. Why would the Mukhabarat detain her son?

Bassam did not regain the weight he'd lost during those five days and nights he'd been held, but in time, everyone grew accustomed to his thinner, leaner silhouette, and, just as Kenan Pasha had decreed, neither his weight loss nor the circumstances that provoked it were spoken of again. In any case, there were other, more pressing concerns. In due course, Irène gave birth to the twins, Wajeeha and Mona, and the family returned to the flat in Lazoghli, and later, to a spacious five-bedroom villa in Zamalek, where they were joined at the weekends by Khaled and Soraya, and their daughter Fatimah.

A few years later, when the twins were nearly six and Fouad was a tall, sensitive young boy of ten, Egypt went to war with its neighbour, Israel. The Kenan sons narrowly avoided being called up. By then, Ibrahim was in Paris, furthering his studies; Khaled was exempted on account of his accident, and Bassam's name did not appear on any call-up list. Egypt lost the war, but Nasser's standing and popularity remained high. In 1970, after a series of border skirmishes with Israel, he died of a heart attack whilst hosting the Arab League summit in Cairo. He was succeeded by Anwar Sadat. Sadat dissolved Nasser's United Arab Republic, proclaiming the birth of the Arab Republic of Egypt in 1971. Later that same year, Bassam disappeared for the second time. This time, he did not come back.

It was announced on the news. Dr Bassam Kenan, son of Achilles Kenan and his wife Houda Al-Aswamy Kenan, was a spy, working for the

Israelis against the interests of the Egyptian state. The revelation swept through the upper-crust circles in which they moved like a hurricane. Irène, using her Italian passport, fled the country with their three young children and resettled in Milan. On the orders of the state, Bassam's two brothers were placed under surveillance, an edict that was to be observed for the rest of their lives. Kenan Pasha died of a stroke – and, some said, the shame – not long afterwards. Fifteen years later, his widow too passed away. The house and garden in Maadi were left unoccupied after her death, the gardens slowly returning to a state of impenetrable neglect.

PART NINE

July–August 2011

51

Her father's voice stopped. Inès swallowed hard. She was struggling to take it all in. 'Is … is that why you sent us away? Here, to school?' she asked finally.

Her father lifted his head slowly and blinked, his eyes refocusing on hers. 'Partly, yes. But it wasn't true, Inès. None of it was true. Bassam wasn't working *against* the state, not in the way they said. He was working *for* it, at least for some version of it that he believed in.'

'What do you mean?'

'After that first time, when they picked him up on his way to Rome, things changed. He never said what happened to him, not once, not to anyone. Not even to his wife. But everyone knew he'd been tortured. You only had to look at his arms, his back … his legs. The soles of his feet. He hid those things from us, of course, but … we saw. I don't know when he started going to mosque. More often than usual, I mean. It must have been a year or two afterwards. That's when it began.'

'What are you saying … he joined the Brotherhood?'

Her father nodded. 'Oh, he wasn't as radical as some, not by a long shot. And he certainly wasn't religious. No, his was a *political* decision, not a spiritual one. He believed in a secular state, as we all did. But the men he met at mosque were able to articulate things that we … well, we preferred not to see those things. When Qutb was hanged and the movement went underground, everything seemed to die down. We thought it would all be forgotten. But when Mubarak became president, back in the 80s, he began to crack down on the Brotherhood again and it was all dredged up. We – your mother and I – decided that whatever happened, we would make sure you and Deena wouldn't have to grow up under the shadow of Bassam's name.'

'But you weren't involved! You don't even pray!' Inès burst out incredulously.

'No, but it's enough that my brother was a member. Your grandfather never knew the truth. He died thinking Bassam was a traitor; it broke your grandmother's heart. We were forbidden to speak of him, ever. But the state knew. There was always a question mark hanging over us, just as we knew there'd be one hanging over you. We were determined that you should have an education outside the country, away from it all, from the stigma that has followed the rest of us.'

'But why didn't ... why didn't Uncle Khalu leave? Is that why you ... why you don't get along sometimes?'

Her father sighed. 'Yes. He thought it was the wrong decision. An admission of guilt, if you like. He chose to stay behind and fight the system from within, not run away.'

'We didn't run away!' her mother burst in suddenly. 'We made the right decision. You know that, Ibrahim.'

'Yes, well ... there are times when I wonder,' her father said heavily. 'Look what's happened now.'

'It's not your fault, Abu,' Inès said indignantly.

'Perhaps not. But the two of you ... yes, you had a good education and I'm proud of you, you know I am. Yet when I compare you to your cousins ... married, with children, happy back at home ... I sometimes wonder. Did I make the right decision?'

Inès looked at her hands. Suddenly all kinds of things began to fall into place. Her father's moods, which had constituted the weather of most of their lives, were useless to quarrel with or fight against. They blew through the house like a cold wind, appearing out of nowhere, or so it seemed, dampening everything and everyone in their path. Whole days slipped by when even their mother couldn't elicit a 'good morning' from him and the only sound at mealtimes was the awkward clinking of cutlery and the noise of food being swallowed, as quietly as possible. Inès dreaded those days when he was 'down in the dumps', as their mother put it. He seemed to live in two worlds and there was no traffic between them, or none that the rest of the family could fathom. She began to fathom it now.

Her mother sighed heavily. 'It's been hard on you girls, I know. And I'm sorry for it. But it's been hardest on Deena. She's the most like Bassam, you know. From the minute she was born, we knew. The same determination. She always wants to do what's right. She was always the one to cry if one of the servant girls cut her finger, or if she saw a beggar in the street. We thought sending her here would help, ease her sense of injustice somehow.' She shook her head. 'I think it only made it worse.

Every holiday when you girls came home... the questions! *Why* is it like this? Why don't people have enough to eat? Why is that man beating his son? Why are the streets full of beggars? Why, why, *why*.'

Inès's eyes filled with tears. That was Deena all right. 'What d'you think has happened to her?' she whispered, almost not daring to say the words out loud.

'I don't know, *habibi*. But Uncle Khalu and I will find her. We weren't able to help Bassam when he needed it, but this time will be different. We won't let anything happen to Deena. *Mate'le-ish ya'binti, inshallah hanlei-iha*. We'll find her, my girl, don't you worry.'

To Inès, though, the words sounded hollow, merely an expression of hope; faith rather than fact. They brought her little comfort.

52

Jane flung open the door to her walk-in dressing room and stood peering into the abyss. What to wear. What *not* to wear. The evening stretched deliciously ahead. Drinks, followed by dinner. And Lexi's edict, of course, barked down the line from Heathrow, where she was waiting to board her flight. 'Whatever you do, *please* don't bring him home. *Not* on a first date.'

'But it's our second date. Technically speaking, I mean.'

'Trust me on this.'

'You're reading too much into it. He's ten years younger than me.'

'And your point is ...?'

'Well, what's *your* point?'

'OK, fine. Play it your way. Ring me tomorrow and tell me how it went.'

Jane put the phone down. It was fine for Lexi to talk. She had Mark. Although she wasn't sure it was possible to 'have' Mark, at least not in the conventional way. For all their closeness, he was impossible to pin down. There was something untouchable and unreachable about him, though he wasn't in the least bit aloof or cold ... more that there was a horizon in him that couldn't be crossed. Lexi was like that herself, though she hid it better. Perhaps that was why it worked. But there was no such horizon in Jane. She was desperate for the closeness that both Lexi and Mark seemed to shun. She longed for nothing more than the warmth that a new romance always seemed to promise. A new man, new possibilities, new directions.

She drew in a deep breath. *Stop it. It's a drink, followed by dinner. And he's on probation.* She tried saying it out loud. It sometimes worked. Not always, but sometimes.

Half an hour later, she was ready. A pair of dark blue Diesel jeans – the ones that promised to reshape a woman's derrière and redistribute lumps and bumps to give the optimum curvaceous impression. Unfortunately, there was no easy way of knowing what she looked like from the rear, but she poured herself into them anyway, hoping for the best. A champagne-coloured silk blouse with a ruffle at the neck, and a pair of delicate vintage earrings. She looked sexy and demure, yet grown-up. She picked up a fawn trench coat, slipped on her high-heeled black pumps and grabbed her bag and keys. She was ready.

She peered out of the cab window. 'D'you think this is it?' she asked the driver anxiously. They'd circled the block three times, looking for a sign, and she was now fifteen minutes late.

'No idea, love. Not much of a bar person, to be honest. It says Argyll Street, though, don't it?'

She paid and got out of the cab, and walked into the foyer. A doorman sprang to attention from behind a red velvet curtain, seemingly knowing where she was headed without her saying a word. 'Aqua Spirit? This way, ma'am,' he said, ushering her into the plush upholstered lift.

Phin seemed to know a thing or two about London bars, she thought as they whizzed smoothly upwards. She had no idea what they paid IT geeks these days, but he clearly had expensive tastes. The entrance was spectacular, all gleaming wooden surfaces, mirrored walls and thick, fluffy carpeting. The doorman pulled back a pair of giant ruby-red silk curtains and the bar and dining areas were revealed. An enormous circular bar took up most of the room, with a vast multicoloured glass chandelier hanging over it, sending thousands of rainbow-coloured reflections dancing around the space.

'Jane!' She turned. Phin was making his way towards her. She was struck once again by his height and his boyish good looks. He'd dressed up for the occasion too, she noticed. A dark blue suit with a pale grey shirt and dark tapered trousers. He looked good. Good enough to eat. 'You're here!' he said, with a smile as wide as his face. She stared at him. He couldn't be *that* pleased to see her, surely? 'I'm so glad you came. Have you been here before? Did you find it easily enough?' He seemed ridiculously nervous.

'You've got good taste,' she said, looking around. 'I've never even heard of it.'

'It's brand new. I spent the whole week thinking about where to take you. I asked a couple of mates—'

'You told your friends you were taking me out?' she interrupted him.

'Yeah. Why?'

She hesitated. He had an endearing openness that she'd forgotten a man could possess. There was no edge to him, as her mother would have said. No side. 'No reason,' she said firmly. She turned to look at the bar. 'So, how about a cocktail?' 'Excellent idea.' He picked up the drinks list. 'Shall I suggest something?'

'Go ahead. I'm in your hands.'

He actually blushed at that and she felt her stomach turn over, flip after slow, painful flip. 'Right,' he mumbled. 'They do some of the best cocktails in town. How about a Carrabbas?'

'Which is …?'

'Rum mixed with fruit liqueurs, fresh orange juice and cinnamon syrup,' he read from the menu. 'Too sweet?'

She nodded. 'Give me something with a bit of a bite. I like my cocktails sharp.' She snapped her teeth playfully and was amazed to see his face redden again.

'Japanese Velvet. Pear-infused vodka, nashi pear fruit, lemon grass and lemon juice. How's that sound?'

'Divine. Bring it on.'

Over dinner, she got the facts. Phineas Harman. Twenty-six years old. Born and raised in Fulton, a small village – 'more like a hamlet, really' – just outside Cambridge. Two older brothers, Barnabas and Tristam. His parents, both academics, were still alive and together, and lived in the same comfortable rectory that Phin had lived in all his life. When he went home, he went back to the room he'd grown up in. Like his brothers, cousins, father and grandfather before him, he'd gone to one of the better public schools, just outside Cambridge, and then, unlike Barnabas and Tristam and most of his forebears, had turned down a place at Cambridge and opted to study computers at Westminster University instead.

'Mum and Dad were horrified,' he confided chattily, spearing a piece of sushi and popping it into his mouth. 'Westminster wasn't exactly what they'd planned.'

'It's a good university,' Jane demurred.

'"But, darling, it used to be a *poly!*"' he mimicked, grinning. 'That's Mum talking. They're Oxbridge types. I enjoyed it, though. It was good to get away, get out of that orbit, y'know? And I like computers. Anyhow, that's enough about me. We've been talking about me all bloody night. Tell me something about you. Tell me something *important* about you.'

'Like what?' She didn't think she'd ever been the object of such interest to anyone before.

'Like ... I don't know. OK, what sort of pet did you have as a kid? A dog or a cat?'

'A cat,' she said, laughing.

'Thought so. What's your favourite pizza?'

'Quattro stagioni.'

He raised an eyebrow. 'New York or Berlin?'

'Both.'

'*X Factor* or *Strictly*?'

'Neither.'

'You know what?' he said, grinning. 'I'm beginning to like the sound of you.'

'Only just beginning?' she asked teasingly, and was rewarded with another blush. He was like an open book, she thought, both flattered and puzzled by the attention.

He got up suddenly. 'I'll be right back.' She watched him walk off, presumably in the direction of the toilets. She fished her mobile from her bag and quickly texted Lexi. *He's lovely. And I won't take him home. Not tonight, anyway, Jx.* She pressed 'send', smiling to herself. There was a single piece of *maki* roll left on the enormous white platter between them. She'd been so busy listening to him talk that she'd hardly eaten anything. She picked it up with her fingers, half guiltily, and popped it into her mouth. She was suddenly ravenous. She looked around for a waiter, and before she'd had time to even raise her hand, he'd appeared at her side.

Five minutes later, a fresh plate of succulent California rolls was laid in front of her, but there was no sign of Phin. A spasm of discomfort flitted across her face as she looked around. The bar area was packed with bright young things; girls with long blonde hair, perfect make-up, high-heeled shoes, tanned bare midriffs and flashing jewellery. She took a gulp of wine and helped herself to a roll. And then another. There was still no sign of him. Five minutes lengthened into ten, then fifteen. A tremor of worry rolled upwards through her stomach. Surely not? Not again?

Suddenly her mobile phone bleeped. It was a text message from Phin. Relieved, she opened it. *Daffy Duck calls reception for a condom. Receptionist asks, Shall I put this on your bill? Don't be thucking stupid. I'd thuffocate. Be there in 5! Sorry!* She frowned. It was the oddest text message she'd ever received. She read it again. She took another mouthful of wine, feeling distinctly uncomfortable. A few minutes later, Phin finally appeared. He hurried up to the booth.

'Sorry, sorry ... got held up. Did you get my text?'

'Er, yeah.'

'Good, isn't it?' He grinned at her. 'My flatmate sent it to me the other day. I just about killed myself laughing.'

Flatmate. Text jokes. Daffy Duck. The fact of his age suddenly hit her again. He was a *child*. He'd either stopped off on his way back from the toilets to chat or flirt with one of the long-legged blondes, or he'd gone to make a surreptitious phone call to his girlfriend. *This will go absolutely nowhere*, she thought, suddenly feeling deflated. 'Yeah. It's great,' she murmured. She looked around the bar. 'Look, I've got a pretty busy day tomorrow, Phin ... why don't we get the bill?'

'Tomorrow's Saturday,' he protested. 'You can't be serious.'

'I am, I'm afraid. Perks of the job.' She stood up.

He got to his feet awkwardly. 'You're not angry, are you?'

'Angry? Why on earth would I be angry?' she said, as lightly as she could.

'If it's about that joke I sent you—'

'Phin, don't be silly. Of course it's not about the joke. I've just got a lot on tomorrow, that's all. But *you* don't have to go. Why don't you hang around for a bit? Lots of talent here tonight.' She gestured at the girls clustered around the bar. 'Take your pick.' She picked up her bag, feeling unexpectedly close to tears.

He ran a hand through his hair, looking decidedly dejected. 'I shouldn't have sent you that stupid text. I'm sorry. You probably think it was childish.'

She shook her head. 'No ... it's not that.'

'Then what is it?'

She looked away. 'I ... I don't know, Phin. I mean, I'm more than ten years older than you!'

'So? Look, we get on, don't we? We have a good time together. You seem to enjoy my company and I really enjoy yours. Come on, what's the big deal? Let's just see how it goes. No pressure.'

She sighed and bit her lip. He was right. She *did* enjoy his company. He was fresh and funny and honest. He seemed kind. She glanced up at him. He looked so panicked that she put up a hand to touch his cheek. He caught it, and held it against his face. His skin was like fine sandpaper under her fingertips. It was an oddly sensual moment. They stood like that for a moment, looking at each other, neither saying a word, then he bent his head and very slowly, very gently, he kissed her. It was everything a kiss should be. Soft, tender, full of passionate promise. His hands went around her back, drawing her in. She hesitated, just for a second, then let herself fall, slowly and voluptuously, into the warmth of his embrace.

53

The lift was broken. Inès waited for a few minutes, then pushed open the door to the emergency stairwell. The sour smell of urine hit her as she began to climb, just as it had done the last time she came. She got out at the fifth floor, gratefully gulped down a few mouthfuls of fresh air, then walked along the gangway until she reached the door she sought. Number 15. She drew in a deep breath and knocked softly. There was no answer. She waited a few minutes and knocked again, harder this time. A few seconds passed. There was no answer, but she felt someone watching her, felt the weight of his gaze through the closed door. A small bubble of fear rose in her chest. She cleared her throat. It was up to her to announce herself.

'It's … my name is Inès. Inès Kenan. I'm Deena Kenan's sister and—'

The bolt was suddenly drawn. The door opened a crack, just enough to reveal a bearded man standing in the hallway. 'What do you want?' he asked in Arabic. His tone was neutral, neither friendly nor unfriendly.

She swallowed again. 'I'm … I'm alone,' she stammered. 'I was hoping you could … could help me. It's about Deena, my sister.'

'OK. Come in.' He held the door open for her. 'Quickly.'

She stepped into the dimly lit hallway. The sharp smell of cigarette smoke and something else – sweat? Tension? – hung in the air. The curtains were drawn, and although it was still light outside, the crisp freshness of the early summer's day had not made it past the front door. 'Thank you,' she murmured shyly.

'Go ahead.' He indicated the closed door in front of them that led to the sitting room where they'd gathered on her last visit. 'Go in.'

She pushed open the door. The room was full. Two young men she didn't recognise were seated at the desk at the window, staring at a computer. They looked up at her briefly, then back down at the screen again. In the corner of the room, a couple were arguing fiercely. They broke off as she entered. The woman looked at her, frowning. 'You're Deena's sister, aren't you?' she asked finally.

Inès nodded. 'Yes. I'm Inès.' She edged closer. 'I was just … I was hoping you might have heard from Deena. Anything at all. We … my parents and I … we've heard nothing.'

The woman got up suddenly. She was young and slight, Inès noticed, with dark eyes and hair covered by a patterned headscarf. She nodded at Inès. 'Come with me,' she said. 'Let's talk in the kitchen.'

Inès followed her into the corridor. She pushed open yet another door, that led into a small, tidy kitchen. There was a table by the window, with two chairs. 'Have a seat,' she said, pulling one out. 'Would you like some tea?' She was not Egyptian, Inès could tell from her accent, though she couldn't have said exactly where she *was* from.

'No, thanks. I … I just want to know … have you heard anything?'

'I'm Huda, by the way,' the woman said, switching on the kettle. 'I worked with Deena last year.'

'At the hospital?' Inès asked in some surprise. She looked too young to be a qualified doctor.

Huda shook her head. 'No, on the campaign. I'm from Bahrain.'

Inès was silent. By now she knew better than to ask questions. Each day seemed to bring a fresh set of revelations about the people closest to her. 'Have you heard from them?' she asked.

Huda nodded. 'We know where she's been taken,' she said slowly, 'but nothing more, unfortunately. We've got someone on the inside who's keeping us informed, but the government's shut down the internet several times in the past couple of days. It's not easy for him to get word out.'

Relief flooded over her like a crashing tidal wave. 'So … she's … she's all right?' She couldn't bring herself to utter the word 'alive'. To say it out loud would be to give shape to a fear that was so great it was unnameable, unpronounceable.

'Yes,' Huda said gently. 'She's alive. We don't know what her situation is, if she's going to be charged, or even when … but she's alive, thank God. She's got a British passport. It's too risky, even for them.' There was no mistaking the contempt in her voice.

Inès watched her making the tea, marvelling at her composure. 'How … how can I get in touch with you again?' she asked.

Huda reached for her phone. 'Give me your number. I'll call you if we hear anything. But please don't mention this place to anyone.' She gestured at the flat and the surroundings. 'Anyone at all. Not even your parents.'

'I won't,' Inès promised. She watched as Huda tapped in her number. Somehow, the visit had reassured her. There seemed to be so much about her sister she didn't know – or hadn't wanted to know, perhaps – but one thing was clear: whoever the group was to whom Deena belonged, they were utterly dedicated to one another, and to their cause. Whatever else, her sister wasn't alone. 'Thank you,' she said, her throat thickening with tears.

'*Mate'le-ish.*' *Don't worry*. Huda reached across the table and touched Inès's forearm lightly. '*Insha'Allah*, everything will be OK.'

Inès nodded automatically. Not for the first time, she wished she had some of the group's unwavering belief. Just like the night before, she wanted desperately to believe that Deena's safe return was a matter of fact, not faith.

54

Seven days. One hundred and sixty-eight hours, give or take. *Ten thousand and eighty minutes.* His mind baulked at calculating the seconds, though in truth it would give him something to do. He lay on the narrow bed in the room on the third floor that doubled as his bedroom and the medicine store, and stared at the ceiling, exactly the way he'd done every day since the day he'd come back to find Deena gone, Christos Pitsillides dead in the hallway and the young French doctor turned hysterical with fear. In that maddening way of time stretched to breaking point with waiting, his mind spooled backwards and forwards, sideways and straight, looping between past and present until he was no longer sure which was which.

It had been almost twenty years since he'd last seen Deena Kenan. He wouldn't have recognised her if he'd passed her in the street, but her voice and mannerisms remained the same. The same sideways flick of the head; the same lack of guile. When she'd presented herself to him in the clinic that first morning, there'd been no indication whatsoever that she was trying to make an impression. He remembered that about her immediately. She had no understanding of the need to please. Her clothes were uninteresting, but in spite of it, a strong physical presence remained. Those dark eyes, drops of clarity in a smooth, olive-tinged face; the glossy accent of her eyebrows, which appeared smooth and refined, not plucked into some awkwardly fashionable shape like so many of the women he knew. She'd stood there with her head balanced carefully upright, no trace of coquetry when she spoke to him or listened. She was either so open or so self-possessed that nothing could shake her – same thing, really. After a month, he knew he was in trouble. After four months, her presence had shaken him to his very core. And then he'd come back that afternoon to find her gone.

Seven days now, and counting. He felt her absence more keenly than he could ever have imagined. It wasn't just the calm she brought to their working lives. In the four months they'd worked side by side, thinking, breathing, operating together as one, he'd come to rely on her in ways he'd never expected. There were times when, looking at her across the inert body of a patient, he would catch her gaze upon him and it would seem to him as if she were trying to see past him, through him, right through to the person he sought to hide. As if she were not only aware of who he really was, but of why he'd chosen not to reveal it. Absurd, really. She had no more idea of his real identity than she did of Aiden's.

He shifted uncomfortably in the narrow bed. *Seven days and counting.* He had no one to turn to, no one to ask. His position amongst the doctors he worked with was precarious enough. No one other than Patrice, his immediate boss at MSF HQ in Geneva, knew who he was. Lieutenant Colonel Níall Stewart, RAMC, attached to the Royal Anglian Battalion since 2007 in Helmand Province, was now known as Dr Neil Stuart, a specialist in conflict medicine and emergency surgery. During his tenure at Camp Bastion, there was little he hadn't seen. Nothing shocked him. No injuries, no matter how gruesome, ever rocked the smooth professional exterior. Death was an accepted and acceptable fact of his everyday working life. He went where he was sent, did what he was ordered to do and that was the end of it. Until the day he heard his estranged brother's voice on the radio – completely out of the blue – and walked straight into his superior's office requesting a leave of absence. After some wrangling, it was agreed. Lieutenant Colonel Stewart was simply too valuable a surgeon to be allowed to quit. He flew out of Helmand on a Hercules bound for Brize Norton, and three days later he was in Geneva, interviewing with Médecins Sans Frontières, with whom he'd been ever since.

His leave of absence period came and went; to his superiors' dismay, he resigned from his army commission and elected to stay on at MSF, voluntarily deciding to carry on in Egypt. No one, least of all those who worked alongside him, knew anything of the turmoil that welled beneath his calm exterior, flammable, like oil. He spoke Arabic, French and English and could be counted on to display the utmost impartiality when it came to treating civilians, police and soldiers alike. He took no sides, expressed no political opinion, angered no one. To Patrice he was a godsend, a saviour in a time of extreme need. To his colleagues he was cold but compassionate, and competent in the extreme. And to Deena Kenan? He didn't know what he was to her. Only what she was to him. And now she was gone. He had no idea where, or even if she were still alive. There was only one person in the entire world he could turn to, and although the very thought of it made him sick to his stomach, not knowing where she was or *how* she was made him sicker still.

He pushed aside the cover and swung his legs out of bed, reaching automatically for the cigarettes that lay on the windowsill. He stepped out on to the tiny balcony and lit one, watching the light come up through the clouds, staining the horizon pink. He saw Deena as if she were in front of him, looking at her dark, shining eyes, her mouth with the beginnings of her most habitual expression forming at the corners of her upturned lips. Her features swam before him.

The garden in Zamalek. Bougainvillea, pink potted roses, tall swaying palms. The mothers, sitting at the spindly-legged table on which teacups and plates of sticky, sweet baklava had been set, gossiping comfortably as their offspring ran around the dense, jungle-thick garden. Umm Soraya calling for them. Inas. Dafiyah. Aiden and Niall. The only people he knew who belonged to that same half-world that he and Aiden occupied, neither one thing nor the other. Not Egyptian, not English. Not entirely at home in either place, either language, either culture. Two boys, two girls. One for each. Deena. Inès. Aiden. Himself. A circle with no beginning and no end.

It took him a few minutes to work out why his cheeks were suddenly wet.

55

The man sitting opposite her took off his glasses. Holding them delicately between thumb and forefinger, he polished them with precise, careful movements before settling them back on his plump, jowly face. There was no sound in the office other than the rattle of the air-conditioner. She swallowed as quietly as she could. Mark was outside in the corridor, pacing up and down, probably chain-smoking. Predictably, he'd been refused permission to enter the room with her. Lexi didn't care. After two days of relentless questioning, she'd finally inched her way up the command chain, and if it meant she had to go in alone, so be it. She wasn't about to pass up the opportunity.

'So, Mrs Sturgis,' the police chief said finally, sarcastically emphasising the 'Mrs'. 'What can we do for you?' His English was good, but the undertone of suppressed menace in his voice made Lexi's skin break out in goose bumps. She'd been around men like him countless times during her working life, but there was something deeply sinister about his soft-spoken reserve. She thought about the way he'd polished his glasses, and watched him stroke his luxuriant moustache with thick, hairy fingers. The sleeves of his uniform were rolled back to reveal stocky, muscular forearms. The contrast between his obvious bodily strength and the delicate, almost feminine gestures was unsettling. She looked at his hands, and for a split second, she had an image of them working their way over some young woman's body, inflicting the most unimaginable pain in the most intimate way. She brought herself up sharply. He would smell the fear on her, she knew. He was the type.

'*Miss* Sturgis,' she corrected him, hoping her voice was steady. 'It's about Dr Kenan. Deena Kenan. Your guards seemed—'

'*Enti bitisali alla el bint Kenan?*' He interrupted her, addressing the men behind her. They all laughed. 'You're asking about that silly Kenan girl?' He turned his attention back to her. 'Mrs Sturgis, I can't tell you anything about her.'

His unctuous manner was too much for Lexi. 'But my sources tell me she was last seen being taken into *your* custody!' she snapped. 'Come on, she can't just have vanished into thin air! The British government won't rest until they find out where she is. You *know* that.'

It was a mistake. He stopped stroking his moustache. Suddenly his finger shot out, jabbing at the air between them. Lexi made an involuntary move backwards. The sound of her chair scraping against the tiled floor made her shudder. 'Don't presume to threaten me, Mrs Sturgis,' he said coldly. 'Your government has nothing to do with this. She's an Egyptian and this is an internal matter. You have no jurisdiction here, none whatsoever. Now leave. I have many more important things to do. Much more important than another one of those traitorous Kenans.'

'But—'

'*Leave*, Mrs Sturgis, or I'll have you removed.'

Lexi stood up. It wasn't clear whether he was referring to his office or the country – not that it mattered. There was nothing further to be gleaned. He knew where Deena was, Lexi was sure of it. But he wasn't about to divulge anything. Not to her, or anyone else. She knew when she was beaten. She picked up her bag and made her way to the door under the watchful gaze of the two guards, whose expressions behind their dark sunglasses couldn't be glimpsed at or understood. Mark whirled round as soon as the door opened and looked her up and down anxiously. Together they hurried down the corridor, not speaking until they were on the ground floor, with the safety of the exit in sight.

'So? Did you get anywhere?' he asked as they burst out into the sunlight.

Lexi shook her head. 'He knows where she is but he's not about to tell *me* anything. He keeps referring to her as "that silly Kenan girl", in the present tense, which means at least she's still alive.'

'So what do we do now?'

'Let's go and see Ahmad. I've got a few questions for him.'

'Lexi!' Giovanna answered the door with a smile as wide as the Nile. 'And Mark! Come in, come in! Oh, it's so *good* to see you! We never know who's going to drop by these days ... police, friends, family, secret service. Come in, come in!'

'I should've called,' Lexi said apologetically. 'We got in a couple of days ago. I should have let you know sooner, but you know what it's like.'

'I do, I do. Welcome.' Giovanna kissed them both as though they were old friends. 'Ahmad's not in. He's at his brother's. I'll call him. He'll be so pleased to see you!'

'Is he busy?'

Giovanna laughed. 'They're always busy. Busy talking, planning, dreaming. But not working, not earning *money*.' She gave an exaggerated sigh. 'But what can I do? I didn't just marry him, I married *all* of it!' She threw her arms out to encompass not just the beautiful old flat, but the whole of Cairo and Egypt beyond. She laughed. 'Will you have coffee? An espresso?'

Lexi nodded gratefully. 'Just what we need after spending the morning at the Central Security Forces,' she said with a heartfelt sigh.

Giovanna raised an eyebrow. 'I'll just give Ahmad a ring and let him know you're here,' she said, moving towards the kitchen. 'Tómas is asleep, thank God. He won't wake before four. There's plenty of time.'

*

The coffee was sharp and fragrant, the flavour curling its way around her tongue, flooding her mouth with its heady aroma. She drank it slowly, savouring each mouthful, her mind drifting back to the conversation that morning. Across the room, Giovanna changed Tómas's nappy. In another world, an ordinary, everyday domestic scene.

When Ahmad arrived home, he kissed Lexi gravely on both cheeks and gave Mark a bear hug, then walked over to his wife, gazing down at Tómas as if he'd never seen him before. For a brief moment, the chaos outside ceased to exist.

'So,' he said, accepting a cup from Giovanna and turning to Lexi. 'What's new out there? How're things?' It was a rhetorical question. His face bore the weary expression of one who has seen too much.

'Difficult. You know why we're here?'

'You mean, aside from watching us tear ourselves apart?' He said it with a wry smile. 'It's happening everywhere. Yemen, Libya, Syria, Bahrain … you name it. We've started something that can't be stopped, but they're doing their best to stop us. They're cracking down everywhere. And what do we do? We just fight amongst ourselves.'

'It's a stage, though, isn't it? That's what good old political theory tells us.'

'Fuck political theory. This is *us*, Lexi. This is our life – our lives – and we're destroying each other and everything we fought for. It's a fucking mess!'

'Ahmad,' Giovanna said gently, pointing at Tómas.

Ahmad laughed bitterly. 'As if he can understand, Gio! Maybe it's better he does. Maybe by the time he's old enough to say "fuck", we'll have sorted it all out. Ah, I wish I had the answers. I wish *somebody* had the answers. So what's your angle this time?' he asked Lexi, swallowing his coffee in one gulp.

'Actually, I'm here looking for Deena Kenan. The missing doctor. I've just been to see Colonel Mahmoud at the CSF.'

'You went to the CSF? In Darassa? When?' Ahmad's voice rose incredulously.

'This morning.'

'Lexi, are you insane?'

'Well, where else was I supposed to start? That's the last place she was seen.'

'The CSF!' Ahmad shook his head, half in disbelief, half in admiration. 'Even *I* wouldn't go there.'

'Come on, what're they going to do to *me*?'

'You don't want to know, that's the whole point. Look, they've got Deena. I'm sure you already know all this. Her uncle was one of Sadat's most famous arrests, and the suspicion here, of course, is that she's the same. Maybe not an Israeli spy, but working for one of the foreign intelligence agencies at any rate. Britain, America, France ... take your pick.'

'But why? She's done nothing wrong,' Lexi pointed out quickly. 'She's a doctor, for crying out loud.'

'It's more than that. They're an interesting bunch, the Kenans. It's not a typical Egyptian name. They're one of those old Ottoman families, you know? Arrived in Alexandria after the war with Russia, God knows how or when. No one knows where they originated. Some say Turkey, others Armenia, Austria, Greece. When her uncle was arrested, there was a rumour going round that the family name was actually "Cohen". Who knows? All I can tell you is that the family have a long history of switching sides. I think the general consensus here, at least amongst government, is that Deena is exactly the same.'

Lexi stared at him. 'That's ridiculous,' she said finally. 'I've met her sister. That's not the family of a spy.'

'How would you know?' Ahmad asked irritably. 'What makes you so sure?'

Lexi hesitated. She could feel Mark's eyes on her. Ahmad was staring at her, frowning, as if he knew what she was about to say. She took a deep breath and then let it out slowly. Her mouth opened on the words. 'Because I come from one.'

56

They walked past the families crowded together on the ground floor and the waiters, gliding gracefully between tables. It wasn't their habit, but they were holding hands. She felt his calloused palm against hers. He found a table by the window and pulled out the chair for her. There was an odd formality between them that hadn't existed before.

'What'll you have?' he asked, looking over the menu. 'No wine, I'm afraid.'

'I'd need something stronger, in any case. I'll have a coffee. Arabic.'

He ordered for both of them and then turned to her. He slid his hand across the table and took hers again. 'You said to me once that you weren't worth analysing, d'you remember?'

She nodded slowly, unsure of what he was about to say. 'I'm not.'

'I'm not interested in analysing you, Lexi. I just want to *know* you. Properly. There's a difference. You tell me next to nothing about yourself ... just a few bare facts, trivial things, inconsequential things. I put together some sort of picture of you from the bits and pieces you let drop and I think I've more or less got a handle on who you are. And then you go and drop a bombshell like this one ... What am I supposed to do with that?'

She swallowed. 'I ... I just don't like talking about it, that's all.'

He laughed shortly and shook his head. 'I'm not talking about what your father did for a living. Who cares if he worked for MI5? I'm talking about what it meant to you. What was it like growing up like that? What did it *do* to you?'

Lexi looked away. Her eyes were suddenly blurry with tears. 'I'm not the one who—' She stopped. Her hands were shaking.

'Who what?'

There was a long, painful silence. Lexi opened her mouth several times but couldn't manage to get the words out. 'I ... I ... had a brother,' she said finally, her voice almost a whisper.

'What happened to him?' Mark's eyes didn't leave her face.

She took another deep breath. 'He's dead. He killed himself. B-because of him, my father. And because I wasn't there for him.'

'Tell me what happened, Lexi. Just *tell* me.'

PART TEN

1991–1998

57

Currents blew through that house, fresh as those that brought the storms off the oceans in the various cities around the world in which the Sturgises lived. They'd been to the coast once – to Beira, a seaside town in Mozambique, a day and a half's drive from Lusaka. She remembered the holiday still. It was perhaps the last time she'd seen her parents speak to one another aside from the commands that in that house took the place of conversation. *Pass the salt. Is there no butter? Ask your mother where the girl's put the whisky*. On the long drive to the sea, she and Toby sat in the back, the soft, warm shape of Anna sandwiched between them, playing I Spy and hilariously mispronouncing the unfamiliar names they encountered, mile after mile. *Lusaka–Harare–Mutare–Chimoio–Lamego–Mafambiasse–Beira*. 'Harare–Mutare! Harare–Mutare!' Toby shouted incessantly until he was told to belt up.

The beach, with its line of wavering tamarisks and the crescent of pale sand that curved around the headland, was sufficiently new and exciting to be viewed as a place of resurrection: laughter, childish games and the absence of rules that marked out all holidays. But the holiday was long since past, and whatever truce had been in place, intended or accidental, was gone. Now it was back to open warfare, fights in the night and in the daytime, angry, barked-out commands.

She'd always known the stark truth of her family, always. Her father loved her mother above all else, above everyone, including his own children. Always had, always would. It was no wonder, either. Her mother was beautiful, astonishingly, extraordinarily so. Kitty Cowan was one of two daughters whose looks surprised everyone, including their own parents. Neither could be said to be anything other than ... well, ordinary. The Cowans were resolutely upper middle class. James Cowan was an accountant, like his father and grandfather before him; Jean, his wife, was a homemaker. The arrival and care of the two beauties they'd produced together took up every moment of her waking day. The girls were shepherded carefully through the various phases of their lives – childhood, teenage years, boarding school, finishing school and secretarial college – comfortably certain of making good matches. Neither lacked for anything, except perhaps Julia for her sister's affection, which Kitty manipulatively withheld. When Kitty met Matthew Sturgis, the dashing young marine who was thinking of applying to the Foreign and Commonwealth Office, her parents were horrified. Working class? With no background to speak of? It wasn't the match they'd planned.

Kitty was adamant. They eloped. A funny, faintly old-fashioned term for the manner in which the nineteen-year-old, already three months pregnant, walked into the Kensington and Chelsea Town Hall and married her marine. The pregnancy didn't hold; neither did the subsequent ones. Kitty despaired. Matthew threw himself into work, showing an aptitude for languages that pushed him up the Foreign Office's notoriously greasy pole. After he'd mastered German, Russian and French, MI6 came knocking. The postings followed quickly: Berlin, Sofia, Belgrade and Helsinki. By the time Alexandra finally arrived, some ten years later, the marriage had long since started to crack.

When Lexi was six, a second child, Tobias, was born. A surprise to both parents, for all sorts of reasons, not least the fact that they no longer slept together, except for the odd, rare occasion when they were both drunk … which was precisely what had happened. Or at least that was what Matthew chose to believe. By then they were in Singapore, on their first Far East posting. It was common knowledge amongst the expat community that Kitty Sturgis was 'fast'. Fast and loose. Loose and fast.

'Mum?' asked Lexi one day, home from the school she attended a mile and a half down the road from their small but picturesque house in Bukit Timah. Her ayah, Lucy, walked there with her, to and fro, leaving Kitty to do whatever it was she did during the day. One-year-old Toby had his own ayah, Soon, who looked after him from morning till night.

Kitty was fixing herself a drink. Lexi watched as she expertly cracked the steel ice tray and plopped two cubes into an already fizzing glass. She left the tray in the sink, cut a thick slice off a lemon, throwing the rest of it in the sink too, and turned to her daughter. She took a long, hard gulp. Lexi could hear the liquid going down her throat. 'What?' she said impatiently. She was on her way out. Lexi could see her bag and car keys sitting on the console by the door.

'What's a whore?' Lexi asked innocently.

Two bright spots of colour blossomed on Kitty's cheeks. Her eyes narrowed. She put down her drink. 'Where did you hear that?' she asked, and her voice was dangerously quiet. Lexi began to wish she hadn't opened her mouth.

'N-nowhere,' she stammered, tracing an invisible circle on the ground with her foot. She didn't want to look up.

'Answer me, you little liar! Where did you hear that word? Did someone say it about me?'

Lexi shook her head mutely. There was an angry, tense silence. She could hear her mother take gulp after gulp. Then Kitty bent down so that her face was on a level with Lexi's. 'Listen to me,' she said, and her breath was lemony and sharp. 'They're just jealous, that's all. Every single one of them.'

Lexi tried not to look at her. Something was being said that wasn't just about the word she'd overheard, but at five, she was too young to grasp it. It had something to do with the fights between her parents and the way her mother left the house at night, sometimes not returning until the early hours of the morning. Lexi knew, because her mother's headlights would sweep round the walls of her bedroom as she turned into the driveway, often at dawn. 'OK,' she mumbled. She looked quickly into her mother's face, inches from her own, and saw with fascination something in it that she thought could never happen in an adult's face – the fear of being caught out. Her mother tried to pass off the instant, alert wariness as indifference, but she'd been trapped. They stared at each other for a moment, but it was her mother who was forced to drop her gaze and turn away.

'I'm going to play tennis,' she said quickly. 'Tell Lucy to make you something simple for supper. I don't want you getting fat.'

Somehow Lexi understood the comment – something that was about as likely as being struck by lightning – as a way for her mother to momentarily claw back the authority she'd just conceded. She said nothing and watched Kitty grab her bag, the colour high in her cheeks, and flounce out of the front door. Without her tennis racket, either.

She looked over towards the corner of the living room, where Toby lay in his cot. Soon was in the kitchen, preparing his lunch. She wandered over and looked down at him. In that placid, knowing way of his, he stared back at her, his dark-brown eyes as unfathomable as the night sky. There was depth there, and light and understanding, too, but it was always unspoken, unvoiced. At least she'd had the dubious benefit of some of their mother's attention as a child, however fleeting it might have been. Toby had had none. She couldn't remember the last time she'd seen her mother even pick him up, much less cuddle him. He seemed to know it; he made so few demands on her attention. It hurt Lexi terribly to think of Toby as unloved or unwanted, and it made her lavish attention on him in a way that, even at five, she knew wasn't altogether normal. But no one seemed to notice, much less say anything. Soon and Lucy just looked blankly at her when she crushed him fiercely against her chest, smothering him with kisses and cooing into his silent, placid little face. That was their house all over. A house where there was lots of noise – doors slamming, voices raised, the radio playing too loudly in the background – but no one ever said a thing.

58

She forced herself upright, her heart beating fast against the thin cotton of her pyjamas. She clutched the sheet in one hand. Across from her, perched awkwardly on the edge of the bed, sat her father, his whole body slumped with defeat. She'd never seen him like this. He looked up, and his gaze slid past her to the window that looked out on to the driveway. The driveway along which her mother had sped, leaving them all behind.

'I've discussed it with Julia,' he said. 'It's decided. It'll be the best thing.'

Lexi forced herself back to the present, to what he was saying. She felt his attention momentarily down the side of her body. 'Wh-what?' she stammered.

'For Julia to take you. And Toby,' he added hastily. 'She knows the schools you'll like.'

'School?'

'Yes, boarding school. It's all been decided. You'll stay with her in the holidays. Anna's young, Lexi. She can't be expected … it wouldn't be fair to her, you do see that, don't you?'

Lexi struggled to follow him. Anna? What did Anna have to do with it? 'But ...'

At last he looked away from the window. He was silently pleading with her, she saw, not to make a fuss. Not to ask questions. To do as she was told. Even now, when their whole world was tumbling around them, the important things – the real truths – were left unsaid. She felt a fierce stabbing in her chest that took the form of bewilderment, but was, in fact, the beginning of her longing for, and terrible drive towards, the truth. 'Now?' she asked, her voice suddenly cold and hard. 'When d'you want us to leave? Now?'

'No, it's not like that, Lexi. It's just ... it'll be better—'

'When?' she asked flatly.

His eyes came to rest full upon hers. She'd won, she saw. There was fear in them now, not just of Kitty and the mess she'd left behind, but of her. An eleven-year-old girl. He dropped his gaze. 'Soon ... just as soon as we can get things organised. Aunt Julia's waiting for you ... at home.'

She nodded. Everyone knew, anyway. It would be a surprise to Toby, of course, but it would be up to her to break the news in a way that he could handle. It would take the form of a story, an adventure of sorts ... something with a happy ending, of course. It was the only way he could manage. 'Fine.' She slid her legs down underneath the sheet and turned her back. The discussion – if it could be called that – was over. As was their life as they knew it. From now on, it was her and Toby, no one else.

Aunt Julia met them at Gatwick Airport on a cold and rainy November morning. Rain sluiced down from a leaden sky that looked as though it might fall on them at any moment. The High Commission had arranged for someone to accompany them on the flight. At the arrivals hall their aunt bent her head awkwardly to kiss Toby, but Lexi was already gone, striding impatiently ahead. She had begun to torment herself with what she called 'the hard facts'. *One*, she would never again see the woman whose name she'd declined to remember. What was the point of pretending she was sorry to see her go? *Two*, Aunt Julia had been forced against her will into taking them in. What was the point of her pretending she was pleased to see them? *Three*—

'Is that all you've brought with you, Lexi?' Aunt Julia said, interrupting her. 'Just the one suitcase? Surely not?'

'Yes, that's all.'

'All right. Then we'll go shopping together tomorrow. That'll be fun, won't it?'

'No.'

'Come along, children.' Aunt Julia swept them both up in her gaze. She talked all the way to the grand, shiny black car driven by a man in a stiff peaked cap, much the same way they'd been driven around in Lusaka, only the driver here was an Englishman called Mr Wigglesworth. Lexi and Toby giggled over his name. Aunt Julia talked all the way into London too. She had a series of bright, carefully authoritative answers to Toby's hundred and one questions. Lexi was quiet. Adults talked. They talked all through childhood, saying nothing. A monologue without end.

59

London

On another blustery November morning, twelve years later, Lexi wandered into the kitchen of the house she shared with Ruth and Maxine, two students she'd met on her Master's course at Goldsmith's. It was a small, cosy two-bedroom place at the wrong end of St Mark's Road, one of a row of terraced houses on a Peabody estate. Lexi and Maxine had a room each; Ruth, who paid a little less, occupied the sitting room. The kitchen, at the rear of the house, doubled as their living room. The back door opened on to a garden that hadn't seen a scythe or lawnmower in a decade – it was an overgrown tangle of brambles and long grass that no one looked at, let alone bothered to tend. The landlord, a cheerful Greek Cypriot whom everyone called Johnny, came round once a month to collect the rent. In cash. 'No cheques, girls, no way. I'm a strictly cash business. Only way to operate.' The rent was considerably cheaper than they'd have found anywhere else in the area, so no one complained, although Aunt Julia commented acerbically that Ladbroke Grove wasn't quite what she'd had in mind when she recommended west London.

Ruth looked up from the pot of something unidentifiable that she was busy stirring. 'Oh, hi. Your brother rang again, by the way. Said it's urgent and can you call him back today?'

Lexi's heart sank. 'OK, thanks. What's that?' she asked, pointing to the pot.

'Vegetable curry, can't you tell? You in tonight?'

Lexi nodded. 'Yeah, I've got an essay to finish for tomorrow. I've been putting it off for weeks.'

'I know what you mean. Stay and have a bowl with us. Maxine's bringing a bottle of red. She's on her way.'

Lexi looked dubiously at the contents of the pot. 'Maybe. I'll … I'll just go and ring Toby. I'll see you later.'

'I'll save you some,' Ruth sang out cheerfully, undeterred.

'Thanks,' Lexi called back weakly as she closed the door to her room. She eyed the telephone beside her bed. She ought to call Toby. She really should. She just didn't feel like it. Their conversations were always so fraught. He'd rung the other night with a string of questions that still made her frown.

'So you don't think it's odd?' he'd said, lowering his voice as though he was afraid he might be overheard.

'What?'

'That he retired so early. He was forty-two. No one retires at that age!'

'Well, he did.'

'Yes, but doesn't it make you wonder?'

'No, Toby, it doesn't. I don't really think about him at all, to be honest,' she said warily. It was the one topic guaranteed to end in an argument. Toby was convinced their father was a spy. Lexi couldn't have cared less. She wished Toby would just let it go, let everything go. He'd gone from being an unhappy, insecure child to a deeply angry young man, and she didn't know how to deal with him, or make things better. He was in his first year at art college in Brighton, studying film, and he saw conspiracies everywhere. Lately he'd been getting more and more agitated when she refused to be drawn in.

'You should, Lexi. He's your father.'

'He's your father too,' she pointed out mildly, but the comment only served to annoy him further.

'Why d'you make a joke out of everything I say?' he asked crossly.

'I'm not making a joke out of it,' she sighed. 'I just don't think about him, that's all. Did you have classes today?'

'Don't try and change the subject.'

'I'm not. Look, I'd better go, Tobes. I've got an essay to hand in and—'

'Fine,' he snapped, and hung up, just like that. She'd stared at the receiver for a few minutes, then shrugged. She did have an essay to finish and his distinctly odd line of questioning wouldn't lead anywhere other than an argument ... and she just didn't feel up to it. Now she looked at the phone guiltily. She ought to ring him. She really ought to. But she didn't.

She was walking from the library to the lecture hall through the cloisters the following afternoon when she saw Maxine running towards her. There was a look on Maxine's face that made her stop. Maxine had a mobile phone; Lexi didn't. She was holding it out as she reached her, breathless with agitation. 'Lexi ... Lexi ... it's Ruth. She's at home. You'd better go.'

'Go where?'

'Home. Y-you've got to go home.'

'Why?'

'Y-your aunt ... your aunt's th-there.' Maxine's teeth were chattering. 'You've got to go.'

'Why?' Lexi asked again, a cold, horrid feeling of dread slowly making its way up through her stomach. She hadn't known that fear could be cold.

'I-I don't know.' They both knew Maxine was lying. She put out a hand to touch Lexi, but Lexi was already gone.

Aunt Julia was in Ruth's room, the living-room-that-was-a-bedroom, when she finally got there. She stood up as soon as Lexi walked in. She was wearing a light blue suit – a stylish boxy jacket and an above-the-knee skirt. Her slim, tanned legs were bare. It was November, but Aunt Julia had just come back from her summer holiday, wherever it had been. Lexi tried to focus on the details as if they might stall whatever it was she was about to say.

'Lexi. Oh Lexi, darling.' To Lexi's horror, the two cleft lines on either side of Aunt Julia's nose deepened and she began to cry.

'Wh-what is it ... who ... is it Toby?'

Aunt Julia nodded wordlessly. Out of the corner of her eye Lexi could see Ruth's shocked expression. 'D-darling, we've been trying to reach you all day,' Aunt Julia said, her voice wavering unaccustomedly.

'I ... I was at college. I had a lecture first thing in the morning and then I was in the library.' It seemed important to establish exactly where she'd been.

'I know, I know. It … it happened this morning, darling. Just after nine. The police called me.'

Lexi turned to her open-mouthed flatmate. 'Ruth, would you mind leaving us alone?' Ruth fled without a word. Lexi turned and found that her legs could no longer carry her. She sat down heavily at Ruth's desk. She put her hands up to her ears, but no amount of pressing against them could blot out what Aunt Julia went on to say.

It was a simple ceremony. The vicar, an avuncular, kindly-looking man with the face of one who had seen it all, spoke well. 'As we reflect on Toby's life, it is all too easy to dwell on the last few weeks and months. But today we need to remember all of that life.'

Lexi listened to the words without taking them in. Her mind was full of Toby. Of his expressions. His turns of phrase. *Harare–Mutare!* She looked around guiltily as though she had spoken out loud. *Tell me a story, Lexi. But make it a good one. Make it one with a happy ending.* She'd obliged him all the way through their childhood, but the truth of it was there was no happy ending, not for Toby.

At approximately seven thirty on a sunny but chilly morning, he'd gone down to the beach at Hove, a couple of miles west of Brighton. According to a statement given by someone passing by, he'd walked into the sea fully clothed. At first the passer-by hadn't paid him much attention: Brighton was full of young people doing odd things, especially in the first few weeks of term. The stranger, whose name Lexi immediately forgot, as though she wanted no part of him, was walking his dog. He stopped as the animal peed against a lamp post, and that was when he noticed the head bobbing up and down in the waves, already quite far out. He watched for a few minutes, wondering if he ought to call someone. He didn't have a phone, though, and the nearest phone box had been vandalised. He saw the figure once more, flung high by the waves, and it occurred to him that something was seriously wrong. He stopped another dog-walker who did have a phone. Together they called the police. But it was too late.

The passer-by stayed on the beach until the body was brought back in. Accidental death by drowning. A NUS card was found in his wallet, still tucked safely inside the back pocket of his jeans. It took the police just over two hours to contact the university. Neither of the young man's parents appeared on any university register. They failed to reach his sister, Alexandra Sturgis, Tobias Sturgis's appointed next-of-kin, but there was a legal guardian listed, Julia Mahon.

It was left to Aunt Julia to break the news to Lexi.

PART ELEVEN

July–September 2011

60

'I was supposed to take care of him,' Lexi said flatly. 'It was just me and Toby and I was supposed to look after him and I didn't. I'm the strong one. Toby wasn't strong. That was the difference between us. That's what matters. In the end, I didn't look after him the way I was supposed to. I let him down.'

It's not your fault. That was the conventional line offered in situations such as this one. But not him. He didn't say it; he couldn't. He made no routine murmur of protestation, offered no platitudes of sympathy. He saw how an emotion she couldn't identify came over her. She put her arms around his waist and buried her head in his chest, taking the scent and feel of him deep into her body. He caught the longing and misery coming off her skin like a vibration, a faint buzz or a film of sweat. His own head was a jumbled mass of emotion.

The gun ... where's the fucking gun? On the floor, now covered in two sets of prints. Someone is screaming. Is it him, or his father, trousers still around his ankles, literally caught with his pants down? On the bed is Tumaini, or what's left of her. He's seen death before, of course. Animals: dogs, game, birds ... usual stuff. But never a human being, never that. The funny thing is, apart from the red stain spreading outwards from her chest, she looks exactly the same as she always did.

Those eyes – huge, dark, unfathomable – staring blindly from underneath the mound of his father's huge, flabby body; the eyes of a child who has been catapulted out of childhood into a place of adult desires and pain. He knows he won't be able to explain to anyone just what it is about seeing those eyes that fills him with a rage so clean, so pure, there's only one option. He has to kill him.

He backs away, crossing the landing to the tall cupboard where the guns are kept, and opens the glass door. The little key – stupidly, the prosecution say later – is hanging beside the cabinet. He takes out the handgun, the Walther

P88, checks that it's loaded, and walks back to the bedroom. He's still on top of her, heaving and grunting. She lies there, not moving, her thin dark legs propped ridiculously around his bulk. He shoves his whole weight into her, grabbing at her legs, which would otherwise have fallen away. She makes a sound; she's seen him. His father stops suddenly, abruptly, halfway to his twisted satisfaction, and turns … and it all seems to happen at once. The scream, the sound of the bedsprings creaking and the thud as someone's feet hit the floor. He feels his father's hand on his arm, the arm that is pointing the Walther at him, straight and true, square and solid, just as he's been taught. There's an almighty bang, the sound of a thunder crack, and then nothing. Absolutely nothing. Just the silence and the seeping red fluid that spreads outwards from where Tumaini lies. Her lifeblood, draining away.

Seventeen, not yet a man and therefore ineligible to be tried as one. There is some plea-bargaining to be done. In his more lucid moments, his father wants to take the blame. An intruder. She surprised him. It's a remote farm. Whites are vulnerable, you know. The excuses tumble from his lips like spittle. Mark refuses. His father, unable to hide behind the cloak of youth, is jailed, bail refused. At the trial, he is sober for the first time in years. The charges are read out; the circumstances narrated. Two sets of prints on the gun. Who shot whom? Only two people know what happened that afternoon, and neither speaks. The legal machinations go on and on.

Mark listens to the court proceedings with a sense of detachment so profound he wonders if he is actually present. It is only when his eyes move upwards – away from the ring of faces, their gazes trained on the judge and the trio of lawyers who have come up from 'down south' – and land on his father that he feels a surge of revulsion spiralling upwards through his gut. He can't meet his father's eyes.

When the sentence is pronounced, he gags. Basil Houldsworth, 4th Baron Fermeroy, charged with the rape and murder of a ten-year-old. As Mark's lawyer says in an aside, 'The bastard's clearly guilty of one; what difference does the other make?' His father is led down to cheers from the public gallery and silence from the cluster of whites in the balcony.

At the time, he thought it was anger that prevented him from gazing upon that face. Now he understood it differently. It wasn't anger; it was fear. The same fear that he saw in Lexi now, with a clarity that startled him. It was her eyes. Eyes that had seen too much. Eyes that were capable of absolving all sin. If there was anyone on this planet capable of understanding him, and what he'd done, it was Lexi. He needed her in more ways than he could rationally express.

It's not your fault. It wasn't his either.

61

The huge beech tree whose branches sometimes caressed Inès's window appeared silhouetted against the white netting. She'd forgotten to draw the curtains again. She lay in bed watching the branches dance across and against the light as dawn broke over London. For the past three weeks she'd been overtaken by an impossible, debilitating inertia, but it couldn't go on. *She* couldn't go on sitting with one hand on her mobile in case it rang and the other on the television set. It had been almost a month since she'd opened her textbooks or even thought about her coursework. Everything hung in limbo. Her final exams had come and gone; her lecturers knew what was happening – hell, the whole country knew what was happening, but she couldn't go on sitting there like a statue any longer. Something had to be done. Something had to give. Her parents were paralysed, made immobile with fear. Now that she knew what lay behind it, it was all she could do not to give in to it herself.

She pushed the bedcovers aside and stood up. It was nearly seven o'clock. She showered quickly, picked a sweater and a pair of jeans from the cupboard and pulled them on. Her cupboards had never looked so neat and tidy. It seemed to be the one task that brought her mother the tiniest measure of relief. She washed and ironed their clothes incessantly. She pulled her hair into a rough ponytail and opened her bedroom door. The flat was quiet and still. The door to her parents' room at the end of the corridor was closed. Her father was usually up before her mother, who worked late into the night cooking and cleaning, sewing and mending … anything to help pass the time. She tiptoed down the corridor and carefully opened the kitchen door.

'Oh!' she gasped.

Her mother turned at the sound and frowned, motioning to her to be quiet. 'Shh! I don't want to wake your father.'

'But … where are you going?' Her mother was dressed as though ready to go out. She had on her smart fawn Burberry trench coat, and her hair was carefully hidden behind one of her 'good' scarves – a Hermès, Inès noticed.

Her mother looked embarrassed, as though she'd been caught out. 'I'm … I'm going to visit a friend,' she said finally, picking up her handbag. One of her expensive handbags, too.

'At this time? It's not even eight o'clock!' Inès protested. 'Which friend?'

Her mother looked even more embarrassed. 'Shh!' she repeated, pointing at the door.

'But what'm I supposed to tell him when he wakes up?' Inès asked in bewilderment. Her mother was behaving in the oddest fashion. Her face was carefully made up and painted in a way it hadn't been for weeks. 'Where should I say you've gone?'

Her mother appeared to be weighing something up. She gripped the handles of her bag and Inès saw that her knuckles were white. One corner of her mouth was tucked in, the way it was when Deena or Inès asked for something – a second helping of pudding, or permission to go to a friend's house when they were small – and she was unsure whether or not to grant it. 'All right,' she said finally. 'Fine. I'll tell you.'

'Tell me what?' Inès asked in alarm.

Her mother sat down at the kitchen table and motioned to Inès to join her. There was a pot of still-warm coffee in front of them, and her mother carefully poured Inès a cup. She seemed to be stalling for time, preparing herself to say something. Inès's stomach growled as the lukewarm coffee hit. 'Do you want something to eat?' her mother asked.

Inès shook her head vigorously. 'No. I just want … I want you to tell me what's going on, Mummy.'

Her mother sighed. She picked up the now-empty pot and took it to the sink. For a few seconds she busied herself with rinsing it, setting it carefully on the draining board before turning round. 'Do you remember the Stewarts?' she asked in a low, cautious voice.

Inès frowned. 'Who?'

'The Stewarts. They lived a few doors down from us in Zamalek. There were two boys, Aiden and Níall. Their father was Scottish. Their mother was Egyptian. You used to call her Tante Yara, do you remember?'

Inès nodded slowly, still frowning. 'I ... I think so. Wasn't he a doctor or something?'

'Yes, a paediatrician. I knew Yara's family from my own schooldays. You and Deena used to play with the two boys ... they were a bit older. Deena had a crush on Aiden. He didn't bother much with her ... she was too young.'

'But what do they have to do with all this?'

Her mother hesitated again. 'Inès ... I'm going to visit someone. It was arranged yesterday. I think ... well, perhaps you'd better come along too.'

Inès felt something clutch at her insides. Over the past few weeks, almost everything she'd ever thought of as true and solid about her family and its history had been turned upside down. She felt as though she were treading water rather than standing on firm ground. 'But where are we going?'

'Not far. Just across the river. Battersea.'

'Battersea? Why? Who's in Battersea?'

'Do you remember Madame Abou-Chedid?'

Inès frowned, struggling to remember. 'The fat one?'

Her mother smiled faintly. 'Yes, that's her. She lives in London now.'

'But why are you going to see her?'

'Because she's the only person I can think of who'll know where the Stewarts are.'

'But why do you want to get in touch with the Stewarts? What do they have to do with it?'

'Oh, Inas, Inas,' her mother sighed. 'I don't know. But I can't sit here any longer doing nothing. Mrs Stewart had a brother ... he was someone high up in the police force. He's dead now, but she must know *someone*. Your father would kill me if he knew what I was about to do, but I can't carry on doing *nothing*. You understand that, don't you? I can't sit here waiting, waiting ... I'll go mad.'

Inès swallowed. She nodded. 'I'll get my coat. I'll leave a note for Abu.'

She got up quickly from the table and went to her room. She scribbled a note for her father, put on her coat and together they left the house. They walked down Iverna Terrace in silence, each buried in their own thoughts. How did that Irish proverb go, Ines asked herself? *Things will be all right in the end. And if they're not all right, it's not the end.* Well, they weren't at the end of anything right now, that much was clear. They were only at the beginning.

They caught a cab easily. As they climbed in and her mother gave the driver the address, it occurred to Inès that it had been years since she'd seen her mother go anywhere alone. In spite of her mother's education and liberal outlook on life, she was of the class and generation that rarely went out by herself. She had a small circle of friends in both Paris and London – women in their fifties, like her, who'd married young and given up their studies to look after their families – but the idea that Mrs Kenan would go anywhere outside of the narrow group of exiled Arabs that made up her parents' social network without her husband's knowledge, if not his tacit approval, was unthinkable. How different things were for Inès and Deena's generation, Inès thought to herself. Neither her mother nor her father had any idea whom Deena knew – not that *she* had any idea, either. The taxi pulled away from the kerb and began to speed down Kensington High Street, still quiet at this early hour before the rush hour began. Questions welled up in Inès's mouth like saliva, tears. She swallowed quietly, frequently. As they headed for the river, she looked at her mother. Her face was closed, her lips tightly compressed, and her knuckles were white and clenched over the handles of her expensive handbag. She was lost in her own private anguish. Whatever answers Inès sought, they would have to wait.

They pulled up outside one of the handsome red-brick buildings on Prince of Wales Drive overlooking Battersea Park. Primrose Mansions. White-painted entrance, neatly manicured hedge and a fancy brass plaque that listed the building's inhabitants. Her mother peered at the scrap of paper that held the address and painstakingly went down the long list of names.

'*Aiwa*. Here it is. Third floor.' She glanced across at Inès briefly for confirmation.

'Go on, Mummy. I'm right here,' Inès said encouragingly. Her own heart was beating fast. She had no real memory of Madame Abou-Chedid other than a dim recollection of someone soft and large. In her mind, the Lebanese widow and the next-door patisserie were inextricably linked.

Mrs Kenan pressed the buzzer. A few seconds later, a voice crackled through the grille. '*Oui? Nam, me'en da?*' As soon as Inès heard the woman's gravelly voice in her mixture of French and Arabic, the memories started to flood back.

'*An'na Lateefa. Lateefa Kenan.*'

'*Ah. Aiwa.* Come up, come up.'

There was a uniformed maid standing halfway down the hallway. She bobbed respectfully as they approached and led the way in. Inès's nostrils widened to take in the scents of cardamom and lilies, redolent of Beirut or Zamalek, places where Madame Abou-Chedid had lived and whose aura she brought into her homes. Inès had forgotten who Madame Abou-Chedid's husband had been, or when he'd died. She remembered now the elegant home and the many cats that strolled up and down the thick Persian rugs, weaving their way around the antique furniture and visitors' legs. Madame Abou-Chedid had no children; God had not been so kind as to favour her, Inès remembered her saying endlessly, but she had *so* many nieces and nephews and the sons and daughters of her neighbours and friends whom 'I look on as my own'. It all came flooding back now as she and her mother stood in the thickly carpeted hallway, waiting for Madame Abou-Chedid to appear.

'*Lateefa? Inas? C'est vous?*' A short, almost impossibly round woman in a light-pink-and-yellow Chanel suit marched into the room. Inès stared at her. It had been twenty years since she'd seen Madame Abou-Chedid, but she looked exactly the same as she'd always done, a curious mixture of matronly and girlish, her face heavily made up and her bouffant-style hair dating from the fifties. 'Inas!' She held her arms wide, painted lips parting in a smile. '*Mon Dieu!* Look at you! Just look at you! *Comment tu es belle!* How *are* you, Lateefa?' She turned to Mrs Kenan. '*Quelle surprise!*'

Inès found herself smothered against the great shelf of the woman's bosom. She was alternately pulled close and thrust away, held at arm's length for inspection, questions and exclamations tumbling out of Madame Abou-Chedid's mouth like gunfire. 'Yes, you're just like your mother. Beautiful, beautiful! Come my dear, let's have some tea. Sit, sit. Yes, over there, by the window. My eyesight's not what it used to be, I'm afraid. Mireille!' She broke off to bellow at the maid, who was standing stiffly to attention only yards away. 'Mireille! Bring tea! Hurry, girl, *hurry!*'

Madame Abou-Chedid led Inès and her mother to two plump chairs by the window. 'Sit, sit … make yourselves comfortable. There … and perhaps a stool for your feet, *chère Lateefa*? Mireille! Bring a stool for Madame Kenan!'

The maid darted back in, did as she was told and then disappeared, returning a few minutes later with a tray. She carefully placed cups and saucers on the little wooden side tables with their intricately patterned pearl inlays that were a staple of every Arab home. Madame Abou-Chedid settled herself into the window seat like a great clucking hen, overseeing the elaborate preparations.

At last it was done. An engraved silver teapot with a long curved spout stood waiting. Mireille served them quickly and efficiently, and silently withdrew, closing the door behind her. Every situation had its protocol. Inès knew her mother wasn't about to launch into an immediate explanation of the reason for her visit. There were questions to be asked and answered, first. How was dear Ibrahim? And his health? How long had it been since they were in Cairo? Her mother answered patiently, waiting for the moment. Finally, it came.

'And your lovely sister? Deena? How is she? Married by now, I expect. Oh, I look upon you children as my own, you know. God didn't favour—'

'That's why I called, Aisha,' her mother interrupted her. 'I've come to see you about Deena.'

'Deena? *Pourquoi?*' Madame Abou-Chedid's eyes grew wide. 'There's no … trouble, is there?' she asked, lips automatically pursing in disapproval. In the tightly monitored circles of Cairo's upper-class society, 'trouble' could mean only one thing.

Her mother shook her head violently. 'No, no … nothing like that.' She took a sip of tea, composing and preparing herself. How best to explain? 'She's missing, Aisha. She's been taken.'

'Missing?' Madame Abou-Chedid's eyes grew even wider. 'What do you mean, *missing*? Taken by whom? What are you talking about?'

For fifteen minutes, as her mother spoke, Madame Abou-Chedid was silent, pausing only once to light a cigarette, a long, thin cheroot which she smoked elegantly, gently wafting the smoke away from her face.

'It's been nearly three weeks now,' Mrs Kenan said finally, heavily. 'All we know is that she's being held by the police, but we've no idea where, or what the charges are. There's a young reporter – I'm surprised you haven't seen the news, to be honest – she's in Cairo now, looking for her, but no one seems to know anything.'

'I don't watch the news these days, I'm afraid, Lateefa. And when I do, it bears so little resemblance to what really goes on … what's the point?' She stubbed out her cheroot. 'I switch between the stations, as we all do. You pick between them … Al Jazeera, BBC, CNN … somewhere in the middle lies the truth … or so you hope.'

Inès looked at the two women uncertainly. Something had changed between them. Gone was the formal, almost girlish hospitality that characterised every social event she'd ever attended with her mother. Her mother was leaning forward, listening intently to Madame Abou-Chedid, who in turn had dropped the coquetry of her manner. Suddenly they were two intelligent, politically aware women discussing matters that she was more accustomed to seeing her father occupy himself with.

'I thought I might ask you something, Aisha,' her mother began slowly. 'Something big.' She looked up. Inès watched Madame Abou-Chedid carefully. She nodded and reached for another cheroot. 'I want to contact Yara Stewart,' Mrs Kenan went on. 'I have no idea where she is. I thought you might be able to help me.'

There was an uncomfortable pause whilst Madame Abou-Chedid lit her cheroot. She picked delicately at something between her front teeth with her pink-tipped nail and then took a sip of tea. She darted a look at Inès. 'She knows?'

Mrs Kenan gave a small shrug of her shoulders. 'Some of it. Part of it. Not all.'

'Not all what?' Inès couldn't help herself. 'What don't I know?'

Madame Abou-Chedid gave a strange little smile. 'You didn't tell them, Lateefa?' she asked.

'Tell us *what?*' Inès burst out.

'Inès, Inès … don't be rude.'

'I'm not being rude! But you're hiding something from me! What? What is it?'

'She has a right to know, Lateefa,' Madame Abou-Chedid said quietly. 'It was a long time ago, yes, but she has a right to know.'

Her mother looked down at her hands. 'How could I tell them?'

'*What?*' Her tone was sharper than she intended but she couldn't help it. They were talking as though she were invisible, elsewhere.

'*La famille Pierre,*' Madame Abou-Chedid broke in. 'You wouldn't remember.' She turned to Inès. 'They always thought themselves a cut above, you see. That's how it is with certain Egyptian families, the so-called "French" ones. Mind you, we have the same thing in Lebanon, of course, with the Christians. Phoenicians, they call themselves, not Arabs.'

'Who are you talking about?' Inès asked, bewildered.

'Why, Mrs Stewart, of course. Yara Stewart. Her own mother was Egyptian, *une vrai Egyptienne. Real* Egyptian, the daughter of a *fellahin*, a peasant. That's why they called her Yara and not Antoinette or some such nonsense. But her father was a Pierre. He was a Copt, a Christian. They were so proud of Yara's marriage to the Scottish doctor. It was the right sort of match for a girl like her. Everyone was pleased, everyone. They felt elevated. She'd moved them *up*, so to speak … in society. Her brother was more problematic. One of those in-between types, you know.'

'In-between types? What does that mean?'

'*An'na ba'sud*, neither one thing nor the other. Not Christian, not Muslim. The Pierres weren't quite aristocracy even though they would've liked to be. It was the mother's family, you see. They made things difficult. They were only a step or two above the peasants. Their relatives were semi-illiterate, rural people. So the children always had this difficulty of fitting in, Hassan more than most. I always said *that* was the reason he joined the police, and it was the reason he rose so high, too, and so quickly. He would do things others wouldn't. Unpleasant things. Things you Egyptians don't like to talk about. But *we* knew. Oh yes … we knew. Your parents more than most, you see.'

Inès's heart was thudding. 'Did he do something to … us?' she asked. Madame Abou-Chedid looked at her mother questioningly. Mrs Kenan gave a barely perceptible nod, then got up slowly.

'I'd like to use the bathroom,' she said. 'No, no … don't get up. I'll find it.' She left the room before either Inès or Madame Abou-Chedid could protest. It would be up to Madame Abou-Chedid to tell her, Inès realised. Her mother couldn't, or wouldn't.

Madame Abou-Chedid turned back to her and nodded. 'Just as well,' she said heavily. 'It was a difficult time, Inès. We had the riots in February in Cairo … you must have learned about it in school, no? Then later there were the bombings in Damascus. Everyone was nervous. The brother saw conspiracies everywhere. He became obsessed with the Brotherhood, with tracking them down, exposing them … killing them, even. I think he wanted to prove to his superiors that he was just as committed as they were, even more perhaps. He was fanatical, and his theories began to infect everyone, including his sister Yara. It was Hassan who brought your uncle's name up again.'

'Uncle Bassam?'

Madame Abou-Chedid nodded. 'More tea, my dear? I'll get the girl to bring us a fresh pot. And some pastries, perhaps? It's long past breakfast time and I'm hungry. All this talking, remembering. We'll have some petits fours. Delicious. You must try some.' She picked up a silver bell and jangled it loudly. 'Mireille!'

Inès could only nod. Her heart was hammering against her ribcage. She was about to hear something terrible, she could sense it. 'What about my uncle?' she asked. 'What did he say about him?'

'Ah, who knows if it was true ... or even *what* was true. Everyone thought Bassam Kenan had been hanged by the Mukhabarat – everyone within *our* circle, that is. Most ordinary Egyptians believed he'd fled to Israel. But Hassan was convinced he was still somewhere in Egypt, working for the Brotherhood. He claimed he'd seen your mother with him, not once, but several times, so he had her followed. When the riots happened in the spring, people were afraid that the Brotherhood had infiltrated the army and the police, and when the bombings started in Syria, the government panicked. Someone gave the order to arrest your mother. I don't know what happened to her whilst they held her. But they picked her up from the beauty salon, the one we ladies all used to go to, at the bottom of Mahfouz Street. You remember the salon? She'd gone there that afternoon with Mrs Stewart. We didn't know about it until a few days later, but one of the girls who was doing Mrs Stewart's hair – those silly highlights she used to have put in, remember? – well, this girl remembered Mrs Stewart asking her to use the phone. She claimed Yara had spoken to someone in French. "*Elle est là.*" That's what she overheard her say. *She's here.* Of course Yara didn't know the girl understood French. Typical Yara. So snobbish! Anyhow, five minutes later, the police arrived and took your mother away.'

Inès suddenly felt faint. She could scarcely take it all in. The words kept going round and round in her mind. *Her mother. In prison.* 'She betrayed her?'

Madame Abou-Chedid nodded. 'She and the brother. When your mother finally came home from the police station, it was Dr Stewart who was the first to see her. He saw what they did to her. He packed the whole family up the following afternoon and they disappeared.'

'Where did they go?'

'Back to Scotland. He lasted a year, maybe two. Cancer. It was the guilt that killed him. That's what your father always used to say.'

'And Mrs Stewart?'

'She's here.'

'Here? Where?'

'In London. Just outside, actually. In Windsor. She moved there when her husband died. She had an older brother, Walid. He'd worked in England in the early eighties and left her the house. Hassan was killed in '93. They never found the killers. They ambushed him in broad daylight, cut his throat, *pouf*, just like that. Like a goat.' She made a slicing movement across her neck.

Inès thought for a second she would be physically sick. 'D-do you have an address for her?'

'Yes, we're in touch every once in a while. You know, Christmas cards … something on my birthday, still. She's become quite devout. Doesn't surprise me, to be honest. Not with everything that's happened.'

'The two sons, where are they?'

Madame Abou-Chedid gave a mirthless chuckle. 'Isn't life funny sometimes? Now Mrs Stewart's in exactly the same position as your mother is. A missing child. No one knows what happened to Aiden. He disappeared three or four years ago. Not a word, nothing. Just dropped out of sight. Vanished. He was an engineer, like his uncle Walid. Degrees from everywhere … London, MIT, Princeton. Bright young man. *Very* bright. But angry, too, just like his other uncle, Hassan. Another in-betweener. Not Arab, not British, not Egyptian, not Scottish. A real loner.'

'And the other one? What was he called? Neil?'

'Níall,' Madame Abou-Chedid corrected. 'He's in the army. A colonel, I believe.'

'The *army*?' Inès couldn't keep the surprise from her voice. 'Why on earth would he join the army? Everyone knows how corrupt it is.'

'Not the *Egyptian* army, you silly girl, the *British* army. He's an army surgeon. One of the best, or so Mrs Stewart says. He's been everywhere, too … Iraq, Afghanistan … fighting against his own, some say.'

Madame Abou-Chedid rang the bell again. 'Mireille! Bring us

something to eat! And bring me my address book. The one by the phone in the hall.' A minute later the maid reappeared, bearing the book reverentially. Madame Abou-Chedid quickly flicked through the pages. 'Ah yes. Here it is. Yara Stewart. Do you have a pen, my dear?'

Inès shook her head but took out her phone. 'I'll put it straight in,' she said, her fingers shaking.

'Ah yes. You young people. No one knows how to write any more. Well, it's 11 Clarence Crescent, Windsor. That's the phone number. Here, I don't see too well.'

Inès took the book from her. There was a sound at the door. She looked up to see her mother standing there. A look passed between her and Madame Abou-Chedid that Inès was unable to decipher. Gratitude? Shame? Relief? She suddenly felt dizzy. Her family's history was spread before her like an enormous jigsaw puzzle with all the major pieces missing. All around her were fragments of other people, other lives, other circumstances, other explanations ... other versions of events. Now Deena too had become part of the complex story of belonging and betrayal, mistrust and suspicion, half-truths and incomplete histories. She put a hand to her cheek, and wasn't in the least bit surprised to discover it wet with tears that had only just started to fall.

62

Life with a twenty-six-year-old boyfriend was very different from life on her own. Aside from the fact that Phin was the least complicated person she'd ever met, there was the matter of his energy, and not just in bed. His sheer enthusiasm for everything was both touching and frightening. Had the past ten years taken more of a toll on her than she realised, or had she always been so cynical? She suspected the latter. In comparison to Phin's childhood, hers was a minefield of loss and struggle. Not that his had been perfect, she corrected herself quickly, but still ... there was something so reassuring about the simple continuity of things – Sunday lunches, his childhood room still at his disposal, his mother's cooking, and the chess game with his father and brothers on winter evenings when he happened to be 'home'.

'No.' He shook his head, laughing, whenever she tried to express her admiration for what she imagined was his life. 'No, it's not always like that.'

'No, of course not. But … still. It's there. Always. Whenever you want it.'

'Sure, but you've also got a home, haven't you? I mean, I know your mother passed away and everything.'

Jane was quiet for a moment. 'It's not the same,' she said finally. 'I'm older than you, don't forget, and—'

'How can I forget?' he laughed. 'You only mention it every other day!'

'I don't. Do I really?' she asked after a moment, colouring.

He nodded. 'Yeah. I just don't understand why it's still such a big deal.'

She shook her head, unsure of how to respond. 'It's just … no, nothing. It's nothing. It's just taking me a while to get used to it, that's all.'

'It's been over two months, Jane. And there was me thinking you were the quickest thing off the mark that I'd ever seen,' Phin teased.

'I am. Just not … not about this.'

'So what's going to make you change your mind?' Phin grabbed hold of her hand and pulled her towards him. 'This?' He placed it squarely on his hard-on.

She blushed now, thinking back on this morning. She was in her office, struggling to finish editing Lexi's report, due to be aired that evening, and here she was thinking about Phin. She bent her head to the task at hand. The footage Lexi had sent through of yet another forbidding police station where they thought Deena Kenan might be held was excellent – dark, omnipresent, menacing. Mark was equally adept as a cameraman as he was a photographer, managing to convey perfectly the atmosphere of fear and desperation that made Lexi's reports so compelling. They worked well together, each attuned to the other, complementing each other with exactly the right balance of empathy and hard-nosed facts.

The phone rang suddenly, breaking her concentration. She glanced at her watch. It was nearly four. The half-hour segment was almost ready to go out. It would be aired after *Newsnight* later that evening. Not the most prestigious slot, granted, but it would do. She picked up the phone. 'Hello?'

'Jane. It's me. Short notice, I know, but we're going out to dinner. You, me, Oliver and Draycott. He wants to meet you.'

Jane almost dropped the phone. Scott Draycott was their elusive American investor. He lived in New York or Aspen or Zermatt, depending on the season and the tax regime. In the six and a half years she'd been with NNI, she'd seen him in their London offices once, and only at a distance. Well, it could mean only one thing. Jane Marshall had finally impressed her impossible-to-impress bosses. 'Where … where are we going?' she asked faintly.

'Mandarin Oriental. Bar Boulud. Dress to impress. Seven sharp, Marshall. Draycott hates people who're late.' He hung up before she could reply.

She stared at the phone, panic beginning to set in. It was nearly four. She had a couple of hours, no more. She looked down at her Stella McCartney jacquard skirt, now stretched tight across her knees. The red-and-blue floral pattern was so bold and bright it made her eyes hurt. It wouldn't do. Too loud, too trendy, too … too much. It had been a bit of a scramble getting out of the loft that morning. Phin's parting comment to her as she thrust her feet into her shoes and flapped wildly around for her handbag was a mild 'Sorry. I know I've made you late, but it's not my fault. I can't help it if you're the embodiment of every teenage fantasy I ever had.' What could you say to that?

There was no time to go home and find something suitable to wear. It was Selfridges. Again. Quickly.

Thirty minutes later, she was on the second floor, trying things on. 'It's not too … well, Eurotrash?' she asked the sales assistant anxiously.

'Eurotrash? Darling, it's Giambattista Valli. How could it *possibly* be Eurotrash?' The girl was genuinely nonplussed.

Jane nodded. At just over two thousand pounds, it wasn't cheap. But if the salesgirl was to be believed, it was perfect. Made of silk shantung, the off-white, black and taupe patterned dress had slightly puffed shoulders and a close-fitting cut that clung to her waist before flaring ever so slightly over her hips and thighs. 'Shoes?' she asked, hoping the answer wouldn't run into triple digits.

'I've got the *perfect* pair of heels for it,' the girl cooed. She reached behind the counter – no doubt she'd had them waiting all along – and produced them with a flourish. 'Charlotte Olympia. These've *just* come in. No one does heels better than Charlotte, I *promise* you.'

Jane eyed them nervously. 'How much?' she croaked.

'Just six hundred and ninety-five pounds. An absolute *bargain*, an *investment*. You'll wear them over and over, I *promise* you.'

She was full of promises, Jane reflected drily. She picked up one of the skyscraper-high slingbacks and slipped it on. She turned slowly. 'OK. I'll take 'em.'

'Oh, they look *great*, I *promise* you! Oooh, one more thing. You've *got* to have a piece of statement jewellery to go with that dress and those shoes. You've just *got* to. You'll look positively *naked* without one and ... guess what? I've got just the thing.'

'I'll bet you have,' Jane murmured, but without rancour. The girl was good at her job. She, of all people, couldn't hold that against her. 'OK, let's see it.'

'Hervé van der Straeten. I can hardly pronounce it,' she added breathlessly, producing an enormous brushed-silver cuff, 'but isn't it *divine?*'

'Mmm. How much?' Jane asked briskly, admiring it. 'And don't you dare begin by saying "just".'

The girl had the grace to smile. 'Five hundred and eighty. And that's with a thirty per cent discount. Seeing as you've bought so much.'

'All right. Total it up and let me get out of here.' She glanced at her watch. It was nearly five thirty. Just enough time for a quick shower at the office gym in the basement and for her to reapply her make-up. She handed over her credit card and waited for the girl to finish reverentially packing her boxes. Ten minutes later, she pushed her way through the revolving front doors, glossy yellow bags swinging jauntily from each arm, and jumped into the first available cab.

'Ah, Jane. Lovely to see you.' Both Oliver and Donal stood up as she approached. 'Great *dress*,' Donal murmured as she hurriedly slid past him and settled herself into the booth. 'You know who Scott is, of course. And this is Mike Harding from Starlight Pictures – the competition – not sure if you've met before. And this is Bryan Rusedski, Scott's lawyer.'

'Nice to meet you,' Jane smiled, shaking hands in turn, wondering where to put her handbag. Five men; she was the only woman. She stole a quick look around her. The bar was the epitome of understated elegance. How her father would have loved it, she thought suddenly.

Waiters gliding silently by; muted, discreet conversations around them; no shrill voices or strident mobile phones. Men in sombre suits, women in elegant dresses and high heels. She was glad she'd splurged on her outfit. Scott Draycott clearly thought so too, she noticed suddenly. He was staring openly at her. She coloured a little under his direct gaze. He was in his late forties, she knew, one of those Californian wunderkinds who'd made a fortune in Silicon Valley in the nineties and then cashed in his shares, becoming the sort of venture capitalist that men like Donal depended on. When he met Scott at a technology conference in San Francisco, it seemed as though all his prayers had been answered. Draycott was looking for a project and Donal was looking for money. Draycott provided the cash; Donal came up with content.

'So, Jane,' Scott said, leaning slightly towards her. 'Donal tells me you've come up with a winner, sending that blonde reporter out to Cairo – what's her name again? I've looked at a few of the reports she's been sending over. She's doing a great job. Well done.'

'Oh. Well, let's hope there's a happy ending,' Jane demurred. 'But thank you.' She looked up as a waiter placed a champagne flute in front of her.

Mike Harding was smiling. 'Yeah, well done. We've actually had our eye on Lexi Sturgis for ages, but we just couldn't come up with the right vehicle for her. Outstanding reporter. Good-looking, too.'

'Cute as a darn button,' Scott agreed. 'Always a good combination. My favourite, in fact.'

Jane glanced nervously at Donal. She wasn't sure quite how to respond. She grasped her champagne flute firmly by the neck and gulped down a mouthful, waiting for the bubbles to hit. Why the hell had she been invited? The first segment hadn't even aired yet. She had no idea what Scott Draycott and his creepy lawyer, Bryan whatever-his-name-was, were doing here. Nor Mike Harding either. She took another gulp. 'So, er, how long are you over for, Mr Draycott?' she asked, wishing she could think of something slightly more original to say.

'Depends. I have some business in London to take care of. I kinda like it here, weather aside, of course. Man, I don't know how you guys stand it.'

Everyone laughed politely. 'Oh, you get used to it,' Jane smiled. 'And if you don't know any different … well, that's probably a good thing.'

'You ever been to San Francisco, Jane?' Scott asked.

Jane shook her head. 'No. New York, of course, and LA and Chicago. But I never made it to San Francisco for some reason. I don't know why.'

'Well, we'll have to rectify that, won't we?'

'We will?'

'Absolutely. You must come out and visit.'

'Scott's place is outstanding,' Bryan interjected smoothly. 'Just outstanding.'

'Lucky you,' Oliver murmured oilily. 'A *personal* invitation.' He couldn't have looked more pleased with himself. What on earth was going on?

'More champagne?' Hugh looked around the table expectantly. Everyone nodded enthusiastically. Jane demurred.

'No, I think I'll ... I'll hold off for a bit, I'm—'

'Nonsense.' Scott batted away her reluctance firmly. 'Not to your liking?' he asked, peering at their almost empty glasses. 'Whad'ya order, Ollie?'

'Bottle of Pol Roger. Thought it was appropriate.'

'Why's that?'

'Churchill's favourite drink.'

Scott roared with laughter. 'Man, that's what I love about you, Ollie. So fucking *smart*. How d'you know I was a fan? I just *love* that fat old man. Greatest leader ever.'

Jane nearly choked on her drink. Oliver's smile grew even wider. 'Oh, just a lucky guess,' he murmured, his voice dripping with false modesty.

'Well, let's get something even better.' Scott didn't even have to raise his hand. A sommelier materialised immediately, bearing the wine list. Scott ran down it quickly and pointed something out. 'That one. Yes, that looks good to me.'

'Very good, sir.' The waiter reappeared almost immediately with a bottle and six glasses. He bent deferentially towards Scott. 'Krug 1928, sir. A *very* fine choice.'

Jane's eyes almost popped out of her head. 1928? She turned to Donal, who was staring at the bottle. 'That's ... *old*,' she squeaked finally.

Scott seemed gratified. 'What's the point of making money if you can't enjoy it?' he said, watching the waiter pouring the pale gold liquid with exquisite care.

Jane had no idea how to respond. 'Thank you,' she said finally, lifting the fresh glass. 'Cheers.'

'Cheers,' everyone murmured.

There was silence for a few seconds as the first sip hit the tongue. Jane had never tasted anything like it. It literally exploded in her mouth, a heady, sensual rush of perfume and flavour that was practically physical, like a caress. It took her a moment or two to work out that the faint buzz against her calf actually *was* physical. It was her bloody phone. She put her flute down carefully and slid a hand down to her bag, switching it off.

'Something wrong?' Scott's eyes were on her.

She shook her head. 'No, no … not at all.' Whoever it was could wait. She lifted her glass again. 'It's divine.'

'Ain't it just?' He smiled. 'To NNI, girls and boys. And to you, Jane.'

They lifted their glasses. 'To Jane,' they echoed.

Jane took another mouthful and felt her smile slowly slipping out of control.

She had no idea whose suggestion it was, or how she'd been persuaded to get up from the table and follow them upstairs to Scott Draycott's penthouse suite. Donal had cried off, sensibly, leaving her alone with Oliver and the Americans. All she knew was that at some point after midnight, she found herself sitting next to Bryan Rusedski on an enormous couch with the television on, and Oliver and Scott huddled together discussing something with serious and deadly intent. Amidst the noise and music and laughter, a strange feeling of desolation suddenly swept over her. What was she doing in Draycott's suite with three men she barely knew, two of whom she disliked intensely? She knew why. It was the childish fear of being left out that had accompanied her all her life. When had it started? She could see herself, standing at the window in the living room at Ashampstead Road, looking longingly out at the neighbourhood children walking en masse to the swings. 'Can I go?' she asked her mother, even though no one had called at the door for her.

Her mother shook her head firmly. 'Not with that lot. Wait until you start school and make some *proper* friends.'

She never did. None of her classmates from St Augustine's lived in Southcote, and she'd have sooner died than take any of the girls with whom she shared her lessons, if not her confidences, back to Ashampstead Road. That was the crux of it. In Southcote, where she might have made the sort of friend she was desperate for, her parents held themselves apart. The invisible distance they created was the same distance she'd been desperate to cross in her friendships ever since. It was why she never said no, never put her foot down, never put herself first. She was desperate to please, desperate to fit in, desperate just to be *liked*. The strangest thing of all, she sometimes thought in moments like these, was that when someone *did* like her, like Phin, she couldn't quite bring herself to trust it. She thought guiltily of her mobile phone, switched off all evening.

'So … what're ya drinkin', Janey?' Scott Draycott's accent, mouth and face were slipping. He crossed the room to the minibar and flung it open, peering in at its contents. 'Whad've we got here? Whisky, anyone?'

'Yeah, she likes a whisky, does old Jane.' Oliver piped up from his semi-comatose position on the couch.

'How come you know so much about Jane?' Scott slurred. 'What is it with you two?'

'Us two?' Jane felt her smile slipping. 'There is no "us two".' It was an important point to make.

'Me and Jane? Oh, we go *way* back, don't we, Jane?' Oliver winked at her.

Jane eyed him frostily. 'We've worked together for quite a while,' she explained to a indifferent Scott. 'That's all.'

'Oh, come on, Jane … that's not all there is to it.'

'Where's the bathroom?' Jane stood up abruptly.

'Thataway.' Scott waved a hand in the general direction of the bedroom. She hesitated for a second, then grabbed her bag. Scott wandered over to Oliver and Bryan and the three began a huddled whispered conversation. She paused uncertainly at the bedroom door and looked over at them. They seemed to be negotiating something between them. She caught a snatch of the conversation.

'You're sure?'

'Absolutely. Right to the door. Quality guaranteed, boys, guaranteed.'

'And he's safe? You trust him?'

'Absolutely.'

She wondered what on earth they were talking about. She pushed open the door. The bathroom, typically, was on the other side of the massive room. She hurried through and closed and locked the door behind her, then pulled her phone out of her bag. There were four missed calls from Phin and half a dozen text messages. The last one had come in only ten minutes before. *Gotta dash out. Bk in 30. U home yet? Can I stop by? Where r u?!?* She smiled to herself. It was what she liked most

254

about him. Eager, happy-to-please, totally and utterly unpossessive. She hurriedly typed out a reply. *At some boring business dinner. Should be home in an hour. Come over! Jx.*

'What are you *doing* in there, Marshall?' Oliver's voice came through the door. 'Get your splendid arse out here. Your drink's melting. *And* we've got a little surprise coming up.'

Jane rolled her eyes. 'Be out in a minute!' She straightened up and put away her phone. One more drink, she promised herself fiercely. And then she'd tell them she had to go. She opened the door and hurried across the thickly carpeted bedroom. All three were sprawled out on the low leather couches, half-full tumblers in hand. Oliver waved his languidly. 'Yours is on the counter, darling. And bring a couple more ice cubes whilst you're at it. Bucket's on the table next door.'

Jane swallowed down hard on her irritation and picked up her own glass. She walked through to the dining room and fished several cubes out of the silver ice bucket. She walked back into the living room just as the doorbell went. Oliver jumped up, tapping the side of his nose, grinning inanely.

'Ah! Delivery boy's here,' he said, hurrying to the door. 'Wait until you get a taste of this stuff. Best in London.'

Jane looked up from the couch. Surely they hadn't gone and ordered *more* food? Oliver flung open the door.

There, standing in the hallway, framed by the light, stood Phin.

'Aloha,' Oliver said, a warm note of welcome in his voice. 'Come on in. You got here quickly. Then again, you always do,' he added. He turned to face the other three. 'Gentlemen – and Jane, of course – let me introduce you to Phineas. Fastest dealer on two legs. Well, two wheels, at any rate. Top-quality drugs, anywhere you want 'em. I don't know what we'd do without him.'

The sensation of ice-cold liquid spreading across her lap and trickling down her legs brought Jane back abruptly back to herself. It was hard to tell whose confusion was greater. She and Phin stared at each other for what seemed like an eternity before she got to her feet. She'd spilled whisky all over her Giambattista Valli dress, but she didn't care. In a flash, so many things about Phin suddenly started to make sense. The unexplained absences. The phone calls in the middle of the night. The restaurants and bars that he frequented on an IT worker's salary.

The fact that his phone rang almost constantly but she'd yet to meet a single friend.

She kicked the tumbler away from her and picked up her bag. No one stopped her, no one said a word. She brushed straight past Phin, not looking at him, and walked quickly down the corridor to the lifts. He was a drug dealer. A twenty-something drug dealer. She was a desperate going-on-forty professional woman whose desire to be loved was so strong it had blinded her, completely and utterly. It was such a fucking cliché. If it wasn't so painful, it'd be funny. The lift arrived and she stepped gratefully into it. She turned to press the button for the ground floor, her eyes blurry with tears.

63

Inès looked defiantly at her mother. 'I'll go,' she repeated firmly. 'I'm the only one in this family who ... well, who hasn't *done* anything.'

'That's not the point, *habibi*,' her mother said wearily. They were in the kitchen. Her father was getting ready to meet yet another group of officials from the Foreign Office.

'It *is* the point. I've got the address ... I'll take the train from Waterloo and I'll be back later this afternoon. *You* can't go. Not after what she did to you. I won't let you, Mummy.'

'It's not up to you, darling. I don't care about that. It's all in the past. What matters now is Deena. If there's a way Mrs Stewart can help us, I don't care what I have to do. When you have children of your own, you'll understand.'

Inès's eyes filled with easy tears. 'I *do* understand, Mummy. Deena's my sister. I will do anything to help her. Anything. You know that. So don't try and stop me. I'm going, and that's the end of it. I'll be back before tea.'

'Going where?' Both women looked up. Her father was standing in the doorway, shrugging himself into his tweed jacket.

'N-nowhere,' Inès stammered. 'I'm just going to the library. I ... I haven't been for weeks. Mummy was just saying I ought to go.'

Her father nodded distractedly. 'Lateefa, you don't think this is a bit too casual?' he asked, his mind on the meeting ahead.

Her mother shook her head, relieved that his attention was elsewhere. 'No, but let me iron your scarf,' she said, getting up. 'It's crumpled.'

Inès saw her opportunity. She picked up her bag and coat and quickly left the kitchen while her mother attended to her father's outfit. She was gone before either of them could stop her.

She took the Tube to Waterloo and bought a ticket to Windsor. There was a train leaving in twenty minutes, enough time to buy a paper and a bottle of water. She chose an empty carriage and settled down for the short journey, looking for all the world like any well-dressed, pretty young woman on her way to or from a city centre whose selection of shops and cafes might be the sole reason for a Saturday morning visit.

At Windsor and Eton station, she got out and walked up through the town, clutching Mrs Stewart's address in her hand. It was early September but the air was still warm. At the top of the high street, with the castle behind her, she spotted a cafe across the road. She pushed open the door and walked in to the warm, coffee-scented interior. She took a table by the window, wrapping her hands around her hot mug, and tried to focus on what lay ahead.

She had no idea if Mrs Stewart would be in. It was a Saturday morning – she could be anywhere. She would leave a note if no one was at home, but she hadn't wanted to give her the benefit of preparation. She had no idea what the woman even looked like. Inès had been two or three years old when the Stewarts disappeared; she couldn't picture the boys, either. She wondered what they would look like now. One an army surgeon, the other an engineer. She smiled faintly, wryly. Education was the obsession of the post-independence Egyptian middle classes. *And what does your son do? And your daughters? Are they educated?*

She looked at her watch. Quarter to twelve. It was time to see if the woman was indeed at home. She left the cafe and followed the road round the castle to Clarence Crescent, an elegant half-moon of Georgian houses painted in pastel colours. She stopped outside number 11, an ivory two-storey house with a blush-pink spray of roses splashed against the facade. She pushed open the little front gate, walked up the short path and pressed the bell. A tangle of white honeysuckle clung to the wall; a whiff of its sweet perfume caught at the back of her throat. There was no answer. She pressed the bell again, her heart still racing. Its chime echoed hollowly on the other side of the door. She was just about to turn away, heavy with disappointment, when she heard footsteps, slow, measured, and then the sound of a chain sliding across.

'Who is it?' A woman's voice.

'It's ... it's Inès Kenan.'

'Who? Who is it?' The woman's voice rose a fraction.

'Inès. Inas Kenan. *An'na coont mea-addy min Windsor.*' She spoke in Arabic. *I was just passing through*, a lie if ever she'd told one.

The door opened to reveal a short, plump woman, grey-haired, eyes wide as saucers. She fixed her stare on Inès, travelling up the length of her body and coming to rest on her face. She put a hand to her own face, patting her hair awkwardly. 'Inès? Inès Kenan?'

Inès nodded. She felt her throat grow alarmingly thick. 'I ... I was just passing through Windsor,' she began again. 'Someone ... Madame Abou-Chedid ... do you remember her? She ... she gave me your address and—'

Mrs Stewart seemed rooted to the spot. For what seemed like ages, the two women stared at each other, each struggling to comprehend the other. 'Well, you'd better come in,' she said finally, opening the door properly. 'Come in. Through here.'

She led Inès through a narrow hallway into the front living room. It was bathed in a rosy light that came flooding in through the ornate curtains at every window. There was an alcove on either side of the ornamental fireplace, one with an elaborate rococo gilt mirror, the other holding a table and a porcelain vase-turned-lamp, topped with an enormous ivory silk bonnet. Although Inès was too young to remember anything about the Stewarts' home in Cairo, there was something strangely familiar about the atmosphere.

'Have a seat, yes ... that one,' Mrs Stewart instructed her. 'It was my late husband's favourite chair. You know he passed away?' she asked, her tone almost accusatory.

Inès nodded. 'Yes, Madame Abou-Chedid told me. I ... I'm sorry,' she said, not knowing what else to say.

Mrs Stewart sighed heavily. 'Do you know, I've been a widow longer than I was a wife. Terrible, terrible.'

Inès looked away. The atmosphere in the room was unsettling, at once nostalgic and tense. Mrs Stewart regarded her fiercely, tilting her head a moment. Now was the time for her to enquire about the rest of the Kenan family – mother, father, sister – but somehow, both women were aware that such a simple question would open up territory between them from which it would be impossible to return. Inès had already let slip that she'd spoken to Madame Abou-Chedid; Mrs Stewart must know that what had happened over twenty years ago had already been divulged. All this was acknowledged without a single word being exchanged.

'My sister's missing—'

'I suppose you've heard about—'

Both of them spoke at once. Mrs Stewart glared at her. 'My son. Aiden. I suppose she told you about him. You remember Aiden? My eldest.'

Inès nodded. 'Of course. Yes, she did—'

'I don't know where he is.' Mrs Stuart interrupted her angrily. 'It's been three years now since I've seen my firstborn. Can you imagine that? He's alive, thank God, otherwise I wouldn't be able to stand here and talk about him. Every six months or so, I get something –flowers, a bottle of perfume, little things. Things he knows I like. But no word from him. Not a single word.'

'Deena's missing.' Inès said suddenly.

'Yes, I heard. Who hasn't heard? They're not making the same effort with my son, I can tell you,' she said bitterly. She withdrew a handkerchief from her inner sleeve and Inès saw that her hands were shaking. 'What did I do to deserve this? What son doesn't want to talk to his mother?'

'What about Níall?'

Mrs Stewart's face hardened. 'What do you know about Níall? You heard, didn't you? You heard what he did. How could he think of joining the British army? The *shame* of it, you can't imagine! Everybody knew … *everybody*. I was ashamed, so ashamed. He fought against his own, can you believe that? Against his own people. How could he?'

'But they're half British,' Inès protested. 'He has every right—'

'Ah, yes, you Kenans, always so quick with those big words,' Mrs Stewart interrupted her angrily. 'Rights. Duties. Responsibilities. That's all you know how to talk about.'

'Mrs Stewart.' Inès looked up at her, her eyes fixed squarely on the woman's face. 'I didn't come to argue about Níall. You must know why I'm here.'

Mrs Stewart's face took on a sly, evasive look and she put a dainty hand to her mouth, like a little girl who'd suddenly been made aware that she'd said too much. 'Listen to me,' she said, shaking her head. 'Bringing up the past. My friends say I live too much in the past. Come, I'll make you a cup of tea. You can't go back to Kensington without at least a cup of tea. What would your mother say? Come, come. Let's go into the kitchen. It's warmer there.'

Kensington. It was a glaring slip. She obviously knew more about Inès than she was letting on. A minute passed, then another. The two women eyed one another warily. They were in a game of cat-and-mouse, hide-and-seek, give-and-take, where what was not said was just as important as what was admitted to. Mrs Stewart was no fool. She had grasped immediately that Inès had come to ask for something specific.

Eventually Inès got up from her chair and followed Mrs Stewart to the kitchen. There was a collection of framed photographs sitting on the console halfway down the hallway. Inès stopped and stared at them. There was one in particular, a large photograph of a man standing on the edge of a cliff somewhere, his face turned towards the camera, his arm slung around someone who was out of the frame. A stunned shiver of recognition travelled up and down her spine. She gasped, and took a step backwards. *A face of extraordinary beauty, saved from a Hollywood plasticity by one or two oddities: a slightly crooked front tooth, a scar that ran across his left eyebrow, ploughing a narrow furrow in what would otherwise have been a thick, glossily smooth dark line.*

'What is it?' Mrs Stewart looked at her sharply.

'N-nothing,' she stammered. 'I ... I'm just ... I don't remember your sons, that's all. I ... I'm surprised. That's Aiden, isn't it?'

Mrs Stewart's eyes narrowed. Inès kept her face absolutely neutral. She knew where Mrs Stewart's eldest son was. She knew *who* he was, too. So now she had something more than she'd arrived with. A bargaining tool.

64

Inès sat at the kitchen table with her parents, feeling in her father's stunned gaze his disbelief and anger at what she'd done, what she'd taken upon herself to do.

'So you weren't going to the library. You went to see Mrs Stewart instead. Why? Why did you lie to me?'

Inès swallowed. It was the particular feature of their upbringing. *Don't lie. Always tell the truth, no matter how painful, how hard.* She wasn't sure which she was more afraid of – her father's anger or his disappointment in her.

'I ... I just didn't want you to worry,' she said finally.

'Worry?' Her father barked out the word, making both Inès and her mother jump.

'Ibrahim,' her mother murmured.

'And you.' He turned on her. 'You knew, didn't you? You were in this together!'

'No, Abu ... it was my decision, I promise you. Mummy didn't know.'

'Don't lie to me!' he roared. 'Both of you! I won't stand for it!'

'I *did* know,' her mother contradicted Inès, making matters worse. 'I told her about what happened ... I told her about Mrs Stewart. She has a right to know, Ibrahim. We shouldn't have kept so much from them.'

'And you *still* went?' Her father glared at her, seemingly unable to grasp it. 'Knowing what she did to your mother, to *us* ... you still went to see her?'

Inès nodded, too afraid to speak.

'She had no choice, Ibrahim.' Her mother spoke gently. 'She had to do something. She couldn't help it.'

Her father stared at them, speechless with rage. He passed a hand over his face, and Inès saw that he was shaking. Suddenly she saw him not as the angry, outraged patriarch whose wife and daughter had defied him, but as a man driven to helplessness by his own inability to protect his family from what was surely every father's nightmare. Her eyes pricked with hot tears. The protection and care of their womenfolk was such an ingrained part of the culture of every Egyptian male … she understood now, perhaps too late, that he felt he'd failed not only his wife when she needed his protection, but now Deena too. 'Abu,' she said hesitantly, laying a hand on his arm, a gesture she would normally never have made. He looked at it as if unsure whether to slap it away or cover it with his own. 'Please … I know I should have told you. Remember what you said to me when you told me about Uncle Bassam? You said you should have told us but you wanted to protect us. It's exactly the same. Don't ask me why or how, but I just *knew* Mrs Stewart would know someone who could help us. I felt it when we went to see Madame Abou-Chedid.'

'You went to see Madame Abou-Chedid?' Her father looked at them incredulously.

'Yes.'

'We had to.'

There was a moment of carefully held tension as both Inès and her mother waited for him to erupt, but the explosion didn't come. He turned away from them, though not before Inès had caught a glimpse of his reddening eyes. She looked away. She had never seen her father cry. Never. She wasn't sure she could stand to see it now. She got up, clumsy with emotion, and ran from the kitchen.

'Let her go,' she heard her mother murmur as the door closed behind her. 'Don't be angry with her, Ibrahim. Someone had to do something.' It was the first time she'd ever heard her mother address him in that way.

She blundered down the hallway and pushed open the door to Deena's room, shutting it behind her and walking over to the bed. She kicked off her shoes and lay down, pulling the eiderdown over her, completely covering her head. She could almost feel her sister's presence. 'Deena, Deena,' she whispered, her voice catching on a sob. 'What have you done? What have *I* done?' How had it all come to this? In the contracted space of half a year, everything about their lives had been turned inside out, upside down. She could scarcely remember what life before Deena's departure for Cairo had been like. Was it really only a matter of months since they'd giggled over things like the endless parade of suitors brought before Inès, or the drama of a haircut? That life seemed about as remote as Cairo did … another world, literally. She couldn't recall a single day since the news of Deena's disappearance that hadn't been dominated entirely by fear.

But there was hope. Faint, perhaps, but hope nonetheless. Inès was surprised to discover in herself a capacity for driving a hard bargain that she'd previously never suspected. She'd extracted a promise from Mrs Stewart that she would see what she could do. It was up to her to deliver on that promise. Once she had, Inès would do the same. Between a sister and a mother, whose need for reassurance was greater? She prayed they would never have to make the choice.

65

Her fellow inmates were used to being ignored. It was one of the things she noticed immediately. Detention forced its own intimacy. Amongst the women who'd been arrested were doctors, like herself, lawyers, teachers, university lecturers ... but there were others, too. Cleaners, servants, the poor and illiterate ... even prostitutes. For the first few days, the rigid social hierarchies that governed life as they'd previously known it held fast, evidenced in the way they responded to their enforced incarceration. To the educated and affluent, officialdom was petty and ridiculous. They argued with the policemen sent to deliver food and messages. They argued with the warders and the women sent in to empty their slops. They argued over the quality of food and the length of time they were allowed out in the tiny yard each day for 'exercise', in reality a quick walk around a courtyard whose walls almost screened out the sunlight. But to the poorer, less educated amongst them, their jailers were all-powerful. They submitted meekly to the demands imposed upon them, sometimes purely for the enjoyment of their captors. *Sit. Stand. Face the corner. Recite from the Koran.* The list of ways they could be humiliated seemed to grow exponentially with the men's boredom.

One day, one of the young prostitutes who'd been arrested on God-only-knew what charge fell ill, and it was Deena who intervened, arguing successfully to have her transferred to the clinic. 'Believe me, it's the last thing you want here,' she said in a low but commanding voice to the hesitant warder. 'An infection like that starts out with one person ... before you know it, the whole section's gone down. Your men won't be

exempted, you know. That's the thing about disease. It doesn't discrimin-
ate. If we're ill, you're ill.'

The warder looked at her angrily, but he sensed his own defeat. It was
true. The last thing he wanted was an epidemic on his hands. He was
already short-staffed. The girl was taken away that afternoon. Without
anything being said, it was assumed that Deena would speak for those
who couldn't – or wouldn't – speak for themselves. The new-found
camaraderie established between the dozen or so inmates squashed
into the four cells that made up Block B, as they'd heard it described,
made the long, drawn-out days go by a little faster. There was so much
to hear and learn from each other, and whilst it wouldn't exactly be
true to say that Deena enjoyed it, it made the waiting more bearable. It
stopped her mind drifting back to Dr Stewart, or worse, to her family.
She couldn't imagine what they must be thinking, fearing, waiting to
hear. She concentrated instead on those around her, listening to the
stories of the women who'd been peripheral to her life, the childhoods
of those who'd been left behind with relatives whilst their mothers and
fathers worked for Deena's parents and their kind.

The warders and guards who kept their eyes fixed on them were not
blind to this new form of partisanship. It amused them to reverse the
roles, throwing out commands to Deena, Maryam and Zuleika, the two
doctors and the university professor who'd been arrested for distributing
subversive material in the form of a prescribed psychology textbook.
Deena was handed a bucket and a scrubbing brush one morning and
told to wash the floor. She accepted both with a calm grace, infuriating
the policeman who'd brought them in. 'Here,' he shouted gruffly. 'Clean
this place! Now!' Under his hard, angry gaze and the frightened but
embarrassed glances of Layal, one of the women who'd done a similar
job every day for years, she dropped to her knees. Layal waited until the
guard had left the cell, then darted forward with a bundle of rags.

'Here,' she whispered. 'Put these around your knees. It'll help.'

Deena took the bundle from her and quickly did as she was told. How
or where Layal had found them was a mystery; she was too grateful for
the temporary relief from the hard concrete floor to ask. She had just
enough time to pull her skirt back down and kneel again before they
heard the sound of oiled bolts being drawn back and the door opened
once more.

A woman stood in the doorway. Her long cream-and-yellow silk skirt reflected off the dark, dank walls so that Deena was compelled to look up. The scent of fine soap and perfume, of fresh flowers, lavender sachets and good coffee impregnated the air in the same way the smell of bad cooking and unwashed hair had permeated the walls and floors of the cells. She stared at the woman, who was holding out a plastic box; through its milky sides, Deena could make out the shape of a cake.

Before anyone could speak, the warder appeared.

'Who let you in?'

'I've got some things for the detainees,' the woman said briskly, her eyes catching and holding Deena's.

'No, no gifts allowed.'

'It's not a gift,' she said patiently. 'It's a cake.'

There was a moment's hesitation. The warder was clearly nonplussed. 'It's the rules,' he said finally.

'Yes, of course. I understand. But it's only a cake. I'll cut it open in front of you, here … just like that. You can see … there's nothing inside. Surely you wouldn't begrudge these poor young women a slice of cake?'

The warder drew himself up to his full height of five foot three inches. No woman – however cultured or upper class she might appear – was about to outdo him in etiquette. 'No, of course not.' He very nearly added the word 'ma'am'. 'I'll see that they get some straight away. Yes, straight away.' He barked out a command to one of the officers standing behind him. The cake tin was carried away almost reverentially.

'*Tout va bien*, Dafiyah?' As she smiled her thanks to the warder, rewarding him with a flash of perfect white teeth in her beautifully painted mouth, the woman suddenly addressed Deena directly, quietly, in French.

Deena stared at her. She'd heard that voice before. But where? She nodded quickly, afraid to speak.

'Thank you, Mr Abbas.' The woman smiled again. 'I'll let my husband know how helpful you've been.'

The remark drew a puzzled frown from the warder. Who was her husband? But before he could stammer out a question, she'd rapped loudly on the door. It was opened immediately. She bestowed one last smile on the women and their jailers and stepped through it.

The after-image of the woman's skirt and hair swam before Deena's eyes as she bent back to the scrubbing brush and the floor. The sound of her voice rang in her ears. She obviously knew who Deena was – knew her well enough to speak French *and* call her by her childhood name. But who was *she*?

66

The five a.m. call to prayer drifted across the city, mingling incongruously with the sound of gunfire still cutting across Tahrir Square. Lexi lay in bed, her skin cooled by the gusting fan, listening with half an ear to Mark's soft, regular breathing beside her, her mind elsewhere, running over the events of the previous few weeks. Her enquiries into Deena Kenan's whereabouts had drawn a complete blank. She'd tried everyone, every contact, every insider, every informant. The young woman had simply vanished. By now, Lexi knew enough about the Kenan family's background to understand that this was no ordinary detention. Whoever had taken her, had done so for a purpose, whatever that might be. But Egypt was a place of utter confusion. Alliances were made, broken and betrayed in the space of twenty-four hours, and there was no guarantee that whoever had taken her would be able to hold on to her. If she was valuable to the regime, she was equally valuable to its opponents.

She turned over, careful not to disturb Mark. His energy and commitment matched hers, there was no doubt about it. Watching him the previous day, she'd been struck again by his complete immersion in the job at hand. For him, the camera was a second set of eyes, as integral a part of his own body as his limbs, his mind, his heart. He'd shown her the footage he'd filmed over the past couple of weeks, and she'd been astounded by what he'd captured – things she'd missed altogether and things she hadn't even seen: the young boy sitting with his father in the corridor of one of the police stations they'd visited, eyes wide with distrust; the plastic bags of clothing bundled in a corner with the unmistakeable gossamer fabric of a woman's abaya peeking out amidst the men's trousers and jackets; corridors that led to nowhere; burnt-out lights and windowless panes. She'd looked over his shoulder, astonished.

Because of the way they'd met – knowing nothing about one another

– an odd, unexpected ease had been established between them that allowed them to approach each other without the usual circling around reputations and achievements that characterised almost every other encounter she'd ever had. But the ease had left her unprepared, not just for who he was and what he'd done, but for his extraordinary charm. Part of it was the fact that he understood things about her that she had difficulty understanding herself. But another part of it was physical: the way he used his strong, lovely body to express the things that his words couldn't. Everyone had some cache of trust, she realised, when everything else fell away – family love, love of country, of home. Mark's cache was his body. He'd talked to her about it the night she told him about Toby. He felt it was all he could rely on.

'It's funny, really. I mean, I never gave it much thought, growing up. We got it drummed into us: don't look at it, don't touch. I grew up on a farm ... suffered all the usual shit ... scrapes, cuts, broken bones, that sort of thing. But when I started doing this sort of work, well ... it changed.'

'How d'you mean?' she whispered. It felt strange to be lying next to him, talking drowsily into the hidden, folded parts of each other's bodies about their bodies.

'Well, bodies are just bodies. Things. Objects that can be blasted apart, ripped up ... you can't imagine what it's like. Well, you can. When I was in Chechnya that first time, I used to come back to the hotel and strip off and just look at myself ... check my ribs, my face ... legs still working? Still breathing in and out? Silly stuff.'

'No, it's not silly at all.'

'I was wild when I came back sometimes,' he admitted sheepishly. 'I don't know how anyone could stand me.'

'Women, you mean?'

'Yeah. I ... I just couldn't square it, you know? Seeing all that stuff, filming it, talking to people and being right there in the thick of it, and then the next minute you're back at Heathrow and on the train and you look around you ... and it's like you're an alien. As if you've landed from another planet.'

'That's how it is, Mark. You know that. It's what we do. It's *all* we do, actually. We just shuttle back and forth. We bring cigarettes and alcohol and money to one set of people and we take back images and stories of death and suffering to another. That's all. I used to think it made a difference ... now I'm not so sure.'

'So why do it?'

She was silent. 'Because I don't know how to do anything else,' she murmured after a while.

'Well, that makes two of us. I thought I could get out. And then I met you.'

She smiled against the warm skin of his throat. 'So you're doing this for me?'

His laughter was a rumble against her cheek. 'How else am I going to hold on to you?'

67

You only count the days if you are in prison or waiting to have a baby. Deena had no idea where she'd heard that line, but it came back to her with depressing regularity several times a day. The thought of what Inès and her parents must be going through was enough to make her physically ill. She knew her decision to come to Egypt had upset her parents, especially her mother, but at least she'd been safe. Now, they must be imagining the worst. She had no idea who was behind her arrest or what they wanted. Aside from that one frightening encounter with the commanding officer, whoever he was, the day she'd been brought in, no one else had paid her any more attention than any of the other detainees. No one in their block had even been charged. It was now nearly a month since she'd been brought in; some of the other girls had been there for much, much longer. The previous night, she'd overhead Zuleika, the university lecturer, say to one of the others that the worst thing about being detained without charge was the waiting. 'It can last forever,' she'd said with a depressed authority that made Deena's skin crawl. 'I know people who've been inside for years. No one knows what happened to them.'

'You're lying.' That was Najmeh, a student.

'I wish I was.'

Deena had turned away from the conversation, sick with fear.

Suddenly there was a faint noise at the end of the corridor. The bolts on the outer door were being carefully drawn back. She lay on the thin mattress, her breath coming in shallow, frightened spurts. She could hear footsteps approaching her cell. Her stomach contracted and she closed her eyes tightly.

'Kenan,' a voice whispered into the darkness. 'Get up.'

She recognised the voice. It was Mustafa. Within a matter of days, they'd learned the names of their guards, what each one was like, who was most likely to slip them a cigarette or a quick slap ... just as they'd quickly established amongst the prisoners who was most likely to give them trouble. Deena kept herself to herself. She'd quickly understood that for all their bluff and swagger, the warders resented having to stand guard over women. To restore their own sense of honour and power, they would suddenly lash out – at times verbally, at other times with their fists – and there was no way of knowing whom they would strike, or why. But Mustafa was different.

'Kenan,' he whispered again. 'Get up. Quick. Are you dressed?.'

She slid out of bed and hurried to the door. 'Yes.'

'I'm opening the door. Come with me and hurry up. We don't have much time.'

She stared at the cell door in disbelief. Was it possible that he was actually helping her to escape? The door opened a crack. In the pitch darkness she could just make out his face. 'W-where are you taking me?' she whispered, her teeth chattering.

'Just come with me. Don't be afraid.'

She swallowed. She could hear Zuleika moving about in the cell next door. She hesitated. Was it a trap? But what sort of trap? Was it connected in some way to the woman who'd mysteriously appeared the day before? There was only one way to find out.

Lexi's mobile buzzed suddenly, dragging her straight out of sleep. Disorientated, she fumbled for it, hoping it hadn't woken Mark. It vibrated wildly on top of the bedside table. She grabbed it and pulled it down into the sheets beside her. It was an incoming message from one of her contacts. She read it quickly, her heart racing.

'Who is it?' Mark's voice punctured the darkness.

'It's from Zuhair. The intern at Al Jazeera, remember him? He says something's going on at Abdeen police station. A female prisoner's escaped. He thinks it might be Deena.'

'Where's Abdeen?' Mark was already out of bed.

'Not far from here. It's by the Ahmed Maher hospital. About ten minutes by taxi.' Lexi kicked the sheets aside and stood up. 'Let's go.'

By four o'clock that afternoon, Lexi was sure of one thing: Deena Kenan had indeed escaped, either with or without the help of one or more of her guards. From the reaction of the police officers she tried to interview, it was clear that heads were rolling. It was clear too that the tip-off had been sent to half a dozen other news agencies as well. The precinct was crawling with journalists, reporters and cameramen. They were still milling around aimlessly when the late-afternoon call to prayer sounded, sitting in groups in the nearby cafes, pretending to share information with one another, forcing small talk. At the Elbaraka bakery a few streets away, Lexi and Mark sat down at a table a few yards away from a noisy group from CNN who were busy uploading their reports. For once, the cafe's Wi-Fi seemed to be working.

'Two coffees.' Mark ordered for them both. 'And a couple of pastries. Yeah … those'll do.' They hadn't eaten all day. Lexi was furiously typing up her own report to send to Donal. 'So what now?'

Lexi shrugged. 'We wait, I guess. I'd hate to go back to Ahmad's and miss something.'

'Any ideas on who helped her?'

She shook her head. 'I need to speak to Inès Kenan first. The family must be going out of their minds.'

The waiter appeared with their coffees just as one of the CNN reporters took a call on his mobile. He listened for a few seconds, then stood up. 'Let's get out of here,' he muttered to his colleagues.

Lexi and Mark looked at each other. Seconds later, Lexi's own phone began to ring. She picked it up, listened for a moment and then signalled urgently to Mark to follow her. She began to thread her way through the tables, almost running. He jumped up, grabbed the pastries and had enough presence of mind to leave a few notes for the surprised waiter. Outside, most of the foreign press could be seen scrambling for taxis.

'What's going on?' he shouted to her as she ran towards a battered old Mercedes taxi, still listening to whoever was on the line.

'The Israeli Embassy's just been attacked,' she shouted over her shoulder, flagging down the driver. Within seconds, they were speeding through the streets towards Giza.

Lexi was on the phone to Donal when the driver stopped just below the on-ramp to the Al Gamaa Bridge and refused to go any further. 'You can walk. Too much peoples. They spoil everything, also my car.'

There was no arguing with him. Reluctantly, they got out, Lexi still arguing with Donal. Mark whipped off his cap and stuck it on her head as they merged into the crowds streaming towards the embassy in the centre of Giza. It wasn't a headscarf, but at least it hid her blonde hair. She flashed him a quick smile. The pavements were already thick with crowds coming from every angle, every direction, all heading along the left-hand bank of the river. It was like swimming in a strong tide. She felt herself being pushed and jolted, first this way, then that. She gave herself up to the general movement, did not try to fight her own way forward. Cries of '*Allahu Akbar!*' reverberated around them in waves. People linked and swayed, chanting, laughing, shouting, crying ... men, women, teenagers ... even children. It seemed as though the whole of the city was on the streets.

As they neared the heart of the protest, Mark's hand began to lose its grip on hers. Twice he reasserted it, grasping hold of her firmly again, but finally, after the third or fourth time, she felt his hand slither along the length of her forearm and contact was broken. She fought against the urge to panic, but when two men suddenly stood in front of her, blocking her path, fear rose in her throat. She stumbled as they moved towards her, the musk of sweat and sweet soap so strong it was as if something had been placed over her nose. She gasped and struggled to push past them, lifting her arms. Someone snatched at her cap; she felt it lift off, felt the cool evening air ruffling her hair. There was a murmur of shocked recognition from those around her at the presence of a foreigner. A young woman tried to reach out and hold on to her. Lexi snatched blindly at the woman's hand, but they were forced apart. Another hand grabbed her from behind, forcing her to turn around. She found herself in front of a phalanx of bearded men in long white kurtas. *Stay calm*, she told herself fiercely.

Somehow the men who'd blocked her path had managed to separate her from the bulk of the crowd. As she was pushed and shoved along, she realised she was being forced, slowly but determinedly, towards a side street. This time there was no question of staying calm. Fear broke out all over her, pimpling her body like a sweat. 'Please,' she gasped, not knowing what else to say. Someone laughed. She heard the words 'foreigner', 'journalist', 'whore', and the fear rose again, sending a nausea of panic rippling through her throat. She looked up into the ring of faces staring down at her. She could hear her own breathing, a ragged, desperate pant dredged up from the pit of her belly. From somewhere further down the main street came the sound of pounding, hammering blows against a barrier of sorts, and the wild, frenzied chant of the crowd. There was a sudden roar, like a furnace blast of heat, and someone rushed past them, shouting in Arabic, 'The wall's gone! They're inside!'

There was a second's pause. Indecision flitted across the men's faces: stay or run. It couldn't have lasted more than a minute, but in that lingering moment of hesitancy, a young man standing next to them saw his chance.

'Go!' he shouted to them, grabbing hold of Lexi by the arm. 'I've got her! I'll wait for you, brothers. The embassy is more important than this stupid woman. *Go!*'

The two ringleaders looked at each other questioningly, then nodded and melted into the crowd surging towards the embassy. Lexi was left standing in the doorway of a shop with the man who'd grabbed her still holding on fast. Both were breathing heavily. She looked up at him. He was young, dressed in jeans and a grey hooded sweatshirt. His face was covered with a keffiyeh, Palestinian-style, and there was a large black rubber watch on his wrist. She took in the details quickly, automatically.

'Let me go,' she said suddenly, taking a chance. 'I'm on your side. We want to show—'

'I know you who are,' he said quickly, in American-accented English, cutting her off. 'Come.'

'Wh-who are you?' she asked in panic, as he half pushed, half dragged her towards a waiting car.

He ignored her. 'Get in.'

She glanced inside. There were two men in the car, one in the driver's seat, one waiting in the back. Both were young, dressed similarly to the man who was busy trying to shove her into the car.

'Give me your cell phone and get *in*.' There was an undertone of impatience in his voice. Suddenly she realised it was a voice she'd heard before. He ran around and jumped into the passenger seat. '*Yala*. Let's go,' he said to the driver. He turned round to Lexi. 'Your phone.' She handed it over, her mind racing. Where had she heard his voice before? She hadn't been able to see his face beneath the keffiyeh, but there was something about his manner, his voice …

'Faisal! You're Faisal! You took me to Alexandria that night!' she gasped.

'Yes.'

'But ... but how? How did you know I'd be here?'

'Call it a lucky coincidence. You're not exactly difficult to spot.'

'Can I make a call?' she asked finally. 'My friend ... he'll be worried about me.'

'No. Not from a cell phone. We'll arrange for a message to be sent when we get there.'

'Where? Where are we going?'

'You're looking for someone. We're looking for a story. It seems like a fair exchange.'

'You know where Deena Kenan is?' Her heart was racing.

But Faisal wouldn't answer. 'Wait and see.'

68

Almost two months had passed since she'd looked up to see Phin standing in the doorway of Scott Draycott's hotel suite, motorcycle helmet in one hand, brown paper bag in the other and a look of utter dismay on his face. Since then, she'd cut off all contact. She refused to take his calls or answer his text messages. For almost a fortnight, Susie silently deposited stacks of yellow Post-it notes, reminders of Phin's calls, none of which she read or returned. She half expected to see him walking towards her office, or in the lift, but fortunately he'd had the good sense not to do that. For days, she couldn't get the fact of it out of her head. Phineas Harman, her boyfriend of nearly two months, was a drug dealer. She longed to talk to someone but the only person who knew about their relationship was Lexi, and she was still in Egypt. There was no one else to turn to. She'd been so paranoid about anyone at NNI finding out about their relationship that she'd kept it absolutely under wraps. It was doubtful Susie knew that the young man who rang incessantly was the same young man who'd come to fix her computer, and thankfully Donal hadn't been there to witness the look on Phin's face as he stood in that hotel doorway. But Oliver knew. She couldn't quite bring herself to believe he had done it on purpose, but the whole scene was so typically Oliver that it was hard to believe he hadn't. She hadn't stopped that night to find out what was *in* the brown paper bag, but Oliver was only too keen to fill her in the following morning.

'Coke, a couple of Es and some Vicodin. That's all. What's the big deal? I didn't even know you knew the guy.' She'd mumbled some incoherent answer and escaped to her office. No big deal? It *was* a big deal. Her boyfriend was a dealer of Class A drugs. She didn't even know what Vicodin was.

One Saturday morning, she woke up late with a headache and a sour taste in her mouth, the result of the half-bottle of wine she'd drunk the night before. She lay on her stomach, breathing in the scent of her own hair on the pillowcase, trying to order her chaotic thoughts. She groaned. Her mouth suddenly flooded with water and she sat up. She was actually going to be sick!

She threw the covers aside and only just made it to the bathroom in time. Up came the contents of last night's meal, including most of the wine. The bowl was a particularly vile shade of puce by the time she'd finished. She leaned back, exhausted, then staggered upright and looked at herself in the mirror. She looked absolutely dreadful. She fumbled with the latch on the medicine cabinet and opened the door, looking for a bottle of mouthwash. She gargled away the horrid taste in her mouth, tucked her hair behind her ears and bent her head to the tap to drink. For a dangerous second as she straightened up, her stomach heaved and quivered again, but the nausea thankfully passed.

She pulled on a dressing gown and walked downstairs. Camomile tea and a digestive biscuit – that was all she could face. She switched on the kettle and the radio and pulled out a stool, leaning her elbows on the smooth marble counter and burying her face in her hands. The soft, buttery sounds of the Radio Four news being read flowed over her. She took a deep breath, opened the cupboard and pulled out the jar of tea bags. She made herself a cup, watching the pale yellow liquid slowly intensify, added a sugar cube, watched it dissolve, and then brought the cup to her lips. She longed to talk to someone. *Anyone.* For the first time in her life, she had no idea what to do next. And the awful thing was, she missed Phin. More than she could say.

69

She'll be fine. She's a pro. She knows what she's doing. She'll be fine. The more he repeated the words, the more he believed them, or so he kept telling himself. It had been almost an hour since they'd lost sight of one another in the crowd. Her mobile went repeatedly straight to voicemail. She'd either switched it off or it had run out of battery ... he didn't allow himself to think beyond that. He knew the rules. They both lived and worked in the eye of the storm, the centre that meteorologists always said was safe, a place of security rolled up in a ball of fury. They were certainly in it now.

He ran into the crowd, watching events unfolding around him with his second eye, the camera lens that never lied. An hour passed, then another, and another ... and still she didn't call or appear. He followed a group of French reporters, concentrating only on his footage and blocking out the fear. *She's a pro. She knows what she's doing.* The crowds surged and roiled like a roaring sea, tearing through the building right up to the top floors. Somewhere in there, he heard, there were embassy staff, hiding in a strongroom. The rumours flew around him like gunfire. The army had been sent in. Israeli commandos were en route. The ambassador had been killed although no one seemed to know where his body might be. He took frame after frame, forcing himself to stay only in the present.

Sometime long after midnight – he couldn't have named the hour – his carefully held composure cracked. He was in the entrance, crouched down and hidden by the enormous pillars, filming the arrival of the Egyptian army in those precious few moments before everyone was evacuated from the complex, when he felt his mobile buzz dully against his thigh. His heart pounding, he reached into his pocket and pulled it out. It was a text from an unknown number. *All gd. Nthg to worry abt. Fllwg a lead. B in tch. L.* Then, almost as an afterthought, a single *x*. He stared at it.

Suddenly gunfire erupted somewhere behind him. The army were storming through the building, screaming at everyone to get out. It was time to go. He thrust the phone back into his pocket, switched his camera to 'record' and ran towards the exit doors, through the swaying, heaving mass of protesters and soldiers, activists and bystanders, the curious and the committed.

Three hours and a lifetime later, the day had a second morning. He found himself sitting with two-hundred-odd foreign correspondents in the bar at the Ramses Hilton as dawn came up over the city. He was absolutely exhausted. After elbowing his way through the crowd to get a drink, he took his double-whisky-*no-ice-please* and stood to one side, swallowing it practically in one gulp. The loud, excited voices around him disappeared with a knife-stroke abruptness. The voluble, vitally alive faces of those who'd come from the embassy siege appeared as some high-coloured hallucinatory dream unfolding around him. All he could think about was Lexi. Where was she? Whose phone was she using? He'd tried the number every few minutes since his arrival at the hotel but, like Lexi's, it went straight to voicemail, and in Arabic, too.

A man's voice cut across his thoughts. 'Githerton! What the hell are you doing here?' He looked up, irritated. A large, sandy-haired man with the ruddy, beefy looks of a hardened drinker, was standing in front of him. He struggled to place the fellow. 'It's me. Paul. Paul McFarlane. We were in Basra together ... don't tell me you've forgotten?'

It came back to him in a flash. Basra. 2002. Of course. 'Yeah, sorry ... mind was elsewhere. How're you?'

'I'm fucking great, mate. Great. Have you met Eric van Veerden? He's with the *Mail & Guardian*. Out of Cape Town. Eric, meet Mark Githerton. He doesn't need an introduction, right?'

'Pleasure to meet you, Mark.' Eric grinned and shook his hand. 'Welcome to Paradise. Can I get you guys a beer?'

Mark sighed. Any hopes of a quiet morning spent nursing a drink and a hangover were rudely dashed. He didn't know whether to be pleased or irritated. It would help pass the hours until he heard from Lexi again, but making small talk was the last thing he wanted to do. 'Yeah, why not? Thanks.'

Eric promptly disappeared. 'So ... who're you with?' Paul immediately turned to him. 'Heard you'd come back to the fold, actually.'

Mark shrugged. 'Yeah. You know how it is. Can't stay, can't stay away.'

Paul snorted into his beer. 'Don't I just. You're with Lexi Sturgis, right?'

But Mark was saved the agony of a response by Eric's arrival, bearing several bottles of beer. He took one by its already sweating neck and had a long swig. He was back in the same bar where he'd bumped into her again, and he was suddenly overcome with a longing for her that was like hunger, or worse, thirst. He felt sick with it. He nursed his beer, the worry and longing rising like a fever, a *maladie*, a delirium of sorts. He heard the voluble, excited voices all around him discussing the day's events and their implications.

'I thought the wall would collapse on top of me ...'

'I heard there were Israelis on the scene ... someone said ... he could tell by their voices, apparently.'

'Fuck, if the Israelis get dragged into this, the whole region'll go up in flames. That's the worry.'

'That's not the only worry, come on!'

Sounds of nervous laughter, glasses chinking, cell phones going off ... a distant rumble that might be thunder, might be gunfire, probably both.

'Another one?' Eric looked at him.

Mark shrugged. 'Go on.'

Lexi had been gone for over twelve hours. The feeling of dread that sat at the base of his stomach intensified. Eric reappeared, triumphantly bearing yet more beers, followed by a waiter with food that looked processed rather than cooked. He chewed and swallowed mechanically – bread, *ful*, tomatoes, olives – his mind anywhere but with his companions, neither of whom seemed in any hurry to go to bed. He ought to try and find a room. Get some sleep. Ring Donal. Jane. Anyone. Confusion and the sense of slowly intensifying dread brought a momentary blankness, as though the room around him had suddenly been blotted out.

'Here, mate, take it easy. You got a room?' Paul's face was at a level with his.

Other voices, that he didn't know.

'He can take mine. He looks like he could use it, poor fucker.'

'Yeah, let's get him up there. Come on, mate ... let's go. Easy now.'

He allowed himself to be led away to someone's room – he didn't know whose – where he drifted away from the cacophony of voices, sinking down until he lay like a stone on the seabed.

70

Dawn came up, and the city began to fall away as they drove along the old Cairo – Alexandria desert highway. Newly built clusters of smart town houses and brand-new roads gave way to decaying industrial buildings, vehicle repair shops, and roadside cafes where men sat under striped awnings, smoke curling from their cigarettes, looking blankly at the car as it came to a stop at one traffic light or another. Lexi kept her face pressed against the window, her heart thudding lightly with its usual mixture of exhilaration and nervous anticipation. She was doing what she loved best, following a lead, following the story. But this time, her excitement was tinged with worry – for Mark, for what he must be thinking, and for what he was missing.

As soon as she'd seen and recognised Faisal, she knew that her separation from Mark had been planned. There was no room for him where they were going. Faisal had allowed her to send one text message from a phone whose SIM card he'd destroyed as soon as the message was sent. She'd hesitated over the wording. *All gd. Nthg to worry abt. Fllwg a lead. B in tch. L.* When it was done, she still hesitated. *I love you?* She'd never said it, certainly not to his face. Her fingers itched. An *x*. He would understand, surely?

They were coming to the very edges of habitation. The last few traffic lights were abruptly left behind and they entered the sea of sand. There were no palm trees here, no roads, no buildings ... just the occasional stray dog, and a donkey-and-cart ridden by youths with sticks in their hands who surveyed the passing cars with contempt. Where were they going? There were few road signs, and those they did pass, she couldn't read. She knew better than to ask, but curiously, she wasn't afraid. She knew the men she was with. She trusted them. An image of the man they'd taken her to meet suddenly floated up through her mind. *Dark brown eyes fringed with impossibly thick lashes, the shadow of a beard coming through his golden skin.* She shivered, even though she wasn't cold. She had the strange sensation of a man lying low somewhere, not a stranger exactly, but a man who belonged to the present, and only to himself.

There was a bus station on the periphery of one small village that suddenly loomed up out of the misty sands. Lexi asked to stop and use the toilet. Amidst the ageing buses and the clusters of people, women swathed entirely in black, she was led to a small outhouse past cages of live chickens and enormous blue-and-red-checked nylon bags into which a lifetime's worth of possessions had been stuffed. She squatted in the sand with relief, like any nine-year-old. In the small tin bucket of water tactfully provided for those seeking to pray, she washed her face, neck and hands to rid her skin of the fine sand that clogged her pores. Walking back to the car, she found Faisal leaning against it, a carton of bottled water stacked on top of the bonnet. They all drank thirstily, eyes blinded by the white, white sunlight.

'*Yala*,' he said briskly, as soon as they'd finished. 'Let's go. It's a long drive.' The man who sat beside Lexi, and who hadn't yet uttered a word, collected the plastic bottles and deposited them carefully in an overflowing bin.

Just before noon, they stopped again, at a cafe attached to the side of a building, itself perched tentatively at the edge of the desert. A faded Coca-Cola sign glared down at them from across the road. It was less than a village – a cluster of white cubist buildings with the thick finger of a minaret pointing skyward, a petrol station, a few houses, and the shop-cum-cafe at which they sat. The driver and the man sitting next to Lexi disappeared, probably to pray. Faisal kicked out a chair at the little tin table underneath the awning and offered it to her.

'Here,' he said, holding out a patterned scarf. 'You'd better wear this from now on. People are more conservative around these parts.'

'Where are we?' Lexi asked, winding the ends expertly around her neck. 'By my reckoning, we're near the Libyan border.'

Faisal said nothing. 'Coffee?' An elderly man in a long white *thawb* came out to serve them. He eyed Lexi nervously, but silently poured two glasses of cardamom-scented coffee from a long-handled pot. Behind him, in the darkness that was the shop and kitchen, objects were strung across the ceiling and music blared from a radio placed on the counter. The coffee was strong, and was followed by food – simple fare, bread, *hummus, ful.* The driver and the other man joined them. They ate quickly and without comment. When they were finished, the three men wiped their fingers fastidiously, then pushed their chairs back to smoke. A crow materialised out of nowhere and landed on the ground not far from their feet. Lexi watched in silence as it pecked aggressively in the dirt for scraps they might have left behind.

When they were getting ready to go, she stopped Faisal, putting out a hand instinctively to touch his forearm. He looked at her in surprise. 'Please,' she said. 'Let me make a call. Just to let my friend know everything's fine. I won't say a thing about where we're going, I promise. You can speak to him if you like.'

Faisal looked at her, his expression unreadable. 'OK,' he said finally. 'But no calls. It's too easy to track a call. You can send an SMS. Here, use this phone.'

Her heart lifted and she took the phone from him with shaking hands. This time she tapped out her message without thinking. *Hope ur ok. I'm fine. Not sure when bk, but will call. Love, L.* She pressed 'send' before he could change his mind.

'Let's get going,' Faisal said impatiently as she handed back the phone. 'I want to cross the border before dark.' He quickly disposed of the SIM card and inserted another one in its place. He seemed to have an endless supply.

She looked up at him in surprise. The border? So they were about to cross into Libya. It was the kind of detail he shouldn't have given away. She followed the men back to the car, her mind racing ahead again. Misrata was the nearest large town to the Egyptian border. Was it possible that Deena Kenan was there?

The sun tracked their progress across the tedious landscape. The road they travelled along was the only one, a long, thin ribbon that stretched unwaveringly in front of them, and behind. Once or twice Lexi turned her head, now hampered by the flowered polyester scarf, and tried to gauge the distance they'd come. It was impossible. The desert offered no landmarks, no sense of scale or distance or time passed – it was sameness from beginning to end. Where the tar ended on either side, the sands began. It was unsettling. In London, there was always another road, and another, and a street behind that one, and a railway line that linked suburb to village, village to town. Here there was nothing. When the road ended, so too did life.

Up front, Faisal and the driver were arguing over something; their Arabic was too fast and too colloquial for Lexi to grasp. She began to doze, lulled into sleep by the heat and the monotony of the landscape, which acted upon her senses like a drug. She drifted in and out of lucidity, swaying with the car's rhythm, her head slowly drooping forwards on to her chest. Every once in a while, when she turned her dazed, bleary eyes to the window, a dark speck somewhere in the distance would slowly reveal itself as a woman in black, herding goats. The figure was come upon at speed, and left behind just as rapidly, turning once more into a speck on the horizon. She tried to think, but it was impossible, like gazing out to sea and being overcome by the vastness of the element surveyed. She closed her eyes. It was better not to think too much, either about where she'd just come from or where they were headed.

71

The following morning, she was woken by the same feeling of nausea. This time she didn't quite make it to the bathroom. She threw up en route and then stood still, too shocked to move. She walked to the bathroom as if in a daze and looked at herself in the mirror. The pallor as she withdrew into herself made her freckles stand out all over her face like a rash. She put a hand on the trembling softness of her abdomen and burst into tears.

She waited two more days. On the Wednesday morning, she got up early, ate a dry piece of toast to keep the nausea at bay and put on her coat. She'd already phoned Susie to say she wasn't well and wouldn't be in that day. She hailed a taxi and clambered in. It was a twenty-minute ride from Clerkenwell to the Devonshire Place Medical Clinic, just off Harley Street, where she'd booked a nine a.m. appointment with the practice nurse. She paid the fee, filled out the forms and was ushered into a small, pleasantly furnished room that looked more like her father's bedroom in his expensive Oxfordshire nursing home than a gynaecologist's office. At the thought of her father, her eyes filled with tears. The nurse came in, tactfully ignored her obvious distress and skilfully drew a blood sample.

'More reliable than a urine test,' she said cheerfully, dabbing Jane's arm with a small cotton swab. 'And I suspect you've done one already, anyway.'

Jane shook her head. 'No. I ... I've only just ... well, I've only just noticed.'

'When was your last period?'

Jane blinked. She couldn't actually remember. 'A few weeks ago?' She hazarded a guess. 'I'm not sure.'

'Don't worry. We'll have the results in about ten minutes. If you'd like to go back into the waiting room, I'll call you in as soon as I have them. And then we can discuss what you want to do.'

Jane nodded, too overcome to speak. She stood up, clutching the spot where the nurse had inserted the needle, and left the room. She stopped in the toilets before going back to the waiting room and shut herself away in one of the sterile white cubicles. She knew. The test was simply a formality. She put her face in her hands and tried to dispel the knot of despair at the pit of her stomach. How on earth could it have happened? She'd been careful. Phin had been careful, hadn't he? It wasn't the first time she'd fallen pregnant. Twice before, years ago ... everything taken care of discreetly, expensively, silently. Neither of the two one-night stands involved – if that was the right term – knew anything. She'd never seen either man again. But this was different. She was nearly thirty-eight.

Despite the age difference, and the fact that they'd only been together a couple of months, Phin was the closest thing Jane had ever had to a 'real' boyfriend. Although they didn't socialise together, and she could hardly picture taking him along to a work event the way, say, Lexi and Mark moved around together, still ... he was *there*. He was kind and funny and reliable. He didn't play games. He was inordinately happy to see her. He was thoughtful, generous. *He's a drug dealer*. Her stomach gave a lurch. She tried to picture her mobile phone without the habitual twice- or thrice-daily text messages from him, or her inbox without his name. Her stomach gave another lurch. She'd grown *used* to him. She'd grown used to hearing from him without even thinking about it. Unlike every other bloke she'd ever dated, there was no edge to Phin, no hidden darkness, no baggage constantly weighing him down that she had to take into account, overlook, excuse. *He's a drug dealer*. She put a hand to her mouth. A wave of nausea crashed over her, and she took a deep breath, trying to steady herself.

'Jane Marshall?' The door to the toilets opened and a woman's voice broke into the silence.

'Yes, I … I'm just coming. I'll be right th-there,' Jane stammered hastily, wiping her cheeks.

'No rush, I was just checking to make sure you're all right. Your results are in. Dr Kessler will see you as soon as you're ready.'

'Th-thanks.' Jane waited until she'd closed the door, then blew her nose, trying to stem the flow of tears. She washed her face with cold water and brushed her hair. She looked dreadful. She felt even worse.

'Yes, you're about nine weeks pregnant,' the doctor said, peeling off her gloves. 'Have you had any thoughts about what you want to do?'

Jane nodded. 'I … I'm not … I can't keep it,' she said awkwardly.

'That's absolutely fine. You seem perfectly able to make a decision. I'll just sign off the paperwork for you and you can discuss with the receptionist when you'd like to come in. Any questions?'

Jane shook her head. 'No.'

'Then I expect I'll see you in the next couple of weeks.'

'Will you … are you the one …?' Jane didn't know how to ask the question. It suddenly seemed important.

Dr Kessler smiled. 'Not necessarily. It depends what day you come in. But you're in very good hands.'

Jane swallowed. She felt like crying. 'Th-thanks.' She slid off the bed and slipped her shoes back on. Her legs felt wobbly and weak. Dr Kessler smiled at her again briefly, professionally, and left the room.

'When would you like to come in?' the nurse at reception asked. Her voice was kind.

Jane blinked. It was as though they were discussing a dentist's appointment. A visit to the hairdresser. She cleared her throat. 'As … as soon as possible. The earlier the better.'

'We could do Monday afternoon or Wednesday morning. Those are our surgery days. You indicated that you'd rather have a surgical procedure, am I right?'

A surgical procedure. She cleared her throat again. 'Er, yes. Yes please. Monday would be best.'

'You'll need to have someone here with you to take you home afterwards. It doesn't take long. You should be in and out within a couple of hours, depending on how fast you recover from the anaesthetic.'

'That's fine.'

'And did they mention the fee?'

Jane nodded. 'That's fine too.'

'We'll see you on Monday morning, in that case. If you could be here by seven, that would be great. Doctor likes to get started early.'

Get started early. The bland terminology was almost too much to bear. 'I'll … I'll be there at seven.'

She pushed open the door and walked out into the bustle of early-morning shoppers heading for Marylebone High Street. Oblivious to the traffic and the conversations that flowed around her, she concentrated instead on putting one foot in front of the other, step after step. Soon she found herself at the edge of the Euston Road. A red bus sailed by. Without thinking, she walked to the bus stop and got on board. She didn't stop to see where it was headed. She went upstairs and took the front-row seat. It had started raining softly, drops streaking against the window as the bus jerked forward and began its slow crawl towards King's Cross. She sat alone, taking in the view from the top deck as if she'd never seen it before. Regent's Park, leaves just beginning to turn; the steel-and-glass buildings around Euston Square; the pale green glass and white concrete panels of the new University College Hospital and the gracefully aged stone of the Wellcome Institute and UCL. They trundled along, past Euston Station, past St Pancras and King's Cross, and began labouring up the hill. She had no idea where the bus was going, nor did she care. She sat staring out of the window at the city slipping past, too numb to actually see.

She fell asleep in front of the television when she got home, something she hadn't done in years, and woke up disoriented. It was early evening and dusk was beginning to descend. She drew her legs cautiously under her, afraid of disturbing whatever balance her body had managed to find and setting the nausea off again. Outside, the rain had cleared and the loft was flooded with evening light. Dust motes circled lazily in the air where a shaft of low sunshine fell through the window panes. Her long, pale curtains bellied convex, then concave, on the open window. She

284

drew breath in time with the breeze ... in and out, in and out. Presently she levered herself to an upright position and reached for her phone.

'Zoë? It's Jane. Jane Marshall. I hope I'm not disturbing anything? Listen, sorry to ring you out of the blue like this, but I need a favour ...'

72

Just when she thought her body wouldn't be able to take the jolting and bumping for another second, the car finally came to a sudden stop. It had rammed up against something, a bollard or a stone kerb, Lexi couldn't tell which. It was pitch black outside. There was a quick, intense exchange between the three men. They'd been driving in the dark for almost two hours, no headlights, no inside light ... just the eerie greenish light of a digital compass to guide them as they skirted the border post, several miles to the south and deep in the rocky desert.

'Yeah, this is it,' Faisal said softly. 'We've hit the kerb. It must be the road.' There was a grinding sound as the sump scraped the asphalt, and suddenly they were on a tarred surface again. The driver shouted in relief and switched on the headlights, and the ghostly beam picked out the open tongue of road. For Lexi, it was simply enough that the juddering had stopped. Her whole body ached and her head was pounding. She thought longingly of a glass of water. In that desiccated, parched landscape, water had no place. The desire for it seemed foreign.

They picked up speed on the open road. She picked out a sign – *Tubruq, 47 km*. Headlights zoomed past, once or twice they were overtaken, and as they drew closer to the city, the traffic began to thicken. They stopped under a street light and the driver killed the engine. Faisal took out his cell phone and switched it on. There was a second's wait, then a string of messages flooded in. He dialled a number and spoke for a few moments; again, the dialect was too fast for her. She leaned her head wearily against the glass. They'd been travelling for nearly twenty-four hours and in spite of her barely suppressed excitement at the thought of what might lie ahead, it was the first time in months that she'd gone a whole day without being in touch with Mark in one way or another.

She was suddenly aware that she missed him, and shivered slightly, as though waiting for him to put his arms around her. It was around nine in the evening and the temperature outside had dropped.

They were inside Libya now. Somewhere along the way they'd veered off the highway and entered through the vast, borderless desert, porous as a sieve. She looked at the signs of habitation – the tarred roads, small buildings, clusters of 4x4s and burnt-out shells of abandoned cars – as they neared the town. The streets had the charged air of a place that had seen nothing but fighting in recent weeks. The shops were barricaded and shuttered, buildings had been blasted apart, their innards – electrical wires, pipes, even furniture – spilling out messily. The butterflies in her stomach began to flutter, sensing danger.

They drove fast; the driver seemed to know where he was going. Lexi struggled to read the road signs, but the car whipped around the corners too fast, and they came and went in an analphabetic blur. Eventually they stopped outside a blank apartment building, surrounded by an impossibly high wall. The driver sounded the horn impatiently as Faisal dialled a number. There was the dragging whine of metal scraping along the ground and then the gate slid open and they rolled in. It was immediately dragged shut behind them. They all got out of the car stiffly, stretching limbs that had been cooped up for hours.

'*Salaam aleikum.*' A tall, bearded man in jeans and a sweatshirt was standing in the entrance. He beckoned to them to enter. *Quickly.*

'*Aleikum salaam,*' Faisal answered for them all.

One by one, they hurriedly filed in. The bearded man embraced Faisal with a kiss on either cheek, then looked Lexi up and down quickly. She suddenly became aware of herself again as a foreign object, a blonde woman in a room full of dark-haired men. He led them into a large, high-ceilinged room, lit by strips of harsh fluorescent light. She blinked quickly, her eyes adjusting to the brightness. Aligned neatly against the wall was a long row of ornate high-backed chairs, like dowager aunts waiting grimly eagle-eyed for the start of a ball.

A door opened in the far corner of the room and a young woman entered. Her head was covered, but it was clear from her manner that she was no servant. She looked at Lexi. 'Come with me,' she said in clear, mildly accented English. 'I will show you to your room. And then you can eat with us.'

Lexi glanced at Faisal. She had a hundred questions for him, but she was exhausted. Water, food and possibly a phone call? She was longing to hear Mark's voice. She would ask Faisal later.

'I'm Khadija,' said the young woman as she led Lexi down one darkened corridor after another. The building was a maze. From the rooms they passed en route to wherever it was she was to sleep came the sounds of muted conversations. The place was clearly full.

'I'm Lexi.'

'I know who you are. We've been following your reports,' Khadija said, almost shyly. She stopped and reached into her pocket for a key, handing it over. Lexi opened the door on to a small, neat room with an en suite toilet and shower. A pair of badly hung blue curtains took up most of one wall; the narrow bed was made up with sheets and a towel, like any hotel room. They'd clearly been expecting her. There was a dressing gown hanging behind the door, and a clean T-shirt, a pair of jeans and a packet of underwear, still in its shop plastic covering, lying on the bed. Lexi looked around her cautiously.

'How long am I supposed to be staying?' she asked.

Khadija's shoulders rose and fell. 'I don't know. When you meet the others, you can ask them.'

'What others?'

She shook her head. 'I don't know. I ... I'm not really supposed to say.'

'Is Deena Kenan here?' Lexi looked straight at her.

Two conflicting expressions chased each other across Khadija's face: open admiration and panicked hesitancy. 'You can have a shower,' she said finally, by way of an answer. 'I'll wait outside. I'll take you to where we eat.'

Lexi was too tired to pursue it. She nodded her thanks and picked up the towel. She felt as though her pores were clogged with dust. She opened the door to the shower, turned on the tap and stepped inside.

Ten minutes later, her hair still wet, she followed Khadija back down the same corridor and across a small courtyard. They walked in silence, Lexi taking in great mouthfuls of the cool, dry desert air. Khadija opened the door on to a large room where a dozen or so young men and women sat at tables in the manner of a refectory. Faisal and the two men who'd come with her from Cairo occupied a table in the corner. Faisal nodded at her as they came in.

'Come,' Khadija said, indicating a seat at a table occupied by two young women. 'Sit with us. This is Mona, and this is Leila. They both speak English.'

They exchanged tentative smiles as Lexi sat down opposite. Both women were in their late twenties, Lexi guessed, possibly students. The food was already spread out along the table: neat triangles of paper-thin pitta bread; plates of thick hummus sprinkled with a dusting of paprika; a salad of chopped tomatoes and cucumber and a bowl of creamy white *labneh*, the soured cheese that was a staple in these parts. Lexi's stomach growled angrily, reminding her that she'd barely eaten all day. She accepted a plate and began to eat.

She was almost finished, her mouth tingling pleasurably from the unaccustomed combination of spices, when a door at the far end of the room opened. There was an abrupt lull in the conversation. She looked up. The room was filled with an odd electricity, as if a storm had blown up whilst her attention was elsewhere and when she looked back, everything seemed bathed in a new, more vivid light. A man walked in. Her pulse started to race. He looked across the room straight at her and his slow, rare smile opened his face up like a leaf in the sun. *That* smile, she realised suddenly, dazedly. The smile she hadn't quite been able to forget.

73

If Zoë was taken aback by Jane's request, she hid it well. 'You all right?' she asked kindly, sitting down opposite Jane.

'Yeah. Sort of.'

'It'll be over soon. You won't remember a thing. It literally takes five minutes.'

Jane looked at her. 'You've had one as well?'

It was Zoë's turn to look surprised. 'Yes. Oh, I thought … I thought you knew. I thought that's why you called me.'

Jane shook her head. 'No, I didn't. Your private life isn't my business.' She stopped, aware just how pompous – not to mention ridiculous – her comment sounded. Here she was in the waiting room of an abortion clinic, and the person accompanying her was one of her own staff. It didn't get much more private than that. 'I'm sorry. I didn't mean that. I don't even know why I said it.'

'Jane, it's fine. Don't worry about it. It's a difficult decision. Well, at least it was for me.'

Jane looked away. In an hour's time, it would all be over. So why did it feel as though she was holding her breath?

'Jane?'

She looked up. A smiling nurse was standing in the doorway. 'Yes?' Fear and nausea pumped through her like a heartbeat.

'We're ready for you now. If you'll just come this way ... your friend can wait for you here. There's coffee and tea. She won't be long,' she said to Zoë with a quick, professionally sympathetic smile.

Jane got up. Her legs felt wobbly. She saw Zoë glance up at her, her face full of concern. She pulled herself together abruptly. She didn't need anyone's pity. She'd got herself into this situation, she would get herself out. 'I'm fine,' she insisted. She clutched her bag firmly to her chest and followed the nurse through the doors. *It's the right thing to do. It's the only thing to do.*

She was still murmuring the words to herself when she felt the sharp prick of a needle being inserted into the back of her hand and the soothing touch of the anaesthetist as she fed the Propofol through the catheter. *It's the right thing.* She felt herself sinking as the world around her grew fuzzy, fading sharply to black.

Two hours later, almost to the minute, it was all over. 'Are you sure you don't want me to come in?' Zoë's anxious face hovered inside the taxi. 'I'd be more than happy to, Jane. Make you a cup of tea or something?'

Jane shook her head firmly. 'I'm fine, thanks. Really.'

'Call me if you need anything.' She paused. 'Anything at all. I mean it.'

Jane felt a lump harden in her throat. 'Thanks,' she mumbled, wanting only to turn away before Zoë saw the reddening of her nose and eyes. 'But I'm fine. You need to get back to the office. And ... thanks for coming, Zoë. I ... I appreciate it.' She gave her a quick, half-hearted thumbs-up and practically ran to her front door.

Once inside, her legs gave way completely. She closed the door and slid down it until she was practically sitting on the ground. A terrible fear had lodged itself somewhere deep inside her. She was thirty-seven years old and still single. *Terminally* single. It might be her last chance to have a child, have a relationship, settle down to a normal, more or less fulfilled life. To have what everyone else seemed to have. What was wrong with her? She was intelligent and kind, generous to a fault. She was more than capable of looking after herself, and of someone else too, if it came to that. She had so much to *give* and she asked for so little in return. Perhaps she made too few demands. But how could *that* possibly be a problem?

She put a hand up to her wet cheek. Christ, what had she just gone and done? The truth of it was that the past couple of months had been the happiest of her life. For the first time, there was someone to talk to. Properly. Whenever she wanted. She let out a soft, animal groan. It was a memory she tried to suppress whenever it came up, but there was no suppressing it now. About a year before she met Phin, Paul, her old friend from university, had come to stay. He, Amanda and Jane had hung out together for almost the entire duration of their degrees. Immediately afterwards, he'd gone to work for one of the big aid agencies – Oxfam, Christian Aid, something like that – and they'd drifted apart. She still got the odd email, now that everyone was 'connected'. Then last year, he'd rung up out of the blue and asked if he could stay for a week. He was on his way to take up a new post in Pakistan after four years somewhere in East Africa.

She'd been only too delighted to have someone come and stay. She'd run to John Lewis in her lunch break, bought as many 400-thread-count Egyptian cotton sheets, feather pillows and duvet covers as she could stuff into the back of a black cab, and instructed her cleaner to come every single day that week until there wasn't a surface in her loft that couldn't have doubled as a dining table. It was spotless. Spotless and sparkling. And despite the fact that they hadn't met up in years, Paul had been so much fun. They sat around late at night watching reruns of *Friends* with the sound turned off, eating sushi and drinking Prosecco out of crystal champagne flutes. When he left, she craved his physical presence like a drug. She continued to talk across the room as if he were still there for days and nights after he'd gone. After a week or so, the intensity of the longing for company began to leave her and she found herself slowly returning to sanity. But the pain of loneliness could rear its ugly head at any moment, striking out at her with a viciousness that stunned her, left her shaking with hurt. She'd been out with Lexi and Mark one night, just before they left for Cairo. Watching them, heads inclined towards each other, talking softly, sharing a private joke, she'd had to bite down on her tongue so hard she tasted blood.

What's the matter with me? Why doesn't anyone want me?

74

'Neil … why do I get the feeling there's something you're not telling me?'

Dr Julio Hernandez-Munné, MSF's Deputy Head of Emergency Operations and Níall's immediate boss, swivelled round in his chair. They were in his cramped office in Villereuse, close to Geneva. Outside, rain was falling in slow, steady swathes against the window panes. The two men faced each other. Níall was the first to drop his gaze. He turned to look at the dismally grey weather. The steely, frothy Lac du Genève was just visible across the rooftops.

'I … there's not much I can say. It's complicated,' he said finally, with a rather Gallic shrug. 'But I think I know where she is.'

'You *think* you know?'

'I'm pretty sure.'

'So why can't you tell me?'

He paused. 'It's complicated. I'd be compromising someone.'

'And you won't say who?'

Níall shook his head. 'I can't.'

'So … what do we do now? I'm assuming that means she's safe?'

Níall nodded. 'Yes. For the moment.'

'What do you mean?'

'Well, no one really knows how this is all going to end, do they? She's fine for the time being. I imagine she's being put to good use and I imagine she's chosen to remain where she is. But whether the people she's with will be safe … well, that's anyone's guess. The whole region's in flames, Julio. I just don't know. No one knows.'

Julio looked at him carefully for a moment, his hands steepled in front of his mouth, fingers interlocked. He nodded to himself, then stood up. Níall got to his feet too. They were both aware that there was something more to be said, and yet there wasn't. Julio wouldn't press him further.

Whatever his reasons for his reluctance to say where Deena Kenan was and why she'd been taken, he respected them. All this was understood without either saying a word. They shook hands.

'But you'll stay with us?' That was all.

Níall nodded. 'Yes. I ... I can't go back to the army. Not now. Maybe not ever.'

Julio was quiet for a moment. 'You're a strange one, Neil. I've never been able to work you out, you know? But I'm glad Deena's safe. And I'm glad you're staying on. When do you go back?'

'Tomorrow morning. I've got a couple of things to do in London, and then I'll catch a charter to Sharm el-Sheikh. I'll make my way overland from there.'

Julio shook his head. 'Difficult to believe the resorts are still open. People lying on sunloungers, drinking cocktails, snorkelling ... it's hard to fathom.'

Níall shrugged. 'Some would say it's a good thing. For a country that depends on tourism, the whole episode's been a disaster. We ... I mean, they ... there's not a whole lot else. Especially there, along that Red Sea coast.' He stopped, embarrassed. Had Julio noticed the slip? 'Well, I'd better get going. Thanks, Julio. I'll ... I'll be in touch. If I hear anything more about Deena, I'll let you know straight away.'

'Please do. I never met her, but from all accounts, she's an exceptional woman. And a damn fine doctor.'

'Yeah, she is.' He turned and walked out of the room before he could say anything else that might betray him.

It was September, but it might as well have been December. Switzerland had been gripped by a fist of cold rain and thick grey cloud ever since he'd arrived. He exited the building and walked down Rue d'Italie towards the Jardin Anglais, right at the water's edge. It had stopped raining, and the blanket of cloud hovering above the rooftops was beginning to break up, revealing flashes of blue sky. As he walked, every now and then the lake gave an enormous bright wink in the sunlight and for a brief moment the city become loud and summery. Then the cloud moved over, the blue merged to grey and the brightness disappeared.

There was a little pizzeria sitting incongruously between the road and the edge of the lake. It had started to drizzle again, so he walked inside and chose a seat by the window. A group of Japanese tourists sat at the table opposite, preoccupied with the painstaking translation of the short menu into something they could identify or understand. He ordered a coffee from the unsmiling waitress and turned to look at the wrinkled skin of the water. As always, the transition from the chaos and adrenalin-soaked atmosphere of the places in which he chose to live and work to the smooth, polished surface of his temporary sur-rounds – Geneva, London, Paris – unsettled him. His body made the necessary leaps – put on a sweater here, take it off there … a tie in one, a stethoscope in the other – but his mind couldn't. He found himself staring at the silver pot of sugar cubes in the centre of the table as if he couldn't quite bring himself to believe in its existence. Couples strolled slowly up and down the Proménade du Lac, oblivious to the rain. The murmur of a woman sitting with her back to him cut into his thoughts like a radio that had suddenly been turned up. *'C'est très bon. Oh, oui, c'est très bon.'* He turned his head; she was alone, eating a cream-filled gateau with small, careful bites.

He was filled with a sudden, almost immeasurable sadness. He thought of his mother, alone in her elegant house in Windsor stuffed with furni-ture, memories, relics of their Cairo lives. Her brother's house. The house from which he'd been banned almost a decade ago. He hadn't seen his mother in all that time. He hadn't seen Aiden, either. His memory gave one of those sudden violent jerks backwards in time. *Be a guid lad now, Níall.* It was his grandfather's voice, his hand heavy on Níall's shoulder. The whispered instruction on the day of his father's funeral. All through childhood he'd been encouraged to be a *guid wee lad, a guid wee soldier* in the frequent matters of scraped knees and bloodied noses. But no one had told him how to be when he had to stand beside the coffin that contained his father and watch it being lowered into the earth. He'd watched Aiden, standing very still and straight, looking solemnly ahead. He'd tried to copy him, but standing up straight and looking ahead were the last things he felt like doing. He wanted to feel the weight of his father's hand on his shoulder, not his grandfather's, and bury his face in the soft cardigan that smelled of cigar smoke or the hot woollen suit he wore in all climes, everywhere.

He finished his coffee in one gulp and stood up, his head spinning. *Deena. Aiden. His mother. His father. Her mother. Her father. Her uncle. Him.*

Circles with no beginning, no end.

75

Adnan leaned back in his chair, surveying her without speaking. They were in a room somewhere in the compound that appeared to be his office. Just as in Alexandria, this room too was filled with computer and telecoms equipment, a dozen fax machines and modems buzzing furiously. A hundred questions darted back and forth through her mind. but she found herself unable to speak. He seemed older. Behind his glasses, his eyes were deeply shadowed, heavy-lidded. He laid his hands, palms down, on the table between them and spread his fingers, a gesture that seemed to invite something from her but she didn't know what. She waited for him to speak, her whole being held taut within his silence.

'So, here you are. Journey all right?' He might have been enquiring after a holiday trip. He got up, pushing back so that his chair scraped loudly against the tiled floor.

'What am I doing here?' she asked, struggling to bring things back under her control.

He turned away from her and walked towards the window. It was past midnight. He drew back the curtain and looked out at the night sky, sporadically illuminated by flashes of gunfire. He clasped his hands behind his back, contemplating the scene, before turning back to her. 'Same as before,' he said quietly. 'We've got something to say. You seem to be good at getting our message out there.'

'Who's "we"?'

He shrugged. 'Different groups, different leaders ... different players. You know that already. But the same message. That's the important thing.'

'And what's the message?'

He walked back to the table and sat down. He took a packet of cigarettes from his pocket and flipped open the lid, proffering one. There was an electric moment as their hands touched; she pulled her fingers back as though she'd been burnt. He noticed, but didn't comment. He lit up. A moment passed, then another. They smoked together in silence. Then he leaned forward, suddenly animated. She felt the full force of his gaze and knew that he was searching for something beyond the neutral, non-judgemental face of the professional reporter that was her habitual expression. He *wanted* her to judge. He *wanted* her anger.

'Things have changed, Lexi. We've started something they can't stop. No one can stop us, not now. It's too late.'

The sound of her name in his mouth was almost too intimate to bear. She swallowed. 'Who's "we"?' She asked the question again.

'You're missing the point.' There was an almost sardonic smile playing around his mouth.

'I just want to get the facts straight.'

There was a moment's pause between them. 'The facts,' he murmured, blowing smoke delicately out of the side of his mouth. 'Ah, yes ... the facts. Well, these are the facts, as you call them. Two thousand, six hundred and forty-two detentions in the past three months. One thousand, one hundred and eleven deaths. Three hundred and sixty-two missing persons, including women and children. Seventy-four people went out to buy coffee, cigarettes, whatever ... none of them returned. Number of reports filed at police stations—'

'I get your point,' Lexi said quietly, stopping the flow of words.

'So why d'you ask?'

'I just want to get things straight. *If* I'm going to do the story – and it's a big "if"—'

'There's no "if" here, Lexi. You wanted to come.'

She had to smile. His confidence was overwhelming. 'How do you know?'

'Because you wanted to see me again.' It was said boldly, not flirtatiously. She tried to make out the expression behind his beard and glasses. His eyes were a curious mixture: hazel, green, brown – impossible to say what colour they were.

'Maybe so.' She shrugged with as much nonchalance as she could muster. 'But that's not the only reason I'm here. I'm looking for someone.'

'Ah. Deena. Yes, of course.'

Her heart began to beat faster. 'She's here, isn't she?'

He nodded. He took off his glasses and pinched the bridge of his nose in an expression of unimaginable weariness. Then he settled them back on his face again and looked straight at her. 'Yes, she's here.'

'What's she doing here?'

'Why don't you ask her yourself?' He swung round in his chair and got up. Again her eyes travelled up the length of his body, coming to rest on his face. It was a face that belonged to another time, sculpted with the classical symmetry and beauty of an eighteenth-century painting. There was an indeterminacy about him, she realised at last. Neither Arab nor Westerner, not quite Mediterranean yet not Egyptian either. His face was a perfect melange, so that it was impossible to say where he was from, what race, what ethnicity, what caste ... no certainties that would have placed him in any meaningful context. The result was an identity all of its own.

She broke off her gaze and tried to focus on something else. He unsettled everything around him, including her. For the first time in her professional life, she was finding it hard to concentrate on the reasons why she was there.

'Wh-where is she?' she asked, breaking the silence. Her voice was unnaturally loud, even to her own ears.

'Follow me.' He opened the door and stood aside, letting her pass. He led her down the corridor and opened the door to an outside courtyard. They stepped out together into the chill of the night. She looked up as they crossed the courtyard to another building, and she was struck by the vastness of the sky overhead. It was so close she could almost feel the weight of the stars hanging there in the dark, velvety nothingness, glowing and turning.

They stopped outside a two-storey building made of raw, unfinished concrete with crudely constructed doors and windows. He looked down at her, then rapped loudly on the door. There was a muffled answer from within. He pushed it open slowly and they stepped inside.

They were in a long, low-ceilinged room that was arranged like a dormitory, with rows and rows of beds seen as vague shapes in the semi-darkness. A soft light from the courtyard spilled in from a fanlight above the door. In a puzzle of shadows and highlights, the bodies of sleeping children were displayed, some curled up knee to chin, others spread-eagled face down with only a foot or a bare sole protruding from the sheet, others laid out straight, their breathing light and steady. A woman stood by the window on the far side of the room, her back turned to them. Her hands were busy, and when she held one up to the light, Lexi saw that she was holding a syringe.

She looked to her left and right. She found it difficult to interpret the details in the dim light. There were perhaps twenty or thirty children in there, the room thick and full with their presence. She pieced together what she could as her gaze travelled from bed to bed, separating shadows from substance, limbs from pillows and their rounded, slumbering forms underneath the sheets. They made sounds, too, murmured snatches of a dream or a grunt or a moan. One of them, in a bed close to where the woman stood preparing her injections, began to whimper words out of some imaginable hurt. It was in Arabic, which Lexi couldn't follow, but the expression of pain was all too evident. The cry started a ripple that gathered up the rest of the children, and soon they all began to whimper. The whole dormitory was alight with their groans, making Lexi almost sick with the unsteadiness and suffering of it all.

The woman at the window turned, expertly administering the shot. She put a hand on the child's brow and bent over her, whispering something. Slowly, slowly the whimpering stopped – not just the child she'd touched, but others nearby – and the room began to settle once more. She waited until all was quiet, ignoring Lexi and Adnan, who stood at the entrance. Then she quickly and efficiently disposed of the needles and vials and washed her hands. All this was carried out in semi-darkness, her shape the only solid fixture amongst the ghostly shadows. She walked towards them, humming softly to herself, then stopped and lifted her face up to the light. No one said a word.

'Buprenorphine,' she said finally, shoving her hands in her pockets. 'I wish I had more. It's the only thing that'll help.'

'Deena, this is Lexi Sturgis. She's—'

'I know who she is.' Deena held out a hand. 'I hear you've been looking for me. Welcome.'

76

They walked back to Adnan's office in silence. Two young men were already inside, setting up the interview equipment – camera, tripod, recorder. Lexi couldn't tear her eyes away from the slight but commanding figure of Deena Kenan. In her stained white medical coat and grey rubber Crocs, she looked like any other doctor calmly going about her ward rounds, her mind and attention focused on something beyond everyone else's everyday gaze. Adnan stood by the window, smoking quietly, his dark eyes flitting between the door and the two women.

'Ready?' He spoke suddenly. The young men nodded their assent. One finished adjusting the microphone, placing it at the correct level and making sure it was switched on. Adnan ground out his cigarette underfoot and took a seat. He indicated to Deena to do the same.

Lexi sat opposite them, checked that the camera was recording correctly and that the lighting levels were all OK. 'All set,' she confirmed.

'Good. Let's get started.'

She looked at her watch. It was past midnight, but there was an urgency and energy about Adnan that made the question of sleep seem ridiculous. 'Just one thing before we start,' she said quickly. 'I know this is your interview and that you've got a whole list of things you want to say to the world. But it's also *my* interview and there are a couple of things I'd like to ask *you*. So here's the deal. I'll start off asking you a few questions – without prep – and then you can take things where you like.' She looked directly at Adnan. 'You chose *me*, remember?'

It was a bold statement. She saw Deena and Adnan exchange a swift, wary look. The ground outside rumbled with the sound of a rocket being launched somewhere not far off. She heard the dull whistling sound, then the moment's silence before it exploded. There was a burst of artillery fire, and the answering racket of machine guns. Deena's eyes closed briefly, as though in acknowledgement, then she opened them again. They were like Adnan's, dark pools of silent, knowing depth.

'Fine. Go ahead,' she said at last. Adnan's lips opened on a note of protest, but Deena quickly stopped him. 'No, let her ask what she wants. It's only fair. And you trust her. You said so yourself.' She smiled, and Lexi saw the likeness between the sisters. It was a poignant reminder of the different paths siblings sometimes took. Inès, the historian, watching from the margin of unfolding events; Deena, the doctor, fully immersed in them. For a second she thought of Toby. Despite the death and suffering she witnessed and reported in her job, she'd chosen life, in all its messy, violent complexity, whereas Toby had chosen to walk away from it.

She blinked suddenly. There was something else present in the room with them, she felt suddenly, some emotion other than fear or excitement. She looked at Adnan and Deena in turn, at the likeness each drew out in the other. The high emotions of the past hour had brought an apricot-grained warmth to Deena's small, delicate face, matching Adnan's colour. Her skin was satiny smooth, like his, the cheekbones and the shadows under the eyes finely hollowed. Her hair swung loose as she bent forward, clasping her hands around her knees, revealing a pair of small diamond studs, perfectly and carefully centred in each earlobe.

'Go ahead,' she instructed Lexi. 'Fire away.'

It was almost two in the morning when Lexi finally switched off the camera and pressed 'stop' on her tape recorder. Adnan's final sentences were still ringing in her ears: *You cannot judge us by your own standards. Democracy isn't simply a numbers game. Its real value is in its commitment to upholding a plurality of voices, perspectives and beliefs. You don't march or protest, because in the end, your systems and your freedom to remind your leaders when they are failing work. Ours don't. It's that simple.*

Then Deena's voice, an accusation aimed not just at Lexi but at the world outside. *We're ... no, sorry, you're just too comfortable, that's the problem.* The slip-up, 'we' in place of 'you', was one she made frequently, as if she could no longer determine whose side she was on.

'When do you want this to air?' Lexi asked.

'As soon as possible,' Adnan said, lighting a cigarette.

'This is just the first episode,' Deena warned. 'We have a lot more to say.'

Lexi swallowed nervously. She'd been gone for more than a day. Although she'd managed to send Mark a couple of messages, by now he'd be out of his mind with worry. 'How long am I expected to stay?' she asked steadily.

Adnan shrugged. 'A few days ... a week, I can't tell. Getting you out may not be as easy as getting you in. Is there somewhere else you'd rather be?' he asked sardonically.

A small tremor of fear ran lightly up and down her spine. The adrenalin that had kept her going all day was almost gone. From the moment she'd been bundled into the car, her professional self had taken over. She'd thought of Mark sporadically during the long journey, but the journalist in her had managed to push down her emotional response. She had to focus on the story ahead. That was the way it was with her, always had been. Her own safety was secondary. It was the only way to work, the only way she *could* work.

She clamped down on the fear and shook her head firmly. 'No. This is what I came for.'

'Good. Deena will show you back to your room.' Adnan's eyes flickered over her briefly. He seemed about to say something, then changed his mind. He opened the door, barked out an instruction to the two men waiting outside and disappeared.

His departure caused a sudden shift in the atmosphere, as though the temperature had dropped. Lexi glanced at Deena.

'I saw your sister,' she began hesitantly. 'I—'

'Please. Don't say anything more,' Deena stopped her immediately. She shoved her hands in her pockets. 'I couldn't bear it.' She opened the door. 'I'll show you back to your room.'

Lexi followed her in silence. She felt as though a web was slowly being spun around her, but instead of being able to grasp it fully, she could only see strands, flimsy filaments that didn't quite add up to a whole. Something was missing, some important detail that she'd failed to see, that would bring the picture into focus. Like Adnan's gaze, a look that was at once languid and fiercely concentrated. She couldn't grab hold of it and yet she couldn't put it to one side either.

After Deena had shown her to her room, she sat down on the edge of the narrow bed, overwhelmed. She was too tired to undress. She pulled back the covers, burrowed herself deep into the pile of blankets and willed herself to forget what she'd seen and heard. She'd been promised she could make a phone call the following morning, and with any luck, one of the young men would be able to upload the file of the interview and send it out to Donal. She thought briefly of Jane and Donal in London, eating at their favourite restaurants, watching a film, talking to friends on the phone. She thought about the dormitory of wounded children for whom Deena had given up everything. She thought of Toby, walking into the cold, heaving sea. She breathed deeply, her throat clogged, eyes aching with unshed tears.

77

There was absolute silence in Donal's office when the tape ended and the man's face faded from view. Donal was the first to break it.

'Well.' He took off his glasses and pinched the bridge of his nose. 'At least she's alive.'

'Who? Lexi or Deena Kenan?' Oliver tried to make a joke.

'Both of them,' Jane said simply, shaming him. 'But there's no way of knowing where exactly they are?'

Donal shook his head. 'One of the conditions of the interview, apparently.'

'It's the same guy she interviewed last time, isn't it? You can't really see his face, but I'm pretty sure.'

Donal nodded. 'I imagine that's why they chose her, however they did it. I spoke to Mark earlier. He said there wasn't any indication that they'd sent someone for her. They were covering the storming of the Israeli Embassy when they got separated. He's had a couple of text messages from her ... always from an unknown number ... but she doesn't say much.'

'Typical.'

'What are you talking about?' Jane rounded on Oliver immediately.

'Now, now. Let's not get into that.' Donal quickly deflected any trouble. 'Just focus on what's important. Deena Kenan is alive and well. And it looks as though Lexi will get an exclusive with her.'

'Sooner the better, if you ask me,' Oliver couldn't help but interject. 'She's high on the news agenda at the moment, but she won't be for ever.'

'Is that all you ever think about?' Jane snapped at him. 'Ratings?'

'What do you think?' Donal interrupted again. 'Should we leave Mark where he is for a few more days? I'm assuming Lexi'll be in touch pretty soon.'

'Yes, leave him there. He'll find something to do. Christ, he'll find plenty to do. I can't imagine him sitting in the hotel just waiting for a

301

phone call.' Jane looked at her watch. 'OK, I've got to run. I've got a . . . a dentist's appointment in half an hour.'

'Let me know if you hear anything from Lexi,' Donal said, briefly looking up. 'Will you pick up the latest budget figures from Susie before you go? We've got a meeting tomorrow with Finance and I want to make sure we've covered everything.'

'I will.' She beat a quick retreat before he could think of anything else to throw her way. She grabbed her coat and bag and headed for the door. It was four o'clock. She had a four thirty check-up at the clinic in Harley Street, and – unusually for her – she'd invited Zoë for a drink at six. It seemed a better way to say thank you than a bunch of flowers. And with Lexi gone, she'd missed having someone around to talk to. She turned the collar of her coat up as soon as she reached street level. Unbelievable. It was September and it felt like February already.

At six on the dot, she was seated comfortably at the bar in Hix, on Brewer Street. *Hix at six.* She'd texted Zoë as soon as she came out of the clinic. She looked at it and gave a quick, rueful smile. It was the sort of message that Phin would have sent.

'What's so funny?'

She looked up. Zoë was standing in front of her. She hadn't seen her come in. 'Nothing,' she said, reddening. 'Just . . . oh, nothing.'

Zoë slid on to the bar stool next to her. 'What're you drinking?'

'I got us a bottle of Amarone.' Jane smiled. 'And don't worry if you'd rather have something else. I'm sure I can polish it off on my own. After three weeks of sparkling water, it tastes like nectar.'

'Everything was all right, then, was it?' Zoë asked delicately.

Jane nodded quickly. 'Yeah. Fine. No . . . complications.'

'Think I'll join you.' Zoë nodded at the big, beautiful glass of red that Jane was holding. 'What a day. Did you see the report Lexi sent through? Donal circulated it. It's going out tonight.'

'Yeah. Fantastic job. Thank God she found her.'

'Or they found *her*. I heard it was the same guy who asked for her earlier on this year. They obviously trust her.'

Jane nodded again. 'Who wouldn't? She's brilliant.'

'You're pretty close, aren't you?' Zoë asked curiously. 'Thanks.' She picked up the glass that the attentive bartender had just poured. 'You and Lexi, I mean.'

'Yeah, we … we're friends.'

'I have to admit, we were kinda surprised.'

Jane looked at her. 'Surprised?'

'Yeah. When you and Lexi became friends. Don't get me wrong …
she's great. All the writers like her. It's just … you're quite an unlikely
pair.'

Jane blushed. She wondered if it was entirely proper to have been
drawn so quickly into a discussion of her private life with someone she
worked with. Someone who worked for her, she corrected herself quickly.
She took a careful sip of her wine. Oh, fuck it. She'd asked for Zoë's
help at a time when there wasn't anyone else to ask, and she'd given
it, willingly. Relax! But it was difficult to let her guard down. She just
didn't know how to *be* with other people. At school, she remembered,
her cheeks warming as she dragged the memory up, she came away
from the group of girls who used to tolerate her presence with tears of
frustration in her eyes. She'd got it wrong. Again. She'd either been too
loud or too flippant or too sulky. She was oversensitive to other people's
remarks but not sensitive enough to her own … she didn't know how
to just be one of the gang, one of the group. Lexi was different. It was
easier with her because she was so damned difficult herself.

'Don't worry,' Zoë said quietly. 'Nothing you tell me will go further
than tonight.'

Jane swallowed. Zoë had somehow read her mind. 'Th-thanks,' she said
shakily, reaching for her glass. 'I … don't usually like to … you know …
socialise at work.'

'But you met Phin through work?'

Jane almost choked on her wine. 'How … how d'you know about
Phin?' she asked weakly.

It was Zoë's turn to look embarrassed. 'We … we all know him,' she
said hesitantly.

Jane's face was on fire. 'You mean … because of … because of what
he does? On the side?'

Zoë nodded. '*I* don't buy from him, but … yeah, some of the others
do. Look, we don't have to talk about him if you don't want to,' she said
quickly. 'Phin, I mean. Oliver's an asshole, we all know that. I don't know
how you put up with him, to be honest.'

'It's my job,' Jane said defensively. 'I have to put up with him.'

'*I* wouldn't.'

'Well, that's why—' Jane stopped herself just in time. 'No, you're right. I don't know why I do either.'

Zoë gave a half-smile. 'It's fine. You're allowed to say it. You're the creative director. I'm just a lowly staff writer. There's the difference. Anyhow, let's not ruin a perfectly good evening talking about Oliver. Or Phin, if you don't want to.'

Jane shook her head slowly. 'No, I ... I don't mind.' She took a deep breath. 'It's nice. It's ... helpful, you know? Just to talk. Lexi's the only other person who knows, and she's so clear about everything. I wish I could be like that.'

'You're not?' Zoë prompted. 'You seem pretty clear about stuff at work.'

Jane sighed. 'That's different. I know what I'm doing at work. Most of the time, anyway. No, when it comes to men, I'm hopeless. I just don't see it coming.'

'See what?'

Jane shrugged. 'All of it. I ... I'm just so goddam flattered that anyone would ... well, you know ... pay attention to me. I guess I just get carried away.' She swallowed. It was perhaps the most honest thing she'd said about herself to anyone, Lexi included. She took a large gulp of wine to cover her acute embarrassment. She hardly knew Zoë! What the hell was wrong with her?

But Zoë didn't seem surprised or uncomfortable – or even amused, which was the reaction Jane most feared. As she took a sip of her own drink, she looked ... well, almost sympathetic. Was that possible? 'It's easy to get carried away,' she said after a moment. 'Especially with someone like Phin.'

'I just don't understand how I didn't *see* it,' Jane wailed. Her relief was so great, the desire to talk was suddenly overwhelming. 'I should have realised. He's ten years younger than me! How on earth did I think it was ever going to work?'

'It's got nothing to do with his age,' Zoë said quickly. 'He just wasn't good enough for you. He was out of his depth and he knew it. That's what all the dealing and hustling was about. He was trying to impress you. I bet he took you to the most glamorous places, didn't he?'

Jane nodded miserably. 'Yeah. I guess it did cross my mind ... how the hell could he afford it? And then he'd keep disappearing ... you know, whilst we were in the bar, or at dinner or whatever.'

'How did you find out?'

Jane winced. 'I went out with Oliver and Donal and Scott Draycott the night Draycott was over. We wound up at his hotel suite and Oliver called Phin. He came round to make a delivery. I don't know who was more shocked, me or Phin.'

Zoë smiled. 'Yeah, that sounds like something Oliver would do. He can't help it. He's got the most awful crush on you.'

'Who? Phin?' Jane's eyes widened.

'No, silly. Oliver. That's why he picks on you. He fancies you. Don't tell me you haven't noticed.'

Jane almost fell off her bar stool. 'Don't be ridiculous.'

'It's true. Ask anyone. He can barely string two sentences together when you're around. That's why he's always attacking you. He's terrified you'll see through him.'

Jane shook her head firmly. 'You're insane. Oliver can't stand me.'

Zoë laughed. 'That's where you're wrong. I bet you don't even notice the way men look at you when you walk past, do you?'

Jane's face felt as though it was on fire. 'I don't know what you're talking about,' she mumbled, mortified.

'Well I do. Wake up, Jane. You're quite something. The only person who doesn't seem to get it is you. And *that's* your problem. It's not Phin, or how old he is. And it's not Oliver, either. It's you.'

Jane couldn't speak. The scene drifted in front of her and she was powerless to stop it. It was just the two of them. Her and her mother. Her father, relieved to be out of the bedroom, where every surface was crowded with drugs and painkillers, had gone down into the garden to work with the living, his large hands buried in the flower beds he loved so much.

'Janey, love,' her mother said suddenly, her voice cracking through the parched muscles of her throat.

Jane looked up from the book she was reading. 'What is it, Mum?' She reached across to the bedside table for the glass of water that was kept habitually full. 'Here, take a sip.'

Her mother lifted her head slowly and complied. 'There's something I want to tell you,' she said, falling back heavily against the pillow.

'Anything, Mum, anything.' Jane slid off the chair next to the bed and knelt down beside her mother, just the way she'd done as a child.

'Don't be taken in by them.'

'By who, Mum?'

'Men.' Her mother smiled faintly. 'Don't be fooled. They'll promise you the earth, you know. They'll promise you all sorts of things. But don't be taken in. You're meant for more. For better things. I want you to have all the things I didn't have.'

Jane swallowed painfully. 'Mum, what are you talking about? You and Dad ... you've been happy, haven't you?'

'That's not it. I didn't have the advantages you've had, love. I didn't have any ... options. I'm just saying. What happened to me isn't going to happen to you. Promise me. You'll make something of yourself, won't you, Jane? Don't be like me. I want more for you, you hear me? Don't be fooled.'

Her mother's voice grew hoarse with the effort of speaking. Jane swallowed down on the lump in her own throat and nodded, laying her head very close to her mother's arm. They stayed like that for a few moments, until her mother's breathing lengthened and deepened and finally she dropped off to sleep again. Jane levered herself up from the floor and went into the bathroom, where she turned on the taps and cried as silently as she could against the noise of running water.

78

He touched down at Heathrow just after noon. He collected his bag and was through customs within twenty minutes. Skirting the line of waiting chauffeurs, friends and relatives, their expectant, hopeful faces turned towards the doors that flew open nervously every minute or so, he was almost at the ticket machine for the Heathrow Express when he stopped suddenly. He looked at his watch. To the casual observer, he appeared to be weighing something up, deciding. He walked towards the lifts instead and rode up to Departures. He scanned the list of flights, then walked over to the British Airways desk. Ten minutes later, ticket in hand, he moved through security in the opposite direction. He stopped briefly at World of Whiskies and picked up a bottle of Bunnahabháin, then walked quickly to Gate 5.

His flight took off on time. He declined the offer of a drink from the smiling flight attendant and closed his eyes. Less than an hour later, just after three, he disembarked at Glasgow International Airport and headed straight for the car rental desk.

The road led him away from the city, through the late-afternoon traffic and the industrial estates made of corrugated metal that no longer produced anything worth buying. *Hillhead, Anniesland, Drumchapel, Kilbowie.* The signs floated into view and disappeared again. 'Just follow the A82. It'll take ye all the way there,' the Avis representative had instructed. On his left was the dark blue tongue of sea, narrowing to the Firth of Clyde, snaking its way back towards Glasgow; on his right, a rolling line of hills swayed towards the horizon, great swathes of burnt grass and heather, the ground burnished to a coppery gold by the autumn sun.

At Dumbarton, he followed the signs to Loch Lomond, skirting its edges. The skin of the lake wrinkled periodically, prompted by unseen shivers of wind. He followed the winding road, his eyes constantly drawn to the vastness that sloped off into the distance, a blue haze that filled the gaze. He stopped at Tarbet, a small crossroads town halfway up the loch, and sat in the front room of the Lomond View Country House with a pot of steaming coffee and a plate of home-made scones, the only guest in a room full of stuffed green armchairs. Every now and then a car zoomed past, the noise a muffled yawn through the double-glazed windows. He saw from the way the receptionist had looked at him, trying to work out where he'd come from or where he might be headed, that this wasn't the sort of place where strangers often found themselves. He passed a hand uncertainly across his chin, fine, sharp bristles pricking his fingertips.

Lomond, Arkaig, Garry, Cluanie, Duich. Back on the road, the unfamiliar-sounding names were come upon and passed, one after the other. *Loch Tulla. Lochan nà h-Achlaise.* The syllables couldn't be guessed at, but the sense of estrangement was oddly pleasing. At Ballachulish he crossed the sturdy bridge and continued up the flank of Loch Leven until he reached Fort William and turned left on to the A380, which would take him to the western edge of the mainland, to Mallaig. From there he would catch the ferry to Skye.

'Where're ye headed?' The ferryman, a bearded man in yellow oilskins, spoke to him suddenly from underneath the broad brim of his cap.

'Armadale.'

'Och aye. Nice wee town.'

Níall said nothing. After a second or two and a quizzical glance, the ferry operator turned away. Níall moved to the stern and looked back at the mainland. Rain leaned in from the horizon, gusting over the sea, which churned up its own froth and spray so that all became one, sea and rain and rain and sea, and the sound of it came and faded with the wind's breath, like the sound of a door being slammed far away. The clustered-together clouds hung low and close over a single line of slate-roofed cottages clinging to the lower slopes of the island, and beyond them, the dark outline of hills protecting the loch.

Armadale, the ferry terminal on the other side, began to swim into view. A terminal building, a car park, not much else. The hills of this part of the island were low and rolling. He took in a deep breath; the bracing sea air plunged deep in him, sharp and crisp. Once, as a child, he'd gone for a walk along this very seafront and somehow lost his way, absurd as it sounded on an island. He'd wound up tramping along a path through the heather, the darkness so dense he could feel it on his tongue. Turning his head slowly from side to side, all sense of direction gone, he'd stopped, unsure of his next footstep and where it might take him. Suddenly the moon came out from behind a gossamer-thin cloud, illuminating his way. To his surprise, he saw that he was almost at the water's edge. A thin shimmer of light on its surface showed that he was on dry land, but only just. Since then, he'd never been able to shake the precarious sense of falling whenever he visited Skye.

The crossing was nearly over. A mournful horn blast preceded an announcement to car owners to go below deck and start their engines. He shoved his hands in his pockets, took one last look at the gently heaving sea, and grasped the cold handrail. He was almost there.

It was just past ten. The light was fading slowly, leaking out of the sky as the clouds rolled in, settling over the shore and the grass and the houses with a fine mist. Everything smelled of rain, of water, of damp. As they approached Armadale, the strong, smoky scent of peat and wood curled around his nostrils. *The peaty coal fires in the tiny living room of his grandfather's home in Fife. His father's father. The view of the Tay Bridge and the patch of grass outside that his grandfather called a garden, so different from the lush, semi-tropical gardens at home. The strangeness of it all.*

*

There was a small hotel just next to the jetty. He parked the car in the forecourt and hauled his bag out of the boot. The door to the main entrance was stiff and swollen with damp but it eventually gave way. The woman behind the desk looked up, clearly surprised to see someone at this late hour. She was reading a paperback, which she placed carefully on the counter, making sure not to lose her place.

'I'm looking for a room for the night,' he said, newly aware of the Englishness of his voice.

'Oh aye. Ye're in luck. We've no many visitors this time o' year. They're all away by now. There's a nice big one on the first floor ... overlooks the water. It's got a fireplace.'

'Yes, that'd be fine.'

'Is it just the one night ye'll be stayin'?'

'Yes, just for tonight.'

'Is it yer first time—'

'I'm sorry,' Níall interrupted her. 'I don't mean to be rude, but I'm very tired. Could you just show me the room?'

She blinked, surprised. She was obviously unaccustomed to being cut off mid flow. 'Right ye are. If ye'll just come wi' me, sir.' She took a key from the rack behind her and crossed the hallway to the stairs. He followed her up, floorboards squeaking under their weight.

The room was large and spacious and, just as she'd said, overlooked the water. She busied herself lighting the fire whilst he walked over to the window. There was a break in the trees that lined the shore. He could see the trawlers tacking their way towards home. He stood there, listening with half an ear to the sounds of the woman behind him, his mind running ahead of himself, as always.

Half an hour later, the fire was lit, the bed was made up and the landlady or owner – it was hard to tell – had retreated downstairs to her armchair and paperback. He poured himself a small measure of the Bunnahabhaín, took off his boots and jacket and lay back against the headboard. The fire crackled in the grate, sending tiny whirlwinds of glowing sparks shooting up the chimney. There was a radio on the bedside table. He picked it up; it took him a few minutes to tune into a station he could understand. Up here, Gaelic took precedence. He finally landed on an English-speaking voice. He picked up his glass and took a sip, letting the soft, hot liquid slide around his mouth and teeth before swallowing.

It burned pleasurably down through his chest and stomach. He hadn't eaten all day, he realised. He hadn't thought to ask the landlady if she had any food. No matter. It wouldn't be the first time he'd had a glass of whisky in lieu of a meal. It probably wouldn't be the last, either.

The fire leapt and danced; outside, the wind picked up. He took another sip and, for the first time in months, felt a warmth steal through him that wasn't to do with the heat outside, the daytime temperatures that soared above anything he'd ever known and the ever-present stench of death.

An unexpected bar of sunlight shone through the bedroom window and came to rest on his eyelids, waking him. He looked across the room to the window. It wasn't a dream. The sky was blue and cloudless, the sun coming up slowly into the fullness of its autumn warmth. He pushed aside the covers and stood up, stretching his arms, feeling the pull of his muscles as if for the first time. He got out of bed and crossed the room to the window. Yesterday's rain had disappeared. He looked at his watch. It was just after eight.

He turned away from the window and walked into the bathroom. He stood under the scalding spray of the shower for almost ten minutes, seeking temporary relief from the tension that had built up in his neck and shoulders over the past few months. He shaved in poor light, using the small mirror above the sink, feeling his way across his two-day stubble. It took him only a few minutes to dress; he'd brought very little with him. By eight thirty, he was finished. He cleared the room, stowing the whisky in his rucksack, and closed the door. The agreeable scent of frying bacon and fresh coffee drifted up the stairs. His stomach gave an angry growl. He was starving. He made his way to the dining room, nodded at the room's only other occupants, a middle-aged couple who sat together in almost total silence, and sat down by the window. The landlady brought over his breakfast with a cheerful 'Guid morning!' and filled both his coffee cup and the toast rack several times without comment but with a smile.

He finished, settled the bill and took his bag out to the car. He slammed the boot shut, slid the keys into his jacket pocket and started walking. Although it had been nearly five years since his last visit, he knew the route to his grandfather's bothy like the back of his hand. Along the tarmac road that ran beside the water's edge for half a mile;

turn left into the bracken and mossy grass until he came to the footpath that led up the hill and over it. The ground underfoot was rough with tussocks, springy and unsteady, but as he broke into a run and began to find his pace, he ceased to notice it, moving instead deeper into the solitude of the land and its calm stillness that he soon realised wasn't a stillness at all but the interweaving of background noises that faded then disappeared. The clear, perfect day hung above him, waiting to draw breath. A flock of birds rose from the distant silvery glint of a small pond, and dragonflies, hanging on the breeze, darted about, their wings illuminated in flashes of fire as they caught the sun. As capriciously as it had landed, the great bird of distress lifted off his shoulders and flew away.

He walked for about half an hour, climbing steadily. At last he came to the crest of a hill, where he slowed to a halt. Below him lay the small crofter's cottage he'd come all this way to visit. Even at this distance he could see that no one had been near it in years. The garden was tangled and overgrown, and the hedge that ran all the way around it had all but disappeared, swallowed up in the weeds and long grasses that this side of the island produced. He looked to his right. The mainland seemed closer than ever, all smoky blue outlines and deep, crevassed ravines. A metallic light bounced off the water. He leaned over, resting his hands on his knees, catching his breath, and then slowly sank to his heels. The purplish heather beneath him was soft and spongy and he lay back into it, letting it take his full weight, the shape of his body's presence. He closed his eyes, the landscape shrilling in his head.

There was earth on his lips. He woke with a start, his body giving one of those tremendous, violent jerks, every muscle in his body gathering to make the leap between the terror of sleep and the harmless safety of wakefulness. He must have dropped off. For a second he didn't know where he was, only that there was grit in his mouth and that he was staring straight into the eye of the earth. He got up stiffly, brushing bits of heather and bracken from his sweatpants, dusting himself down. It was a long walk down to the cottage. He picked up his pace and began to jog towards it.

79

Her telephone rang, late at night. It was on the bedside table, where it lay every night, just in case. She was pulled straight from sleep. 'Hello?' Her heart was beating like a wild animal. She held the phone away from her for a second: *No caller ID*. It was a man's voice. English. Deep. A stranger's voice.

'Inès? Is that you, Inès?'

'Who is this?' She was instantly awake and alert.

'Something's about to happen, Inès. Something big. When the news comes out ... I didn't do it because of her. It was because of *him*. Don't forget that. It's important.'

'Who is this?' Fear rising up through her throat.

But there was nothing more. Just silence. That voice, urgent and quiet, echoing emptily down the line.

80

Dawn broke on her third day in Tubruq, bringing with it the sound of the muezzin calling the faithful to prayer, and those without faith to work. Lexi's eyes flew open, and for a second she struggled to remember where she was. The sounds of fighting drifted by, at times alarmingly close, at others distant, as if from miles away. She was used to the background noises of war: automatic gunfire, the whistling *ping* of a sniper, the low rumble of artillery and the steady, blood-thumping sound of exploding mortars. Occasionally she heard the tinny voice of a radio presenter from a transistor left somewhere in the building, but the reports were in Arabic and were hard for her to follow. Often she heard the screech of tyres and the rolling back of the gate that indicated someone leaving, or entering … she had no idea. She lay in the narrow bed, sweating lightly with the rising heat. What was she? Prisoner? Guest? Sympathiser? Reporter? It was almost impossible to know.

The morning after the interview, Khadija had taken her through to an office somewhere in the rear of the building, where Faisal and a couple of other young men had helped her upload her files and send the interview back to Donal. She'd been allowed to send sporadic emails since then, but she found herself curiously at a loss for words. *Hi, all fine here. Should be back soon. Hope everything's well with you.* What else? Mark wanted more. She knew that as soon as his replies came back. Donal's only concern was that she was unharmed. Jane was oddly distracted, and Aunt Julia was probably not even aware she was gone.

In some ways, Lexi's story was over, almost before it had properly begun. Deena Kenan was safe and well and appeared to be working here entirely of her own volition. In her own, guarded account of her release from detention, there were few clues as to how or why it had come about. Yet Lexi was acutely aware of another, deeper story buried beneath the layers of the young doctor's quiet competence that was to do with Adnan and the curious hold he appeared to have over her – over everyone.

She turned impatiently on to her side, pushing the sheet away from her. Adnan was the last person she wanted to think about right now. Suddenly there was a tap at the door. She sat bolt upright, clutching the sheet rather comically to her chest. 'Who is it?'

'It's me, Khadija.'

'Oh. Come in.'

The door opened a crack. Khadija stood hesitantly in the doorway. 'Good morning,' she said, evidently surprised to see Lexi still in bed. It was nearly eight o'clock. 'Please come with me. You can help us today.'

Lexi looked up at her. 'Doing what?'

'We work in the kitchen,' Khadija explained earnestly. 'You can help.'

'In the kitchen?' Lexi repeated, as though she hadn't quite heard right.

'Yes. We prepare the food. For the men.'

'Me? You want me to help you cook? I can't even boil an egg!'

Khadija wasn't to be budged so easily. 'It doesn't matter.'

Lexi was so astonished by the request that she simply gave in. 'OK. Give me ten minutes. I need to get dressed.'

'I will wait for you.' Khadija closed the door softly behind her. Lexi shook her head. Cook? Her? But she got up and got dressed anyway.

She followed Khadija down the corridor to the kitchen, a low-ceilinged room adjacent to the dining room where she'd eaten every night since she'd arrived. There were half a dozen young women already in there, many of whom she knew by sight. Some were conservatively dressed, in scarves and chadors; others wore jeans and sweatshirts emblazoned with the names of American colleges.

'You can cut, yes?' One of the young women indicated a chopping board and a knife. Lexi nodded doubtfully. 'For tabbouleh.' There was a plastic shopping bag full of parsley and a handful of pearly-skinned onions. Lexi grasped the knife. The other woman watched in dubious silence as she began to chop. 'No, smaller.' She smiled indulgently. 'Like this.'

For almost an hour Lexi diced and sliced onions and tore the refrigerator-cold parsley leaves into tiny shreds, which were chopped and chopped again until all that remained were thin slivers, crisp and sharp against the tongue. Preparations for the meal took up the whole morning. Although the work was monotonous, she found that there was some comfort in the soothing domestic rituals. The women chatted quietly amongst themselves, mostly in Arabic, occasionally in French or English. Like the men she'd met so far, they were a mixture of Egyptians and Libyans, with the odd Algerian or Moroccan thrown in. They were all in their twenties and thirties, some students, some already working; one or two were married, and there was one woman, older than the others, who held the keys to the storeroom, over which she presided like a jealous matriarch. It was hard to gauge exactly what their respective roles might be. Khadija was a law student at the University of Tripoli who'd broken off her studies to join the movement. But any further enquiries into the nature of the group – its founders, its aims and objectives, its history – no matter how gently she put them, were met with the same tolerant silence. If there was a story to be had, the women seemed to imply, it wasn't theirs to tell.

Finally, the tabbouleh was done. Khadija inspected the three large bowls that Lexi had filled and smiled her appreciation. 'You can help me with the kibbeh,' she said, motioning towards the mounds of pale mincemeat and bulgur wheat waiting to be shaped. Lexi nodded and moved over.

She had just finished washing her hands when she heard the noise, a high-pitched whistle, singing through the air. She lifted her head.

She knew that sound. It was a rocket launcher. She turned just in time to see two of the women standing by the sink instinctively raise their arms, cradling their heads protectively, and then the first shell hit. The impact could be felt right down to the foundations, a shudder that went through everything. There was a second screaming whistle and then a dull, thundering crack as the front of the building was blasted apart.

Lexi didn't hesitate. Grabbing Khadija by the arm, she dragged her towards the door and yanked it open. There was a courtyard between them and the next block. She kept hold of Khadija's arm, pushing her forwards. The sound of running feet burst around them as people poured out of the block that had been hit. A shell landed somewhere behind them, forcing everyone to the ground. She could hear people screaming and shouting, and the constant low wail of missiles and artillery shells flying overhead. Someone was targeting the apartment complex. A shower of rubble and debris rained down on them. She turned her head to look at the kitchen behind her and almost retched. It had been reduced to a smoking crater.

She waited for a few seconds, then scrambled to her feet, hauling a terrified Khadija with her. Behind them, vehicles sprang into life as people began to beat a mass exodus from the building through the main gate. Lexi's instincts told her otherwise. The front of the building had been hit; shells were coming from across the street and the main entrance was the target. There had to be another way out. 'Where's the back entrance? The back door?' she yelled at Khadija.

Khadija's teeth were chattering. She looked around wildly, then pointed towards the doorway in front of them. 'Th-there! Th-through that door!' They made a wild sprint for the doorway as another rocket landed somewhere close by. They burst into the corridor, Khadija leading the way. They were running in the direction of the dormitory where Deena's children slept, Lexi realised. At the end of the corridor was another courtyard, with a small gate set in the high wall leading to the narrow alleyway behind the building. It was open. Deena and three or four other adults were frantically helping those children who could walk through it. Lexi and Khadija sprinted towards her.

'What the hell's going on?' Lexi screamed over the noise of gunfire. 'Who's doing this?'

Deena turned to her. Her face was pinched and white with fear and anger. 'Help us get these kids out of here,' she said through gritted teeth.

She motioned to Khadija to take two of the older ones by the hand. 'There's an abandoned building at the end of the alleyway. It's a safe house. Take them there! Come on! We've got to get as many as we can out of here!'

Lexi grabbed two little girls firmly by the hand. They were too shocked to even cry. She shepherded them through the gate, shielding them with her body as best as she could as they ran across the narrow alley. Shells were still exploding behind them and the air was beginning to fill with the smell of smoke. In a heartbeat, the compound had turned from a calm but efficient centre of refuge and industry to a place of appalling, unimaginable carnage.

For fifteen minutes, as the air continued to be ripped apart, they ferried the children across, until every last one was out. There were seventeen in all, Lexi counted, frantically scribbling notes to herself as the evacuation took place. Her iPad and camera were in the room she'd left behind, most likely blasted to smithereens, but there were enough people around her with electronic devices to be able to put some sort of testimony together and get it out to Donal and Jane. Her phone, which was wedged into her back pocket, still had enough battery life to film something … anything. She whipped it out and took a few precious minutes of footage, forcing herself to look straight into the oddly calm faces of the children, who sat huddled together in one corner of the abandoned building.

More people joined them. She caught snatches of conversation, urgent discussions and half-finished arguments about where to go and what to do. Deena moved between her charges, soothing them as best she could. Lexi put the phone away, mentally calculating how much longer she'd be able to film before its power ran out. As she looked around, wondering if there was anything even resembling a working socket, a movement in the doorway made her look up. It was Adnan. He was covered in dust and there was a bloodstained gash in his left shirt sleeve, indicating a wound, but there was no dimming the energy that came off him, a sort of vitality that could have powered not only the dying phone but the whole of the dark, hollowed-out place they had come to.

'How much of this are you getting?' He came over to where Lexi was crouching and squatted down beside her.

'Some. Enough. My editor will want more, of course, but my

equipment's back there.' She glanced over her shoulder at the smoking ruin of the compound some fifty metres behind them.

'We've got to get everyone out of here. They're bracketing us.'

Lexi swallowed. She knew what the term meant: firing on a target and using an observer to relay information about the hit back to the artillery gunners, who would then adjust their sights and fire again. She knew too what it meant about who was doing the shelling. The only way to observe what was going on was from the air. They'd heard no planes or helicopters anywhere overhead, which meant that drones were being used ... and *that* meant the military. Government forces. A small bubble of fear rose in her throat. 'Wh-what are you going to do?' she whispered.

He looked around. 'There's a hospital about half a mile away. There'll be a lull soon ... I know the pattern. As soon as it's safe to move, we'll get everyone out. I've got half a dozen vehicles waiting at the end of the alley. The guys will load up the kids. You stick with me. I'll get you another camera.'

There was a lull in the shelling. The group left the building and ran at a crouch down the alleyway to where the cars and battered 4x4s were waiting, engines revving nervously. The children were put in first, Lexi marvelling at the disciplined, orderly way they were passed from one set of hands to another until all seventeen were safely on board. The vehicles moved off in a jagged convoy, people hanging on to the sides and off the backs like limpets stuck to the hull of a ship. There were only a handful of them left sheltering behind the shells of burnt-out cars and barricades. Deena had gone with the first convoy but Khadija was still somewhere in the group behind her, waiting for the signal to sprint across the open road. Someone came up behind Lexi and pressed something into her hand. She turned. It was Adnan. He'd somehow found her camera and the small pouch containing her iPad and battery chargers.

'Get it all,' he murmured. 'As much as you can. Who knows where or how this is going to end.'

She nodded, grabbing hold of the bag. He touched her arm lightly and moved off. She was left crouching in the debris, her heart in her mouth but her mind only half on the terror and destruction raining down all around her.

81

Lexi's face swam in and out of the misty static. 'With no medical facilities whatsoever, Dr Kenan and her colleagues have somehow, against the most unimaginable odds I've ever witnessed, managed to keep everyone alive.' There was no mistaking the anger or the admiration in her voice. There was another burst of static and the screen shook, then the transmission ended abruptly and she disappeared.

'That came in this morning,' Donal said, getting up. He paced to the edge of the room, then turned back. 'But it was filmed last night. Mark got a message from her around midnight. She's OK, he said, but only just. The house they were staying in took a number of direct hits ... it's not clear how she and Deena Kenan got out, but they did. They've taken refuge in a hospital close to the centre of town, but who knows how long that's going to be safe.'

'We've got to get her out.' Jane spoke up suddenly.

Oliver looked at her as if she'd gone mad. 'Are you insane? That was some of the best footage I've ever seen!'

'This isn't about *footage*, Oliver,' Jane snapped. 'This is about Lexi. She needs to leave, end of story.'

'Haven't you forgotten something? Without her, there *is* no story. We've invested—'

'Who gives a fuck about that now? Didn't you see the report? Someone was targeting them ... Christ, for all we know, they've already been hit, or worse.'

'That's her job. She *chose* to do this, remember? That's what she signed up for. That's why *she's* behind the camera and—'

'I don't believe what I'm hearing.' Donal stopped pacing and turned to face them. Jane saw Zoë and Martin, the finance manager, exchange an uneasy glance. Donal's voice was suddenly quiet. 'I'm pulling her out. End of discussion.' The door slammed shut behind him. No one spoke for a few minutes.

'Oh for God's sake,' Oliver began wearily as three pairs of accusing eyes landed on him. 'I *know* it's dangerous! I know they've just been shelled, but, Jesus … d'you know how much money's been—'

'Fuck you, Oliver.' Jane got up from her chair and left the room. She grabbed her jacket from the rack next to the front door and headed up the stairs. She needed a cigarette and some fresh air. Lexi's footage was wonderful. Raw and unflinching, yet charged with emotion. Donal was right: she had to leave Tubruq. Now. But Donal hadn't seen it. Jane knew Lexi well enough to know two things: one, that there was no way in hell she would voluntarily leave a story behind; and two, that there was something else going on that Lexi had taken great pains to conceal. It was there in her voice. Jane had seen it, even if no one else had.

82

There is a line, thought Inès, struggling to make sense of her own fears as she brushed her hair and prepared to meet their visitors. *On one side is what we all are, and on the other is what we don't admit to.* Next door in the sitting room, her parents were surrounded by friends and relatives. Since Lexi Sturgis's story had broken on the Sunday evening, the flat had been inundated with friends and relatives. Inès had heard from her cousins in Cairo that there were now Facebook pages dedicated to Deena. Her profile had 'gone viral', whatever that meant. Lexi's boss, a very nice woman called Jane Marshall, had been in touch to say that the sudden exposure could work in Deena's favour – *if* she was prepared to leave Tubruq. She'd come round to the flat to tell Inès so. After a few minutes, it was clear to Inès that there was another reason why she'd come. Lexi Sturgis had refused to leave the hospital where they were holed up. Jane Marshall was hoping to enlist Inès's help in persuading her sister and Lexi to leave together.

'You don't know my sister,' Inès said slowly, after Jane had stopped speaking. She'd listened politely to everything she'd had to say, making no comment.

'No, I don't, I'm afraid. I'd very much like to meet her. Perhaps when this is all over I'll get the chance, but for now, I'm concentrating on getting them both out as soon as we can.'

Inès shook her head. 'No, she won't listen. Not to you, not to me. She'll leave when she's ready, not before.'

Jane hesitated. 'Tell me something,' she said after a moment, a note of curiosity in her voice. 'The man they're with … we only got his first name, Adnan … what do you know about him?'

Inès felt the heat start to mount in her cheeks. She was powerless to stop it. Jane's eyes were on her. She didn't look the type to miss things. What did she know? Inès wondered. She took a gamble. 'Not much,' she said slowly. 'He was part of the April 6th Youth Movement … but I think he left them and started on his own.'

'Started what?'

Inès shook her head. 'I … I'm sorry. I don't know much about him or what he does. I don't even know how Deena got to know him.'

'But you know his mother? You paid her a visit a couple of weeks ago.'

Inès looked at her. Her heart started to beat faster. 'H-how do you know that?'

Jane gave a faint smile. 'We're reporters, Inès. That's our job. Not mine, personally, of course, but that's the business I'm in. But I should also point out that if *I* know, others will too. And they might not be so circumspect about how they choose to use that information.'

Inès's heart was thudding. The thought of a reporter rooting around and digging up her family's past was enough to make her feel sick. What would Abu say? She only just stopped herself from reaching out to clutch Jane's arm. 'Look, I … I can tell you that we knew each other as kids. *I* don't remember them … I was too young. But Deena might have. He was here in London, almost a year ago. Deena took me to meet them—'

'Them?' Jane interrupted, quick as a flash.

Inès bit her lip. 'There was a group of them … they were staying at someone's flat. Look, no one's going to get into trouble, are they?' she asked anxiously, thinking of Huda, the young woman from Bahrain in the King's Cross flat who'd seemed so brave.

Jane shook her head. 'No, no … I'm not about to run to the police or anything like that. I'm just looking for clues that'll bring this story together. It's all so fragmented at the moment. Deena hasn't done anything wrong. On the contrary, she's a bloody hero! No, this isn't about *punishing* anyone. It's just about getting to the truth.'

The truth. She looked at her reflection in her dressing table mirror. Whose truth was Jane Marshall referring to? Deena's? Lexi's? Her own?

'Inès? Where are you?' Her mother's voice came down the corridor.

'Coming.' She hurriedly finished brushing her hair and got up.

'Ah, Inès … there she is.'

'Poor thing.'

'Such a worry for her. But she's borne it so well.'

'Yes, though look how thin she's become. They're so close, you know … so close.'

The comments reverberated around the room. Her mother was sitting in the centre of the sofa, stoically accepting the odd mixture of congratulations and condolences from the crowd who'd gathered at their flat, morbidly anxious to be part of the unfolding drama. Inès kissed and was kissed in turn by the half-dozen aunts, uncles, friends-of-the-family and sympathisers, and took her place dutifully to one side, sitting with a cup of tea balanced awkwardly on her knees. Her mind kept returning to the strange telephone call she'd received a few nights before. Had she dreamed it? Who had made the call?

Mrs Stewart wasn't amongst the guests, Inès noticed, although Madame Abou-Chedid was sitting next to her mother, her hand resting possessively on her mother's knee. The television was on in the corner of the living room. People chatted to one another with one eye on the screen. Everyone was waiting … For the phone to ring. For Deena's safe return. For life to go back to normal, for the madness to come to an end. In the midst of the animated chatter around her, the line came back to her again. *Things will be all right in the end. And if they're not all right, it's not the end.* Despite everything that had happened, she knew they were still – always – only at the beginning.

83

From: Donal Pearson <donal.pearson@nni.com>
Date: 17 September 2011 11:00
To: Lexi Sturgis <lexi.sturgis@nni.com>
Subject: Leave

Lexi, I want you out of there. Mark's waiting for you in El-Saloum, just beyond the border. Your last report was excellent but the situation's deteriorating and it's just too dangerous for you to stay. Try to persuade Deena Kenan to leave with you. Her family will fly to Cairo to meet her, if you can only get her to agree. You've done enough and the risks are—

She looked up from the screen. Adnan was standing in the doorway. He walked over to her and crouched down, opening his palm. Two cigarettes. She took one and they lit up in companionable silence. They were alone in the bombed-out shell of an apartment building a few blocks down the road from the hospital where they'd been hiding for the past twenty-four hours. Earlier that morning, Adnan had managed to secure safe passage for Deena and the seventeen children in her charge through one of the many tunnels that ran between Tubruq and Al Karam, the nearest small village on the main road to Egypt. The local area commander had arranged for transportation on the other side. They would be safe in Egypt, he promised.

'She's not coming?' He'd pointed to Lexi.

Lexi answered before anyone else could. 'No. I'm staying.' She saw Deena's head jerk up, but it was Adnan who spoke.

'Take the children and get out of here. I'll see you in Cairo. Go on. That's more important than anything else right now.'

'Someone's got to show the world what's happening here,' Lexi broke in, shoving all thoughts of Donal's email to the back of her mind. 'I'll manage. I can hitch a ride back to the border later on in the week.'

Deena's hesitation was written all over her face, but she allowed herself to be pushed into going. Khadija would accompany her. At the last minute, Lexi scribbled a note for Mark. 'If you come across a photographer called Mark Githerton,' she said to Deena, 'would you give him this?'

Deena nodded and slipped the rather grubby envelope into her bag. There was no time for an elaborate goodbye – a hug, a 'take care' salute and they were gone.

And now she and Adnan were alone. They'd fashioned somewhere to sleep at opposite ends of a room on the second floor. There were a handful of mattresses stacked against the wall which they dragged out and threw down, Lexi opting for what had once been the dining room – a handful of souvenirs remained: broken plates, the lid of a rice cooker and two chairs, both missing a leg. Adnan's mattress was wedged between the door and what was left of a wardrobe, a few yards away. She'd been in situations like this with more men than she cared to remember. After a night spent sheltering from gunfire, all attempts at modesty and privacy were forgotten. It was comforting to feel the presence of other human beings close by.

'Who's it from?' he asked presently, glancing at her screen.

She shrugged. 'My boss. He wants me out of here.'

'And you?'

'I don't think I *can* leave,' she said slowly. 'Even if I wanted to. I feel as though only half the story's been told.'

'Which half is that?' He smiled faintly.

She shrugged and looked away, across the ragged balcony to the city now illuminated by flashes of fire, both real and artillery. 'Well, there's all the usual stuff, if you can call it that. The suffering of ordinary people, lives being blown apart and destroyed … that's the sort of thing viewers want to see and it's what makes my boss happy. But there's another story here that I can't quite get at.' She hesitated for a moment, but Adnan said nothing. She bit her lip, then continued. 'It's to do with you and Deena and Faisal and everyone else. All of you. Why you've chosen to give up everything – your careers, your studies, your families, everything you know. You're six hundred kilometres from home, in someone else's country, and yet you're part of this … this *struggle* as if it were simply part of *you*. As if there were no other choice. I don't understand.'

He smiled. 'There *is* no other choice. You're right. This struggle across the region is part of us. We're all connected. That's what you in the West don't get. What use is freedom if it's not shared by all of us?'

She took a deep breath. Something had been niggling at her for days. She took a risk and opened her mouth. 'You say "you in the West" as if you're talking about a completely different culture. But it's not, is it? I sometimes wonder … are you full Egyptian?' She stopped suddenly. He'd got to his feet. There was a strange expression in his face as he looked down at her. For a moment, neither of them said anything. Then he turned on his heel and walked off.

Lexi ground out her cigarette and slowly leaned back against the wall. Had she offended him in some way? There was a sudden sound behind her. She looked round. Adnan was standing in the doorway again. There was a hardness in his face that frightened her. 'You should go back to Cairo. There's a convoy leaving this evening. The Red Cross will be waiting for you and they'll escort you to the border. Once you reach Al Karam, you'll be safe.'

'Adnan, I—'

'No. You're done here, Lexi. You've done your job. It's time to leave.'

She'd gone too far, she realised. She'd pushed too hard and touched something in him that had only made him close up again. She levered herself upright, getting to her feet, but as she balanced precariously on the lumpy mattress springs, she felt something rush past her ear, pinging wildly off the wall behind her. There was a second's stunned silence, then she dived, palms forward, to the ground. Someone was firing at them. The apartment block was immediately plunged into darkness.

'Stay down!' Adnan hissed. 'And cover that fucking screen.'

She shoved her iPad under the mattress, her heart beating wildly. Above the rat-tat-tat of machine guns, she could hear vehicles approaching. 'Who is it?' she whispered, fear seeping through every pore. Shelling and rocket fire was one thing: gunmen was another altogether.

'Come with me.' Adnan was at her side in a flash. He grabbed her by the upper arm, hauling her to her feet. 'Run!' He pulled her through the doorway after him, pushing her towards the staircase. Below them, they could hear a door being kicked in, followed by rapid firing. The blood thundered in her throat as she and Adnan raced towards the rooftop. He shoved her through the narrow doorway at the top of the stairs, pausing to jam it shut behind them with a pipe he'd spotted lying on the ground. They were on the flat roof of the apartment building. Adnan sprinted ahead of her to the edge, looking over, then motioned to her to join him. 'See that?' He pointed to the gap between their building and the next. 'Can you make it?'

Lexi looked across at the next-door building. Tubruq was an old city, and fortunately for them, the buildings were precariously close to one another. It was a jump of about a metre and a half over a low wall. She swallowed and nodded. 'I ... I think so.'

He gave her no time to change her mind. He held her firmly by the forearm. 'Let's go. There's a pickup truck in the alley. Someone'll be waiting. Come on.'

She closed her eyes, said a hurried prayer and grabbed hold of his hand. And then, together, they jumped.

They took the fire escape on the far side of the building, clattering down in the darkness, her ankle aching from the jolt of landing. He was still holding on to her as they burst out of the front entrance. A battered pickup was indeed waiting, engine running. Two men were up front. As soon as they saw her and Adnan running towards them, they threw open the back doors and the pair of them scrambled inside. The driver took off before they'd even had time to close the doors. Careening wildly, they screeched across the darkened street. In the distance, tracer rounds scored enormous streaks across the sky. The three men were shouting at the tops of their voices, but it was too fast for Lexi to follow. Her ankle was beginning to throb and the blood pumping hard through her heart was almost painful.

Not a single light shone in any building as they snaked their way around the neighbourhood. An occasional flash of torchlight signalling the all-clear was the only thing to break the thick blackness. There was a momentary barrage of fire as a sniper let off a round in the darkness, then the vehicle swerved off to the left and tore wildly down a bumpy road.

'Where are we going?' Lexi whispered, only half expecting a reply.

Adnan's mouth was very close to her ear. 'There's a safe house about a mile down the road. We'll sleep there tonight and leave at dawn.'

Lexi swallowed. 'Are you coming too?'

'Yes. I'll take you as far as Al Karam.'

'*Shukran*,' she managed to say. *Thank you.*

'*Afwan*.' She could hear the smile in his voice. *No worries.*

*

A few minutes later, they screeched to a halt. The driver flicked the headlights once, and a second later there was an answering flash from the darkened building in front of them. '*Yala.*' The other man turned round. 'Let's go.'

Adnan helped Lexi out of the truck. Her ankle was now throbbing fiercely. She hobbled up the steps on his arm. Two bearded men were standing in the doorway. They greeted Adnan with the traditional kiss on either cheek and the bear hug that signalled common cause. There was a rapid exchange of opinions about what to do with Lexi – all three kept turning to look at her, Adnan shaking his head vigorously. Finally, when she thought she would pass out from the pain, Adnan broke away from them and came towards her.

'Come on. Someone'll take a look at your ankle. I think it's only sprained, but you need to get it taped up. Tomorrow will be a tough day. We'll have to go through a stretch of tunnel to get you to the Red Cross. You need to rest.'

She could feel a sob welling up in her throat. The high emotion of the previous few days had finally caught up with her. She jerked her head away. 'I'm fine,' she muttered, avoiding his look of concern.

'No you're not. Stop arguing with me. Let's get this seen to. Come on.' He offered his arm for support. Lexi had no choice but to take it, and together they hobbled down the corridor to a kitchen at the rear of the house.

Half a dozen armed rebels were sitting around a table, smoking, including a man in a bloodstained white coat with the tiredest eyes Lexi had ever seen. 'Dr Abu Hanim.' He held out a hand. 'I know who you are. Welcome to Tubruq, Miss Sturgis. I trust you've had a good stay?' There was a loud guffaw of laughter from the men around the table. Lexi stared at him. His voice had the faintest trace of Liverpool. 'Yes, I trained at the Royal,' he grinned, reading her mind. 'So ... how are you?'

'Her ankle. I think it's sprained,' Adnan said tersely, kicking out a chair and collapsing into it. 'We're going through the tunnel at Al Karam tomorrow. She'll need it taping up.'

Dr Abu Hanim pulled a face. 'Tunnel, eh? You ever been in one of those before, Miss Sturgis?'

Lexi shook her head. Again the men around the table burst into laughter. All save Adnan. She lifted her eyes and met his. There was something unreadable in them that made her look away.

Dr Abu Hanim touched her swollen foot. 'Yeah, it's a bad sprain. Lucky you. Could've been worse.' He stood up and asked one of the rebels to fetch something. Seconds later, the man reappeared with a roll of bandage and a bottle of pills. Someone else jumped up and filled a basin with water, placing it carefully on the table. Lexi looked around her at the battle-hardened young men standing to attention, waiting for the doctor's next order. There was a tenderness and concern in their faces that made her want to weep. 'Take four now. No, go on, all of them.'

'Wh-what are they?'

'Pain relief.' He wouldn't elaborate. He made sure she swallowed all four pills, then bent down and eased off her boot. She was too tired to protest as he began carefully and methodically to wash her filthy foot. Someone was preparing coffee. A bitter, wonderfully sharp aroma filled the small kitchen. A cup was placed in front of her. 'Drink,' he urged her. 'It's strong. It'll give you a kick, you'll see.'

He was right. Within minutes, the adrenalin had kicked in and the pain was beginning to subside. She closed her eyes, hoping the tears wouldn't force their way through, and surrendered herself to the strange luxury of having her feet washed by someone she'd only just met.

Half an hour later, having eaten everything that was placed in front of her, and downed a tumbler full of whisky – no ice – she was shown to a room at the rear of the house. The young rebel who escorted her spoke no English, but between her poor Arabic and his vigorous sign language, he let her know that there was a large bucket of hot water in the adjacent bathroom and that the toilet worked. She had to physically prevent herself from throwing her arms around his neck. He grinned and left the room, his gun swinging jauntily from his hip as he walked back down the corridor.

Lexi closed the door behind her and looked dazedly around. There was a low bed in one corner – with sheets! – and an old armchair in the other, balanced precariously on three legs. A small bedside lamp stood on the floor beside the bed. The floor was dusty with footprints and the single light bulb hanging from a cord in the ceiling had no cover, but it was the most luxurious accommodation she'd seen in ages.

She hobbled into the bathroom and stood staring in disbelief at the huge bucket of hot water standing in the middle of the salmon-pink tub. There was a sliver of soap beside it and a towel that more closely resembled a piece of cardboard. She didn't care. Within seconds, she'd stripped off her filthy clothes and stepped in. The first sluice of warm water made her gasp in pleasure. She soaped herself down, washed her hair and finally scrubbed as much of the dirt of the past four days as she could out of her clothes. She hung them carefully on the bare pole that had once housed a shower curtain, then, shivering from the cool air, hurried back into the bedroom.

She wrapped the bed sheet firmly around her, tucking it under her arms, sarong-style, switched off the bedside light and lay back against the flat mattress, staring unseeingly into the dark. She closed her eyes but although she felt physically exhausted, her mind moved on, skittering and skimming, jumping over the events and images of the past few days. She had the sensation of falling. It was as though her mind had lapsed, laying her open to the flow of things. She felt she'd lost control over what she'd seen or how she felt. The feeling surprised her, but she had no time to dwell on it. Someone had stopped outside her door. She lifted her head cautiously. She knew even before the door opened that it was Adnan. He closed it quietly behind him and stood with his back to it, waiting for some sign from her that would indicate whether or not he should proceed.

What are you doing? The thought moved slowly, hazily across her mind. *What are you doing?*

He crouched down beside her and switched on the lamp. The room was suddenly filled with its soft yellow light. They stared at each other, neither moving, neither speaking. Lexi's heart slowed, almost to a stop. Adnan slid his long, jeans-clad legs into the bed beside her and took her face in his hands, turning it slowly this way and that. She couldn't breathe. Desire rose in her like a great suffocating tidal wave.

'What are you afraid of?' His voice punctured the silence.

She swallowed painfully. 'Ev-everything,' she stammered.

'Lexi, there's nothing to be afraid of.'

She felt the heat break out all over her, a blush that travelled up her body into her neck and face. She clenched her fists, trying to conceal it, pushing down on the urge to thrust his hands down the plane of her stomach and into the hot, pulsating centre of her body that seemed to be the very core of herself. He began to kiss her. She thought wildly of Mark. There was no way to know how it would be, that first touch. No way to know how the tongue would be, or the taste ... no way to know anything about the man lying next to her. Stunned, she followed him, blind with gut-wrenching desire. She gave herself up to it, wallowing in his embrace, grabbing at him with greedy abandon. He broke the kiss and rolled away from her, hurriedly shedding his clothing, his second skin. She raised herself on an elbow, drinking in the sight of him – the naked torso with its ripple of ribs under the smooth golden skin; dark-brown nipples on the pad of muscle at either side, the chest powerfully cleaved by thick brown hair that swept outwards, away from the single indentation that ran from his breastplate down the flat stomach, disappearing into the curly thatch below his belly button … Her eyes moved down to the thick, erect penis, proudly jutting in front of him.

He tugged impatiently at the sheet still covering her until at last they were both free of the envelopes of clothing and modesty that hid one from the other. He might never have been presented with a woman before, or she a man. His arms went around her, sliding agonisingly slowly down the small of her back. He lifted her deftly on to him and slid inside her, deeply, without warning or preparation. She needed none. She'd been waiting for this for longer than she could remember, she realised dazedly. The realisation freed her, and the tempo between them suddenly changed. She wanted more of him, all of him. He couldn't push hard or deep enough. She clawed wildly at his back until he rolled them both over, turning her around so that she looked up into his face and saw for the first time the achingly beautiful smile that he kept hidden from everyone. The flash of white teeth, eyes fluttering open on thick, fringed eyelashes. His eyes, now hazel, now brown, now green, searched out her own, confirming what they both knew. The pleasure he was taking so fiercely from her was matched equally by her own.

84

He recognised her even before she'd opened her mouth to address him. 'You're Deena, aren't you?' He stood up so abruptly his chair toppled over backwards. The crash was loud in the quiet little cafe where he'd been

329

waiting, day and night, for nearly three days. He bent down to pick it up, his heart accelerating so fast it was painful.

She nodded. 'Yes.'

'Is she here? Did she come with you?'

'No, I'm sorry. She didn't want to leave, not just yet.'

'But she's coming? At some point?' He could hear the desperation in his voice and it made him wince. 'I'm sorry ... I haven't even asked ... are *you* all right? When did you get here?'

She nodded. Her dark hair was a curtain over her eyes and face, hiding not just her image but her thoughts. 'I'm here with the children I've been looking after. Seventeen of them. We came through one of the tunnels yesterday. Lexi asked me to give you this,' she said, producing the crumpled letter.

'How did you find me?'

She smiled. 'It's a village. Everyone knows where everyone is.' She turned to leave.

'Wait, don't go. Is she ... all right?' he asked, holding tightly on to the note.

She nodded. 'Yes, she's fine.'

He didn't know why he asked the question. 'Is she alone?'

She put up a hand to tuck her hair behind her ear, and one side of her face was revealed to him. She looked at him out of the darkness of the past few months, shaming him for having given in so readily to his fears. She shook her head, but the expression in her dark eyes was impossible to read. 'No, she's not alone.'

He watched her wind her way back through the cafe, only just managing not to call out her name, begging her to stay and answer the question now running incessantly through his head. *She wasn't alone.* That was the answer he'd sought. He hadn't known he feared it until it came. The door closed behind her and he was alone again.

He sat down heavily and unfolded Lexi's note. Her looped, scrawling handwriting leapt out at him. He read it through quickly, twice, his eyes drawn to the last sentence. *I should be back by the weekend, if nothing goes wrong.* He read it a third time, staring at it as though trying to squeeze a message for him alone from between the lines, but there was none. For a second he was reminded of the moment he'd gone to the reception desk at the Peponi in Lamu and found her gone. A cold wave of dread washed over him, leaving him almost trembling. He pulled himself up short. He was being ridiculous. That was before.

He folded her note away and slipped it into his pocket. He was gripped with longing for her that was like a thirst, or worse. He lifted his arm and summoned a coffee. Unfortunately there was no alcohol to be had in this part of the world. Especially not now.

85

As soon as she saw the question in Mark's eyes, even before he'd voiced it, she knew she was right to worry. She'd sensed it the moment Lexi Sturgis arrived. She'd seen Adnan's swift catch of interest, though he'd quickly suppressed it; not just because she, Deena, was present but because it represented a side to him that he continuously fought to suppress. There was no time for personal feelings to get in the way of their cause, or at least that was what Adnan's very being seemed to suggest.

Deena was neither slow nor stupid. Adnan's extraordinary appeal lay not just in the politics of what they all believed in, but in *him*, in some raw, essential part of him that none of them could resist, men and women alike. It was evident in the way people around him worshipped him, they way they hung on his every word, every command, every gesture. No one was exempt from the power he exuded, least of all Deena. There was something in him that was both strangely familiar and yet powerfully distant, a shifting horizon that she longed to be able to cross; part of his charm was that he fooled you into thinking you *had* crossed it, only to withdraw immediately afterwards, leaving you confused and unsure. Was it something you'd said? Done? Failed to do? The more he demanded of you, the more you gave, until the point was reached where he suddenly stopped demanding ... and then you longed for the full weight of his gaze upon you again, no matter the cost.

She had never met anyone like him, a man whose body and mind were so poised and intense that he radiated an energy that was a new kind of heat, separate from everyone else, hard-edged and perpetually alert. When he turned his head to look directly at her, she felt her heart begin to beat faster, the blood in her veins warm up. Yet the warmth in him had nothing to do with kindness. The heat in Adnan was a fiery, hot-headed madness, of the kind that burned. Once, long ago, when she'd started going round to the King's Cross flat, she'd found herself alone in the kitchen with him as she prepared to take in a tray of tea.

'So you're Deena Kenan,' he'd said to her, standing with his back to the window so that his whole body was framed by light.

'Y-yes,' she stammered.

'And you're a doctor?'

'Yes.'

'Ah. That's good to know.'

She'd understood right there and then that there was no question she wouldn't join them, irrespective of what was needed. 'Have we met before?' she blurted out suddenly. Just then, just as he spoke, there was an expression on his face that reminded her of someone ... but who?

He shook his head. 'No, we've never met,' he said firmly. He held the door open for her. She ducked her head under his arm and felt the blush of desire travel all the way through her body. Her face was on fire when she walked into the room and placed the tray on the low coffee table with shaking hands. She prayed none of the others would see her stunned expression or know how to read it.

That same blush had been on Lexi Sturgis's face. When Adnan appeared a few seconds later, Deena understood its source.

She turned away from the mirror. The expression in her eyes sickened her. She looked at her watch. In less than half an hour, the representatives from the Red Cross and MSF would be there. She'd had a call from Valérie to say that she too would be coming. They would take the children directly from Al Karam to Alexandria, from where the Red Cross had organised a flight to Rome. Valérie would stay with them in Rome whilst Deena would be flown back to the UK to be reunited with her family.

'What about Dr Stewart?' she asked. 'How are things ... back there?'

'Haven't you heard?'

'No, what?'

'He left.'

'He *left*? What are you talking about?'

'He left MSF. We had a message the other day from HQ. He's resigned.'

'Resigned?' Deena had difficulty believing it. 'Because of what happened to Christos?'

'No. No one knows. He left shortly afterwards. Didn't even say goodbye.'

Deena was shocked. No one could possibly have been more dedicated than Dr Stewart. 'Who's replacing him?' she asked finally.

'We don't know yet. Are you coming back, Deena?'

'Of course I am.'

She could almost see Valérie's smile of relief. 'Thank God. We miss you. It's not the same without you.'

'I'll be back before you know it.' As she put down the phone, a small tremor of trepidation ran through her.

Now, waiting in the local hospital for her colleagues, that trepidation was intensified. If something happened to Adnan – and she couldn't quite bring herself to think about what that 'something' might be – did she have the conviction required to see this through?

86

The immensity of the desert blots out any attempt at human habitation. It puts a stop to the houses, streets, shops, cafes, the signs of life to which one is habitually accustomed. It's another kind of life out there.

As they left El-Saloum behind, they came upon a scattering of masonry, the abandoned remnants of the attempt to impose some sort of human will on the sea of shifting sands. She sat in the back seat of the Red Cross vehicle, sandwiched between Mark and one of the three officials who'd been sent to bring her back to Cairo. Mark's arm was drawn tight across her shoulders. Her ankle was throbbing. It had begun to hurt again the minute Adnan slipped away. He'd left her just before dawn, before the men who were to escort them to the tunnel came for them. To her immense distress, aside from a few terse commands as they lowered her down into it, he'd hardly said another word. The last she'd seen of him was his tall, lean body silhouetted against the rising sun as she stumbled towards the car that was waiting to take her to El-Saloum. Now there was nothing left of his presence save the expression of stunned, guilty disbelief that she knew was written all over her face.

She leaned forward abruptly. 'Can we just stop for a second? I need some air.' Mark's arm loosened its grip.

'Here?' he asked, looking around at the sea of sand that stretched in every direction.

Lexi nodded. 'Just for a few minutes. I feel sick.'

The vehicle slowed, juddering over the tarmac until it came to a stop. She opened the door. There was a shift in pressure as she stepped out into the burning heat. 'Thanks,' she muttered. 'I won't be a moment.'

She could feel their eyes on her as she limped around the back of the vehicle and leaned against it, fishing a crumpled packet of cigarettes from her back pocket. She lit one and squatted down by the side of the road, resting against the warm bumper as she smoked. The silence was a roar in her ears, the sandy distance a hazy veil. She turned her head to look at the road behind them. It seemed to run on for ever. It was the last time, she realised that. If she continued to look back, she would be lost. She took a final draw on her cigarette and ground it out under her heel, keeping her eyes dead ahead as she climbed back inside the air-conditioned car and fastened her seat belt. She took a deep breath, then another, and another. *This is how it's got to be*, she told herself slowly, firmly. *This is how it has to be. This is how the story ends.*

He put out a hand to touch her, moving it over her head as though over a piece of sculpture, flattening her short, spiky hair.

'Why don't you grow it?' he asked, the words slipping out as if some-one else had spoken.

'Why?'

He could feel the heat rising in his face. He didn't know what to say. He continued his soft stroking, hoping she would take the request as a murmured endearment rather than a question of any serious intent.

'Why?' she asked again.

He shrugged, turning to press his lips against her hair. 'No reason,' he mumbled. 'I like it long, that's all.'

'You've never seen me with long hair.'

'I … I know. I just thought … a change, that's all.'

'No, it's not practical.' She slipped out of his embrace and stood up.

He watched her walk around the bed, as unselfconscious as she'd always been, and was alarmed to find himself aroused again. She still carried a faint limp – she'd hurt her ankle jumping from one roof to another, she'd explained tersely – and the sight simply made him want her all the more. He closed his eyes, revelling in the pleasure of hearing her move around close to him. He put out a hand to catch hold of her, judging from the sound where he thought she would be passing, but it closed on air. She was gone.

He opened his eyes slowly. Something had happened. He'd been with too many women not to recognise the subtle shifts in mood, tempo, touch that preceded an announcement of some sort. *We need to talk. It's not the same. It's not working out.* He was usually the one to make the sudden announcement, to walk off, walk away.

Not this time.

PART TWELVE

December 2011

87

'Ready?' Aunt Julia stood in the doorway, giving her a final once-over. 'You look lovely, darling. Doesn't really show, you know.'

Lexi looked down at her stomach. 'Only if you're blind,' she said drily. She turned sideways.

Aunt Julia smiled tolerantly. 'You're barely three months gone. It hardly shows, I promise you. Now, are we ready?' She looked across the room at Jane.

Lexi nodded. 'About as ready as I'll ever be.'

'What on earth makes you say it like that?' Aunt Julia asked, frowning. 'I ... it'll be all right, won't it?'

'Darling, what's got into you all of a sudden? Of course you'll be all right. You'll be just fine. It'll be over in an hour.'

'No, not that.' She stopped, putting her hands over the tiny bulge of her abdomen. 'I mean, this.' She rubbed her stomach hesitantly. '*This.*'

There was a sudden silence in the room. Jane and Aunt Julia eyed each other nervously. 'Of course you'll be all right,' Jane said firmly.

'Jesus, don't make me cry,' Aunt Julia said, flapping her hands in front of her face. 'Have you got a tissue, Jane?'

'Here.' Jane fished one out of her clutch. 'Everything's going to be fine, Lexi. I promise.'

'How can you doubt yourself?' Aunt Julia cried. 'You, of all people. After all the things you've done, everything you've been through.'

'That's different,' Lexi said slowly. 'That's my job. I ... I don't know if I can do this.'

'Look, it's *perfectly* normal to have doubts. Perfectly normal,' Aunt Julia said firmly. 'You'll see just how naturally it'll all come as soon as the baby's born.' Lexi looked at her, and then at Jane . All three of them were aware that their certainty was something of a bluff. Between them, not one of them had ever had a child. 'Now, put a damned smile on

339

your face. Let's get this wedding under way. Taxis are all waiting outside. Come on. Take my arm. I'll walk you down the stairs.'

Lexi drew in a deep breath. For once, her morning sickness had kept itself at bay. It was December, but the day had dawned bright and clear. The perfect day to be married. Mark was waiting for her outside the church. It was time to go.

Jane gave Lexi's hand one last quick squeeze as the taxi pulled up next to the kerb. Many of the guests had walked down Portobello Road to the church and were gathered in front of it, waiting excitedly for the bride to appear. She saw Mark, splendidly handsome in his dark grey suit, his hair swept away from his tanned face, and had to draw in a deep breath to steady her nerves. She couldn't have been happier for Lexi – or for Mark, for that matter – but there was no denying the bittersweet quality of her own feelings. It was three months since she'd had the termination, and now here she was at Lexi's wedding, her maid of honour, watching her pregnancy from the sidelines. *Stop it. It's Lexi's day*, she cautioned herself sternly. *Don't you dare ruin it by feeling sorry for yourself.*

Lexi must have caught something of her mood. 'You all right?' she whispered as the driver got out to open the door. Aunt Julia and two of her friends were in the taxi behind them.

Jane nodded quickly. 'Course I am. Come on, let's get you inside.' She took Lexi's arm to help her out of the car. 'Before you change your mind,' she added, forcing a note of laughter into her voice. A curious tremor ran through Lexi's arm as she said, it but before she could comment, Mark suddenly materialised.

'Thank God you're here. I thought you'd changed your mind,' he laughed, echoing Jane.

She felt the tension in Lexi's arm again. For the umpteenth time since Lexi's return from Egypt, it struck her that there was something not quite right. She'd tried several times to probe beyond the cheerful mask, but Lexi carefully and skilfully deflected her questions. When she'd announced she was pregnant, Jane had wondered for a single, mad, fleeting second ... then pushed the thought firmly away. No, of course not. Lexi was nothing if not scrupulously honest. If something had indeed happened back there during the week she'd spent in Libya, she would have said. Of course she would.

*

Breaching protocol, Lexi walked towards the church steps with her arm in Mark's. She caught a fleeting glimpse of the small group of friends and colleagues who'd come to see her and Mark tie the knot. There were the Kenans, standing together, Inès, Deena and their parents; Ahmad and Gio had come over from Cairo somehow; she spotted Donal and Zoë and most of the other correspondents, even Dominic. Oliver was there, standing next to Susie, their hapless receptionist, resplendent in shiny green silk. Several of Aunt Julia's fashionista friends had come too, set apart from the rest by their elegance, fur stoles and pin-sharp heels.

'Ready?' Mark's voice buzzed softly against her ear. She looked at the expectant faces around them. There was one absence that brought a sharp lump to her throat, but she swallowed down hard on it. Toby. She and Mark had already decided on a name for the child they now knew would be a boy. Magnus Tobias Githerton.

She nodded. 'Ready.' The church doors opened. To a loud burst of applause from the onlookers and several passers-by, they walked slowly up the steps together.

88

Aunt Julia had spared absolutely no expense. Jane looked around the ballroom at the Berkeley and sighed deeply. The art deco interior was at its most elegant. Wine and champagne flowed, the food and service were exquisite … she felt as though she'd stepped into the pages of *Vogue* or on to the set of a glamorous film. Everywhere she looked, people were laughing, chatting animatedly, swapping stories, numbers, business cards. Donal and Oliver were huddled together at one of the tables, earnestly discussing their next series, no doubt. Jane herself had spoken to almost everyone, from the Kenan sisters to Lexi's friends from Cairo. She'd played the part of best friend to perfection, disguising the underlying sense of failure that had grown disproportionately – and alarmingly – stronger as the evening wore on. It was the wine, she kept telling herself.

It was nearly ten o'clock and the party was beginning to thin. She'd passed the point of euphoria and was now slipping towards despair.

She could see Zoë, the only person in the whole room who might have guessed at the source of sadness contained deep within her, looking quizzically in her direction. She took another careful sip of champagne. In the elegant foyer of the hotel, the band had started up. The music drifted in through the open French doors. A well-known song, a crowd-pleaser, though she couldn't have said who or what. She listened for a few minutes, her mind gone blank. But it wasn't the crooning words of the lead singer she heard. In her mind's eye, she saw only the face of the doctor who'd assessed her a few months before. *Are you sure about this? I wouldn't normally say this to a patient, but you're thirty-eight, aren't you? There may not be another chance.*

'Bride or groom?' A voice suddenly cut across her thoughts. She looked up in consternation. She was sure her face had registered her distress. A man was standing in front of her. Tall; short dark hair sprinkled with grey; fit; good-looking; a face of serious concentration but with enough laughter lines radiating outwards from the corners of his eyes to reassure her that he knew how to smile. She blinked, confused. Who was he?

'I'm sorry … what did you say?' She managed to gather herself together.

'Are you a friend of the bride or the groom?' He said it patiently, with a faint smile.

'Oh. I'm … I'm Jane. I'm Lexi's friend. Maid of honour, actually.'

'Ah. Can I get you another?' He pointed to her empty champagne glass.

'Er, sure. Yeah, why not?'

'I'll be back in a second.'

She watched him walk across the lobby to a waiter, deposit her empty glass, pick up two full ones and walk back towards her. Her face felt warm.

'I suppose I should ask you the same thing. Bride or groom?'

'Neither. I've never met either of them, I'm afraid.'

She frowned, trying to follow. 'So … how … who invited you?'

'No one. I'm a family friend of the Kenans. I heard they'd be here but I just missed them, it seems. It's a pity. I haven't seen them for quite some time.'

'Oh.'

'I'm Níall, by the way.'

'Jane.' She held out a hand.

'You already told me your name.'

342

'I did?'

'Yes.' He smiled, and her heart missed a beat. He had a slow way of smiling that made her think of a leaf opening itself into sunlight, or a flower coming into bloom. It felt good to have made him smile. No, better than that … it felt great. She was aware of an answering smile tugging at her own lips. Out of the corner of her eye, she could see Zoë looking at her again, only this time her expression was one of cautious delight rather than concern.

She brought her champagne glass up to her lips and took a small, dainty sip. They looked at one another warily, but neither said anything. The silence between them deepened, but it was a comfortable silence, full of words that simply hadn't yet been said. To her surprise, Jane felt no pressure to fill it, but simply waited for him to speak first. He was quick to pick up on her generosity. She saw from his eyes that he'd caught her moment of uncertainty towards him, and there it was again – that slow, sensuous smile playing around his mouth. There was a lightness about him, a little buzz … she could hear it coming off his skin. She looked up at him, at the smile that was in his eyes as well as his face, and began to laugh.

PART THIRTEEN

November 2016

89

She could hear Mark's voice from the top of the stairs as she hurried between bedroom and bathroom, her toothbrush clamped between her teeth. 'No, not today, son. Today's a nursery day.' There was a pause, then Magnus's typically obstinate reply: 'But I don't *want* to go to nursery. I went *yesterday*.' She smiled at that and turned her attention to getting ready. Her flight to Edinburgh was at ten. It was now eight thirty. Fifteen minutes to get out of the house, avoiding a tearful showdown with Magnus; an hour to Heathrow, during which time she'd finish reading her notes … a full day at the Scottish Parliament covering the results of the election, then back down to London on the last flight. With luck, she'd be there at the breakfast table the following morning, ready to go through the whole question again. Magnus was four and hadn't quite grasped the principle of nursery, or of school. '*All* my life? I have to go to school my *whole* life?' he'd asked her the other day in disbelief. '*Every* single day?'

'Except Saturdays and Sundays. And holidays, of course.'

'But that's *ages* long! I'll be *old* before I stop having to go to school.'

'You never stop, Mag, that's the whole point.' Mark had come into the living room.

Magnus's lower lip trembled as he struggled to take in the implications of what he'd just been told. 'It's not fair,' he said finally. 'It's just not fair.'

Lexi had to laugh at that. 'Life's not fair, darling. Now, come on. Dad'll take you on the back of his bike. How's that?' They'd gone off on Mark's bicycle together, Magnus with a helmet that was twice the size of his head. It was a far cry from the way both she and Mark had walked to school every day along a dusty Lusaka road or through the Kenyan bush.

'Hullo, you two,' she said, coming into the kitchen. 'What's new, Mag?'

He eyed her suspiciously from behind his cereal bowl. 'Dad says I've got to go to nursery today.'

''Fraid Dad's right,' Lexi said, opening the fridge. 'Are we out of milk?'

Mark shook his head. 'Behind the orange juice.'

'Are you going away again?'

It was the 'again' that killed her. 'Only for the day, darling. I'll be back by bedtime.' She ignored Mark's frown. He disliked it when she lied to appease him. 'Just tell him you'll be there in the morning. He won't go to sleep until you're back, you know.'

Magnus eyed her woefully. '*Jake's* mummy—' he began with a sigh, but Lexi cut him off.

'Yes, well, I'm not Jake's mummy, thank God,' she said briskly. 'Now, who's going to be first to kiss me and who's going to take my bag to the door?'

Five minutes later, Magnus having been dispatched to get his own bag, Lexi reached up on tiptoe and curled her arm around Mark's neck. 'Why the long face?' she whispered. 'Don't tell me you're going to sulk too.'

Mark shook his head. 'No, but I wish you wouldn't say things like that in front of him.'

'Like what?'

'Like "I'm not Jake's mummy, thank God." He'll start to wonder what's wrong with Barbie.'

Lexi snorted. 'Her name, for a start. Who on earth is called Barbie these days? OK, I'm sorry. I didn't mean it.'

'Yes you did. Barb's a good woman, Lexi.' Mark's tone was unusually defensive. Lexi looked up at him quizzically, but before she had a chance to respond, Magnus appeared in the doorway. Having resigned himself to the idea, he was now impatient to get going. The next few minutes were taken up with goodbyes and kisses, and then, abruptly, she was alone again.

She wandered back into the kitchen, finished her coffee and began to gather her things. Her taxi would be here any minute. She stood for a second looking out of the window. Their small second-floor flat just off Kingsland Road was also a far cry from the rambling ambassadorial houses and farmhouse that they'd grown up in, but Mark had been adamant about buying something that was within their means rather than Aunt Julia's. Lexi smiled to herself. She could still picture Aunt Julia's face as they'd driven down Balls Pond Road towards the flat. 'Is this still London?' she'd asked, looking around her in disbelief. Lexi had snorted but spared her an answer. It was near Jane and Níall and a quick bus ride to NNI's offices at Old Street. Getting to Heathrow was more of a challenge, but ... *you can't have everything*, Lexi reasoned with herself. She was only too aware that she had more than most. A sharp toot of a horn interrupted her musings. She grabbed her bag and laptop and opened the front door. Time to get going.

She boarded the flight with only a few minutes to spare. She flipped open her laptop and quickly scanned through her notes. A full morning of interviews, including one with Alex Salmond that she'd been angling for over the past few weeks; a late-afternoon TV appearance and then a quick early dinner with colleagues before heading back to the airport for her flight home. With any luck she'd be in bed by midnight.

She thought briefly of Mark. She'd already forgotten what he'd said he'd be doing that day, aside from picking Magnus up from nursery, of course. She pulled a quick, guilty face. It was too easy to forget what Mark was doing. They'd made the decision jointly: Lexi would continue to work; Mark would stay at home to look after Magnus. Deep down, Lexi knew the decision had been hers, not his. She had a career worth continuing; Mark did not. It was that simple. He'd come into the marriage with very little. There was no job waiting for him in London ... why not stay home, at least for a while, and take care of the baby? A while became a year, then two ... then three. By then it would have been almost as unthinkable for her to leave NNI as it would have been for Donal. She stayed on; Mark stayed at home. In time, it simply became the manner of their lives.

Twenty minutes to landing. Twenty minutes to landing. The washrooms are now closed. Please fasten your seat belts and put away your tray tables. She came back to herself with a start. She must have dozed off. She fastened her seat belt and pulled the rug up to her chin, suddenly feeling cold. She glanced at her watch. It was ten forty-five. In less than twelve hours' time, she'd be on her way back home.

She was coming out of the washrooms at the Scottish Parliament when her mobile rang. She fumbled with her files, clamping her phone between chin and cheek as she hurried down the stairs. It was Donal.

'All done?' he asked.

'All done,' she confirmed. 'He was on top form. And I got a bit in with Nicola Sturgeon.'

'Great.' There was a momentary silence.

'What is it?' She could hear his hesitation.

'I've got something for you.'

'What?'

'Remember that pipeline that was blown up in September? The one with the six Western hostages?'

Lexi nodded. 'Yeah, near the border with Libya?'

'Yes, that one. Well, we've just had a call from someone in Algiers. Seems he knows who's behind it. He's willing to talk.'

Lexi's mouth was suddenly dry. 'When?' she asked, her heart beating faster.

'Can you get there by tomorrow night? I know it's tight. The guy asked for you. Marwan Kalmichi. You've used him before, haven't you?'

'Yeah. He's sound.'

'Good. Well, let me know when you get out there. If it all checks out, it'll be big, Lexi.'

'I'll speak to him and ring you back.' She ended the call and stood still for a second. Marwan was a fixer, someone who could organise almost anything from vehicles to translators, including safe passage out of any given situation … for a price, of course. Many loathed him; most feared him. Lexi didn't. She liked his directness and the fact that her gender was of absolutely no interest or consequence to him. He would just as happily deal with her as with anyone else, something that couldn't be said of many who operated in the same realm. She had a few questions for him, then she'd make a call to the office to organise the logistics – a ticket, some cash and a hotel room, at least for her first night. Third and last: a call to Mark before grabbing a cab to the airport. Mark. Always the most difficult call of all.

90

Five-star hotels are the same the world over. At such short notice, Pat had said, semi-apologetically, it was all she could get. Lexi looked around her and smiled faintly. There was nothing to be sorry about. Fine cotton sheets, firm pillows, air-conditioning, no matter the outside temperature, an embossed folder with all services conveniently listed A–Z, and the usual neutral palette of colours: taupe, aubergine, cream, mink. In the bedside drawer there was a copy of the Koran and, thoughtfully, a New English Bible. Everything for the modern traveller. 'You're getting old, Sturgis,' she murmured to herself, taking it all in. There was a time when she'd have baulked at such luxury. Not now.

As soon as the bellhop had silently withdrawn, she'd tossed her bag on the bed and begun the ritual of unpacking: a few clothes in the wardrobe, a couple of books beside her bed, laptop and equipment out on the desk. She hadn't brought much. She'd had no idea how long she'd be away.

'How long this time?' Mark had asked the night before, watching her pack.

'Hard to say. A couple of days ... a week? I'll know more tomorrow when I've met him.'

'What'm I to tell Mag?'

She'd had to bite down hard on her irritation. She shrugged. 'Tell him what you like. I mean, I can't change it, Mark. We've been through this a gazillion times. I go away to work. Millions of fathers – mothers, sorry – do. He's got to get used to it.'

He'd looked at her then in that maddening way of his when he wanted her to know he disapproved but wouldn't say it outright. *Fathers, yes. Not mothers.* That was what he meant. What he actually said was 'He'll miss you.'

She had no answer for that. She snapped her case shut and left the room.

Now, remembering it, a wave of tenderness for him, for Magnus, stole over her and she picked up her phone from the bed.

'Hi. It's me. I just got in. Mmm, it was all right. Are *you* all right?' The question, delicately phrased, was intended to cover it all – him, her, their marriage, her leaving, their son ... all of it.

'Yeah. Tired. Took Mag to the park to wear him out, but it's worn me out instead. What's the weather like?'

'Cold. You forget how cold it gets. I always think of Algiers in summer.'

'Yeah.' He had no real answer for that.

'I'd better go,' she said quickly. 'I've still got some background work to do tonight. Kiss Mag for me, will you?'

'Yeah, sure. What about me?'

'What *about* you?'

'I meant a kiss, Lexi. It was a joke.'

'Oh. Sorry. I'm just about all in. I'll make it up to you when I get back, I promise.'

He snorted. 'How many times've I heard that before?' he said, but there was a smile in his voice that sent a fresh wave of tenderness crashing over her. He hung up and she stood for a moment with the phone in her hand, an unexpected lump forming in her throat. She walked over to the window, and after a moment's difficulty, succeeding in finding the button that automatically opened the curtains. Algiers was spread out below her, a cascade of light fanning down the gentle slope of the city towards the glinting, glimmering bay.

The phone rang suddenly, shattering the silence. It wasn't her mobile; it was the hotel phone by her bed. She picked it up. 'Hello?'

'Call for Miss Sturgis. Please wait.' There was a brief exchange in Arabic, and then Marwan Kalmichi's voice came down the line. 'Lexi. *Ahlan*. Welcome back.' She smiled. Marwan was shrewd. He wanted to make sure she was where she'd said she'd be. His professionalism was reassuring.

'Thanks. It's good to *be* back.'

'OK, listen. You need to get to Sidi Aïch tomorrow morning. Take the train. Be there by eight. There's a small cafe on Rue des Frères Chaffa, La Casbah. Wait there. Someone will come for you …'

Once Marwan had finished giving her instructions, she put the phone down and hurried over to her laptop, bringing up a map of Algeria. He hadn't said exactly when the man would pick her up, but someone would be watching out for her to make sure she hadn't been followed. Donal had told Jim to wait for her in Algiers, but the conditions of the meeting were strict. A single reporter. No one else. No photographs whatsoever.

She spent the next couple of hours memorising as much of the area around Sidi Aïch as possible. It was highly unlikely that they would risk bringing their man into town. She would be picked up from the cafe and driven to meet him, and she needed to recognise as much of the topography of the surrounding area as she could in case something went wrong. Standard procedure, standard risks. She'd done it a hundred times before.

It was almost midnight when she finally snapped her laptop shut. She booked a cab to take her to the train station the following morning at dawn, took a shower and hopped into bed. She closed her eyes, thought briefly of Magnus and Mark, and slid effortlessly, as she'd always managed to do, into sleep.

Epilogue

November 2016, Sidi Aïch, Algeria

For a few minutes, Adnan and Lexi simply stared at each other. She could feel her heart beat gathering itself up in her throat before rushing down to the pit of her stomach, tearing at her with such force that she gripped the arms of the chair to stop herself pitching forward.

'It's you,' she said at last, her voice breaking the silence, words shattering like glass. 'You're behind it all. I should've guessed.'

He nodded. His hand went to the pack of cigarettes that was lying on the desk. He picked it up, offering it to her in the gesture she remembered so well. She shook her head.

'I gave up.'

'Sensible. I can't.' He tapped out a cigarette and lit it. She held her breath. He blew the smoke carefully out of the side of his mouth. Everything about him was the same. Face, hands, gestures, expressions, eyes. That kaleidoscope of colours. The commanding presence. The way he silently shifted the room's energies, focusing everyone's attention on him. The tension he generated. It all came rushing back. Neither spoke. Slowly, as she watched his face, the various aspects of his being rearranged themselves so that it wasn't the hunted, weary expression of someone who'd been on the run for longer than she cared to imagine sitting opposite her, but the face that had once hovered above hers, tense with pleasure. A face she'd tried to forget.

She cleared her throat and the sound startled them both. His cigarette was burned almost down to the butt. She saw that his fingers were nicotine-stained and that there were scars on the back of his hand. They hadn't been there five years ago. 'You have something for me,' she said carefully, finally. 'Something you want to tell me. Marwan said you have some ... information.'

He nodded cautiously. The silence between them deepened. Both were aware of the consequences of his disclosure. 'Can I trust you?' he asked.

She nodded. 'You know you can.'

'How do I know?'

She hesitated for a moment, then withdrew her phone, placing it on the desk in front of him. 'That's how.'

He looked at it and frowned. 'What's this? Who is this?'

For a moment they regarded the image together almost politely. It was a picture of Magnus, taken in the summer. They'd gone for a walk in Holland Park, Mark indulging him in what was then his favourite activity: birdwatching. She'd snapped the photograph at exactly the minute all his concentration was focused on the robin that had landed a few yards away from them, drawn by the biscuit crumbs Mark had tossed down on the ground. Magnus was utterly absorbed in the uniqueness of the small creature with its rosy, downy breast, bright flickering eyes and tiny splayed feet. 'Imagine,' Mark had whispered to him, 'that little bird's been everywhere. All over the earth's surface, all the way up to Siberia and across the whole of Europe and then back down again, here, to London. D'you think it remembers where it's been?' She'd pressed the shutter on Magnus's look of delight.

'He's my son,' she said quietly, her heart thudding. 'He's four years old.'

There was a moment of carefully held tension between them. He stared at the photograph again. The truth hit him then, Lexi saw it. She saw the way it was hammered into his lungs and throat so that his whole body took the blow. He lifted his eyes and looked at her. They might have been stepping back into an age-old relationship, its edges worn smooth by habit, time. She remembered the first time she'd seen him smile. It was in Alexandria, six years ago, when they were both younger, more innocent versions of themselves. *Like dawn breaking.* She saw now that it had been her first real glimpse of him, the one that had established for her, whether she wanted it or not, their bond with one another. She hadn't know then that it would be the beginning of something that would extend all the way to the present, to the very moment in which they sat, each warily regarding the other. But she knew now. The thread of connection, taken up so loosely over the years, would extend past this moment, spooling far into the future. *That* was the real price of the conversation. She felt a kind of trembling in herself that was like a fever, not physical at all, but the burning of another kind of emotion. She took a deep breath, then another, steadying herself. What had started out as the straightforward passing on of information had suddenly become an exchange of something infinitely more complex. Love, trust, betrayal, faith, hope, despair … the whole sweep of humanity bound up in the extraordinary history they shared, the extraordinary times they'd witnessed and lived through. A sudden, unexpected wave of lightness swept over her, surprising her. It was as if the weight of the guilt she'd been carrying for so long fell away. They continued to stare at each other. 'Listen,' she wanted to say to him, 'can't we make this easy? So much has happened, so many things we couldn't see or predict. Our worlds have been turned upside down … but it's alright, isn't it? We're both alive. He's here … you can see him, can't you?' She said none of it out loud but he was quick, so very quick. She saw from the look in his eyes that he'd caught something of what she was thinking, what she was trying to say. When she opened her mouth to speak, finally, a kind of calm had settled over her and for the first time in her life, she felt entirely at ease.